THE RACE OF FIRE
Rekindling Truth

ALSO BY THIS AUTHOR

Ella Mortimer

The Race of Fire

Rekindling Truth

MY THANKS TO

My family, especially my children, for believing in me.

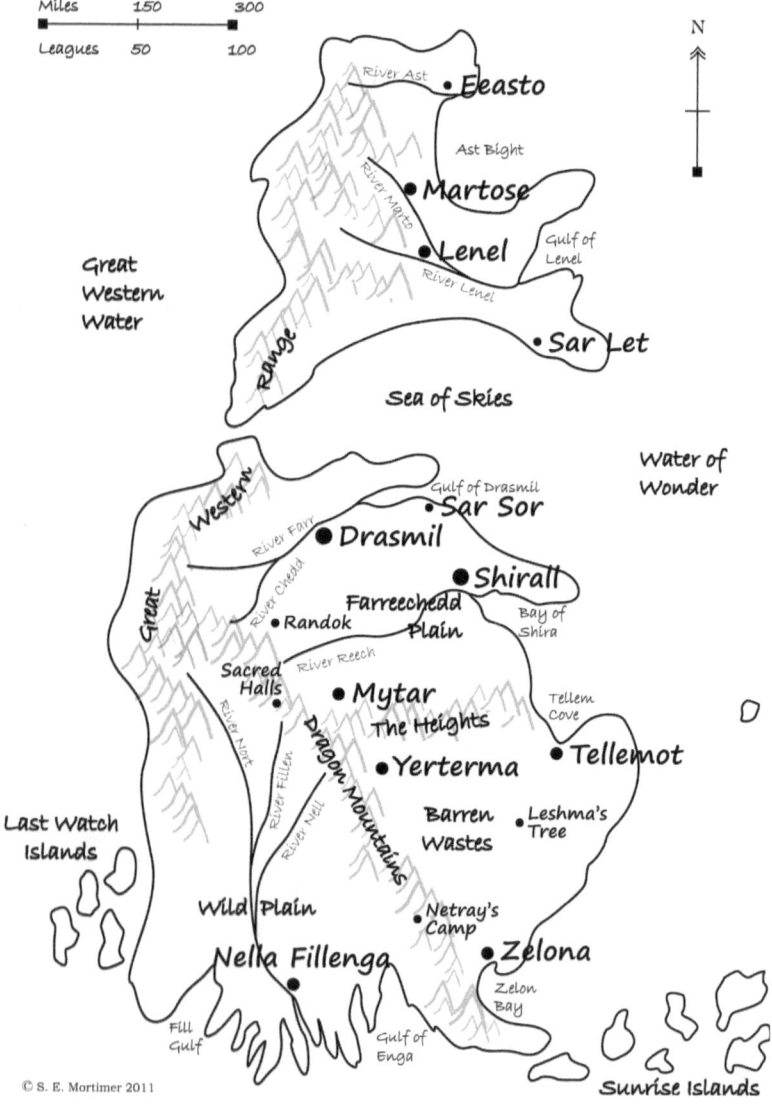

Miles   150   300

Leagues 50   100

N

River Ast

• Eeasto

Ast Bight

• Martose

Great
Western
Water

River Marto

• Lenel

Gulf of
Lenel

River Lenel

• Sar Let

Sea of Skies

Range

Western

Water of
Wonder

Gulf of Drasmil

• Sar Sor

River Farr

• Drasmil

• Shirall

River Chedd

Farreechedd
Plain

Bay of
Shira

Great

• Randok

River Reech

Sacred
Halls

• Mytar

The Heights

Tellem
Cove

River Niat

River Fillen

Dragon Mountains

• Yerterma

• Tellemot

River Nell

Barren
Wastes

• Leshma's
Tree

Last Watch
Islands

Wild Plain

Netray's
Camp

• Zelona

Nella Fillenga

•

Zelon
Bay

Fill
Gulf

Gulf of
Enga

Sunrise Islands

© S. E. Mortimer 2011

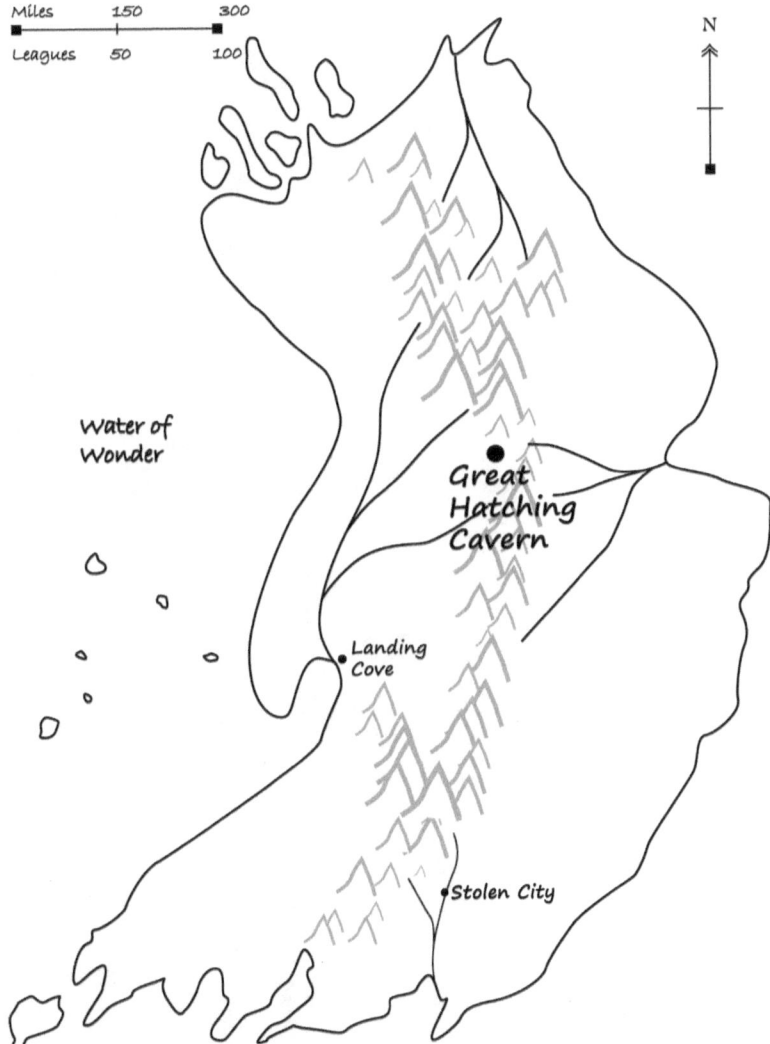

Miles 150 300

Leagues 50 100

N

Water of
Wonder

Great
Hatching
Cavern

Landing
Cove

Stolen City

PROLOGUE
THE MYTH OF THE SANDMAN

In times long past, a world forever gone,
A people journeyed forth and left their home.
No hope of turning back, they travelled far.
For years, they wound their path among the stars.

Lifetimes passed and souls began to sleep,
Taking rest with knowledge buried deep.
Waiting for a new life growing near,
Giving up the past they held so dear.

Soon the time of waking, coming close,
One who stayed nearby will give the dose.
Opening their eyes to life once more,
Remembering the time that came before.

Giving sleep, the Sandman stayed awake,
Entering each new life without break.
Watching others sleep and wake and sleep,
To help preserve the memories they keep.

Sandman kept them safe and gave them life,
To be sure his people would survive.
Never resting, life on life he claimed,
And sleepers watched, until the waking came.

Life returning, cycling round with death,
Saving thought with each one's final breath.
Keeping safe the soul and mind of all,
Bringing back to health from shadow's fall.

Lifetimes without number passed them by,
Living life and sleeping, never to die.
Until at last, the new world they could see,
The journey over, as was meant to be.

Beginning life again, a home at last,
Letting go the memories of the past.
A people changed, the world a different kind,
Their history was stored in just one mind.

His task complete, the Sandman sought his rest,
Taking into dreams the people's quest.
Knowledge stored of lifetimes on the way,
To keep them safe until another day.

When hope is fading and the darkness falls,
The Sandman will awake to hear the call.
To lead his people to a new beginning,
When it seems there is no hope of winning.

The memory of ages long ago,
A life the Sandman must choose or forgo.
He tells the past and brings it back to life,
That people know and so avert the strife.

It is said the Sandman waits alone,
Dreaming of the new life soon to come.
The truth will be revealed to those held dear,
And when the past is vanquished, all is clear.

ONE

The last surviving clone-son of the holy-one led his master down into the rotting heart of Stolen City. Glancing back to check the old priest still followed, he tried to ignore the empty faces, their haunted eyes glimmering from dark doorways and peering out from behind old and tattered curtains.

He was the different one, the outsider, and yet they always seemed so unhappy. He had long since stopped asking why he alone had long arms, a full set of fingers, and a flat, boring face. But he would always wonder. If it weren't for the voices in his head, he might doubt if he was human at all.

He checked the directions on a scrap of paper and pointed down a dark alley.

"This way, Master," he whispered.

As the old priest's corpulent form shuffled its way into the alley, the boy hurried ahead until he found the right door. He lifted a disgustingly perfect hand and knocked twice. A thin, quavering voice called out.

"Who is it?"

"Who do you think?" the boy said. "I knocked twice didn't I?"

"Well you can tell holy-one we're not ready. My husband is fine, he's not dying yet."

"Ma'am, open the door. You wouldn't want the holy-one to refuse to take him."

There was a gasp, and a scurrying of feet. The door opened a crack.

"It's not time!" the woman sobbed. "Please..."

The boy pushed on the door and the woman stumbled back, allowing him in. He glanced around, noticed the table laid for a solitary meal, and spun to face the woman.

"Where's your offering for the holy-one? You'd better have more food than this!"

The woman blinked, her mismatched eyes filling with tears. Her crooked chin wrinkled with her grief as her small lips, bent almost sideways to accommodate the much shorter right jawline, almost disappeared into her toothless mouth.

The boy opened his mind to hear her thoughts. Why did she have to fight it? Her husband deserved peace, and a chance at a new life. She had no right to deny him that. He felt the woman wavering under his persuasion.

"The holy-one will be here in a moment," said the boy.

"Yes," she gasped. "I'm sorry. I'll get everything ready."

The woman bustled about, fetching bread from the larder, gathering more bowls and ladelling out soup from the pot on the fire. The boy slipped out the door and stood waiting for his master, whose dragging steps had brought the priest almost to the poor woman's home.

"Ist all in order?" the old priest huffed.

The boy shrugged. "A little denial, but nothing I couldn't handle."

"Good, good," said the Master. "Then let us begin. I am hungry."

With that, the holy-one entered the dwelling. Without a word, the priest shuffled across the room and sat at the head of the table, pulling the bowl close and spooning hot soup into a sneering mouth.

The boy followed and took a seat, motioning for the

woman to join them. The holy-one ate quickly, spoon seeming to fly from table to mouth, without spilling a drop. The boy filled his own belly as quickly as he could, to be ready when the Master finished. The woman stared over her untouched bowl, tears dripping off the point of her chin.

"Let us take the patient his last meal," said the holy-one with a smirk.

The woman let out a sob, but grabbed the bowl and led the way into the bedroom. A small man lay still, eyes closed, his shallow breath barely moving his grizzled whiskers.

"He hasn't eaten for days," she whispered.

"No matter," said the boy. "A few drops on the spoon is enough, just to send him off."

With a trembling hand, the woman slipped the spoon between the sick man's lips. The boy stepped up, took the bowl from her and laid it on the bedside table. He noticed a chair by the bed, and helped the woman to sit.

"Are you sure it's time?" she whispered.

"The holy-one is never wrong," the boy replied. "Besides, you wouldn't want him to get here too late, would you? If your husband were to die before the holy-one could take him, his soul would be lost forever."

The woman nodded and reached out to take her husband's hand; two fat digits where the fingers were fused, and a thumb. The woman stroked the crablike hand lovingly, bent to kiss it with her crooked mouth, then looked up at the holy-one.

"Will he be happy?" she said.

"He shall have a whole new life," the holy-one said.

"Will he be healthy?"

"I do assure thee, he shall be perfect in every way," the holy-one replied.

"Like him?" she tilted her head toward the boy.

"Just so."

"No more pain?"

"Nought of pain shall plague him."

The woman sighed. "Then I'm ready. Take him now."

The holy-one stepped up to the bed, something gleaming in one hand. The priest stroked the man's thinning hair, then slipped a fine gold chain over his head to rest about his neck, and positioned the shining amulet on his bare chest.

"May thy soul be saved," the holy-one intoned. "Thy new life doth await."

With one hand theatrically raised in the air, the holy-one brought the other hand down over the amulet. The boy watched, trying to catch the exact moment, but no matter how many times he witnessed the farce he had no idea how his master triggered the release of the soul.

From under the holy-one's hand, a blue glow began to form, spreading to engulf the dying man. The dim room seemed bright as day for a moment, then the glow dissipated and the man's light breath was stilled. The holy-one removed the amulet and slipped it unceremoniously into a hidden pocket. The boy sighed. Another soul for his master's collection.

* * *

The Adept known as Tong watched as the Awakener moved slowly along the line of applicants, trying to see the man's face, half hidden by the black border of his hood. Tong frowned at the Journeyer who followed behind, whispering in the man's ear. How could she even be there?

Tong remembered meeting the young woman almost three years before in the palace at Drasmil. She had seemed a quiet, unpromising girl, with no connection to the College of the Art. Nothing could have prepared him for the shock of seeing her there, wearing the green border of a journeyer, trailing in the footsteps of the Awakener.

The man in the black bordered cloak stopped in front of a young man in the red border of artisan, several years younger than Tong himself. Tong strained his ears to listen.

"I'm glad to see you here, Reep," said the Awakener with a smile.

"Thank you, Sir," the young man replied. "I hope I prove worthy."

"I'm sure you will, Reep. You were always more talented than I."

"I highly doubt that, Sir."

"I never want to hear that from you, Reep. And don't call me sir."

"Sorry, Sir... ah Sand." He grinned. "I never dreamed, when we were in the apprentice wing together, that you would be the Awakener and I would be standing before you begging for your teaching."

"Nor I, my friend. May I?"

When Reep nodded, the Awakener slid his fingertips under the red edge of his hood, pressing them to the Artisan's temples, and concentrated. Then he smiled and glanced at the woman beside Reep.

"Is this your wife?"

"Yes, this is Iris," said Reep, eyes glowing with pride. "She's testing for adept five years early."

The Awakener submitted her to the same mental examination and smiled again. Tong saw him glance at the Journeyer at his side and caught the small nod she gave. The Awakener smirked.

"You're in, Reep. Both of you."

The Artisan grinned broadly and caught his wife in a quick hug. Tong seethed inside, unable to hold down his unseemly emotions. The College was overrun with young upstarts joining the higher ranks. It was devaluing the whole order of things. There was a schedule for a reason. An adept was not just powerful in mind and body; he had to be strong in experience and maturity, an artisan even more so. Those two fools would never cope in the Awakener's class.

The Awakener had moved on and was addressing a young girl in a brown edged cloak, a mere apprentice. Tong could not suppress a snort. The child had spent the entire morning staring, doe-eyed at the Journeyer beside her. How could an apprentice ever hope to succeed in an advanced class? Or a journeyer, for that matter. Whoever was preselecting these candidates was out of their mind.

"I assume you are testing this year?" the Awakener said.

"Yes, Sir," the girl whispered.

"You realise I can't accept you into my class until you gain the green," he frowned.

"I... yes, Sir, I start the testing this week. I just..."

"Sand," the woman beside the Awakener murmured. "She has been recommended by the Maestro himself."

He raised an eyebrow. The Awakener touched his hands to the girl's temples and frowned.

"You have an amazing mind," he said and the girl blushed. "When do you plan to be joined?"

"Joined, Sir?" she whispered.

Sand glanced at the young man beside the girl. Tong saw the Journeyer take the girl's hand and snorted again. Children!

"Sir, we've never met before today," said the young man.

"Oh?" Sand frowned. "The energy between you is palpable."

The girl blushed again. The Awakener sighed.

"I like you," he said. "You both have great potential."

The couple grinned at each other and the girl let out a happy sigh.

"But," the Awakener continued. "There are some issues that must be resolved before you can join my class." He raised a hand to forestall comment. "First, you must complete your testing to gain the green."

"Yes, Sir."

"Then, you two need to work things out between you, and get your relationship sorted out."

"Relationship?" said the boy. "But Sir, we've only just met!"

"So?" the Awakener scoffed. "Everyone in this room can feel the spark between you. Get it sorted and come back when you're joined. I don't need you distracting my class with your love-sick murmurings. Hear me?"

Both youngsters nodded and the Awakener smiled. "I do want you both, but not before you have yourselves and each other under control, understand?"

They nodded again and the Awakener moved on. Tong stifled his chuckles and straightened to meet the eye of the man on whom his whole life depended. His future lay in the balance and he needed to impress.

"We've met before," said the Awakener.

"Yes, Sir, in Drasmil, before the old king died."

"I remember. I see you've gained a colour since then."

"Yes, Sir. And hopefully another very soon."

"You're testing for artisan?"

"Yes, Sir. A year or two early," he said with pride.

"Well done," said the Awakener. "May I?"

Tong nodded uncertainly as the man's cool hands touched his temples. He steeled himself for a mental invasion that never came, the touch of his mind so subtle that Tong felt nothing. Then the Awakener was frowning, shaking his head, and Tong's heart sank. The Journeyer touched the Awakener's arm and they shared a long, sorrowful look.

"What's wrong?" said Tong.

"I'm sorry, Tong. I really wanted you to join me, but..."

"But what?"

"Tong, you have an admirable mind. Your potential is staggering. But there's one challenge you have yet to meet. One that is vital for these classes."

"What challenge? I can learn if you just tell me what I need to do!"

"I'm sorry. This is something that can't be learned or prepared for. If and when it happens, you will be welcomed into this class. Until then..."

"What? I'm sure, whatever it is I can work on it..."

"I'm sorry."

How dare the man reject him, for some nebulous 'challenge' that probably didn't exist! The Awakener was making excuses just to get rid of him. The man was nothing but an upstart pup, in way over his head. How Sand had ever been allowed to progress so quickly Tong would never know.

The arrogance of the man, to think he could take on the exalted rank of Awakener before he even reached the age of thirty, when he should barely be ready to test for adept. And that little journeyer, looking all deer eyes at him. How did she get to be assistant to the Awakener? The whole thing was a farce.

Mist hurried to join Sand at the Maestro's office. When she arrived Sand was deep in conversation with the Maestro, and Mist cleared her throat to get their attention.

"Ah, Mist," said the Maestro. "Come in, we have some things to discuss."

This sounded ominous. "What is it, Sir?"

"Sand tells me you have been maintaining your training?"

Mist looked a question at Sand. "Yes, Sir."

"So tell me my dear, are you back at full strength after your pregnancy?"

"I... believe so, Sir. What's this all about?"

"All in good time. What about your fighting skills? Have you mastered left-handed sword play?"

Mist flexed the muscles of her right arm, glancing at the long white scar running the length of her forearm, the only reminder of the injury that had almost killed her and had left her right arm permanently weakened.

"There's still room for improvement, but I can hold my own," she said.

"We should make that your top priority then."

Mist shook her head in puzzlement. "What's going on?"

"I've taken the liberty of putting your name down for testing."

"Testing?"

"For master," said Sand, eyes shining with pride.

Her jaw dropped and her eyes widened, flicking from one to the other. "I..."

"You know you're ready, my love."

"I... suppose so. But what about the advanced classes? I can't spend all my time teaching if I have to prepare for testing."

"I'm sure we can work something out," said Sand with a smile. "We have a few weeks yet. You won't test until the final year apprentices are finished."

"There's another reason I want this for you," said the Maestro. "I've had one or two... enquiries about you."

"I don't understand, Sir..."

"I don't know if I should be telling you this, but..." he sighed. "I had someone in here wondering why a mere journeyer had earned the exalted position of assistant to the Awakener." He shrugged an apology.

"But that's ridiculous!" she cried, glancing at Sand. He said nothing, but his lips thinned and his eyes flashed.

"I know that," the Maestro said. "I made it perfectly

clear that I was not pleased to hear such prejudice from a member of the Art. He has been reprimanded, but I would rather not have to face such questioning again. This is not the kind of behaviour I condone in the College. Jealousy has no place here."

Mist felt like she had been kicked in the stomach. The last thing she had expected was an attack like this, from within the College. This was supposed to be home, a safe place to be accepted and welcomed. A place where partnerships of the kind her and Sand shared were never questioned or doubted. It was enough to bring a lump to her throat and a tear to her eye.

She felt the loving touch of Sand's hand on her arm. Mist went into her husband's arms, the tears falling freely now, bitterly disappointed that the joy of her elevation would be tainted by the pettiness of jealousy.

"I don't want you to think this reflects in any way on my decision to recommend you, my dear," the Maestro said. "I would have done it anyway, you deserve it. But I do think a higher rank will offer you a certain level of protection from the small-minded people of this world. I'm just terribly disappointed that it came from a member of the Art."

The Sandman watched as the invader slipped into his vessel's mind. He held back an angry impulse to fly to the attack. It had taken months to get this far, clawing his way past the vessel's defences. This was his vessel; the interloper had no right to be there. But the Sandman had not the power to repulse the invader. Not yet. Not until he had established control and become truly reborn.

This vessel was not what he had expected. His beloved had assured him that she would complete the transfer without delay, but this body was much older than he remembered. His clone-son had been a child, just ripe for the transfer, but this body was full-grown and at the height of its power.

The Sandman turned his attention to the intruder. The spirit was familiar, yet different. He remembered the last time he enabled the transfer for this soul. He had been eager to be reborn, unwilling to wait until his clone-son was ready. The Sandman had warned him of the danger that he might send the tender young mind into madness, but he had been determined and had refused to go into storage.

But now this spirit carried a new and greater burden. It seemed unwhole, neutered, sexless, referring to itself as It. Obviously a lot had happened while the Sandman had slept. Settling into his quiet corner, the Sandman watched as the intruder followed the mind of the vessel, a fully developed mind with great power and a soul of its own. The Sandman saw the intruder latch on to the thought stream created by the vessel as it linked to another living mind.

He tried to imagine what the invader might be planning, and how he might thwart it. It seemed this vessel would be hard won, with three souls competing for possession. But the Sandman would win; he would take control and be reborn. And then he would learn what had passed in his absence.

TWO

The Awakener lay in the cool, soft grass under the spreading leaves of a simpa tree, his head cushioned in his hands as he gazed up into the branches, completely relaxed. His beautiful wife lay crosswise, her head resting on his stomach as their six month old son sat propped against her, pudgy fingers tangled in the fascinating green stuff.

Sand had never dreamed he would be so content, and he could scarcely believe how much his life had changed in three short years. How had he come to this place, so removed from the closed off, aloof, haunted man he was before? It was all her doing.

Mist had come into his life like a comet, blazing through his hollow work-driven existence and taking control of his well-shielded mind in a matter of days. Instead of taking him away from his work and destroying his equilibrium, as he had feared she would, their partnership had become the most important part of his working life. From the very moment he met her, their minds were perfectly matched, and through her he had become the most powerful revealer ever known.

Now he had an amazing future ahead, bringing knowledge and great power to his fellow revealers and to the world outside the College of the Art. The coming of the Awakener had been foreseen as a great mystical event, bringing change and growth, and an amazing new truth to the world, but he felt none of that. How could he fulfil that incredible destiny if he did not even know where to start?

Mist lifted herself up on one elbow to gaze at him, complete trust in her eyes. "Don't worry, dear, you'll work it out."

The touch of her mind was like a balm to his troubled soul, and he knew she would be right there to help him find the way. The teaching had already begun with the establishment of Schools of the Art in locations outside the College, offering basic lessons to the general public. The Maestro had been against the idea at first, worried that letting some of the secrets of the College be known to the outside world would be dangerous.

Now the head of the College could see that the opportunity to experience a taste of what the revealers already knew would bring new talent to the College. Already this year's intake of new novices had tripled since the program began.

Sand also knew that after the catastrophic events of the year before the people needed something to cling to that would give them hope. With the population decimated by the war with the kalkar, people needed to feel safe.

So many young healthy males had been lost in the conflict. Wives had lost husbands, mothers had lost sons and children had lost fathers. The sudden appearance of Kayus, the spirit of nothingness, in control of the invading kalkar horde, had been terrifying, and the world had been made startlingly aware of the powerful abilities of the mind that the College had kept secret for so long. They knew that those powers would be needed if the dreadful spirit ever returned.

"Stop fretting, dear," said Mist then. "You've made wonderful progress in six months. Don't sell yourself short."

"But it's nothing new. There's so much more I'm supposed to do."

"It's completely new to everyone outside the College! Most of them had no idea that anything like this existed. You have completely blown away all their established knowledge of the universe and their own role within it. You have done everything the Awakener was supposed to do by bringing knowledge to the world. The rest will come, dear, they can't run before they can walk!"

"You're right, as always, my love."

"Which brings us to today's task," she said. "It's time to test the newest applicants for your outsider classes."

"They can wait," he sighed.

Mist smiled, reminded how much he had changed. The Sand of three years ago was a driven man, buried in his work, with a mental shield of iron keeping the world out. She had found herself fluttering like a moth at the light of his mind, compelled to keep trying to reach him. That man would never have kept his students waiting because he wanted to relax in the sun.

The boy ran along the corridor, his yellow-edged cloak billowing out behind him. He only had a few moments between classes to find his sister, and Domyn was determined to catch her this time. It seemed he never saw her these days, even with the baby slowing her down. She was always locked up with Sand's new classes, or too preoccupied with her training to spend time with her younger brother. He wished he were just a little older, more of an equal to his famous sister and her even more illustrious partner.

"Hey, watch where you're going," cried an apprentice as he passed.

"Sorry," he gasped, clutching at his yellow head scarf as it tumbled.

"Hey, aren't you Mist's little brother?"

Domyn hesitated. Sometimes, his sister's fame could be

more of a hindrance than a help. People seemed to forget he had a name of his own.

"I'm Domyn," he said with a frown. "And she's my sister."

"Whatever," said the Apprentice. "You don't know where I can find her, do you?"

"Maybe," Domyn hedged. "What for?"

"I have a message for the Awakener, and he's not in his suite. He might be with her."

Domyn shrugged. "He might. I was just looking for her myself."

"Oh, good," said the Apprentice. "You can help me find her."

"I can do better than that. I can take your message to her myself."

The Apprentice frowned. "I don't know. I'm not supposed to..."

"You can trust me. Sand is my brother-in-law, you know."

"I... well yes, I suppose so."

"I'm sure you have better things to do than look for them."

"I am rather behind in my chores, and I have to get back to studying. I'm testing next week."

"Really? Good for you. What's the message?"

"Oh, just that there's a message from Eeasto. The candidates for the outsider class have been waiting for over an hour and they're getting impatient."

"Is that all? He probably just got busy with something else. I'll tell him."

"Could you? I really don't have time for this."

"Sure, no problem."

"But umm... don't tell anyone, yeah? I'd be in all sorts of trouble if the Maestro found out I let you take the message."

Domyn grinned. "I won't tell. But you owe me."

"Anything, just let me know."

"Oh, I'm sure I can think of something," said Domyn as the Apprentice ran off.

Domyn grinned as he picked up his run again. He knew exactly where Mist was, and that Sand was with her, and that he was quite intentionally late. They were always in the same place at this time of day, but he was not about to let that jumped up apprentice know that.

The Awakener needed to snatch his moments when he could, and Domyn enjoyed being in the know. It made him feel important somehow, to be in the Awakener's private family circle. Bursting out into the garden, Domyn hurried across the lawn and took a little-used track through the woods.

Coming up against a thick hedge full of brambles and weeds, he searched with his hands until he found a thick branch and pulled. A section of bush came away to reveal an opening. Slipping through, he pulled the branch closed behind him, and stepped out into a little clearing where he saw his sister and her family resting in the grass.

"Dom," she smiled as he approached. "What brings you here?"

"I just thought I could play with my nephew for a while," he shrugged.

He loved referring to the baby as his nephew. None of his friends were uncles like him. He bent to smile at Zavvy.

"Aren't you supposed to be in class?" said Mist.

"I've got a break," he lied.

Sometimes being related to the Awakener had its advantages. Domyn knew the masters would not punish him if he said he was with the Awakener.

"Watch it, boy," said Sand with a wink. "You won't be able to get away with that forever."

"I won't stay long. Besides, I have a message."

"Are you doing apprentice work now? I had no idea you were so far ahead of your studies."

Domyn lost his cool as a giggle escaped him. Then he blushed. "Would you rather I had told the messenger about your little escape spot?"

"It's a good thing I like you, Dom," Sand smirked. "What was the message?"

"Oh, just that the outsiders are getting restless."

Sand chuckled. "They always think I have nothing better to do than test new applicants."

"You could always pass it off on someone else, you know," said Mist.

"That wouldn't be fair. It was my idea to start these classes."

"Sooner or later, you'll realise that you're only one man, no matter how exalted you become."

He grinned. "Are you being facetious, my love?"

She returned his grin. "They've waited long enough, dear."

With a heavy sigh, he began to rise. Mist gathered up the little boy.

"I'll take Zavvy to the nursery, if you like," said Domyn.

"Alright, Dom," said Mist. "But you go straight to class afterwards, you hear?"

Sand and Mist watched as Worm, the old gatekeeper, swung the big iron bars wide. Sand held his stallion, Lumen, tightly in check. Mist brushed a calming hand down Cheena's arching neck, the mare picking up on the big black stallion's mood.

With a smile and a nod for Worm, the revealers passed through, and the horses headed down the hill of their own accord, ready for an adventure. The Journeyer pulled back on the reins, a small smile playing on her lips.

"What is it, my love?" the Awakener murmured.

"Nothing, just remembering my name."

"It's Miyam," he said with a wink.

She giggled. "I know that, Evelar, it's just... This changing names whenever we pass through the gate. It's still a bit new for me."

"I know, my love," Evelar smiled. "You'll get used to it. It's like playing a part, taking on a persona."

"Yes, but which persona is real? The anonymous college name or the name I show the world?"

"Both. It's just a name."

"Sometimes I wonder why we have a college name at all."

"For identification, you know that."

"Yes, I know, it confirms us to each other when we meet outside the College. But why isn't it the other way around? I mean... shouldn't we be anonymous outside the College, and show our real selves at home?"

"That's just how it's always been," he shrugged. "It prevents an imposter from gaining access to college secrets."

"It just feels strange, revealing our true names to these new students, complete strangers, while our colleagues and friends know only the anonymous college persona. It just feels backward somehow."

"It won't always feel that way, my love. It gives a personal touch, so the people you meet on the outside will feel they can trust you. Your college name will become the real you, a secret gift known only to your college family. And your real name will become the revealer's mask."

Evelar kicked in with his heels and Lumen leapt forward, heading downhill toward the town of Eeasto, where a new intake of prospective students awaited.

The Awakener moved to the next candidate, and

examined the woman's face before touching his hands to her temples. He smiled, nodded, moved on. In his wake, his journeyer assistant took the woman's hand and whispered reassurance, sending her to join the other successful applicants. Then Miyam hurried after Evelar, a hand touching his arm.

"Evelar, what's going on? You're not usually so dismissive."

He looked at her, his eyes sparking gold. "Mine effort doth grow tedious."

Miyam frowned. "What are you talking about? You never let that affect your work."

"Thy persistence doth wear on my patience."

"What?"

Miyam stopped, staring after him as he lazily tested the next applicant and moved on. Mind racing, she shook her head in disbelief, then hurried after him again.

"Evelar, what's gotten into you? Why are you talking that way?"

The Awakener turned, blinked at her, his brown eyes looking bewildered.

"What way?" he said. "What are you talking about, Mym?"

Miyam shook her head. "You were speaking like the ancients. Don't you remember?"

A snort from behind drew her gaze. "I knew he couldn't do this without losing his mind."

A man in the purple-edged cloak of an adept sidled toward her.

"Tong!" she exclaimed.

"Nashta out here, if you please," he smirked.

"You're the one who complained to the Maestro, aren't you."

"What did you expect? Young upstart like that thinking

he can be the Awakener. And you, a psuedo-journeyer without the basic training of an apprentice, who wasn't even a member of the College two years ago."

"You don't know what you're talking about."

"Don't I?"

"Enough, Nashta," Evelar snapped. "This attitude is unseemly."

"Says the one who rejected me. I'm twice the revealer you'll ever be."

Evelar sighed. "Nashta, you had such promise. I was even going to ask for your help. But since you're too illustrious to accept an offer from me, I'll have to find someone else."

"Offer?" The man's eyebrows rose. "What offer?"

"It's no matter. This job needs tact and patience, and possibly a little humility. I don't think you would want to lower yourself."

"Look," he said, flustered. "I'm sorry. I was stung by the rejection. I really wanted to be in that class."

"And I really wanted you. But as I said, there is something you need to do first."

"What? Why won't you tell me?"

"Are you willing to try something new? Take on a task that might not be quite what you had hoped?"

The man sighed. "Please, Sir, let me try. I promise I will do everything you ask."

The Awakener grinned. "Then we'll see what happens. You never know, this job might bring you precisely what is needed for the advanced class. You might be lucky."

"What do you want me to do?"

The Awakener chuckled. "I want you to teach the outsider classes for me."

The spirit of nothing slipped Its tendrils deeper into the faraway mind of Its greatest adversary. The enemy was collecting more followers, touching more souls, and the spirit could ride his thought waves down into those untrained minds. Not for the first time, the spirit thanked the foresight that had made It wedge the unseen door when It was expelled the last time, when all Its plans had been foiled.

Hiding in the subconscious, the spirit waited, listening for the touch of a new soul. Then, riding on the back of the enemy's searching mind, the spirit sank in Its hook. The new soul, unprotected, closed about the spirit's barb, accepting the link without question. The spirit dropped another hook, into the physical flesh of the soul's corporeal vessel.

As the spirit rode the enemy out, two gossamer threads of thought remained, hooked firmly in the new soul, undetected. The spirit took one thread and attached it in the deepest subconscious centre of the enemy's mind. Holding the second thread within itself, the spirit of nothing gathered the extra threads from all the souls the enemy had touched that day and set Its course.

The spirit slipped away, tracing the lines from the newly captured souls to see them secure in the enemy's mind. The spirit separated from the enemy, taking with It the lines hooked into the physical flesh of the victims, pulling the bundle of threads behind.

It followed the thin line of Its own anchoring thread, over the miles to where the spirit's hated vessel resided. Soon It would have enough souls hooked, enough bodies to claim. Then Its greatest desire would be at Its command.

* * *

THREE

The holy-one paused in front of a panel no different to the rest of the wall, glanced about, and reached a hand forward to press a palm flat against it. A glow spread from the hand, and the panel slid open on its own. The holy-one smiled, reached a hand into a hidden pocket, and pulled out a golden amulet on a chain.

Hanging the charm beside the others, the holy-one ran trembling fingers through a forest of amulets, several hundred already, hearing the faint whispers of the souls stored within.

"Hush, my loyal followers," the holy-one murmured. "Soon thou wilt return, thy new bodies ready for thy coming."

The souls whispered, like a great sighing of wind through the trees.

"Be thou calm and patient. Mine own vessel doth grow and mature. Soon his mind will be strong enough to contain me, that I might leave this sexless thing in which I rot and become young once more, young and male and perfect."

The sighing whisper filled the holy-one's mind.

"Take comfort in thy rest. Thy new vessels will soon be emptied of their souls, ready for thy possession. Then together we shall reclaim this world."

"Master?"

The holy-one slammed the panel shut and spun to face the intruder.

"Why do you need so many souls, Master?"

"Thou needest concern thyself not with such matters, boy. Thy task ist only to learn and prepare."

"So teach me. Why are you collecting souls? Why are you promising them new lives, yet keeping them locked away?"

"Thou shalt know the answers when I take thy body as mine own. With my memories within thy mind, thou shalt be powerful beyond reckoning. And I shall be whole once more."

"I'm not sure I want…"

"I raised thee not to want! Only to be ready and accept. Thou dost wear a borrowed skin, cloned from mine own flesh to accept my soul when the time is right. Thy flesh is mine."

"It's my body," the boy pouted. "I don't have to give it to you."

"Hast thou no conception of the clone-seeds I planted for thee? Of the many failures before mine efforts didst reward me with a clone-son afflicted not with this neutered body? I long to possess it. I long to be whole once more, to know again the pleasures of lust. Thou shalt not thwart me."

"You're mad."

The holy-one fumed. "There was a time when clone-seeds didst know their place, and didst submit to possession with grace and willing. Thou shalt do so for me."

* * *

"So you've heard some unusual stories. Perhaps you've even done a few unusual things, or seen somebody else doing them. Things that involve strange conversations about things you don't quite understand. Like talking to people who aren't there, or talking to people who are there, without any words being spoken. What's going on? Has the world suddenly gone mad? Perhaps you are the one who has gone mad."

Nashta glanced around, noting the wide eyes of his students and almost letting his amusement show.

"Relax," he whispered. "It's not as confusing as it all seems, and you are definitely not mad! You have simply been made aware of a world out there that is totally beyond your previous experience. In short, you have come into contact with people who are open to the idea that there is more to life than the physical realm."

The students stared back at him, variously vacant, bemused, enthralled or just plain scared. One young man's mouth hung open in a look of complete idiocy. A pretty girl licked her lips nervously. Nashta sighed. The Awakener had been right to give him this task. He felt, somewhat to his own surprise, that he would enjoy shaping the immature minds of his students, deriving immense satisfaction from their successes. He could not wait to feel them growing with every lesson, and some showed unexpected promise.

"I will begin with the basics," he continued, "and will slowly expand to reveal to you the secrets of the non-physical world and its interaction with the physical. At this point, there is one thing that I cannot stress too strongly. What I will be teaching is a way of life. Once you start, there is no turning back!"

"So sign me up," came a woman's voice from behind.

Nashta spun, ready with a reply, but what he saw stopped his voice and sent his body into a shiver. His mind reached out to her, a thin finger of thought searching for something his conscious mind could not imagine.

But his probe sank into a soft mass of spongy resistance. He tried to force through, but the more he pressed, the less progress he made. Pushing harder, he felt the resistance push back, and his mental probe bounced out of her mind, snapping back into his own skull. The woman cocked her head, her beautiful face a study in amusement. Nashta tried to gather his wits and stumbled on his reply.

"It... it's too late, the selection is over. You... you'll have to wait for the next intake."

The woman pouted, and Nashta felt a shiver through his gut. "I'm sorry," he mumbled.

"Surely you can make an exception?" she murmured. "For me?"

"I... I'll have to talk to the Awakener."

"Please do," she simpered. "I'd hate to miss any more of your fascinating lectures..."

The Awakener approached Tong where he waited by the enormous iron gate. The Adept appeared nervous, his eyes jumping about as he leaned against the stone wall. Inexplicable fear emanated from his mind. Sand exchanged a glance with his wife, and Mist shrugged, a small smile playing on her lips.

"Come along then, Tong, take me to her," said Sand.

"I..." Tong twisted his hands and shifted his gaze.

Sand frowned as he considered the man. "Is she really that powerful, to have you so skittish?"

"I... no, Sir, of course not, it's just..."

"What, man?" Sand said, exasperated.

"She's... already here, Sir," he said with a tilt of the head toward the gate. "She's waiting outside the gate, she followed me here. She didn't wait down in the village like she was supposed to..."

"Well then, let's go meet her."

"I... I'd rather not, Sir," Tong stammered. "And, if you don't mind, Sir, do you think you could... find a way to reject her? Please?"

Sand raised an eyebrow. "Now, Tong, that's unkind. Now come along."

"I... Yes, Sir," he pouted.

Sand led the way through the gate, noticing a beautiful woman in her mid-twenties who seemed somehow younger than her years yet older at the same time, a hardness about her eyes betraying a troubled past.

When she turned to meet his gaze, the full force of her untrained mind hit him and he almost buckled. Then he gave a laugh and approached the woman, Mist following while Tong hovered just inside the gate.

"No wonder he's afraid of you," he chuckled. "I'm Evelar and this is Miyam. You've already met Nashta, of course. And what might your name be?"

The woman tilted her head. "Can't you read it?"

"Not without breaching college etiquette," he smiled.

"Oh," she sighed. "Really? All that power and you muzzle it just to be polite?"

"If you can't accept that one important rule, we may as well end this right now."

"Oh." She sighed again. "I'm Tinny. Tineya actually."

"Well then, Tineya. May I examine your mind?"

She stared for a moment, then nodded. Evelar stepped closer and placed his fingertips gently to her temples. He concentrated for a moment, a frown settling on his face.

"You will need to release your shield," he said.

Her forehead creased and her lower lip trembled, but Evelar smiled as her mind opened to him. Surprised by his findings, he turned to Miyam.

"Tell me what you think, Mym," he murmured.

Miyam stepped up and took over, her fingers stroking slightly at the woman's temples. Evelar watched as his wife examined the woman, mouth flickering with amusement.

"Interesting," she smiled. "No wonder he's afraid."

"Nashta," Evelar called to the cowering man. "Come out here and join us."

"I... Yes, Sir," he said softly as he sidled over to the little group.

"I'd like to be the first to congratulate you, Nashta," said Evelar with a wink.

"What? Why?"

"You'll see," Evelar chuckled. "For now, let's just say you're one step closer to gaining your place in the advanced class."

"I am? What did I do?"

"Nothing, yet. It's what you're about to do that interests me."

"I don't understand."

"No, probably not." He turned to the woman. "Tineya, you're in. Be gentle, I don't think he's quite ready for you yet, but he will be."

Tineya gave a little giggle and hid a blush. Miyam smiled at her reassuringly.

"Now, Nashta," said Evelar, putting on a serious expression, his eyes twinkling. "Take this woman and train her. I know she scares you, but you need to try. It's very important."

"She doesn't scare me," Nashta said.

"Perhaps not, but she will. And I want you to know that there's no need to be afraid. If you can see past the fear and take on the challenge, your time of testing will be short, with a wonderful reward at the end."

"A place in your class?" he said eagerly.

"Oh, that's just the cherry on top," Evelar chuckled. "You have a much more exciting journey ahead, before you're ready for that. Just promise me one thing."

"What's that, Sir?"

The Awakener winked. "Have fun. Lots of it."

"The powers of the mind are available to anyone who is willing to learn but some, like yourselves, come to the power completely on their own. Some may master it easily, and some may have a natural ability that makes them very powerful, while others may struggle to learn the simplest skills. Everyone is different, but with practice everyone can achieve some level of mastery."

"Well that's good to know!" a woman snorted. "Do we really need this basic stuff?"

"Tineya, you need to understand that your skill is untrained. You don't know everything yet."

"I know that this tedious lecturing is getting us nowhere."

"It is giving you the knowledge you must attain to properly understand your power. Even members of the College spend five years as novices, learning the theory behind the power and experiencing little more than basic training. True mental discipline only begins when they pass the written exams to take on the brown of apprentice."

"Five years of this? I wonder that they stay at all!"

"Tineya, you can either take an interest or you can leave."

Tineya pouted and fluttered her eyelashes. "I suppose I can wait until it gets interesting. I'll just sit here and stare at you, shall I?"

She leant forward in her chair and rested her elbows on her knees, chin in her hands. Opening her eyes wide, she let out a vapid sigh and settled into gazing at Nashta's face. He tried to shut her out of his sight, and addressed the rest of the class.

"It has long been the way of the College to combine two minds for greater power, and we have found that by using this technique we can be assured of well-functioning minds in the field."

"How sweet," sighed Tenaya.

Nashta ignored her. "It is for this reason that our members are always active in a partnership, and it is only on rare occasions that the strongest members are allowed to complete a mission unaccompanied."

"Aww, poor dears, they must be so lonely."

Nashta shivered, shaking his head involuntarily. "For this method to work we must first master the simple skills of mind speak, shielding and linking," he blundered on. "Once these are accomplished we can progress to their main uses of scanning, listening and healing."

"Finally!" said Tineya with a little grimace.

"Perhaps the most fundamental skill for a revealer is scanning. We use this in our primary task of gathering information. Most people, even the clients that employ us, do not give up information easily. We must be able to read the thoughts of those around us to discover the motives, secret plans and hidden agendas of both the people we investigate and the people we help."

Tineya sat up straight as a murmur ran through the crowd. "You mean we're going to read minds?"

"Only at a basic level. There are strict laws and restrictions on its use, and there is no excuse for an invasion of privacy for personal gain. For this reason you will learn to pick out emotion and basic thought patterns."

"What is this? You're supposed to be teaching us how to do what revealers do!"

"That was never the purpose of these lessons. A revealer should be able to reach in to the minds of those around them and pick out thoughts or listen to conversations, not only close by but also over long distances. But that level of proficiency in the general population would be a disaster."

"So you'll continue to lord it over us, reaching into our heads whenever you want, and we can't fight back?"

"On the contrary. You need to let me explain the other side. The people around you, if trained, can look in to your mind and read your thoughts if you let them. This is why one of the first things we learn is how to shield. It is vital that you learn to block out all stray thoughts and keep your innermost mind blocked from all intrusion. In time you will learn to feel when someone is attempting to read you, and adjust your level of shielding accordingly."

"Child's play," snorted Tineya. "I already know how to do that."

"I'm aware of that, Tineya. The one exception to this rule is when you allow a partner to link minds with you for the purpose of enhancement. In this case, you will allow them to see only your public mind. It is advisable to keep your inner mind tightly closed."

"Talk, talk, talk!" Tineya huffed.

"Will you shut up and let him talk?" a young man snapped. "Some of us want to learn."

"But he's so cute when he's flustered," she simpered.

Nashta drew a deep breath and let it out slowly. "We are going to try a simple exercise," he said. "I want you to pair off and take a look inside each other's minds. Now, some of you already have a natural block that will prevent this. I want you to try to lower it and let your partner in, just to the surface mind."

"But Sir..." Tineya whined. "I don't have a partner."

Nashta felt a shiver up his spine, but he pushed the trepidation down. "You... can help me... demonstrate," he stammered.

"Ooh goody!" she cried, clapping her hands.

"I'd like you to lower your shield," he smiled.

"Done," she said, tilting her head and shifting her weight to one hip provocatively.

Nashta sent his thought into her mind, meeting the spongy resistance of her shield. He knew she could release it, as she had for Sand, so she had lied. No matter, he would reach her thoughts anyway.

Instead of a sudden attack, which had resulted in a bounce-back effect the last time he tried to read her, he used a slow, more subtle method, slipping through the holes in her defence completely undetected.

'He'll never get through,' she thought. *'No way I'm letting him in, he might find out... No, better not think that, I need to make him think I'm strong and unaffected. I don't want him to know... He can't find out how I feel...'*

"You think I can't get through," he said. "You lied about your shield, but I got past it anyway. Did you really think you could stop me? You tried to keep me out because you're afraid I might find out something, you're keeping some secret that you don't want me to know."

"How did you do that?" she gasped.

"As I said, you are untrained, and no match for a high ranked revealer such as myself."

He glanced around at his students, all gazing at him, enthralled by what they were seeing. He spread his arms wide and caught Tineya's eye.

"Your turn," he said. "I am unshielded."

As the girl closed her eyes to concentrate, Nashta began a mental litany, painting a picture for her benefit.

'Such a pretty girl,' he thought deliberately. *'A little skittish, but there's something about her. I wonder...'* and he carefully crafted a mental image of her standing before him completely naked.

"Oh!" she squealed, blushing scarlet. "How dare you!"

Nashta chuckled as she slipped away, huddled on the floor in a puddle of embarrassment. He gave her a wink as he turned to the class.

"You have just witnessed a trick, a method of shielding your thoughts without using a conventional block. I painted a mental picture of what I wanted her to see, consciously planting surface thoughts to hide my real intentions. You will need to learn this method to protect yourself from people stronger than yourself. Now, it's time to see what you can do."

FOUR

The Sandman hovered in his little corner, watching as his body continued gathering minds into its core. Every time he tried to break out of his corner and take over, the Sandman found himself battered down, forced to shrink back again.

The mature mind of his vessel was too old, hardened and inflexible, already past the prime age to accept the imposition of his soul. The technology had been misused somehow. The body was right, it was his clone-seed; he could feel it. The code in the amulet matched.

The clone-seed that once had been housed there was used, grown into this body. The vessel was supposed to be occupied before it reached maturity, at a time when the mind was past the fragile growth of childhood but not yet adult, without the strength to resist.

Normally, the transition would be seamless as the stored soul took over the body and became whole again. The Sandman longed to feel that spark of life once more. But the soul transfer had been implemented too late, and the waiting vessel had already strengthened into its own unique soul.

There was something else, something even more troubling. The Sandman could feel that other presence, dark and sinister, hooking into all the minds the vessel touched. If he could only gain control, the Sandman knew he could eject the presence that sunk its threads of thought into the vessel's mind.

But the interloper was too strong, and the vessel's mature soul too powerful to be overcome. The Sandman knew he had to make the vessel's native soul aware. But perhaps he could use this sinister new presence. Perhaps he could let it weaken the vessel's mind, giving him the chance to break through.

There had to be a reason for those hooks of thought. He would have to sit back and wait, see what the dark presence would do. The Sandman had no idea how long he had been stored, but he could wait a little longer if it meant reanimation in such a powerful vessel. He settled back into his corner, watching for his moment.

As the wagon began its long climb up the hill, the woman gazed at the fortress, squatting on its hilltop like a tiger waiting for its prey. The afternoon sun cast its beams across the ancient stonework, reflecting back in bands of light and shadow, and the gate's iron maw roared its silent challenge to the world.

Pulling up at the gate, the woman sat staring, hushing the grumbles of her sleeping child while her husband sprang down to speak to the gatekeeper.

"We are here to see the Maestro," he said in a quiet voice that gave away none of his prowess.

"And who might you be?" the old gatekeeper snarled. "Nobody gets in as doesn't belong here."

"I am King Atwin of Drasmil and this is my wife, Princess Nettayna of Shirall. The Maestro's granddaughter."

The gatekeeper's eyes narrowed. "Have ye any proof?"

"Only my word, Worm," he replied, using the man's secret name with a disgruntled sniff.

The old man's eyes widened and he stuttered uncertainly. "I'll have to check with the Maestro."

"By all means. He is expecting us."

"Wait there," sniffed the man, hurrying off.

Climbing back up to the seat, Atwin gave his wife a grin and she laughed.

"Security still as tight as ever," he said with a shrug.

"Did you expect anything else?"

"No, but one of these days it would be nice if the old man recognised me."

"He is just doing his job, 'Win. Without a revealer's cloak and badge, you are a nobody to him."

The old man appeared behind the gate, huffing and wheezing. He slid the latch without a word and pulled on the thick iron bars, swinging the gate inwards. He gestured for them to pass, eyes downcast. Atwin tried to catch his eye as they passed, but the man had already dismissed them, closing the gate behind them without a word. Atwin chuckled and flicked the reins, steering the wagon through the dark passage and into the bright sunlight of the inner courtyard.

"I wonder if Mym is here," Netta murmured. "I mean Mist."

"It is strange to think of our friends with those college names," Atwin said with a smile.

"It is tradition, we have to respect their ways."

"We will see them soon, I am sure. Let us get the horses stabled and head up to the Maestro's office."

Nearing the end of the corridor, Atwin stopped in front of a door, marked with a sign that simply said "Maestro". He raised a hand to knock, but the door was opened before his knuckles hit the wood. A spry old man grinned at him, the white sash of his rank tied about his bald head.

"Come in, come in, my boy," he said. "My dear Netta, come in, let me see you."

"Hello, Grandfather," Netta smiled and followed her husband into the cosy office, carrying her daughter half asleep on her hip.

"This can't be little Shedissa," the Maestro said. "Will she come to me?"

"Dissa," Netta whispered. "Say hello to Poppy Maestro."

The little girl regarded him with big blue eyes, her lips working on the new words. "Pop-pop?"

The Maestro laughed and held his hands out to her. The little girl went to him happily and reached up to pull the white sash from his head, bringing it straight to her mouth.

"Dissa, no!" her mother scalded.

"It's alright, my dear," said the Maestro.

A chuckle from the darkness by the hearth drew her gaze, and another man stepped forward. His long dark hair was tied back with a black sash, and a black border edged his midnight blue revealer's cloak.

"Ev... I mean Sand," said Atwin with a grin.

The Awakener clasped his offered hand. "It's good to see you, my friend."

"Where is Mist?" asked Netta, looking around.

"She's testing for Master this week. She'll be free later."

"Oh," Netta sighed.

"Perhaps we can go out to the garden?" said the Maestro. "Go and get your son from the nursery, Sand, let the children play for a while. I'll order a picnic tea from the kitchen. Mist can join us there."

"That sounds lovely, Grandfather," Netta sighed. "It has been a long journey."

Mist pushed back the hood of her green-bordered cloak, catching the sash and reaching up to tie it about her head. She checked that her tiny mote knife was snug in its sheath within the sash, grunting as the wound in her side protested. Taking a few shallow breaths, she pressed a hand against the cut and sheathed her sword, gazing down at the assassin's corpse. He had been a worthy opponent, a good swordsman, almost too good.

Reaching out a thin tendril of thought, she located her family and trotted away from the scene of battle. The duty apprentice would clean up the mess. Heading out of the testing wing, she slipped through a hidden door and out into the courtyard, taking a little path toward the walled field to the rear of the College complex, with its well-manicured lawns and extensive gardens.

"Mist!" she heard a cry.

She saw her friend Netta coming toward her, all smiles and waiting arms. She returned the smile and accepted the embrace.

"How long have you been here?"

"Not long. Come along, the food has just arrived."

Netta led her toward the trees, where a little picnic was set, and three men sat on the grass talking quietly. Nearby, little Dissa gambolled about on her wobbly legs while Zavvy crawled frantically after her.

"Mamama!" Zavvy called at sight of her.

Mist caught him up in a hug, stumbling slightly as a wave of dizziness hit her. She sat against a tree near the men to offer a feed. The boy latched on as soon as she lifted her tunic, and she settled back with a sigh.

"Mist, are you alright?" said Netta as she sat beside her with Dissa on her lap. "You look a little pale."

"I'm fine," she smiled. "Just tired. That last test was difficult."

"Can I get you something to eat? There is bread, cheese and salad greens..."

"Thank you, Netta."

The baby squirmed, and she released him to crawl toward his father. Netta brought a plate and Mist gave her a small smile, taking the plate with a trembling hand.

"You are not alright, are you?"

"I'm fine."

Mist watched through a fog as Zavvy clambered into his father's lap and Sand slipped an arm about his son. Then the Awakener frowned and pulled his hand away, staring at it with a bewildered expression.

"What have you done to yourself, little man?" Sand searched about, examining the boy for injury. "It's not you..."

"What is it?" the Maestro asked.

"Blood!" said Sand. "But where did it come from?"

Mist blinked, licked her lips. "It's nothing. Just a scratch."

She felt Sand staring at her, then somehow he was at her side.

"That much blood is hardly nothing," he murmured.

"He got in a lucky hit, before I finished him off. I'm fine."

She tried to focus on her dear revealer as he examined her. Then her eyes fluttered, and she felt herself falling as the world went black.

Something had happened. The vessel was anxious, deeply worried about something. It made him weak. The Sandman climbed out of his corner, glimpsing a crack in the mental shield. The vessel's conscious mind was right there, just within his reach, so close he could taste it.

The Sandman crept closer, slipping a finger of thought through that crack. Slowly, he allowed his consciousness to follow, sliding silently through until he hovered just inside the vessel's open mind. He held still, waiting for the push of rejection.

Silence, just the pang of fear from something external, something the Sandman could not see. Floating further, seeping into the vessel's waking mind, the Sandman felt something he had not experienced since he had been sent into the sleep of soul-storage. He felt about the edges of the feeling, waiting for recognition to come. Was it... love? This vessel was worried about his love?

Just a little more... If he could just control the mind he would be able to see. Suddenly, he had it. Slotting into his long lost home, the soul of the Sandman took hold, imposing himself on the vessel's mind, slipping into a soul-space so familiar and yet so changed. The vessel's own soul was still there, pushed aside yet not vanquished.

The Sandman harnessed the body, feeling his senses returning. The touch of warmth on his skin, the smell of something sweet, the sound of... breathing. The sandman took a deep breath and opened his eyes.

There she lay, his beloved wife, sleeping peacefully. The Sandman sighed, hardly willing to believe she was still alive. She was still there, still young and beautiful, but how could it be possible? His vessel was in the prime of life, but certainly not the man-child he should have been. Yet his beloved was still young, still as he remembered.

He reached forward to brush the hair from her face, drawn and white even in her deep sleep. She must be ill. But... He sat back, sucking in his breath. She looked like his beloved, uncannily so, yet this was not her. The Sandman stared in confusion as the woman's eyelids fluttered, opening to gaze at him, the light of love shining behind her eyes.

"Sand," she whispered.

The Sandman felt a violent pull from within, a sudden shifting of focus. His vision blurred, bright spots flickering before his eyes, and suddenly all was black. Then his other senses disappeared, and he felt a great wrenching and stretching as his connection to the physical body was ripped from his grasp.

Ella Mortimer

Pushed down, out of the vessel's mind, the Sandman was ejected, the door to consciousness slammed shut behind him. Slipping down into darkness, the Sandman curled into his familiar corner, huddling in the cold once more.

FIVE

Sand knocked on the door and entered almost before he heard the reply from inside. The Maestro sat in his favourite chair by the fire, while two revealers, one tall in the purple border of adept, the shorter in blue, stood before him. From behind, all Sand could see was the light frame of a female of average height, and a much taller, more masculine figure at her side.

"Come and join us, Sand," said the Maestro from his chair. "How is Mist?"

"Improving, Sir," he replied as he moved forward.

"Will she be able to complete her testing?"

"I... cannot be sure, Sir."

"I hope so, for both your sakes. I know you realise how important this is."

"Yes, Sir. Was that why you wanted to see me?"

"Only in part. I'd like you to meet your newest students."

Sand approached on silent feet, but before he came close, the taller adept spun to face him. Sand studied him, noting the thin line of a frowning mouth, and a crease between the eyes. Then the stranger's expression cleared and the androgynous face took on a softer, more feminine appearance. Sand paused in his advance, eyes flicking from the taller adept's eyes to the name badge at his neck.

"Iron?" he said, reading the secret characters. "Is it really you?"

"Good morning, Sand," the Adept chuckled, the light

voice a surprise coming from such a powerful frame.

"It is an honour. I've heard so many stories about you, but I never expected to meet you in person."

"I feel, for the privilege of working with the Awakener, it was worth breaking my cover."

"You're something of a legend. You do know that some people don't even believe you exist?"

"I've worked hard to make it so," the Adept replied.

"I look forward to working with you," the Awakener smiled. "But I must test you first."

Iron glanced at the Maestro, another frown knitting his brow.

"I'm afraid you must allow it," said the Maestro. "I can recommend, but the Awakener must accept or reject. I'm sorry, my dear."

Iron took a deep breath and nodded. The Awakener touched his fingertips to Iron's temples. Slipping gently into the Adept's mind, Sand searched for the required qualities. He needed to go deeper than the surface thoughts, to the place where learnt experience settled into the very character of the soul. He paused with surprise at a discovery that was completely unexpected. Pulling out, he met the Adept's eyes with a broad smile.

"You read true," Iron grinned. "I am a woman."

"Why do you hide it?"

Iron shrugged. "I grew up on an isolated farmstead deep in the southern Dragon Mountains. Even as an infant I was big, and without access to proper care my mother died birthing me. With only boys for company, I knew nothing of females, so I dressed and acted as one of them. In the end, even I forgot that I wasn't male."

"But surely when you came here you didn't need to keep up the pretence."

"I knew nothing else. I found I didn't know how to be

a girl. Until I met Path." Iron indicated the woman by her side. "My partner and bond mate. We'd like to join your class together, if we may."

"Provided you both qualify," he smiled, turning to the girl in the blue border of master. "May I?"

The girl nodded, and allowed Sand to test her mind. Then the Awakener gave them both a broad grin.

"You're in."

The two women hugged, smiling at each other.

"When do we begin?" said Iron.

"You can come with me now, if you like. I'm meeting with the rest of the class."

Gathered together in a little grove, shaded by a perfect circle of tall simpa trees, the Awakener's advanced students gazed upon their teacher. Sand's old friend Reep held his wife's hand as Iris shivered slightly in nervous excitement. Iron and Path moved to join them, and the classmates whispered greetings and introductions. To one side, stood Netta and Atwin, outsiders subjected to sideways glances and murmurs from the College members.

"I'm afraid we can't begin lessons yet," Sand was saying. "We have two more couples who will be joining us, but they're not quite ready, and I don't want to get too far ahead before they are able to attend. For now, we can get to know each other."

Sand gestured for Netta and Atwin to stand before the others.

"I know you are wondering why we have outsiders here. I'd like to introduce you to Win and Nett. As is our policy, their identities will not be revealed, but I can tell you they are here as representatives of the royal houses of Sharné."

The class exchanged surprised glances.

"As part of our new teachings, showing our skills to the

outside world, the Maestro hopes that soon we will see more of Sharné's royal children attending classes at the College. Win and Nett are here to observe and to learn. I assure you they are both skilled practitioners of the Art, despite their outsider status. You will treat them with the respect and honour deserving of your fellow members." He nodded to Win and Nett. "Go and join the others."

Reaching an uninviting door at the end of a dark corridor, the Apprentice stood back as her companion tapped lightly. Hearing a voice respond to his knock, she watched as Joss grasped the door handle with a trembling hand. He glanced at her, and she made no attempt to hide her wild eyes, silently telling him she felt the same trepidation.

"It's alright, sweets," he said.

She followed Joss into the cosy room, saw the old man in a soft chair by the fire, the white sash tied about his bare head. On the rug by his feet a young woman sat, smiling up at him. Stopping just inside the doorway, the girl clutched at Joss' hand. The woman rose gracefully and came toward them, the green edge of her cloak flashing in the firelight, a smile sparking in her green eyes.

"Come in, youngsters," said the Maestro from his seat.

"I hear congratulations are in order," said the woman. "On two counts. Sand will be pleased."

"Come here, let me look at you," said the Maestro.

The two young revealers approached the armchair, standing uncertainly before the head of the College. He gazed at the girl with a twinkle in his eye.

"You have chosen your name, I assume," he said.

"I... yes, Sir," she stammered. "I'd like to be Bell, Sir. If that's alright?"

"Perfectly, my dear," said the Maestro with a frown that belied the chuckle.

"You don't like it, Sir?"

"On the contrary, I think it's beautiful. I used to know someone who used that name, but she died a long time ago."

"Oh. I... I'm sorry, Sir, I... I'll choose something else if you think I should."

"Not at all," he said with a wave of his hand. "I'm glad to hear it again. And you can start using it right away."

"But I thought I had to wait until the ceremony!"

"Ordinarily you would, but I want you to join the Awakener's class right away. No point wasting time over a little ceremony, is there?"

"I... no, Sir, I suppose not."

"Mist is heading down there now, so you may as well go with her."

With that, the Maestro settled back in his armchair and closed his eyes. Interview over then, Bell thought, turning to the woman waiting by the door. The famous Mist, who had brought the Awakener back from the dead.

Rumour said she had been absent from the College for years, then was readmitted without explanation and tested for journeyer at the top of her class. She was so young, only a few years older than Bell herself. How had she managed to come so far, to be assistant to the Awakener, and a favourite of the Maestro, yet be so young?

"It's a long story," Mist smiled, reading her thoughts with such subtlety that Bell had felt nothing. "You'll understand soon enough."

Sand turned to meet the newcomers, cutting off his lesson mid-sentence to rush to his wife's side. He touched a gentle hand to her waist, wanting to hold her but concerned about the wound in her side. He slipped his arms cautiously about her, letting her feel his worry.

"I'm fine," she whispered.

Sand felt a pushing from within his mind, an alien thought trying to break through. He held it down, struggling to keep control. This presence was getting stronger. He forced the voice down into its dark corner and slammed the door.

"You shouldn't be here, my love," he murmured. "You need to rest for the mind test."

She shook her head. "I need to work, to keep my mind supple, you know that. Besides, I had to bring your new students. Maestro has cleared Bell to begin."

"Are they ready?"

Mist smiled mischievously. "I believe so."

"Well, that's good news. Are you ready for a full-scale demonstration?"

"Of course," she replied with a wink. "I'm always ready for you, dear."

He caught his breath. "Some days, my love, you are just too distracting for words."

"Just keeping you humble, dear."

Turning to face his waiting students, Sand gathered his thoughts and examined them each in turn. Iron and Path, oddly matched yet somehow right, Iron tall and powerful, Path petite and wiry, each as strong as the other in her own way.

Reep and Iris, perfectly serene, melded together in a gentle union that had stood the test of time, Reep's rash exuberance tempered and controlled by Iris and her gentle grace.

Win and Nett, untrained, but experience had honed them into a powerful team, their latent abilities augmented and controlled by the ancient spirits who dwelt in the amulets they wore.

And the youngsters, Joss and Bell. A new pairing yet to be tested, with the strength of youthful enthusiasm, and the raw energy of newfound lust still sparking about them, showing the promise of a powerful joining.

Time to see what they could do. Sand perused the contents of his box of supplies, pulling out ten candle stubs. Moving to a fallen log, smoothed by years of use as a seat, he arranged the candles along the top.

"Now, first things first. Light the candles."

He demonstrated, by pointing at the first candle and sending a short burst of golden power to light the wick. The students exchanged confused glances. Mist stepped up and promptly lit the second candle, flashing a smile at the bemused students.

"Focus, concentrate, and aim," she said.

One by one, they stepped up and attempted the trick, with various degrees of success. Iron performed the task easily, and Path succeeded on the second try. Reep and Iris both easily lit their candles. Win and Nett reached out together, the faint blue light of the amulets barely noticeable as they lit their candles.

Joss made his attempt, lighting the candle on his third try. Bell stepped up last of all, hesitant, glancing at the other students. She licked her lips, lifted her hand. But no fire appeared. She tried again, and again.

Then on the fourth attempt, something glowed in her hand and the candle was lit. Eyes shifting away from the group, she slipped her hand into a fold of her robe and sidled into the protective arms of her lover, Joss.

"What was that?" said Mist, trying to catch her eye.

"Nothing," she whispered. "Just a charm that helps me focus."

"May I see?"

Bell backed away, hiding behind Joss, shaking her

head.

"No matter," said Sand. "Let's move on, shall we?"

The Awakener returned to his box, pulling out five large wooden torches and planting them in the ground behind the log.

"Now we will pair up, as is normal college policy. But not with our partners. I want you to split up and try to meld with another." His eyes roved over them. "Bell, you're with me."

The young girl gasped, clutching at Joss, eyes wide with fear. Sand gave her a reassuring smile and held out his hand.

"It's alright, I won't hurt you. I promise."

She reached out a trembling hand to take his, face twisting in her anxiety. The Awakener smiled again and Bell felt the magnetic pull of his eyes, a faint twinkle of amusement oddly reassuring beneath his serious expression. She returned his smile with a flush across her cheeks.

"Open your mind and let the meld happen," he said quietly.

Bell closed her eyes and waited for the invasion, but it did not come. The Awakener slipped into her mind, his power touching with the gentleness of a caress. She felt the soft pull, the link taking hold and using her.

Taking a deep breath, she allowed it to happen, swallowing down the fear that made her want to fight with all of her strength. Instead, she gave him her mind, letting him take her meagre power and use it.

At a gasp from the audience, she opened her eyes to see the first torch blazing. The Awakener released her, sliding out of her mind with a whispered thankyou that sent a shiver up her spine. She stood gasping for a moment as the man stared into her face.

"Are you alright?" he said.

She nodded, bemused and thrilled that he had trusted her to meld with him. She thought she understood what made him so special. No wonder Mist loved him. She felt his hand on her arm as he led her back to Joss. Then he was gone, supervising the rest of the class.

When the rest of the students had performed the trick, and all the torches were lit, Sand stood before them and began to explain.

"What you have just experienced was a standard meld, used routinely by all college members in the course of their work. I wanted you to see how it works because you are all used to melding with a life partner, which is a bit different. Now I want you to repeat the trick, this time with your bonded mate. But this time, use the power to extinguish the flame."

He reached out a hand and Mist was there to take it, ready as always. He pulled her close, into an intimate embrace, and as they kissed, the flame puffed out. Pulling apart, they laughed together, forgetting their audience for a moment. Then Sand spoke, addressing the students while staring into his wife's sparkling eyes.

"With your bond-mate, the meld is infinitely stronger, much more powerful. I need you to feel the difference."

His students rose to the task, as each torch was snuffed in an instant, easily and silently. Sand nodded in satisfaction.

"When you applied for this class there was a hidden criteria, something I did not make public. I needed bonded pairs. The deeper psychic bond is imperative for success in these techniques. In time, you will learn to harness this extra power, and you will learn new skills never before taught in the College. You will learn to create a permanent meld, one that will survive time and distance and even death. But first, Mist and I will demonstrate the full force of this meld."

The Awakener raised his hand, and the power began to build. The watchers grimaced as the mental noise roared in their heads. Mist and Sand stood solid at the centre of the silent sound, gathering the power within. Then a great burst of flame leapt from the Awakener's hand, blasting into the trees.

Sand held the sparking flame in a tight burst, aiming the beam of fire at the carefully prepared pyre that only he knew was there. The dry tinder exploded into life, creating an instant bonfire, tongues of flame quickly engulfing the piled wood, blazing for the sky.

Mist stood before the headmaster of mind, ready to accept her final test. Success would put her in the blue of master, one rank closer to acceptance as the Awakener's equal. Not that she begrudged Sand his exalted status, far from it. But people were talking and she needed this promotion.

"We have chosen a member with a rank and status above your own, someone who will be difficult to best. You must use all your skill to infiltrate his mind and switch off his power. Temporarily of course," said the Master. "Here is your target."

He handed her a folded slip of paper. She opened it and immediately recognised the symbol and the name it represented. She stared at the Master, eyes wide. He could not be serious.

"I can't. He'll recognise me."

"That is your task. To get past him unrecognised and undetected. Only then will you pass the test."

She shook her head. "It's impossible. He knows me too well."

"Precisely why he was chosen. This is a test of subtlety and persuasion. If you think you can't do it you can pull out now and try again next year..."

"I..." Mist squared her shoulders. "I'll do it."

SIX

Nashta dismissed his class and packed up his box of props. Turning to leave, he almost slammed into a slight, feminine form and pulled up short. Tineya planted her hands on her hips and shifted her weight, giving him a tantalising glimpse of the promising curves beneath her tunic. Nashta licked his lips and fumbled with his box.

"Did you have a question?" he mumbled.

"Sure," she drawled. "Why do you keep ignoring me?"

"I... what do you mean?" he asked, dreading the answer.

"You know. Every day I try to catch you after lessons are over. And every day you hurry past me as if I'm not even there."

"Do I?" He hugged the box closer, trying to edge past her.

"Don't you dare!" she growled. "Put that box down and face me."

"I don't know what you want from me, Tineya, but I have no time for this."

"What's so important?" she pouted. "I might start to think you don't like me."

Nashta shivered. "I do have other duties. And I have to report to the Awakener."

"I get the feeling he wouldn't mind."

The girl prowled, slinking her way around him as her eyes flickered over him. Nashta felt her hand trailing over his arm, across his back and down to his hip. Dumping the box unceremoniously, he spun to catch her wrist and hold her at arm's length.

"What do you think you're doing?"

"Getting your attention," she purred.

Giving a sudden twist of her arm, the girl broke his grip and slipped under his guard. He felt her hands find his waist and slink in under his cloak, wrapping about his torso with a sensuous caress that sent a tingle racing down his spine. Gasping, he held his arms wide as she snuggled in, head on his chest, her deep throaty chuckle vibrating in time with his own fluttering heart.

"Why are you so afraid of me?" she murmured into his tunic.

"I... I'm not afraid," he stuttered. "I just... can't allow this."

"You know it's meant to be," she whispered.

He shook his head, trying to ignore his trembling knees. "Revealers don't get involved with outsiders."

"Of course they do. My own father was a revealer, and he was faithful to my mother for thirty years before he was killed in the kalkar invasion."

His hands found her shoulders and pushed her back, but she would not be moved. Reaching up, her arms encircled his neck, and she pulled herself onto her toes, planting her mouth firmly on his. Nashta struggled against the compulsion, pushing against her, but she persisted and he found himself responding.

The hands that had held her at bay slipped under her arms and clutched at her back, pulling her closer as he gave in to the desire that had plagued him since the moment he had first seen her. Revelling in the feel of her soft form, his arms wrapped about her, melding her to him. Then her muffled laughter through the kiss brought him to his senses with a gasp.

"You see?" she murmured. "That wasn't so bad, was it?"

"It won't happen again." He pushed her away, staggering for the door and escape.

"You forgot your box," she called after him, the bubbling laughter taunting him.

Nashta fled, forgetting everything in his panic, heading for the fortress on the hill, thinking only of that barred gate and the safety of the College behind it.

Mist watched as the Awakener explained the enhanced power of a permanent joining of minds. Describing the principle of opening the innermost door of consciousness and gaining access to the centre of being, he led the students through a meditation.

Remembering her own connection to Sand, built in just the same way, Mist sighed. Her task lay before her in a cloud of doubt. She wondered how she was to succeed when she didn't know where to start.

She slipped into his mind, and he welcomed her. Together they watched the students delving into each other's thoughts, penetrating into the most private layers of their minds until they reached the sanctum of the soul.

Then, under the Awakener's guidance, the partners swapped essence, taking up residence in each other's centre of being. Watching as the students stared at each other in wonder, Mist smiled in remembrance, her own link to her beloved Sand still as strong as the day he created it, her saviour in many a dark lonely night when he had been forced to leave her behind to pursue the lost princess so many months ago.

'Something is troubling you, my love,' he whispered in the depths of her mind.

'I've been given my target,' she replied.

'And you doubt your ability,' he sighed. 'I'm sure you

can do it.'

'I'm not,' she whispered.

'Trust yourself,' his thought caressed her mind.

Mist sighed, giving a little smile. *'I'll try.'*

She stared at the students, exploring their new world view from within each other's minds, and an idea began to form. In order to infiltrate the mind of a stronger target, she needed to find a back door. Something like the mind link just might be what she was looking for. Carefully closing off her thoughts, she considered her options, formulating a plan that just might win her the blue of master.

Walking hand in hand with her beloved toward the nursery and their waiting son, Mist paused, her mind in turmoil.

"What is it, my love?" he smiled.

"It's nothing, I just..." she sighed. "We've both been so busy lately. It seems we never get to be alone."

"I know what you mean," he said with a chuckle.

"You know, we don't have to collect Zavvy just yet..."

He raised an eyebrow. "What did you have in mind?"

She slipped in under his arm, welcoming his embrace.

"We could go somewhere private," she hinted.

He grinned. "What an excellent idea, my love!"

She wished she could enjoy this moment. Her treacherous body wanted so much to give in to the wild abandonment of a stolen tryst. But her mind had work to do. On the surface, she painted a perfect picture, giving her lover every reason to believe she was caught up in the thrill of his touch.

Retreating into her own subconscious mind, she sought the door to the centre of being. Digging down into her very soul, she found the home of her essence, and there he was, as he always was.

Using his presence, she lingered inside, riding the link back into his centre, where her own shadow-self awaited. She had bypassed his defences, entering his subconscious mind without triggering his awareness. Slipping out of his soul centre, she explored the depths of his mind.

Something watched. A consciousness that was at once alien and yet belonged. Something not him and yet... She shook off the sense of foreboding and continued her careful search. She heard that other presence chuckling its glee.

Burying herself into his automatic responses, she found what she was looking for. Working quickly, she set the block in place, ready to activate. Hesitating, she hoped he would forgive her. Then, she triggered the block, switching off his power. The response was instant.

'My love, what have you done?' he cried silently.

Then her mind exploded in pain. Her beloved slipped from her grasp, his presence pushed aside. The strange other consciousness cackled its triumph as it forced her down, out of the thought centre and she felt her mind come crashing back into her own head.

Blinking back the pain, she opened her eyes to see him staring at her, a golden gleam lighting his eyes.

"I'm sorry!" she moaned.

"Thou hast nought for which to be sorrowful," he said. "Thine action hast freed me from my prison and given me back my body."

"What are you talking about, Sand?" she mumbled.

"Thou mayst call me Sandman, Waker of Souls. Keeper of Memory and Bringer of New Life!"

"What? Sand, please..."

"The one you callest Sand hath control of this vessel no more. I am Sandman reborn!"

Mist gasped. She sent a mental finger probing, searching

for the mind of her beloved. The thoughts that greeted her were unfamiliar, almost alien, with strange memories of a time and place completely unknown. Sand was nowhere to be found. The link to the Awakener that had sustained her in her darkest hours seemed utterly dissolved.

"Who are you?" she whispered over the lump in her throat. "Where is Sand?"

The man chuckled. "Ah, sweet one, thou art fair in thy loyalty. But this vessel doth belong to me."

"No!" she screamed. "You don't belong here! Bring him back!"

"You try my patience. It cannot be done."

Mist flew at him. "You can't do this. He must be in there somewhere. Sand, can you hear me? Come back!"

She clutched at him, his form so familiar yet standing so stiffly before her. The man she loved transformed into this stranger who felt nothing. She sobbed into his unresponsive chest. She felt a great desperation building up inside, her trembling hands clutching, shaking, tearing at him. The gold spark in his cold eyes flickered, the familiar warm brown of her beloved fitfully breaking through before being engulfed in the gold of the stranger once more.

"Let him out!" she screamed.

The stranger pushed at her, breaking her grip on his tunic. As she rushed in again, he raised a hand and sent her sprawling with a back-handed slap to her face. Blinking back tears, she huddled, defeated on the floor, gasping over the painful sobs that threatened to tear her in two.

Floating in darkness, no sound to break the isolation, Sand tried to make sense of his surroundings. Physically, he felt nothing. Mentally, just a vague confusion. He reached out a tendril of thought, exploring his prison. He knew this place, felt a connection to the dark pathways and shadowed corners, as familiar as home. Home, where he and Mist had been enjoying a rare moment together... Mist! If he was here, what had happened to her?

His searching thought touched something. A memory playing its course, imprinting itself on the dormant mind of its host. Suddenly he knew. He was trapped in his own mind, now in the possession of someone else, the interloper imposing its will by implanting memories deep into the mind it had stolen.

More than anything, he wished he had dealt with the strange presence in his head, vanquished it before... this. He allowed his floating thought to infiltrate the strange new memory, and found himself transported to an unfamiliar time and place, completely alien.

He reached forward to open the centrifuge, lifting out the first of many tubes of genetic material. He took out a clean slide, extracted a sample and squeezed a single drop, slipping on the cover and sliding it under the microscope. He hoped this latest batch was viable, but he would not be sure until he could see how the cells multiplied.

He had to find a way to halt the damage caused by generations of cloning. In the early years, the changes were minimal but now, with each successive copy more degraded, time was running out. If they did not find a new world soon the fate of mankind was doomed.

"Well? Is it good?"

He jumped at the voice and cursed, turning to face the crippled officer in his wheelchair. "I know not yet, Kay."

"It had better be. I need my rebirth."

"Your clone-seed must have time to grow. You will have at least ten years to wait, you know that."

"I did think maybe I might be transferred right away, as soon as it is implanted. That I might grow with it."

"You know that's impossible. Imposing your soul on a

fresh seed is too dangerous. The newborn mind is too fragile. You would risk madness or worse."

"I care not, Sandman. I can live like this no longer!"

"If you're filled with such great anguish, you can sleep through it; let your beta take your place right away. I can put you in soul-storage until your clone is ready."

The man shivered. "I hate that place."

"You must go there sooner or later. All souls must be cleansed before they are reborn."

"All except you," Kay spat. "You take your new life straight away. You don't know what it's like."

"You think I want this life? I'd love to get my rest. It's not my fault my beta lost his nerve and pulled out. Be thankful you have someone to take your place while you sleep."

Pulling out of the memory dream, Sand backed away, floating back to the subconscious thought centre and settling into a dark corner to consider what he had heard. The interloper who had stolen his body came from a world he had never imagined and could not understand. What would he do when he realised his world was gone?

A sudden pulling sensation caught his attention and he felt himself floating again, heading for the door to the conscious mind. Somehow, it had opened a crack, and someone was calling his name, drawing him up out of the darkness. He rushed toward the silent call, hope washing over his soul.

'Sand, are you there? Come to me, my boy.'

He surged toward that irresistible pull. 'Sir?'

'The invader is unconscious,' whispered the Maestro's thought. 'And I have restored your power. But you must fight for control. You can do it, boy.'

'Yes, Sir!'

As the Maestro released his grip on the Awakener's temples, Mist chewed her nails absently, her gaze flicking from one to the other. The Maestro held out his arms and she ran into his fatherly embrace.

"Hush, my dear, all is well," he smiled. "Sand responded. He will return to you."

Mist let out a sob. "Thank you, Sir," she mumbled into his chest.

"When he wakes, the intruder will be defeated."

"But you're not certain..."

"He has a battle ahead, but his is the stronger mind. Sand will prevail."

SEVEN

Mist sat in a daze, staring through tear-filled eyes as her little boy played on the floor. She glanced to where her husband still lay unconscious. Occasionally he let out a grunt or a disconnected word, the only sign of life. Mist jumped at a knock on the door. She dragged herself across the room and opened the door a crack.

"Is everything alright?" said Iris through the door. "You missed today's lesson."

"We're fine," Mist mumbled.

"Are you sure?" said Reep from behind his wife. "It's not like Sand to miss a commitment..."

"Yes," Mist whispered over the lump in her throat. "Everything's fine."

The visitors shared a dubious look. "Well, if you're sure," said Iris with a smile. "You know we're here for you if you need anything."

"Thank you," Mist mumbled, closing the door on their concerned faces.

"Mamama!" Zavvy gurgled as she turned from the door.

Scooping up the baby with a stifled sob, Mist sat in the armchair and offered the breast, settling back with a sigh as he suckled. She was dozing when another knock woke her with a jolt, and the baby grumbled in his sleep.

"Mym, can I come in?"

"Netta?" she whispered.

The door burst open and Netta hurried in, followed

closely by Atwin.

"Grandfather told me what happened," said Netta. "You should have sent for me."

"It's alright," Mist mumbled. "We're fine."

"From what we heard, you most definitely are not fine," Atwin sniffed.

"You do not have to be strong with us," said Netta with a smile. "You should know that by now."

Mist looked from one concerned face to the other, eyes flicking to where Sand still lay unconscious. She held her breath on the moan that threatened to break through, the tears flowing freely. Netta slipped her arms about her and Mist sobbed into her shoulder. A groan from the bed drew their gaze, and Atwin moved closer to examine the Awakener.

"I think he is waking up."

Mist shivered, dreading the sight of those cold gold eyes. "What if he's still..."

"He will be fine," said Netta.

Sand groaned again. "What..."

Mist looked up, her breath caught in her throat. The way he formed his words, with that slight accent that she barely heard anymore. In that one word, she had heard her beloved. Netta gave her a pat on the back as Sand struggled to sit up, clutching at his head. He glanced around through squinted eyes, his gaze finally settling on his wife.

"What's wrong?" he mumbled. "Why are you crying?"

Mist flew at him, throwing herself onto his lap, pushing him back down onto the bed, mumbling out something into his chest, indistinguishable through the sobs.

"I will take Zavvy to the nursery, shall I?" said Netta with a laugh in her voice.

She bent to lift the boy from the floor and headed for the door.

"Are you coming, Win?"

"Ah... yes, alright," said Atwin, following his wife. "Glad to see you feeling better, Sand."

The visitors already forgotten, Sand struggled to rise again, gently fending off his wife's clutching hands, his warm brown eyes filled with worry.

"Are you going to tell me what happened?" he said.

"I'm sorry!" she cried. "It was my fault. I blocked your power and he came..."

"It's not your fault," he shook his head. "I should have told you something was wrong. I thought I could stop him myself."

"And then I took your power away," she sobbed.

"You were only following orders. I presume I was your target for the mental test?"

She nodded, a tear sliding down her cheek. "I'm sorry, I should have refused..."

"And wait another year? Of course not. You had no way of knowing what would happen."

He reached a hand to her cheek to wipe away the tears, and she flinched as his thumb brushed against the bruise covering the left side of her face.

"Who did this to you?" he gasped.

"You did," she mumbled. "Or rather, your alter ego."

"What? I would never..." he licked his lips. "Mist, I..."

"It's alright, I know it wasn't you, but..." she took a deep, shuddering breath. "Sand, I was so frightened. Promise me, he's really gone."

Sand pulled back, a frown shadowing his face. "I can't promise that, my love. He's still there, hiding somewhere, waiting for his chance."

Mist shivered. "What are we going to do? Who is he?"

"I don't know. He's from somewhere... different. He left behind memories, of another place, like nothing I've ever seen before."

"Sand, I'm scared. What if he comes back?"

"Don't worry, my love. We'll deal with him."

Nashta, known as Tong, watched the lower ranks milling around in the marshalling room, waiting their turn to take part in the ascension ceremony. As always, the new novices seemed to take forever to file into the great hall, their undisciplined minds full of ten-year-old excitement at joining the illustrious College of the Art.

But finally they were all inducted and sitting among the ranks in their crisp new yellow bordered cloaks, their first experience of college ritual all but over. Next were the new apprentices, the old yellow faded on too-small cloaks, showing signs of wear. The teenagers fidgeted and chattered as they anticipated wearing the brown.

As the last of the youngsters lined up to enter the hall, Tong noticed the ascendant journeyers taking their place in line. He frowned at the sight of the Awakener's favourite, deep in whispered conversation with the child who had taken his place in the advanced class. So the upstart youngster had gained the green. He gave a derisive snort that drew glances from people nearby.

But as the child reached the head of the line and entered the hall, his surprise doubled. The Awakener's journeyer wife took her place in line with the ascendant masters. The green of her cloak, barely worn and almost as crisp as new, stood out amongst the others, who had served their time in service to the College.

Tong grimaced in distaste. Yet another youth elevated before time. It was a ploy to stop the whispers, the condemnation that only he had voiced. Only he had had the courage to take his complaint to the Maestro, and he had been rapped over the knuckles for it.

He saw her conversing with the others, receiving praise

and giving it, basking in her acceptance while he stood alone, the envy of his peers. They would keep. He was twice the revealer she would ever be, and he was going to prove it.

His ascension was only the start. From today, he would wear the red of artisan, the highest active rank and the first step in his plan. If he could not be in the secret Awakener club, he would go higher, and work toward the pinnacle of his profession. He planned to be the next Maestro. Then they would see. They would all pay for dismissing him.

Mist strode out into the hall in front of the entire collected membership of the College. Approaching the line of counsellors, the elders of the College, she removed her green headscarf, palming the small blade she kept hidden there. Handing her old cloak to the waiting apprentice, she stepped up to receive the blue of master.

The new cloak was draped about her shoulders, the blue sash tied about her head to hold the hood in place and her mote knife safely hidden away. And it was over. She caught the Maestro's wink before she melted into the ranks of the College, as the next ascendant master took her place in the ceremony.

Searching for Sand amongst the assembly, she finally found his distinctive black-edged cloak near the back of the hall. She reached out to find his mind, but he was closed off, the familiar loving mental touch denied her. Biting back an irrational moan of grief, she turned to take her place at the Master tables and watch the rest of the ceremony, feeling cold to the bone.

Sand watched his wife accept her new cloak, his heart filled with pride. But as he gazed at her, he felt a pushing from the presence within his mind.

Searching within, he followed the interloper down

into the subconscious, where he lay in wait. The intruder flickered away, refusing a confrontation. Securing his own path back, mentally locking the door to his waking mind, Sand followed, and found himself again sucked into a memory not his own.

Sandman watched his woman dance, feeling her joy in his own heart. She smiled at him as she spun and he somehow knew she wanted him to join her in the dance. She had always loved to dance, even in the confines of the soul-ship.

Every rebirth she grew more graceful, more perfect. He suspected she even danced in the deep sleep of soul storage between rebirths, those long years when she was lost to him because he could not sleep. Those were the times he longed for rest, when his clone-seed was being reared by another family instead of her.

'Come and dance,' she whispered.

But she had not spoken. She had not made a sound. Sandman moved closer as she whispered again. Her mouth did not move but he had heard her speak.

'Try it,' she whispered, speaking directly to his soul. 'Answer me.'

'I... don't know how...' he projected the thought, trying to make her hear.

'You don't have to yell,' she replied in his mind.

'How do you do this?'

'You're doing it too.'

'But how?'

'I think it's another copy error,' she whispered silently. 'A good one this time.'

'How long have you known?'

'Not long. I wonder how many others can do it...'

'It could be the whole batch! I must perform some tests, find out what went wrong and correct it for next time.'

'Why? Why not breed it in, make it stronger?'

'I don't know, beloved. It could be dangerous.'

'I like it.'

Sand fought his way out of the memory dream, struggling to regain his own mind. He heard a faint call, felt a pull from somewhere far away. Floating back toward the door to consciousness, he slipped through and opened his eyes.

The ceremony appeared to be over, and Mist was standing before him with the crowd milling about. Her hands were on his face, fingers at his temples. He blinked to clear his vision and she smiled.

"Thank the spirits, you're back," she murmured. "I thought I'd lost you again."

He smiled and shook his head. "He was remembering, and I saw it like a dream. He made no attempt to take over, but I was entangled for a moment."

Mist frowned. "I don't like this."

"Don't worry, my love."

He took her hand and kissed it, smiling into her eyes. "I just learned how these powers came about, the mental abilities we use in the College."

"You what? I thought we always had them."

"I don't quite understand it yet, but it was some kind of mistake. I can't explain it."

"Just be careful. Don't play around with this stranger. He's dangerous, and you could be taken over again."

He smiled and shrugged, pointing to where the apprentices were bringing out platters of roast meat and vegetables. Sharing a smile, they took their place together at a nearby table, the strict seating order relaxed for this most important of ceremonies.

On this one night of the year, ranks were allowed to blend, mixed-rank couples eating together and unmated members mingling freely.

"Do you think we should postpone our trip to Shirall?" Mist said. "Maybe we should do something about your intruder first."

"I'm sure things will be fine. You don't need to worry."

"But what if something happens? It was only the Maestro's strength that brought you back."

"Nothing will happen, my love. And it will be good for Zavvy to see his future home."

"Are you sure that's wise? It could be dangerous. I don't want to leave him here, especially before he's fully weened, but I'm afraid."

"What could be dangerous about a little family holiday?"

"A working holiday, remember. And you have a way of attracting trouble."

He grinned. "You're not going to hold a little divine possession against me, are you? Kayus is long gone, my love."

"Who knows what this latest possession is all about. Is it worth the risk?"

"Absolutely. I can't wait to get started."

"Well, if you're sure..."

"Of course I'm sure. Now, I command you to enjoy yourself, Lady Master."

"Lady Master? Now that's a preposterous oxymoron if ever I heard one!"

He let out a laugh that brought puzzled glances from others at the table, and winked at his wife. Almost before the meal was over, tables were pulled back, clearing the floor for a night of music and dance, a rare opportunity to relax the rules and have fun.

The first couple on the floor were Bell and Joss. Mist smiled as they swirled into the first movement of the D'Onara, the dance of marriage. Almost immediately, they were joined by three other couples, also declaring their commitment to each other in the sensual movements of the dance.

The ascension ceremony often brought couples together, the festive atmosphere embracing their union. Sand grasped Mist by the hand and pulled her out onto the floor, and she welcomed his embrace.

They had already made the commitment twice before, but the previous occasions had both been in unusual circumstances, and now they performed together as the dance was meant to be. They danced with practised ease, moving as one, bodies intertwined yet barely touching. Ending close together, staring into each other's eyes, they hardly heard the applause.

'Let's get out of here,' he whispered in her mind.

'Not yet,' she sighed. *'We have to congratulate Bell and Joss.'*

'Do we have to disturb them?' he said.

Mist looked to where the young couple stood locked in a passionate embrace. *'They're officially our students now. We have to acknowledge it.'*

She led him by the hand to meet the youngsters, now looking decidedly uncomfortable, as if they wanted nothing more than to escape the hall together.

"Congratulations, you two," said Mist with a smile.

Joss grinned. "Thank you. Same to you."

"Oh, we've done it before. But it's always fun."

"You look so perfect together," said Bell, her cheeks flushed. "I hope one day we can perform the dance as well as you do."

"I'm sure you will," Mist smiled.

"We'll leave you alone now," Sand said with a wink. "But back to work tomorrow, right?"

"Yes, Sir!" said Joss.

Tong watched the upstarts and their back-patting

party with a sneer of distaste. All these youngsters giving themselves more credit than they were worth. And he stood there on the fringe, watching as the world worshipped them.

How did they succeed so easily when all he could do was bluster about getting nowhere? Enough. He stormed across the room, determined to intercept the young couple and find out what was really going on.

"Why?" he exploded at them.

"Excuse me?" said the boy.

"Why you two. What do you have that I don't?"

"I don't understand," said the girl.

"Look at me! Artisan! Right at the top of the tree, red to your green, mere journeyers, one of you barely out of the brown. Why does he welcome you, pat you on the back and chat with you like old friends when I can't get a foot in the door?"

"Is this about the Awakener?" said Joss.

"It's about respect, and acceptance, and recognition. I know I belong in that class!"

"Sir, I don't know what to say," Joss shrugged. "I'm sorry you're disappointed."

"What am I missing?"

"I can't tell you that, Sir."

Tong paced, moving away then spinning back to them. "I'll find out."

Tong caught the girl's eye. She appeared to be genuinely concerned. On impulse, he sent a mental finger probing into her mind. Carefully he slipped past her immature defences, her young mind no match for his well-practiced power. She did not even know what he was doing.

"What about you, little miss?" he snapped.

"I... I'm sorry, Sir."

The girl's mind seemed to spin in circles, constantly settling on her lover then pulling away as if she were trying not to think about him. She was attempting a subterfuge to send him off track.

"It's nothing you can prepare for, Sir." The boy exchanged a secret smile with his girl that set Tong's teeth on edge. "It will just happen."

And there it was, the secret. The girl's mind flicked over the thought before she could stop it and suddenly Tong knew. His heart sank and all his arrogance left him.

"A life partner?" he whispered. "That's it? That's what I'm missing?"

"I... I'm sorry..." the girl stammered.

"It makes the power stronger," said the boy. "So we can learn the new skills. It's a whole new way of working."

Tong shook his head in chagrin. "I thought it was something wrong with me. I thought I wasn't good enough."

"Of course you are, Sir," said Joss. "The Awakener really wants you with us."

"I'll never make the class," he said with a groan. "Where am I to find a life match?"

"Sir," said the girl timidly. "If it helps... The Awakener believes you will join us soon. He thinks you have already found her, you just don't know it yet."

Tong frowned. "I don't understand. Who?"

"I can't tell you that, Sir," she smiled shyly. "You need to trust yourself."

Tong sighed. "I'm sorry for how I've acted. I didn't understand."

"It's alright, Sir."

Tong drifted away, leaving them to their lovesick murmurings. A love match? Impossible. He would have to resign himself to the fact that he would never be privy to the Awakener's teaching. In his despair, he never even considered the woman who already had his heart in her hands.

EIGHT

Retiring early from the celebration, Tong made his way dejectedly to his quarters. Not his much longer, since he would be moving to the artisan wing, with its larger, more luxurious suites. Some newly ascended adept would be given his old rooms, once his possessions were removed. It felt like his whole life was falling apart around him, this last reminder bringing resentment, rather than pleasure.

Why should he be made to feel rejected on the very night of his triumph? Reaching the rank of artisan was no mean feat. He should be basking in the thrill of his success, not slinking away like an outcast.Before he could slip the key in the lock, Tong paused. The door stood slightly ajar.

Grasping the handle, he drew his knife and pushed the door open, ready for a fight, though why there would be an enemy here in the College he did not consider. Stepping cautiously into the room, his gaze was drawn to the window, a slight figure silhouetted against the light from the courtyard below. Nashta frowned, squinting his eyes in the dimness, trying to see.

"Who are you and what do you want?" he said.

The intruder gave a throaty chuckle, low but light and feminine. Nashta felt his blood go cold, a heavy weight sinking deep into his gut, and his heart thudded painfully in his chest.

"What are you doing here? How did you get in here? How did you get past the guard?"

"Your gatekeeper was preoccupied by the noises from your little party. He was quite merry with drink when I slipped through the bars."

"Slipped through... that's impossible."

The intruder laughed again, her soft voice sending butterflies fluttering through his gut.

"You should not be here," he stammered. "You need to leave right now."

"My dear Nashta, I have no intention of leaving."

"It's Tong here, if you please," he sniffed.

"Really? What for?"

"All members use their Art name while in the College," he said defensively.

"Why?"

"Because we are anonymous. All are equal in the College."

She snorted. "So you use a nickname? How utterly silly."

"What are you doing here?"

"Why, visiting you of course."

"If anyone sees you, you'll be arrested as a spy. I can't protect you from college law."

"So shut the door..."

Tong spluttered for a moment, then turned almost against his will and pushed the door closed.

"You can't stay here. I need to work out how to get you out unseen."

"I told you I'm not going anywhere. Besides I can get out again without your help."

"So what are you doing here?"

She snorted again. "Are you really that dense or just deliberately obtuse?"

He spluttered. "I... I can take you out the window, across the roof and over the battlements..."

Striding toward the window, he grabbed her arm, ready

to pull her out behind him. Her face caught the light from the window and he paused, the play of shadow picking out the lines of her cheeks, the light hitting the perfect curve of her jaw. He licked his lips. She pulled him back from the window, slipping an arm about his neck.

"Will you just shut up?" she whispered, pulling him down to plant her lips on his.

Back stiff, he tried to resist the urge to give in. He was not aware of his own arm slipping about her, his hand flat on her back pulling her close. Before he even realised she had won, he was lost in the feel of her, a great pressure building inside threatening to wash over him and send him into a wild wave of sensation.

She pulled at his clothing, and he found himself pushing her backward, moving with her as he drove her toward the bedroom. But something in the back of his mind fought for control.

Even as they fell onto the bed, his hands tearing at her clothing in his desire to feel her soft skin on his, that infallible sense of right and honour already had control of his mind. He calmed his grasping hands with an effort, pulled back from her, fending off her clutching fingers.

"What?" she gasped. "What's wrong?"

"We can't do this," he moaned. "It's not right."

"You can't be serious."

"You're not a member of the College. We can never be together, so why start this now? You have to go."

"I told you, I'm not going anywhere!"

"Tineya, please... I don't know how you got in here, but you need to get out."

"No."

"Then I will," he snapped, heading for the window. "When I come back you need to be gone."

He turned his back on her, climbing out the window

and scrambling up the wall to the roof.

Tong sat in the lee of the roof, back against a chimney for warmth, mind racing, and treacherous body shivering in thwarted lust. He had done the right thing. He had to discourage her, reject her at every turn. He could not commit to an outsider. But he wanted her.

His mind kept going over what the young journeyers had said. That the Awakener thought he had already found his life mate. It could not be her. It was not possible. How could she possibly join him in the advanced class?

If she were of the College, it would be a different matter. It had to be another, but whom he could not fathom. His mind whirled about, circles of thought twisting in a vortex of doubt. It could not be her. But he knew it had to be, somehow. He wanted it to be true.

Somewhere in his tortured mind, an idea began to form. Sand's wife had not been of the College, and now she was. How had he done it? The Awakener had told him to teach her everything. And to have fun doing it. Had he known even then? Perhaps... Just maybe there was a way... If he could only find it.

Slipping down off the roof after hours of indecision and tortured thought, Tong swung through the window into his rooms. Part of him wanted her to be gone, but the greater part desperately wanted her to be there, waiting.

There, in an armchair by the fire, orange light flickering over her beautiful face, sat Tineya, sleep lending a gentle peace to her expression. Tong stared for a long moment, drinking her in. Doubt still pricked at him, but this was the moment toward which all his training had been leading, his whole career. A leap of faith.

Reaching a hand to cup her face, he brushed her lips with a thumb, entranced as her mouth twitched, the corners pulling upward into a smile. Her eyes flickered and opened, shining in the soft light from the fire. Her smile broadened and she sat up, taking his hand in her own. He gently lifted her to her feet, pulling her into his arms, holding himself firmly in control as he allowed himself to study her.

He bent a little and brushed her lips with his, allowing the kiss to deepen as she melted into the embrace. Then, trembling in anticipation, he took her by the hand.

"I knew you'd come around," she murmured as he led her toward the bedroom.

In the cold light of a wintery dawn, an impressive group of revealers and two outsiders gathered in the courtyard, ready to take the passage to the huge iron gate. One artisan, two in the purple of adept, two in blue, two the green of journeyer.

The Awakener in his black-edged cloak stood beside his wife, helping her secure a squirming babe in a sling across her front. Then he helped her mount a golden mare before swinging up onto his own black stallion.

An apprentice fussed about, bringing more horses, freshly groomed, lean but well fed from running at pasture. Bell, the youngest member, was introduced to a new mount, as she was taking her first journey away from the College, while the others welcomed theirs as old friends.

The last of the supplies were loaded into the cart, and the two outsiders climbed aboard, the woman cuddling a toddler on her lap. As the group turned toward the passage, a man ran toward them from the main entrance.

Sand watched the Artisan approach with a small sigh of exasperation. They did not have time for this. He dismounted and strode to meet the man.

"Tong, what's the problem now?" he sighed.

"I'm sorry, Sir, I just... I want..."

Sand placed a hand on his shoulder in an attempt to

calm him. "Tong, it's alright. I know you want to join us, but now is not the time for you. You need to be more patient."

"But Sir, I... I know now. I'm ready."

Sand shook his head. "But she's not, Tong. You can't push her too fast or you'll have a breakdown on your hands. She has ten years training to catch up on. There's plenty of time."

"I... yes, Sir, of course. You're right."

"Tong," Sand smiled. "I want you both, but not until you're both ready. You do understand that, don't you?"

"Yes..."

"So what's troubling you?"

"Sir, she's not one of us. How can she be the one?"

Sand threw his head back and laughed. "Oh, Tong, you sound like me, three years ago."

Tong blinked. "What?"

"You forget how Mist came to be here. Tong, my friend, there is always a way. And a precedent. Speak to the Maestro. He has a plan."

"He does?"

"Of course he does. The Maestro always has a plan. Now, we really must be off."

Pulling up outside the walls of the College, the group of travellers watched as the ancient gatekeeper swung the huge barred gate closed behind them. Mist smiled at her husband.

"Should we do it now?" she said. "Or wait till we stop?"

"Now is probably best," he replied. "Gather close, my friends."

Watching his students obey without question, the Awakener perused their faces, seeing their masked curiosity and hoping they would accept this assignment with good grace.

"First things first," he said. "Introductions. Most of us have never met outside the College, so now is the time to reveal ourselves. I am Evelar of the Sands, son of Shevron, who is nephew to Old One."

"You're a nomad?" Bell exclaimed, then blushed and hung her head.

Evelar chuckled as he gestured for Mist to speak.

"I am Miyam," she smiled. "Daughter of Veroni, who was Mist before me, and of the merchant Ganthus. And this is my son, Zaviar."

"Ganthus," mused Reep. "I've heard of him. A bit of a shady character from what I hear. Is he still running the black market out of Martose?"

"No, he's dead," said Miyam with a sniff.

"I'm sorry, I didn't mean to offend," Reep stuttered.

"No need. I know what kind of business he kept. But I am not my father."

"Of course not," said Reep hastily. "My turn. I am Reeperly of the College. For at least four generations on both sides. That is all."

Iris smiled at her husband and gazed about, the purple of her new rank reflecting in her pale blue eyes. "I am Berkana. I was born in Zelona to ordinary parents. Nothing special."

"Special to me, my dear," Reeperly murmured with a smile.

Iron lifted her chin, a glint of defiance in her dark eyes, her strangely androgynous face a complete mask.

"I am Jumally," she said softly. "Known as Jum, usually. I am the only daughter of farming parents from the southern Dragon Mountains."

"Daughter?" said Reep. "Well that's a surprise."

Jum shrugged.

"I'm Tikki," said Path with a grin. "From Lenel. My

mother was a seamstress and my father a builder."

"Jossep," said Joss. "Street brat from Sar Let. Port beggar and stowaway. Came to the College to get off the streets."

There was a short silence. "What about you, Bell?" said Miyam gently.

The girl stared, wide eyed. "I... I'm Navear. Of the Heights. My father is chief of the Wetsnow tribe. My mother was a bondslave from..." she glanced at Evelar. "The Western Sands."

Evelar smiled at the girl. "Thank you, Navear," he said, stressing the long 'ar' sound in the manner of his people, his slight accent more pronounced somehow.

"Oh, I can hear it now!" the girl exclaimed. "My mother used to speak just like that, only stronger."

He gave her a broad grin, and she blushed again.

"And who are our non-college friends?" said Reeperly with a smile.

"Ah," said Evelar. "We left the best till last. Miyam, would you like to introduce our friends?"

"I have the great honour of introducing Nettayna, Crown Princess of Shirall and Queen of Drasmil, bearer of the Queen's amulet, Leena. Granddaughter of the Maestro and my very dear friend."

After a moment of shocked silence, Navear fell to her knees, and the older members murmured their surprise.

"Then I must assume this is..." Reeperly began.

"King Atwin of Drasmil and future King of Shirall, bearer of the King's amulet, Naali," said Evelar with a grin. "And my good friend."

"The little girl is Princess Shedissa, next bearer of Leena, and heiress presumptive to the throne of Shirall," said Miyam.

"I had no idea we travelled in such exalted company,"

said Jum, one eyebrow raised.

"You travel with friends, that is all," said Atwin with a smile.

"Which leaves us with one question," said Tikki. "Where are we going?"

"To Shirall," said Evelar. "Where we will set up the second outsider school. Then we will continue south to Nella Fillenga to set up another school there."

* * *

The spirit of nothing fluttered about, checking Its hooks and testing Its lines. The enemy was finally on the move, and It had to be ready. The plan was finally taking shape, months of preparation about to be tested.

The spirit stroked the tethered lines with anticipation, plucking a spiritual melody that jangled discordantly in the ether. Soon, the spirit sighed, feeling the lines grow taut and begin to stretch. Soon it would all come to pass, just as had been foretold.

Loyal followers would be rewarded and sleeping souls would be awakened. Just a little farther, the spirit breathed, just a few more miles and it would be done. The shortest lines were buzzing with tension, stretched almost to their limit.

The spirit watched and waited, a mental finger resting on one tightly strung tether, feeling it weakening. It followed the thread back to its source and found the soul clinging to its vessel. The spirit gave it a little nudge, crowed in triumph as it ripped away.

Chasing it as it flew, the spirit of nothing sped after the disembodied soul. Pulled inexorably toward the enemy as the overstretched thread recoiled, the soul collided with the mind of the enemy. More strings stretched to breaking point, more souls clung to life in vain. Cackling in Its victory, the spirit of nothingness danced on the gossamer strings.

* * *

NINE

Nashta followed as his students performed the exercise, walking through the bustling market of Eeasto, gathering wisps of thought as they went. Tineya stayed by his side, one warm hand clutched in his as they moved through the crowd behind the rest of the students.

They were doing well, learning to filter the thoughts of those around them to find what they needed to finish the task. A thief, planted for their benefit, hiding in plain sight. Feeling something tug at his mind, Nashta searched within.

He noted a disturbance in the surface of his mind. A strange rippling of thought, as if the fabric of his mind was being pulled in an unnatural direction. Nashta followed a newly formed ripple, feeling his way. He could sense a fixed point where the waves met, where something pulled at his mind with an insistent stretching.

Reaching the point, Nashta felt about the edges of the disturbance, exploring the way his mind resisted the pull. There. Something was caught, tugging at him. Some kind of mental hook, ripping at his mind.

Nashta explored further. Attached to the hook was a tether, a fine tendril of thought leading... where? Heart racing, he focussed his power and severed the thread. The fabric of his mind sprung back from the point of resistance, the hook still attached but powerless now.

Opening his eyes, Nashta searched for his students. They stood, seemingly frozen in place, oblivious amongst the milling crowd of merchants and customers, townspeople and beggars. Beside him, Tinaya stared, eyes vacant.

Nashta caught his breath. Touching his fingers to her temples, he slipped into her mind, just in time to hear her desperate mental screams as the mysterious tether ripped her away. He tried to follow, chasing after her consciousness, but all trace of her was gone.

"No!" he cried.

He stared around, seeing the other students just as vacant, just as lost, while the business of Eeasto went on around them.

"No!" he cried again.

He had to do something. There must be someone who knew what had happened, who could fix it. The Awakener was far away, travelling south. Who else could help? He reached out mentally to the only other mind powerful enough to do something.

'Maestro, something's wrong,' he called. *'I need help!'*

'Yes, Tong, I felt it,' came the reply. *'Someone will be with you soon.'*

In the College outside Eeasto, the numbers of the taken were growing. Every day more reports came in, and the Maestro sent his trusted few out into the world to collect them. They mingled in the great hall, silent and pliable, vacant eyes staring at nothing.

Apprentice revealers moved among them, spooning cold soup into their slack mouths to be dribbled out again. In their midst, the latest intake into the outsider class, Tong's students, stood staring like the rest. When he tried to read their minds, he found only silence.

All were empty vessels, bodies only, their minds simply gone. Tong spent long hours standing before Tineya's empty body, willing her to return to him, but she remained unresponsive, staring straight through him.

"You should get some rest, my boy," said the Maestro in his ear, one hand on his shoulder.

Tong shook his head vehemently. "I pushed her away, for too long. I won't leave her now."

"There's nothing you can do, son. The apprentices will call if something happens."

Tong stood firm, mouth set in a hard line while his eyes shone with fervour. "I'll stay, Sir."

The Maestro shrugged and moved away, mind already on other business.

"You hear me, Tinny?" Tong murmured. "I won't give up on you now."

* * *

The boy trembled in a corner, watching as the holy-one danced maniacally about the room, rolls of fat jiggling in time to the priest's gleeful steps. The cackling laughter jangled in the air, and the boy covered his ears as the fear threatened to spill out of his own mouth in a tumble of whimpers.

The boy struggled to make sense of his master's disjointed babbling. He could not understand the words, but he could feel the overwhelming emotion behind them, the absolute triumph coursing through the Master's soul.

"Time at last," the Master crowed. "Ah, my loyal followers. Thy reward hast come."

Then the fat priest leapt across the room, moving more quickly than the boy had ever seen the Master move before. The holy-one sprang at the wall, triggering the door to the secret compartment containing all the amulets that had been collected, carrying the souls of the dead.

"Ah my clone seeds, damaged and imperfect, thou wilt soon be whole, as I did promise thee."

The boy watched in fascination as the holy-one reached

into the closet, hands fluttering among the hanging amulets. He heard the voices whispering, the souls trapped inside crying for release, and his tears came unbidden.

The Master clutched at an amulet, bringing it out into the light. Raising it to parched lips, the holy-one kissed the golden charm, whispering reassurance and joy.

"May thou be the first. Takest thou thy freedom. The vessel is thine."

Slipping the fine golden chain over a neck thick with folds, the holy-one pressed the charm firmly against heaving chest with both pudgy-fingered hands. The priest's eyes closed, and the boy closed his own, carefully reaching out with his mind to listen.

In the mind of the holy-one, the amulet shone with its precious burden, the soul recognising a physical match. The spirit found its release from the soul sleep and flew out of the amulet and into the vessel of the holy-one.

But the priest's own soul waited, blocking the possession so desired by the newly freed spirit.

'Thou art denied access to this vessel, damaged as it is,' the soul whispered with the empty voice of its nature. 'But thy vessel awaits, if thou wouldst follow.'

The searching soul of the amulet, desperate for the new life it had been promised, followed the spirit of the Master.

'Takest thou hold of this line. Thy vessel is newly cleansed, emptied of its soul. It is thine to take if thou wouldst but follow the thread.'

The soul clutched at the offered thought string with eager anticipation. Without a backward glance, the newly awakened soul raced along the string, ready and willing to fight for its new life.

'Go, my loyal seed,' crowed the spirit of nothingness. 'Take thy life and use it to do my bidding. We shall be victorious!'

The holy-one opened eyes glowing in righteous fervour. Reaching into the secret cupboard, the pudgy hands fastened on another amulet, choosing another soul to be freed.

Another golden chain hung around that thick neck, another soul recognised its home and grasped its freedom, to be led to its guiding tether by the spirit of the holy priest of nothing.

* * *

A cry awoke the Artisan, who had fallen into a doze against the wall. Blinking to clear his vision, Tong saw people glancing about in confusion. Some still stood in a stupor, but one by one the life returned to their eyes and they shook themselves awake. He sent a mental call to the Maestro.

'*Sir, the people are waking up.*'

Reassured in the knowledge that the Maestro and his helpers were on the way, Tong pushed away from the wall to search for Tineya. He found her in the midst of the crowd, shaking her head and rubbing her neck.

Tong pulled her into his arms, then hurried to take her hand and lead her away from the others. She resisted, staring at him with a confused expression.

"Who are you?" she whispered, her voice thick and heavy, seeming to catch in her throat.

"I... I'm Tong," he smiled. "Nashta. Are you alright?"

"Tong Nashta," the girl murmured, brow furrowed. "Do I know you?"

"Well, yes, of course you do," Tong said, frowning at the strange inflection of her voice. "A little more than know, I should think."

"I... don't remember," she whispered.

Tong tilted his head, listening to the heavy vowels. It sounded like she was speaking with an accent, one he had never heard before.

"Tinny, you're worrying me. What's wrong?"

"Tinny? Who's Tinny?"

"It's you, Tineya... Don't you remember?"

"Me?" she shook her head. "My name's not Tinny or... Tineya, did you say?"

Tong took a moment to decipher her words, that strange way of speaking growing stronger with every word. Then he closed in, hands going to her temples. She pushed him away.

"What are you doing?"

"Something's wrong with your memory, Tinny, I need to scan you."

"You'll do no such thing! There's nothing wrong with my memory, and stop calling me Tinny. I'm Franse."

Tong shook his head, heart filling with fear. "What? Tinny, what's going on?"

"Franse Shorthand is my name, but how did I get here? I was... I was dying and then... I was somewhere white and silent, but someone was talking to me, whispering things I should do. And I woke up here..."

She looked down, brushing her hands across her torso. Then she held her arms out, fingers splayed, a look of shock flicking across her face.

"My arms, they're... long, with... proper hands and... fingers!"

She raised her eyes to the man, mouth working silently before she hurried on.

"A new body! The holy-one promised, but I never really believed... And..."

She ran her hands over her full breasts, cupping them experimentally.

"Female! Oh this is going to be fun!"

'Maestro!' Tong cried silently. *'Something is really wrong*

here!'

"I know, Tong, I'm here," said the old man by his side.

Tong jumped, and turned to face him. "They're... not themselves, Sir."

"Yes, I see that," said the Maestro. "The question is, how?"

Genton awoke to the strange feeling that something had changed. He remembered the sickness, and the holy-one coming, then nothing. He pulled the blanket up over his chest to ward off the predawn shivers and the woman beside him stirred. He stared at her for a long moment, a frown creasing his brow.

He could not remember a woman sharing his deathbed. Just his two cronies, the useless drunkard and the eunuch, keeping watch over his corpse until they could claim the spoils.

He smoothed the blanket with his hands and crossed his ankles, feeling the weight of the blanket on his toes. He wriggled them experimentally. He appeared to have all his limbs intact; no missing right foot, no truncated fingers. And he could see, even in the half-light of dawn; no blurred vision, no white mist before his eyes.

He felt a laugh bubbling up from inside. The old witch doctor had done it. Throwing back the blanket, he planted his new feet on the cold stone floor and stood, heedless of the cold.

Laid on a chair by the door were a rough cotton shirt and grey woollen trousers. They looked very big but he pulled them on anyway, surprised when they fit perfectly. This new body was tall, and well built. Good. That could be useful.

"Samson?" a woman's voice quavered from the bed. "You're awake."

Genton turned toward the sound and a short, squat body slammed into his torso.

"Oh Samson, I was so worried, but now it's alright, you'll get better."

Genton pushed at her, shaking his head.

"I don't know you woman, and I don't know this Samson."

"Samson, it's me, your wife of ten years," she cried, pulling at him. "Come back to bed, it's cold."

"Get off me, woman," he growled, pushing her away.

The woman stumbled backward and fell. Her head slammed into the bed frame and she lay still. Genton stared for a moment as the blood pooled about her head, strands of hair floating in the sticky ooze.

It had happened so fast, there had been no time to catch her. He gave a heavy sigh and headed for the door. He had to find out where he was. He flung open the door and surged from the room, through a small living room and out onto the street. Genton pulled up short.

Two men stood in his path, both dressed in dark cloaks edged in red, the hoods over their heads tied with red scarves. Before he could do more than open his mouth, one had reached forward and touched a finger to his temple, and all went black.

* * *

The boy sat in his corner, watching the holy-one close the secret cupboard and shuffle about to face him. The priest was bent forward, unable to straighten, weighed down by at least a hundred golden amulets.

'Come to me, boy," the holy-one said.

Scrambling to his feet, the boy hurried to help his master, and the priest took hold of his arm. The priest leant heavily on the boy, shuffling toward the low mattress in the corner. The boy helped the Master onto the bed, arranging the mass of gold charms about the priest's body.

"Now thou shalt fetch me some food, boy, I am exhausted."

The boy nodded and hurried off while the priest settled back and took a deep breath.

"Now I needs must pull the strings," the priest murmured.

* * *

TEN

Far to the south, Miyam watched Evelar with increasing concern. He rode stiffly, seeming unaware of his surroundings, occasionally giving a weird twitch of his head. When Miyam voiced her concern, he shrugged it off, but she knew something was wrong.

Then, just outside the bustling city of Lenel, he almost fell out of the saddle. Riding close beside and taking him by one arm, Miyam caught a flash of gold behind his brown eyes, flickering for a moment then gone as quickly as it came.

"He's attacking again, isn't he?" she whispered.

He gave a quick nod. "Yes, but that's not the problem. There's something new and he's just trying to take advantage."

"What's going on?" Miyam frowned. "This isn't the time to keep things from me."

"I know, my love," he sighed. "I keep getting these flashes, thoughts and images, from other minds."

"Other minds?"

"I can't explain it, but that's what they are." He tapped his forehead with one finger. "In here."

"Evelar, this isn't like you. You never get rattled, what's going on?"

"I don't know," he said with a shake of the head. "Every few minutes, there's another one. They..."

His head snapped back, then he clutched his ears,

leaning forward in the saddle, shaking his head.

"Evelar, you're scaring me!"

"I can't stop it," he groaned. "They won't stop, all at once, all these voices."

"Atwin, we need you!" Miyam cried, jumping down from Cheena's back.

She rushed to Evelar's side, clutching at his arm. He lifted his head to gaze at her, the spark of gold in his eyes sending her backward in terror. Then he groaned, blinked, and his own eyes stared back at her, filled with pain.

"What's wrong with him?" said Atwin.

Miyam could only shake her head. Evelar writhed again, head twitching and eyes flashing.

"My head," he moaned. "So many minds, filling my head."

The gold flashed in his eyes again, a deep, maniacal laugh bubbling out of his mouth. Then those eyes went blank and he tumbled from the saddle.

The Sandman handed the amulet to the cripple with a smile. "Glad am I, that you made this choice. Our new world draws near and you need full possession by then."

"Why must you insist on a time of sleep? Could I not take over the vessel now?"

"You know the rules, Kay. The sleeping time allows the soul-space time to cleanse your soul of any corruption obtained in this life."

Kay snorted. "Superstition."

"You know your vessel is not ready, Kay. Don't make me explain yet again."

"Of course not," said Kay with a smile. "Come now, my friend. Will you embrace me before I sleep?"

The Sandman smiled, readily accepting the embrace. "I wish you well, my friend, and I will see you when you awake."

The man's face changed. "May the time be long," he hissed.

The Sandman felt the prick on his chest as the man pressed the amulet against his flesh, saw the blue light expand from the golden charm. His eyes widened as he felt the cold sedative taking effect.

Through a dark fog, the face of Kay laughed. Then the world was gone, and he hovered in a land of white, trapped in the pure place of cleansing.

He had no memory of time passing, only the sudden awakening, opening his eyes to the loving gaze of his mother. Or was it his wife? "What..."

"Be not afraid," she smiled. "Let the memories come."

The Sandman knew those words. He had been coached to receive them when the time came. He had given them a thousand times. Memories warred within his mind. Childhood pleasures of love and comfort from the woman before him, his beloved mother, who had borne him hundreds of times.

But the adult memory was stronger, the love of this woman for her man, his wife through countless lifetimes, sharing the task of keeping the people safe, bearing his clone-seed and helping him transition again and again without rest.

Taking her own sleep times with grace and dignity, ready to be reborn in her own clone-seed and take on the role once again, mothering the new seeds when the time was right.

While generations of travellers slept by his hand and woke in their new bodies, she was at his side, helping him accomplish his transition, then sleeping until her own vessel was ready.

"What happened?" he whispered. "My time was not upon me."

"Kay attacked you, took your soul. Then he took his own vessel, without sleep."

"How long did I sleep?"

"Long enough for your clone-son to mature. You are now ten years old, and my son once more."

"And Kay?"

"He is... changed. He took his clone-son before time. He suffers from a weakness of the mind."

"Then he must be taken into sleep once more."

"It cannot be," she said. "He has staged a coup. We approach the new world with a new and manic leader. I fear for our future."

The scene dissolved and the Sandman found himself once more trapped in the mind of the vessel. He resented the necessity of manually implanting his soul on this too-mature vessel, but he knew this mind now, and the task of implanting memories could continue even before he took control.

He sensed a change in the mindscape, a clamour of voices filling the silence. He allowed his presence to float upward, to slink through the door to consciousness.

Atwin knelt by the Awakener, where he had lowered him to the ground, as the others gathered around.

"What happened?" said Reeperly.

"Is he alright?" said Jum.

Miyam tried to blubber out a response that would not come, shaking her head and clenching her fists against the trembling that would not stop. In the sling across her chest, her son wriggled and yelled, adding to her distress.

She felt a comforting hand on her shoulder and tried to smile as Netta took the child from her. Evelar's body writhed against the restraining hands of Atwin and Reeperly, the eyes glowing golden.

"Mym, you need to get in there," Atwin cried.

"What?" said Miyam.

"Remember how the Maestro brought him back. You need to do it now."

"I..."

"Now, Mym, you have to try."

Choking down a sob, Miyam dropped to her knees beside him, reaching trembling hands to Evelar's temples. The golden eyes stared balefully and the head shook away from her grasp.

Jum took her place at his head and held him still for Miyam to touch his temples again. Closing her eyes, she tried to reach into his mind.

The hostile mind of the Sandman blocked her, but she knew this place. She knew secret paths through the mindscape of this vessel that the Sandman would never know. Dodging his grasping thought, she slipped by and down into the subconscious, looking for a familiar mind.

The noise hit her, almost sending her fleeing from the chaos. So many voices crying out in fear and confusion, all clamouring to be heard. But she gathered her strength and continued on, searching and calling. Voices answered, strangers, lost and frightened. And somewhere amongst them, a familiar mental voice called for help.

'Sand, where are you?' she cried silently, but there was no reply.

She felt a pull, an invisible force dragging her back, denying access into the deeper subconscious.

She found herself back in her own head, cruelly ejected from his mind.

"I can't find him," she whispered. "He can't hear me."

Instantly, a hand touched her shoulder. And another touched that person's shoulder, and beyond those hands, the chain continued, hands on shoulders in a line, as the revealers gave their strength willingly and without hesitation. Taking hold of the extra power, Miyam tried a different tactic.

Using the permanent mind link, she slipped deep into her own subconscious, found the door to the centre of mind, and slipped inside that most intimate place, the home of the soul, where he always waited, and stepped through the link from her own mind to return to her beloved, back into his subconscious mind.

The cacophony rose around her, countless minds crying out for help. And somewhere in all that noise, a faint mental voice called fitfully.

'Mist, help me!'

'Sand! I'm here!' she cried.

But her cry brought more minds, more voices.

'Where am I? What is this place? Help me, I can't see!'

The voices tumbled over each other in their desperate plea to be heard.

'Stop!' Mist cried. 'Please, listen to me.'

The voices subsided, grumbling. Then one voice came through clearly.

'Where are we? Can you help us?'

Mist concentrated on the voice. 'I need you all to calm down. You are all here together, trapped in one man's head. I don't know how you got here, and I don't know how to free you, but I promise I will find a way. You need to keep calm or you will send him mad. Please, I need to find him or none of you will be saved.'

She felt the voices subsiding, the trapped minds content to give her space. She gathered the power of the revealers and sent out another thought. Faintly, she heard the reply.

'Help me, Mist.'

'I'm here,' she called. 'Come to me.'

She felt him rush to join her, welcoming her. She felt his relief wash over her. Leading him toward the door to consciousness, she brought him out, to battle with the

Sandman for control of his body. Leaving him to his task, she pulled out of his mind and collapsed under the weight of her own exhausted body.

When Evelar awoke, he hushed the questions of his companions and insisted they continue their journey. He spoke only to his wife, attempting to quell her worry without success.

A group of revealers and their distinguished companions stood together at the stern of a small ship. They watched as the port of Sar Let diminished into the distance, the full sails of the little ship taking them south across the Sea of Skies.

"Time to get out of sight," said Evelar. "We're making the crew nervous."

Reeperly let out a laugh. "Yes, I was feeling a bit conspicuous."

"People aren't used to seeing such a large group of revealers all in one place," said Miyam with a smile.

"Let's split up, each of us find a spot to ride out the crossing," said Evelar. "But keep in touch, just in case."

In pairs, the revealers slipped away, taking the stares of crew and passengers with them. Netta and Atwin remained on deck, the little princess clutching her mother's skirts as the ship rolled on the swell. Beside them stood Evelar and Miyam, the little boy babbling in his mother's arms.

"Are you sure you are alright?" Atwin murmured to his friend.

"Of course," said Evelar. "Everything's under control."

"Is it? I saw what happened. You were talking about voices, other minds in your head. Then that other one took over. Something is wrong and you need to start letting us help, or we could lose you again."

"I'll be fine," the revealer shrugged. "I have the crowd

under control, they're willing to wait until we find a solution."

"But who are they? And what if that is not all of them, what if more come?"

"I don't know where they came from, but I haven't had any more in a few days so I think it's over now."

"What about the strong one? Is he under control too?"

"He's different. He waits for any moment of weakness and makes a play for dominance."

"So he can come back?" Atwin frowned. "I wish we had known of this before. We could have done something to stop him."

"I can block him most of the time, but the influx of minds was too great and he got through for a moment, that's all."

"That is all? My friend, you need to stop making so light of this. We cannot help if you do not tell us these things. Perhaps we should have turned back."

"I'll be fine, Win, I assure you. It's all under control."

After an uneventful journey from the port of Sar Sor, the revealers made their way up the hill from the city of Shirall to the ruined palace. Facing them at the top of the hill, the newly repaired walls stretched along the ridge, encircling the plateau on which the palace stood. At the gate, King Atwin spoke to the guard.

"Welcome home, your highness," said the soldier as he swung open the gate.

Leading the wagon through, Atwin paused in the courtyard garden to help his wife and daughter alight. A page took hold of the reins and led the rig toward the stables while the rest of the party allowed their own horses to be taken as well.

Looking up at the new tower and the rebuilt accommodation wing, Princess Nettayna smiled, hoping the royal apartments were finally complete. It would be nice to take residence in the grand old building, instead of hiding in the cavern system below ground as the court had done for close to fifteen years.

"Netta, is that you?"

"Mother," Netta smiled, turning to face the woman who approached from a shaded corner of the garden.

"I was just sitting in your father's grotto and I heard the wagon."

"How are you feeling, Mother?"

"Oh, fine, you know me. Now where is my little flower?"

"Nan-nan," the little princess cried, toddling toward the dowager queen.

"Ah, there you are, Dissa," the woman smiled, turning her head in the direction of the sound. "And I sense you have companions. Quite a few, I think. Is that Miyam? And Evelar?"

"Yes, Delsi, it's us," said Miyam. "And some new friends."

"Well then, let us get inside. The new sitting room is ready. You revealers will not want the attention you will get in the formal audience room. Especially with so many of you at once."

"Yes, your majesty," said Evelar quietly.

"Atwin, give me your arm. I am still learning the layout of the new building."

"Of course, Delsi," Atwin smiled. "It is not like you to admit you need help. Is everything alright?"

"Fine, dear, but I do have difficulty keeping the rooms sorted in my head." She smiled up at him, as if she could see his face. "If you guide me, I do not need to count steps."

Evelar sat in the palace garden, eyes staring vacantly as Miyam approached. She paused as she studied him, this wonderful man who had taken up residence in her heart and changed her life forever. Even in the black-edged cloak of the Awakener, the most powerful revealer the world had ever seen, he seemed vulnerable.

She had never seen him falter, never had to worry that he might not succeed in whatever he chose to do, if only he would allow her to help him. But now, she had seen him lose himself in a struggle for his very soul, invaded mind and body by an unknown entity of uncertain origin, and it shook her to the core.

He appeared completely unresponsive, eyes glazed over, and her heart thudded in her chest. What would she do if he were lost to her yet again?

"You don't need to worry, my love," he murmured. "I'm all yours, forever."

She felt a fluttering in her chest, a sparking in her belly. She knelt beside him, snuggling into the circle of his arms and breathing in the scent of him. Even after all this time, she loved him to distraction, and to see the love returned in his warm brown eyes made her shiver in delicious wonder.

"You seemed so... preoccupied," she whispered.

"I was talking to the Maestro."

"Oh!" She sat up to meet his eyes. "What did he have to say?"

"Something's going on. People are losing their minds, going into some kind of trance. And they wake up changed."

Miyam shivered. "Does he want us to go home?"

"Yes, but I don't think we can. It's more important than ever to get the public classes started here."

"I agree," she smiled.

"Do you really, Mym? What if I'm wrong?"

"I trust you. And so does the Maestro."

He pulled her close. "I don't know what I did to deserve you, my love."

"You chose me. I'm the one who doesn't deserve you."

"Don't ever say that. You saved me from myself."

"You were ready to be saved," she smiled. "Why do you think we should stay?"

"We need to continue this work. Shirall is three intakes behind Eeasto, and we still have to get the southern classes set up in Nella. We need to teach people, to prevent this from spreading. They need to be able to protect themselves from whatever is taking their minds."

* * *

ELEVEN

Franse Shorthand listened to the murmurings. A group of men had gathered to make plans and they seemed oblivious to his... her presence. This female business might be useful. He... she might be able to pull some strings, run things from behind the scenes. If only she could get into the right circle. This could be the one. He... she sidled closer to listen.

"So what are we going to do?" said one, young and thin with a crop of unkempt stubble on his chin.

"Why should we stay here twiddling our thumbs?" said another with a surly frown. "The holy-one promised us a new life, not a prison sentence."

"We need to get out of this place," said a tall, well-muscled man. "These monks or whatever they are have no right to hold us here."

"They're not monks," said Franse with a smirk.

"How would you know that, woman?" the surly looking man sneered through a long red beard.

"I'm not a woman... or at least... I wasn't."

"Well you are now," said the thin, weedy young man. "And this is men's business. Go find some young stud to canoodle, we're busy."

"That's just it," she said. "We're not in Stolen City now, things have changed. Women have more power here. But you don't want to know what I know, so I'll leave you to your plotting."

She sauntered away, swinging her hips at them. Ooh, hips! Franse thought. Even better.

"Wait!" the surly one called after her.

She turned, shifting her weight to show off her newfound curves.

"What do you know?"

Franse laughed. "Do you really think I'm going to tell you, just like that? What's in it for me, apart from your sneers and gropes?"

The tall one held up his hands in submission. "I promise you'll get no such disrespect from us. Will she, boys?"

The youngster looked her up and down with eyes much older than his weedy body suggested, licking his lips suggestively.

"No," he drawled. "You'll get the utmost... respect from me, darlin'."

The sneering one just grumbled.

"Forgive me if I don't believe you," said Franse, shifting her weight to the other hip. "You forget I used to be one of you. I know exactly what's in your filthy heads and I'm not interested, so get your eyes off my jugs and your minds out of my crotch or you'll get nothing from me."

The tall man made a placating gesture. "Don't worry, sweetheart, if they step out of line they'll have to deal with me."

"Sweetheart?" Franse growled, eyebrows raised.

"I'm sorry, but I don't know what else to call you. I'm Genton by the way. That's Sniv and Porkis. Do you have a name?"

"I'm Franse, although..." she glanced down at her ample cleavage. "Franse isn't all that appropriate now, I suppose. How about Fransi? Yes, I think I can live with that. Fransi Shorthand... wait, that's not right either..." she let out a little giggle, looking at her perfect hands and beautifully long fingers.

"Ooh I can giggle!" She cried as she did it again, enjoying the high, bubbling sound. "I used to love hearing women giggle like that, now I can do it myself."

She grinned at the men staring bemused at her, and enjoyed the sensation of ultimate control she had over them. She held them in the palm of her perfect hand.

Why had he... she never realised women had such power? But the tall one was more prosaic. He watched, but no covetous gleam lit his eyes. He was cold, calculating, mind always moving behind those piercing blue eyes.

"You said you had something to tell us," Genton said.

"More like something I can do, but I want in. I want to be part of this little coup you're planning."

"Fine by me," said the weedy one.

"You'll keep your hands off!"

"Ignore Sniv," said Genton. "He's all talk. He was a eunuch in his old body, all frustration and no way to let it out. He wouldn't know what to do with his new bits."

Fransi let out another giggle. "That's the funniest thing I've heard all day."

"Now get on with it," said Porkis, the surly one. "What can you do for us?"

"Well," Fransi simpered. "This body was... intimate with one of them. The one who's always hanging around. He's a lovesick puppy and he'll do anything I ask. I won't have to do more than bat my eyelashes at him and he'll fall grovelling at my feet. You want information? I can get it."

Fransi felt the revealer's eyes, his steady stare wearing her down with its intensity. She had promised to get information, but this was getting too surreal. The force of his personality filled the room, her treacherous body reacting to his mere presence with fluttering stomach and rapidly beating heart. How could she manipulate him with this sickness weakening her resolve?

"Go on then," said Porkis. "Get over there and do what you promised."

"I will," she snapped. "Just give me a minute."

"Look, if you don't think you can do it, we can call this off right now," said Genton with a wry smile.

"I can do it," she hissed.

But still she hesitated. She had not the first idea how to seduce a man, nor how to stop before he got too amorous with her. Besides, she was a man on the inside and she did not find him in the least attractive. How could she possibly make her actions believable?

"It's alright, darlin'," said Sniv. "If you don't want him, I'd be happy to take his place."

"I'm sure you would," she snarled. "Just quit it, will you?"

"Are these men bothering you?"

She squealed, almost hitting the roof in her surprise. Clamping her mouth shut, she spun to face him, face going hot and breath coming in gasps.

"I... n... no," she stammered. "I just..."

"Because you know, if you need anything I'm right here."

"I..." she licked her lips, lifting her gaze to meet his.

"Well, there might be one thing," she simpered.

Watching his face light up, she almost laughed before the fluttering in her belly started all over again and she caught her breath in her throat, the laugh squeezing out in a high-pitched giggle. What in hell was going on with her? Such a stupid reaction.

She studied his plain, ordinary face, with its worry lines and skin pallid from a life in the shadows. She could not be attracted to this man. She liked girls. Or she used to when she was male. Her mind had not changed, but this female body reacted to its lover's presence with sensations far beyond her experience. She would never be able to hold her head up in male company again.

"What can I do?" he murmured.

She opened her mouth to speak, but closed it on the giggle that came unbidden at the softness of his voice. She glanced up at him under fluttering eyelashes and pursed her lips. His reaction was instant, his arms slipping about her and his mouth searching for hers.

Her heart nearly burst through her chest as her breasts crushed against him and her knees almost gave way from the sparking fire down low in her gut. Then he was pushing her away, the warmth gone from his eyes, his back stiff.

"I'm sorry," he mumbled. "That won't happen again. I just keep forgetting that you're not really my Tinny."

Fransi barely heard him, fighting to regain control of her body, which had somehow lost all strength as her legs threatened to collapse under her slight weight. She licked her lips, remembering the feel of his kiss, her very female body wanting more as her mind fought against it.

"I'm sorry," he said again, turning to go. "I'll keep my distance from now on."

"Wait!" she cried, one hand reaching for his arm. "I need to know..."

"What?" he asked as she hesitated.

"Why are we here?"

He shook his head. "Why don't you tell me?"

"No, not that," she said. "Why are you keeping us here?"

"Because you are all interlopers in other people's bodies. We need to find out what happened and reverse it."

"No!" she cried. "This is our reward. The holy-one took our souls before we died and gave us new life. We were promised new bodies and you can't take them away from us. They're ours now and the Master needs us."

"You're not leaving," he said. "My Tinny is in there somewhere and I intend to get her back."

"She's not here," Fransi cried. "These bodies were emptied before we ever came here. And we will take them home!"

"You can't stop us," sneered Porkis.

Fransi jumped, finally remembering the men at her back, who had witnessed the whole scene. She frowned, cheeks growing hot again in embarrassment.

"Whatever you intend to do with us," said Genton. "We won't allow it. We'll be freed from this place. The Master is calling and we can't ignore it."

A small group had gathered to watch the exchange, calling for others to join them.

"You won't escape," said Tong, glancing nervously at the gathering crowd. "We have the entire college working on the problem, and you will return those bodies to their rightful owners."

"Never!" Sniv sneered. "You'll have to kill us first."

More people were gathering behind the men, listening with angry stares. Genton turned to the crowd and raised his arms.

"Friends, are we going to stand for this?"

"No!" The word rippled through the crowd.

"Are we going to let them keep us imprisoned here and deny us our reward?"

"No!" The crowd roared, faces set in hostile stares, fists at the ready.

"Are we going to take our freedom?"

The crowd cheered, rushing forward. The commotion in the hall sent the apprentices running. Tong sent a call to the Maestro before backing from the room. As one, the crowd surged forward, toward the open door.

Tong stumbled backward before their charge, pulling the big doors closed and slipping the bolt home. The victims hit the door, pounding and screaming.

"What's going on?" the Maestro said at Tong's back.

"I don't know," he said. "It just started."

"They're angry," said a female voice.

Tong and the Maestro both turned to face the body of Tineya. The stranger's voice coming from her mouth was still disconcerting for Tong. His newfound love, still firmly rooted in the physical, longed for her touch, but his mind rebelled at the loss of his beloved's thoughts linking with his. His body might think this woman was his love, but his mind knew better.

"Why are they angry?" he said with a frown. "We're trying to help them."

"No, you're not," she snapped. "You're keeping them prisoners while you search for a way to destroy them."

The shouts grew louder, the angry voices punctuated by the crashing of fists on the door.

"What are we supposed to do?"

"Accept them as people. Treat them with dignity and give them respect. They may look like people you knew but those people are gone and we are here in their place."

"It is a false possession. Those bodies don't belong to you."

"They were given freely by the Master, who now calls us home. We must be allowed to go free. The Master pulls us, and we can't resist."

Tong jumped at a mighty crash, and the door rattled on its hinges. The trapped crowd were throwing themselves against the wood in an attempt to smash through.

"Who is this master?" said the Maestro.

"The holy-one, who promised us new life and delivered that promise in these new bodies."

"They were not his to give!" Tong cried.

"The Master pulls us home. Hold us and we will do anything we can to escape."

As if to illustrate her point, the doors crashed again, the bolt straining to hold as the wood splintered.

"She's right," said the Maestro.

Tong glanced at the old man. "What are you talking about, Sir?"

"If we don't let them go, they will fight and people will get hurt."

"But Sir!"

"I've made up my mind, Tong. It's inhumane to keep them here. They've done no wrong... yet. Open the door."

The prisoners surged through the open doors, stumbling over each other in their haste to escape. Tong pulled the girl to one side, watching as the crowd pushed past. Tong felt a firm hand take his arm, and a powerful presence filled his mind.

Without warning, the Maestro took hold of his mind, using his power to augment his own, sending a college-wide message.

'All members, take heed. Let the victims go. Do not try to stop them.'

Then the old man's presence was gone, leaving his mind somehow empty. Tong shivered at the power of the man. Such strength hidden behind the old man's quiet gaze.

He remembered his arrogant vow to become the next Maestro. But after feeling the man's mind within his, he knew he would never be his equal. At his side, the girl broke free of his grasp, rushing after the others.

"Wait!" Tong cried.

The woman turned, a wistful look flitting across her face before her mouth hardened to a thin line.

"I'm not your love," she whispered. "I'm sorry."

"I know," he replied. "But I'm still coming with you."

"No, Tong, I forbid it," said the Maestro. "Let her go."

With only a brief hesitation, the girl turned and ran after the others, one wistful backward glance the only sign of her doubt.

"Sir, if we want to find our missing people, we need to find this master," said Tong. "Only the holy-one can bring back their minds. I can follow them and keep you informed."

"Tong, they may not let you. You will be walking into danger. You should not go alone."

"I know that, Sir, but I have to try. I won't endanger anyone else. Please."

The Maestro frowned. "I don't like it, Tong."

"I know, Sir."

TWELVE

At the gate Tong paused, glancing back at the Maestro.

"Take care, my boy," said the old man. "I can't say I like this, but I know you need to do it."

"I can't just let her walk away, not when there's still a chance to save her."

"I do wish you would accept an assistant."

"This is personal, Sir. I wear the red now, I have the right."

"I know. But be careful. They're dangerous and you're on your own.

"Yes, Sir. I'll keep you informed."

Riding through the passage and out into the world, Tong shrugged off the persona of the College and shouldered his own name. It had taken an hour for him to gather his travel pack and prepare for the journey, allowing the possessed to gain a lead.

They had been seen headed south along the main road toward Martose, and his longing for Tineya pulled him after them, toward her stolen body. But he was mounted and they were on foot; he would catch them easily. Kicking in with his heels, Nashta struck out after the possessed.

Tagging along behind Genton and his growing band of followers, Fransi turned to glance back along the road. Stretching far behind, the long line of the reborn trudged in their wake. The call of the Master pulled her forward, urging her to find the enemy, but her body held her back, yearning for something it had left behind.

Her steps slowed and her feet dragged, and the leaders moved ahead. Glancing backward again, she licked her lips. More of the reborn moved past, following after Genton and his band. She had thought her decision was right, that she needed to follow the call, but the physical pull was too strong, dragging at her flesh from deep in her gut.

The reborn continued to file past. Still Fransi stood, watching them go. As the last man shuffled by, she turned to follow, but her feet would not move. A small whimper escaped her lips.

Something pulled at her mind, forcing her to move. She took a reluctant step and whimpered again. Her gut turned somersaults, and her feet refused to move. Time passed as she stood there, slave to the trembling need that took her strength and pulled against the Master's call, tearing her in two.

Finally, someone came. There in the distance, a rider approached at a canter, cloak blowing in the breeze of his passage, horse tossing its head. The sound of the animal's hooves beat a counterpoint to her fluttering heart and she licked her lips again, the longing hitting deep inside and making her knees tremble.

Her breath came in short gasps, tears streaming down her face. He pulled up before her, staring down from the back of his horse, expression unreadable. Fransi cursed inwardly at the compulsion that sent her into a spin every time she saw him, making her forget that she was not really a woman, that her male soul should not be allowing these feelings to take control.

He reached out a hand and her breath caught in her throat. Almost against her will, she stepped forward, took his hand and allowed him to pull her up into the saddle behind him. Slipping her arms about his waist, she settled in, resting her head against his back with a sigh of relief.

Clutching him tightly, she took a deep breath, feeling the conflict dissolve away. He kicked and the horse surged forward, taking them south, answering the call of the Master.

On the road outside Martose, a ragged band of men scouted ahead of the main group. A small herd of sheep grazed in the afternoon shadows, oblivious to the danger. Genton drew his knife and led the men through the scrub lining the road and out onto the pasture.

"Sniv, take Tom and Hart and gather wood, we'll set up camp here. We might just get some real food tonight."

"You got it, Gent," said the weedy young man.

"Porkis, you and Jalnet head on over to that apple orchard we passed a ways back and pick us a good load."

Porkis mumbled something and moved off. As the rest of the reborn began to gather in the field, Genton signalled for another man to join him and headed off to catch a sheep or two to roast.

Sitting his horse with Fransi behind, concealed in the trees at the edge of the road, Nashta watched the camp take shape, shaking his head at the disorganised rabble. Reaching into his pack, he took out two pieces of dried meat and passed one over his shoulder to Fransi, chewing on the other himself.

"Why don't you share with the rest?" she said.

"You think I have enough to feed a small army in that little pack?" he snapped.

"You could give them a meal, surely, instead of lurking here."

"A few sticks of jerky and a handful of dried fruit? Then where would we be? Your lot would be hungry again tomorrow and we'd be right in it with them."

"But they're starving. Those sheep are the first game we've seen since we left your college."

"They're not game. Those sheep belong to someone."

"What are we supposed to do, go hungry again?"

"No, but there are ways to feed these people without stealing."

"Really," she snorted. "What ways?"

"You should be foraging while you travel, split into smaller groups with everyone allocated a task. Taking small animals, berries and grains, some of you gathering firewood. You could travel longer because you wouldn't have to stop to hunt and gather. Then set up individual camps, small fires for your small game and camp in your groups instead of one great big fire that takes more wood than you can find and can be seen for miles around."

"So why are you sitting here watching then, Mister Smartstuff, go talk to Genton. Why did you follow us if you didn't want to help?"

"I'll help when he asks for it, not before."

"Why do you have to be so stubborn?" she growled. "If you won't tell him, I will."

"Suit yourself," he said as she slid down and stalked off.

He swallowed down a sigh of relief, glad of the reprieve from the agony of her presence. His eyes followed her, imprinting her curves on his fevered mind.

Some two weeks after escaping from the College of the Art, the ragged band of the reborn reached the northern shore of the Sea of Skies. They set up camp to the west of Sar Let, the great sea port that ferried all traffic between the two continents of Sharné. Ahead, the sea beckoned, the pull of the Master dragging them forward onto the beach.

Stretching away to the right, as far as the eye could see

and beyond, the gentle curve of the bay disappeared over the horizon. To the left, the bustling port city spread its tendrils across the land and floated its tentacles out onto the sea.

Genton, now the unofficial leader of the whole troupe, gathered his closest minions and made his way into the city. Heading directly to the port, Genton approached the first in a long line of ships moored at the dock.

"Ho the Captain!" he hollered.

A young sailor hung over the rail. "What ya want?"

"Are you the Captain?"

"Who wants ta know?"

"That's for the Captain!"

"Captain's busy."

"Well make him unbusy!"

"Can't, 'is orders is not ta be bothered."

"So bother him."

"Sorry, no can do."

"Ah, forget it," Genton spat.

He moved on to the next ship to repeat the process, with no luck. Finally on the third ship he got to speak to the Captain.

"You lookin' fer passage?" the man called down from the deck.

"Yes, Sir," Genton smiled.

"How many?"

"Can't say exactly," Genton mused. "I'd say somewhere in the region of two hundred."

"Nah, I mean how many passengers, not yer price."

"As I said," Genton shrugged.

"Two hundred passengers?" the Captain scoffed. "Are ye daft?"

"No, Sir, I'm serious. Can you take us?"

"Ye think I'm mad or somethin'? Ye'd need two trips at

least, without cargo. I'd have ta fill the hold with yer people. Ye'd better be willin' ta pay."

"Sorry, Sir, we don't have any money, but we're willing to work for it."

"What? Are ye soft in the head? Two, mebbe three trips with no payin' cargo? I'd be ruined!"

Back in the camp, Genton paced, brow creased as he mumbled through gritted teeth. About the main fire, his men argued amongst themselves with occasional glances at their leader. Fransi huddled nearby, arms crossed to ward off the chill, unwilling to intrude on their circle for fear of their simmering distemper.

No matter how much she wanted to be one of the men, she could not deny the truth. This new body was female, and inferior in the eyes of these men, despite the more enlightened society in which they now found themselves.

Somewhere in the darkness nearby, the revealer lurked, watching everything, offering nothing. She shivered. The only thing keeping him here was the connection he felt to this body, and the desire to bring his love back. But Fransi had no intention of meekly stepping aside for her.

Now that she had her new life and was learning to live with her new body she would be damned if she would give it up. Peering into the darkness, she tried to see where he was hiding, but the midnight blue of his cloak seemed to vanish in the night. But her body tingled with a need that she was still unwilling to acknowledge, a need heightened by his proximity.

Stepping further from the circle of firelight, she closed her eyes momentarily to help them adjust to the darkness, then moved deeper into the shadows. He lifted his head to show his face and suddenly she could see him, plain as day, leaning against the trunk of a tree, as if some spell had been lifted. A smile came unbidden and she moved toward him eagerly. She opened her mouth to speak but he raised a finger to his lips and she heard a voice in her mind.

'Don't give me away.'

She clamped her mouth shut as her heart fluttered in her breast. She shook her head, wondering at the voice. Unable to respond, she tried to put all of her confusion and curiosity into her eyes. She felt silent laughter wash over her.

'I can read your thoughts, you don't need to try.'

She blinked. How did he do that?

'All revealers can communicate mentally.'

She licked her lips. She wanted him to come into the light, to join her at the fire and help her deal with Genton and his cronies.

'They don't know I'm here. I'd like to keep it that way,' he whispered in her mind.

But why? They needed his help. The trip to the docks had been a disaster. Not one ship's captain had been willing to help them. They were trapped here on this foreign shore with only the Master's pull to guide them and no way to proceed.

'If I were to show myself I would lose all power to influence the situation.'

She could not understand how he could possibly have any influence from the shadows. Genton needed a guide, not a spy.

'I am not a spy,' his mental voice hissed.

She gasped, surprised by the depth of hatred and disgust that came with those words. Taking a step backwards, she stumbled slightly and found herself back within the light from the camp fire.

"Fransi?" said Genton. "What've you been doing?"

"I... I thought I heard something," she stammered.

"You shouldn't wander off, you never know who might be out there. Not everyone is as friendly as us."

"Friendly?" she snorted.

"Sure," said Sniv, clutching at her hand and pulling her down to his level. "I'll be as friendly as you like, darlin'."

"Quit it, Sniv," Genton snapped. "We need her to go into the port tomorrow, see if she can charm one of those damned ship's captains."

"What makes you think I'll agree to that?"

Genton came at her, face twisted in an uncharacteristic snarl as he took her by the arms and shook her until her teeth rattled.

"You'll agree to anything I ask if you want to keep under my protection, sweetheart. Half the reborn were murderers and thugs in their old lives, or had you forgotten that?"

"No," she mumbled.

"There's chaos out there, in case you hadn't noticed," Genton snarled, face close to hers. "The ones stuck in women's bodies beaten into submission by the others. You're one of the lucky ones, and don't you forget it."

"I... I know," she whispered.

"Be thankful I haven't taken my due," he murmured. "Do this for me and I'll see the boys don't touch you."

"I don't need your protection," she spat.

A sharp pain sent her reeling. Huddling in the dirt, she touched a hand gingerly to her face, feeling a warm slick of blood from where the back of his hand had connected with her cheek.

Something flew past, a blur of dark fabric and there was a thud. She looked up to see Genton sprawled on the ground, the revealer standing over him.

"You lay a hand on her again and you'll see how much protection she needs," Nashta growled.

"What the..." Genton spluttered. "Where the hell did

119

you come from?"

"She won't be charming anyone, you understand?"

"You're mad!" Genton snapped. "How are we supposed to get a ship then?"

Nashta stepped aside and offered a hand to the man. Genton stared at it dubiously, and the revealer gave a little flick of his fingers. Genton tilted his head and slowly reached up to take the offered hand. The revealer helped him to his feet and gave him a pat on the back.

"I'm sorry I had to do that," Nashta said. "I didn't intend to show myself just yet."

"How long have you been spying on us?"

"Not spying," the revealer snapped. "Observing."

"Whatever. How long?"

He shrugged. "Since I caught you north of Martose."

He moved toward Fransi and she accepted his hand. He lifted her tenderly to her feet, gaze resting on her cheek. Fransi lowered her eyes, unwilling to let him see her tears.

"Where... What's Martose?" said Genton behind him.

Nashta paused. "You really don't know? Where are you people from?"

"Stolen City, mostly. But I can't say I know where that is in relation to this place. Nothing is familiar."

"Never heard of it. And I've been all over Sharné at least twice. You must be a long way from home."

"Sharné?"

The revealer whistled. "If you don't even know that..."

"You didn't answer my first question," Genton interrupted. "How are we supposed to get a ship?"

"You don't need one."

"Don't need... But we have to cross that sea..."

"You'll have to trust me. There's another way. "

* * *

THIRTEEN

The spirit of nothing hovered over Its own prostrate vessel, the golden blanket shimmering white and blue. It would be so good to be rid of that failing body once and for all. If only the new vessel were ready, but alas it was still immature, too weak to accept the transfer. That lesson had been learnt long ago. The spirit turned Its attention to the task at hand.

Following the familiar path toward that other mind, the mind of the enemy, the spirit travelled. Far away, over land and sea, the spirit touched the mind of the enemy, slipped through the open door and down into the dark, subconscious depths. It was greeted by voices, all calling silently for help, tumbling over each other to catch the attention of the visitor.

Ignoring the clamouring voices, the spirit set about securing the threads, sinking them deep into the spiritual fabric of the enemy's soul. Then the spirit took up Its customary position, and waited. The enemy touched a new mind, and the spirit latched on, sinking Its hooks. The minds came in a continuous stream, as the enemy touched one after another and another, over and over again. The spirit cackled to Itself in glee.

* * *

The Awakener moved along the line of applicants, briefly touching each one with fingertips to temples, a quick wave brushing aside some and a nod accepting others. He moved quickly, almost manic in his effort to get through the crowd. This intake would be huge, with probably two classes of forty students eager to learn. And still the testing continued.

Miyam watched him in concern as his eyes glazed over and strange sounds tumbled from his mouth, grunts and mutterings punctuated by harsh, cackling laughter. She frowned. There was something dreadfully familiar about that laugh, but it was not the interloper.

Out of all the minds populating his head, this could be anyone, yet it was strange that it was not the Sandman, the strongest of them all. She could not remember where she had heard that voice before.

Then the voice came again, the mumbling resolving into a coherent sentence. "Ah, Awakener, if thou didst know thou wouldst be ever enraged." Then the cackling laughter came again.

Miyam shivered. Those words, the archaic phrasing, the voice of the spirit of nothing rang in her ears. The spirit she had seen vanquished and banished by the divine council of old.

Her mind raced, filled with images of that horrible battle, when the spirit of nothing and the divine council fought within the body of the Awakener, for control of the free world.

She lived again that horrible moment when the Awakener's body had failed, destroyed by the titanic force of the spirits within, and was taken up by the council to be healed. She knew that laugh, and it made her cold with fear.

"What's wrong with him?"

Miyam jumped at the voice by her side. She had forgotten the presence of the other revealers, the students of the Awakener. She glanced at Jumally and Tikki with a hesitant smile.

"Is he about to lose it again?" said Reeperly at her other side.

"I don't think so," Miyam murmured. "This is something different."

"Different?" said Berkana behind her husband's shoulder. "How?"

"Whose was that voice?" said Jossep, the young journeyer. "It sounded different to the Sandman."

"We've encountered It before," said Miyam. "It sounds like Kayus. But it can't be!"

Navear, Jossep's young wife, gasped. "I thought Kayus was a myth!"

"It was," said Reeperly with a kind smile. "Until last year, when It tried to destroy us all."

"That was Kayus?" Navear whispered.

"Back then, It invaded Evelar's body, and he was killed. Miyam had to follow him to the afterlife to bring him back."

"And now It's back?" the girl squeaked. "Isn't that bad?"

"Yes," said Miyam with a shudder. "If it's really Kayus, it's very bad."

The Sandman watched the screen as the cameras focused on the small island of the western hemisphere, its arid yellow plains and hostile brown ranges staring back in denial. Nobody had known what this world would offer, but none had foreseen the bizarre dichotomy of small desert continents in a vast ocean.

"Multiple lifeforms detected," said the ship's Zoologist, Siren Ferdinand.

"Scans show no evidence of civilisation," said Kay, now in his usurped role as captain.

"Nothing sentient?" said the Sandman. "Are you sure?"

"We've been monitoring the planet since we first entered this system," said Siren with a shrug. "Nothing to suggest

intelligent life forms."

"Launch the pod," the new captain ordered.

The crew held their collective breath as the tiny terraforming pod shot from its launch bay. The spark of light flew in a majestic arc through the starscape, heading for a point near the centre of the western land mass, chosen for its manageable size. A flash of light burst from the surface, signalling the pod's impact.

"Instruments show a distinct cooling at the impact zone," said Siren. "No, wait! The ocean is filling the crater! It's going to fail!"

"Just give it time," said the captain.

As the crew held their breath a small glimmer of blue lit the crater, holding back the rapidly encroaching water. Then a bright circle of blue light burst forth, filling the viewscreen. Siren's fingers played across her instrument panel, checking data. Then she let out a sigh.

"It's working," she smiled.

A cheer rang out and the crew burst into excited chatter, laughter lightening the mood.

"Sandman, begin the landing protocol," said Kay. "Time to wake the first team. Let's get this colony started."

"Sand, don't let him in," a voice broke through the crew's noisy banter.

The Sandman looked about, but it seemed nobody else had heard. He blinked at a haze before his eyes as the memory dissolved around him.

Sitting in their private suite in the new palace, his son sleeping in a cot by the bed, Evelar tried to appear very much in control as Miyam told him of the voice she had heard. Inside he was secretly worried.

If she had really heard Kayus, it meant there was more going on than simply a malevolent spirit looking for a host.

And it explained the change in the other minds.

'It's back. It's doing it again. Don't let It take more of us.'

Evelar sent a soothing thought into the panic, trying to calm the minds so he could think. They forced their way into his consciousness more and more, desperate for him to hear their message and understand. He tried to close his mind to the noise, but only managed to dull the roar of dispossessed souls.

"Are you sure it wasn't the Sandman?" he said. "They have the same archaic speech pattern."

Miyam shook her head. "It was definitely Kayus."

'The Master wants our souls. The Master will take us and use us. There will be no escape from here.'

Evelar pushed the voices down, pressing his palms to his temples. "It can't be Kayus. We destroyed It."

'Set us free. Don't let It take us. We want to go home.'

'Hush!' Evelar cried silently. *'Let me think!'*

"Evelar?" Miyam whispered. "Is it happening again?"

Evelar shook his head, smiling at his wife. "No, my love. They're just being noisy."

"I don't like this. You said they were under control. What if the Sandman takes over again?"

"He won't. They're just worried about something. They want me to do something, but I can't sort it out."

'Help us! Let us go! Why are we trapped here? Don't let the Master win!'

Evelar shook his head, forcing the voices down. "Stop it!" he cried aloud.

"Evelar, I'm afraid. Contact the Maestro. Tell him you need help."

"No, he has enough to worry about."

"Then let me help."

"It's alright, my love. I'm fine."

'Its hooks. Break Its hooks! Before more come!'

'No, thou must not,' came a single voice. *'Let them be. Takest thou notice only of me!'*

Evelar shivered. "On second thought, perhaps I do need you, my love."

"Anything."

"Help me take my mind off them," he grinned, pulling her close.

"You don't need to ask, dear," she whispered, lifting her face to accept his kiss but pulling away at the last moment. "Just don't wake Zavvy!"

He chuckled, remembering many such snatched moments while the little boy slept nearby. "I can be quiet. Can you?"

She gave a little giggle, the sound sending a flutter over his heart. He loved making her giggle.

"Let's see, shall we?" she murmured as he captured her mouth with his.

As the new students gathered, the Awakener pushed down his voices and prepared to begin the lesson. He felt the voices, pushing against the barrier to his subconscious, sending their questing thoughts to pound on that locked door.

He closed his eyes, building a barrier to further muffle the sound. He drew in a deep breath, opened his eyes, and gazed at the gathered students, their eyes wide with eager anticipation.

"It's time to suspend disbelief," he began, seeing them sit forward in their chairs. "If you already accept the fact that mankind is able to do a lot more with his mind than ever previously imagined, then you are certainly ready to embrace a 'new' philosophy."

'Why won't you embrace us? Why do you push us away and hide us from the world? We only ask for your help.'

Evelar pushed down the invading thoughts that had somehow broken through his defences.

"It's important that you realise that no one person can ever know the whole truth. The truth in its entirety is unattainable in this corporeal life."

'What is the truth? We know it and we fear it! The Master will take you all!'

He tried to ignore them. "All we can ever hope for is a fleeting glimpse, caught between the death of one thought and the birth of the next. Just as we only experience the fullness of truth when in that non-corporeal existence between sojourns within the physical realm."

'That's it! That's all we ask! We want our lives back.'

Evelar paused in his lecture, pressing a hand to his temple and mentally pushing against the voices. He jumped at a touch to his arm.

"Sir, you need to let me take over," said Reeperly.

"I'm alright, Reep."

"No, Sand, you're not. What did you train us for if not to help?"

"Your training is for a higher goal."

Reeperly sighed. "This is first year apprentice stuff. Any one of us could teach it."

"He's right, dear," said Miyam at his side. "You're in no condition to teach."

"I'm fine!" he cried.

"No, you're not. Let him take over."

Evelar sighed, studying his friend for a moment. Then he gave a curt nod. Reeperly smiled and turned to the students, continuing the lecture as if the same teacher stood before them.

"Our philosophy concentrates on the realisation of truth within the framework of physical life. This is achieved through the practice of meditation which, when one masters the techniques, enables us to be released from bodily concerns. This opens the way to a realisation of the true nature of the mind."

Evelar allowed his wife to lead him away. Pausing at the door, he turned to watch for a moment.

"It's alright, Sand," said Berkana at the door. "He has me to help, just as Mist helps you."

"Thank you, Iris," said Miyam with a smile.

"Once you are able to glimpse the mind," Reeperly continued, "you can use that knowledge to purify your emotions, and thus your existence. This is the work of a lifetime, and not something you should expect to come quickly. Now, we can use this concept to help us in our own exploration of the truth. I will show you the method, but you must find your own path."

Miyam tugged gently at Evelar's arm. "Let him be," she murmured. "You know he's at least as good a teacher as you."

"Yes, my love," he smiled. "Let's go collect Zavvy and decide what we need to do next."

She returned his smile. "That's the best idea you've had all day."

Together they slipped away as Reeperly's calm voice continued the lecture. "The truth is what you make it. It must work for you, and you must work toward it. Look inside and you will find it."

The little princess squealed as she ran past her mother and around the shrine of her grandfather, while Zavvy toddled after her on wobbly legs. Miyam smiled as she approached, bending to catch the boy as he lost his balance.

"She will be sad to see you go," said Netta. "She has grown used to having a playmate."

Miyam smiled. "Her cousins will be old enough to join

in soon enough."

"Yes, I suspect by the time Kandi is well enough to visit, the twins will be walking."

"Is she improving at all?"

"I believe so. Now that she has a second nursemaid to help she is not so exhausted. She was so sick through her pregnancy, and after the strain of birthing two babies her body is taking a while to heal. Calib says she is more cheerful these days, which is a good sign."

"Perhaps you could visit her in Drasmil when we leave here."

"Yes, that is a good idea. Atwin needs to go soon for an administrative visit. Perhaps we can go with him."

"Of course you can," said Atwin as he entered the grove. "My brother would be thrilled to see you both. And I know Kandi misses you terribly."

"We need to go that way anyway," said Evelar, materialising from the shadows under the trees. "You could travel with us."

"Now that is a good idea," said Netta with a grin. "Just like old times."

"Not quite," said Miyam. "I'd say better than old times. More friends and no kalkar chasing us."

"So you are continuing your journey then?" said Atwin. "I had thought, with those voices keeping you on your toes, you might have returned to Eeasto."

"No point delaying," said Evelar. "And I have them under control."

"Control?" said Atwin, raising an eyebrow. "That sounds more like wishful thinking to me."

"You don't need to worry about me. I'll be fine."

"My friend, I know you want to be strong, but I can see through you. We have known each other too long to hide such things. You cannot blame us for caring."

Evelar sighed as he sat down on the grass beside his wife and son. Pulling his knees up, he rested his head on his hands, hiding his face under the fall of his black-edged hood. Miyam slipped an arm about him, the doubt emanating from him sending a shiver of fear up her spine. It wasn't like him to let his feelings show.

"I think you should tell us what is going on inside that head of yours," said Atwin, taking a seat beside Netta.

Evelar gave another sigh, turning his head sideways to look at his friend, his brow creased. "Imagine you're in a crowded throne room, with too many supplicants, diplomats and commoners all talking at once. Hundreds of people squeezed into a too-small space, all trying to get an audience with you, all at the same time."

King Atwin snorted. "Sounds like a normal day..."

"Really? Well double it. No, triple it."

"Alright..."

"Now imagine one of your advisors has done away with all of your staff, and now that one man is standing behind you, whispering in your ear. You can't quite hear him over the noise, but whenever there's a lull his whispers carry over the hall, echoing in the sudden silence before being drowned out again as the crowd move in closer, sensing weakness. And you know that man is just waiting for the right time, to do away with you and take your crown for himself."

Atwin let out his breath in a long sigh. "You sound like me."

"There's more," said Evelar. "That crowd of people. What if there was another, someone none of them knows is there, not even you. But that someone is pulling the strings, controlling the crowd like some puppet master, with an agenda even you don't understand. They can feel him pulling, and you can see them being pulled. But you don't know who or what the puppet master is."

Atwin gave a low whistle. "And all this is in your head?"

"All the time. It's so noisy, my head hurts."

"But where have they all come from?"

"I wish I knew."

* * *

FOURTEEN

With the rising sun at their backs, the possessed struck out in a new direction, leaving the main road behind. Riding at the head of the column, the revealer led them on, mile after mile, ever westward along a narrow road lined on one side with impassable woodland and to the left, the never-ending shore.

Genton glanced nervously behind as the reborn whispered and bickered, their agitation growing more intense with every passing mile.

"My head!" a woman cried. "It hurts! Don't make me go any farther."

Genton turned, searching the crowd for the voice. A group milled about, staring at the woman who huddled on the ground, her hands over her ears and her face screwed up in pain.

"She's right," a man cried. "I feel like my head will break open if I take another step!"

"It's the Master," a young man said. "We're going the wrong way."

"The Master is angry at us!"

"Silence!" yelled Genton. "Move on."

"I can't take it any more," the woman cried.

"Just block it out and keep going," he said. "We have to go this way to get where we need to be. The Master will have to see that soon. Just keep moving."

At the end of the third day they made camp outside a

small village that smelled of rotten fish. Nashta bartered for a portion of that day's catch, using money from his own ample purse, and the band of possessed ate well for the first time since the stolen sheep of two weeks earlier.

"Are you sure this is the way to go?" said Genton around a mouthful of succulent fish. "Every fibre in my being tells me this is wrong."

"Sometimes a detour is necessary," Nashta replied. "You must trust me."

Genton grumbled but held his tongue. The people were content, and he should be too. They had full bellies and a warm fire, and a guide to take them where they needed to go. He would follow the non-monk until he was given reason to doubt him.

Continuing west for the better part of a week, they walked from before dawn until late at night, fighting against the pull in their heads. But as they travelled the pain eased, the Master's hold weakening as the people refused to yield.

But for the occasional outburst of despair, they were almost merry. The Master's anger was most painful when they were weary, at the end of the day. When their feet would no longer fight it, they camped overnight.

They passed two more fishing villages, where they ate well. But Genton struggled with a sense of unease he could not dispel. When the revealer led them off the road and onto an overgrown dirt track, Genton pulled up short.

"Where are you taking us now?" he growled.

The man in the red-edged cloak frowned. "I thought you had learned to trust me."

"I gave you the benefit of the doubt, but that was when we followed a well-trodden path. But this…"

"I'm keeping to the path. I'm sticking to the coast instead of following a road that would take you miles inland in a sweeping detour costing you several days."

"But we're still going the wrong way! The Master shouts in my mind, taking my ability to think, and tearing at my sanity."

"I assure you, by the end of today you'll feel the turn as we round the bay and take a more southerly route."

"You're sure?"

"Of course. But I must warn you, there are no villages for several days, no easy food. You'll need to forage as you go. We may even have to trudge through sand and surf at some point. Are you willing to trust me that far?"

Genton frowned, considering. Then he gave a curt nod and began bellowing orders to his men.

A week later, a bedraggled band of travellers dragged themselves up off the beach toward a little fishing village on the west coast of the Sea of Skies. At their head, a man in a midnight blue cloak edged in red led his beloved gelding onto the grass, where the horse lowered its weary head and cropped listlessly at the fresh stalks of green.

The revealer stroked the poor animal's neck, murmuring words of comfort while the long line of possessed set up camp around him.

"Sir," said Genton quietly. "The people need a good meal."

"Yes, of course, there should be fish here."

He opened his purse and gave the man a handful of coins, then returned to comforting his horse, loving hands running down the animal's side, feeling the ribs beneath the thinning flesh.

"Will he be alright?" said Fransi beside him.

Nashta smiled at the girl. "Yes, he'll be fine. He's strong and healthy. But I should have sent him home from Sar Let."

"He's your companion, I understand," Fransi smiled.

"You're used to fast travel, not this trudging along in a huge company."

"Nevertheless, he should go home. There's worse to come before it gets easier."

"Worse?"

The revealer said nothing, tending his horse in silence.

Heading south-west they joined the road once more. The pull of the Master took hold as they took a more correct direction. Three days later the road ended unexpectedly at the walls of a city, perched on a ridge below a mountain range that met the sea at a high promontory.

"Welcome to Landsend," said the revealer. "Genton, I need to pick up some supplies. I'll need a hand or three, if you don't mind."

"I'll come," Fransi said quickly.

"It's heavy work."

"I don't mind."

With a dismissive shrug, the revealer headed into the city, leading his horse, with Fransi and two men following. First, he found a neat little inn with a clean and tidy stable out the back.

"I need board and lodgings for my horse," he told the innkeeper. "I'm willing to pay whatever you feel is fair for an extended stay."

"Yes, my lord," the grizzled innkeeper smiled. "How long?"

"Shouldn't be more than a few weeks. Someone from the College will be along to pick him up."

The innkeeper settled on a price and money changed hands. Then the revealer led his companions deeper into the city, where they sought out the market.

He bought several lengths of rope, handing them out to be draped over their shoulders. Then he filled their hands with axes and other tools. Ignoring their bewildered looks, he guided them once more out of the city.

"What's all this for?" said Genton on their return to camp.

"You'll see."

The travellers continued south, forced to take a rocky path between high cliffs and the foothills of a great mountain range. Behind the leaders, the ranks of the possessed struggled to keep moving forward over the treacherous terrain, while the call of the Master, stronger every day, forced them to carry on.

Eventually, the revealer called a halt. They closed ranks, clustered on a rocky promontory overlooking a churning sea.

"Where are we?" said Genton.

"The southernmost tip of the kingdom of Lenel," said Nashta. "On a clear day you can see the clouds forming over the northernmost point of the kingdom of Drasmil. Between is the Straight of the Sun, flanked by the Sunset Gate, the northern side of which is the point on which we stand."

"Why are we here?"

"This is where we will cross."

"But we don't have a ship."

"No. We're going to walk."

"What? Are you mad? We'll drown!"

"Not if we do it right. These mountains continue just under the surface, worn down by the power of the sea, and it's actually quite shallow. If we time it right we can use the tide to our advantage."

"I don't know much about tides, but I do know we have a full moon in the sky and I can see the height of that swell."

"We're not crossing tonight. We'll spend some time here, making rafts. It's a long way, longer than we can cover in a day, so we will take turns resting on the rafts while the others pull. We'll tie them all together so we don't lose anyone."

Genton shook his head. "It's suicide."

"By the time we finish building the rafts, the moon will be more favourable. There's a high point half-way across, usually covered in a sandbar at this time of year; we can ride out the high water there. With the moon at quarter it won't be so high, though the ebb will be deeper."

"We won't make it. We're going to lose people."

"I have no intention of losing anyone. We'll be wading across a high mountain ridge, with water no more than chest height at its deepest point. Hopefully, we'll reach the deep water at low tide. It will work."

As the cold light of dawn tinted the eastern sky, the first raft was pushed off the sand into the dragging tide. The first load of passengers climbed aboard as the waders guided it into the surf while the next raft followed, attached by a short rope. A long, snaking line of heavy log rafts slowly made their way into the water, each raft guided by a team of walkers.

"I'm not going out there!" a woman shrieked.

"Calm down, Beth, the revealer knows what he's doing," an old man murmured.

"Oh really?" said Beth. "Making us walk out into the ocean with nothing but a few rafts?"

A crowd had gathered around her as her voice carried out over the water.

"She's right! We'll all die out there," an old woman yelled.

"He's mad and I won't follow him any further," Beth cried.

"But the Master calls. We have to go." the old man took hold of Beth's arm, dragging her toward the rafts.

"I don't care what the Master says, Druck, I'm not drowning for him!"

"Well I'm not going to risk his anger if we don't!"

"Please, everyone," the revealer smiled as he approached the group.

He reached a hand to the woman, fingers brushing her temple briefly. She sighed, and a smile lit her face.

"I'm sorry," Beth murmured. "Everything will be alright."

"We can't ignore the Master," said a young woman.

"It is the right way," said Druck. "I'm willing to risk getting wet."

A third of the company took the first shift on board while the rest struck out into the cold water. The passengers sat around the edges, some holding long poles to help guide the clumsy craft, while in the middle of each raft a nest of reeds protected piles of supplies, including food, blankets and firewood.

By the time the sun kissed the water to the east, they had left the shore far behind, its only reminder a haze of green on the horizon. Nashta called the first shift and the passengers slid off their rafts into the water.

The second shift were helped up onto the rafts, while the third continued in the water with fresh help from the first. A few of the new passengers reached for blankets but the revealer gave a shout.

"No blankets!" he yelled. "The sun can warm you. Leave the blankets dry for the night shift!"

Amid mumbles of discontent, the precarious flotilla bobbed along in the great expanse of water, soon leaving all sight of the shore behind. As the day wore on, the sun inched its way across the sky, the hourly change of shift the only indication of passing time. By the time the sun passed its zenith, the walkers were almost neck-deep, struggling to keep a foothold on the rocky sea floor.

"The tide's coming in," said Genton.

"Not yet, but it's turning," said Nashta, taking hold of Fransi's arm as she spluttered on a mouthful of water. "We're at the deepest section of the crossing."

Genton shook his head. "How can you possibly know that?" he said. "I can't help but wonder what event led you to this place, that you know it so well."

The revealer said nothing, ignoring the question. The swell had increased even in the few moments they had been talking. Several people lost their footing as a wave washed over them. Scrabbling back to their feet, they clung to the dubious safety of the rafts.

"Walkers, keep hold of the rafts," the revealer called.

"I can't find Beth!" a man cried.

The revealer struck out toward the man, swimming strongly against the current as the waves came again.

"There!" a woman cried. "The wave took her."

Beth waved her arms, screaming in terror as her legs seemed to fail under her. She disappeared for a moment, resurfacing even further away, coughing up water as the current took her.

The man named Druck dove toward the woman. Another wave washed him forward, taking him closer, but the same wave took her even further from the safety of the rafts.

Pushing himself along with feet on the seabed and arms pulling through the water, Druck finally reached her, just as she sank beneath the next wave. His clutching hand caught at her hair, but the current pulled her away and she disappeared beneath the waves.

"She's gone!" he cried.

Feeling a hand grasp at his arm, Druck spun around to find the revealer at his side.

"Where is she?"

"Gone," Druck moaned. "The waves took her, I couldn't hold her."

The revealer dove beneath the waves. Druck held his breath, counting the seconds as he watched. Minutes passed, and he began to fear the revealer was lost too. Finally, Nashta burst out of the depths, gasping for air.

"Did you find her?"

The revealer shook his head, face dark with anger. "She's gone," he snarled. "I'm so sorry."

Druck groaned. "I hardly knew her. We only became friends because we were both reborn in older bodies. She was so afraid of drowning out here."

"Let's get back."

They turned toward the rafts. The current had taken them even further away. A cry came over the water and something sailed through the air to splash down a few feet away. A rope, tied to a short branch taken from the stock pile on one of the rafts.

The men grabbed the branch and were slowly pulled through the rising swell, back to the safety of the rafts. Willing hands dragged them up and they sat staring out to where the woman had disappeared.

Druck glanced down at his hands, where strands of the woman's hair still clung to his fingers. With a long, shuddering sigh, he plucked at the hair, winding it into a small wad and lifting a hand to drop it into the water. But, as it began to float away, Druck grabbed it up again, curling it up reverently and tucking it safely into a pocket.

Slipping down and wading slowly back to the lead raft, Nashta wiped at his face, removing all sign of emotion to become the hardened revealer once more. He found Genton frantically splashing around in the chest deep water.

"What's wrong?" said Nashta.

"Where's Fransi?" said Genton in a tight voice.

The revealer cast about, looking for her. "No, don't tell me..."

He cocked his head, listening. He thought he heard a frantic knocking, muffled and faint. He took a breath and dove under the water. Feeling along the edge of the raft, he found the rope that bound the logs together and followed them, pulling himself underneath.

Searching forward blindly with his hand, he caught hold of a flailing limb and dragged at it as the girl's struggles grew weaker. He burst back to the surface, pulling the girl up with him and leading her to cling to the raft as she gasped for air, coughing up sea water.

"Up onto the raft," he said gruffly, then raised his voice. "Anyone who's struggling, onto the rafts! Tall people on the rafts, take their places in the water. Now. I won't have anyone else drowning here!"

FIFTEEN

For the better part of an hour, they struggled through the deep water, the rafts held on track only by the pole bearers digging their poles into the sand five feet below. Then finally, the revealer raised a hand and the walkers came to a stop. As they watched, the revealer took a step up, and the water dropped to his waist.

"There's a ledge, so watch your step," he called. "We're through the deep water. Just a few more hours and we should be on dry sand for the night."

A pitiful cheer bubbled up from the crowd, quickly petering out as they summoned up a renewed effort to put the deepest passage behind them. But the shallow water soon gave way to the rising tide. As they struggled ever forward the current pulled at their legs, dragging them down. The rafts drifted off course and the weaker walkers were knocked off their feet.

As the sun sank slowly in the west, the roar of breakers heralded the promised sandbar, and the sea bed rose sharply, the water finally dropping below their knees as the first raft dragged on the bottom.

"Right, everybody off," yelled Nashta. "Pull the rafts right up onto the sandbar, as high as you can go. The last thing we need is to lose them to the tide overnight."

As the setting sun cast long shadows across the sandbar, a sorry camp huddled within a circle of soggy rafts. Wood carried with them from the forests of Lenel was piled into a pyre at the highest point of the sandbar, around which the travellers warmed themselves, while chunks of day old meat and various roots and greens simmered in the troupe's only large pot. Around them the ocean raged, the rising tide ripping at the edges of the sandbar, licking at the rafts pulled up onto the sand.

The revealer moved among the people, the cloak he had retrieved from the raft flapping in the evening breeze. He offered words of encouragement, seeing that they shared blankets and received food. He came across Fransi, huddled in wet clothing at the edge of a group of men who sat plotting their next move. Removing his thick woollen cloak and draping it over the girl, Nashta sat beside her to listen. She rested her head on his shoulder and he absently slipped an arm about her.

"Why did you let him bring us here?" Sniv was whining. "We'll all die before we reach land."

"Sometimes you just have to trust someone," said Genton. "He knows what he's doing."

"But look at us. We've been in that water all day and where's it got us? A flimsy patch of sand in the middle of the ocean."

"Not ocean, not really. It's a land bridge. Submerged, but a bridge nonetheless, wide and safe. If it were just a narrow ridge, we'd be surrounded by surf, all the time, but it's been fairly calm so far. If he's right, it will bring us right where we want to be."

"Calm? Tell that to the woman who drowned."

"You really can't expect a passage like this to go without a hitch."

"Well, at least we're heading in the right direction."

"That we are. And the Master is pleased."

"But how much longer do we have to swim? I've got wrinkles on my wrinkles. It's only a matter of time before something else goes wrong."

"I'm not sure. What say you, Nashta?"

The revealer smiled. "We leave again as soon as the tide turns, and by midday we will be in sight of land."

In the deep of night, with a sliver of moon high in the sky, a rough surf tore at the edges of a flimsy sandbar, where a glow from the dying fire touched the huddled forms of a band of travellers, sleeping fitfully in the protective ring of their wooden rafts. As the breakers thundered about them, the rafts bobbed and floated, breaking free of the sand that clutched at them. A cry rang out over the sodden camp.

"Look to the rafts!"

A handful of bodies rose from their slumber, rushing with shouts of alarm, tugging at the rafts, desperate to keep hold of their only lifeline in the middle of a raging sea. Men held tight, digging their feet into the sand. Waves crashed over them, drenching the precious cargo and dragging the rafts deeper.

"Don't give up! We must not lose them!"

The angry sea roared, its foamy teeth biting at the sand. Men fell and were sucked forward into the swell. Scrambling to their feet, they caught hold of the rafts once more as the sand seemed to fall away beneath them.

Woken by the commotion, more bodies lent their hands, and they began to feel they might actually win against the raging tide. Feet found greater purchase and toes dug into sand. Rafts settled more securely and breakers fell short of their prey.

"It's turning!"

Sand took hold of wood, clasping it close, wrapping it in a firm embrace as waves gave up the attack and retreated into the sea. Men fell to their knees, gasping against the cold and the terror that constricted their breath. Rafts creaked and groaned, but sat snug in the sand.

"Wake the rest," said the revealer. "It's time to go."

The afternoon sun dipped in the west, its last rays picking out the tops of the rippling waves and making the sea sparkle. In the deepening shadow, the first of a sorry band of travellers dragged their raft up onto a rocky beach and threw themselves down to sprawl out on the welcoming shore.

Behind them, the rest of the troupe followed, sad and bedraggled in their exhaustion, but alive and miraculously unscathed. In the midst of the lead group, a man pealed himself off the ground to begin giving out orders to his resistant followers.

The revealer claimed his cloak from the raft and slipped away, glad to let the tall man resume leadership of the possessed. He heard Genton sending men out to collect wood, directing others to set up camp and to forage for food.

"Wait!" a woman cried, running after him.

Nashta paused, turning to watch the girl approach, her curves accentuated by the saturated clothing that clung in all the right places.

"Where are you going?" she gasped, eyes wide and lip trembling. "You're not leaving us?"

He frowned, licked his lips as he considered his answer. He wanted to leave. He needed to leave, before he gave in to her. He felt constantly off balance as his physical need warred with his mental discipline.

No matter how much he wanted to feel her familiar body against his, her mind was that of a stranger, his beloved lost to him. His self-imposed mission to keep her safe was proving too difficult, and he wanted nothing more than to get away.

"Please don't go," she moaned. "If you go, I'll be at the

mercy of Genton and his cronies. You're the only thing keeping them under control."

"I... just need to scout ahead," he said, stalling for time.

"Sniv can hardly keep his filthy eyes off me, his hands always itching to follow. Please."

"I promised to protect you, and I will," he sighed. "But I need to... think for a moment."

"But you'll be back?"

He hesitated, eyes shifting involuntarily over her inviting form. He gave a curt nod, then spun away to stumble into the forest.

Behind him, the girl took a shuddering breath, throat aching at the anguish that wanted to rip its way out of her. It had not been easy to admit that she needed him, a soul who had always been so strong as a male now reduced to begging for protection from those same men she would have once joined as an equal. But her fear was real. She wiped away a tear before returning to camp.

"Why are we sitting here twiddling our thumbs?" Sniv whined. "The Master's call is so strong I can hardly stand it."

"Now Sniv, you know why. The people are so exhausted from the crossing we'd be risking illness and worse to make them move now. They need time to rest and regain their strength."

Sniv shrugged. "Suit yourself. But you'll have a riot on your hands if we don't move soon."

"It's been less than a day, Sniv," said Fransi as she entered the circle by the fire. "You'll get your action soon enough."

"Oh I will, will I?" said Sniv, leering up at her. "Come sit by me and we'll make action sooner than you think."

"You'd like that, wouldn't you," she said as she slipped

past him.

He grabbed at her hand, forcing her down to his level. "Right now, little minx, a bit of action from you would go a long way to keeping me happy."

She pulled against his grip, struggling as he dragged her closer, his weedy face twisted in naked lust.

"Let me go," she gasped.

"Oh, sigh some more," he moaned. "Just for me."

She fought against his iron grip, battering him with her fists and turning away from his looming face. She called out in her fear and Sniv laughed.

"Let her go, Sniv," snapped Genton.

"Oh, right, and let her run to you?" he scoffed. "Why should you have her?"

"I mean it, Sniv, she's not for you."

Taking advantage of his distraction, Fransi twisted out of his grip and scurried out of reach. Sniv growled and scrambled to his feet.

"How dare you," he snapped. "You don't have the guts to take her, but you don't want anyone else to have her either. You can't have it both ways."

"Sniv, you're letting your frustration get the better of you."

"Too right, I am, and justified too. You stall and fumble, you hesitate even against the Master, yet you expect us to do as you say. You couldn't have led us this far without that priest or whatever he is."

"Are you saying you could do better? I took help where I got it."

"Help? He took us weeks out of our way and darn near drowned every last one of us."

"I suppose you would have just stormed the port or something and got us all killed."

"It would have been better than sitting around doing

nothing with you."

"An attitude which will be your undoing, sniveller."

"One day, you'll get what's coming to you," he snarled. "Both of you."

As Sniv stormed off, Genton reached out to the girl with a soothing hand. Overwhelmed by gratitude, she sank into his embrace, trembling with the remnant fear that left her weak with relief.

Genton chuckled softly, and Fransi gasped as his hand slipped under her skirt. Fumbling at his belt, she found the hilt of his dagger, pulled it out of its sheath and aimed it at the most sensitive target.

As he pushed in closer he stopped, suddenly aware of the sharp point threatening to unman him. His hands stopped their wandering and he held them aloft, stepping back with a wry shake of the head.

"Alright, sweetheart, I get the message."

Sniv slumped his way through the camp, mumbling as he went. The girl needed a lesson in humility. If that pseudo-monk were not constantly following her around like a lost puppy, Sniv might have got his way with her by now. He longed to show her he was not the sorry outcast he once had been.

Every time he looked at her he saw countless women passing by his hovel, women who sneered down their noses at the sexless vagabond. None of them had seen his tortured soul crying out for something he could never have.

Now he finally had the body of a man, with the ability to exercise his lifetime of thwarted desires, and the bitch denied him. He paused, listening to the whispers in his head. He whimpered, shivering at the Master's pull. The sooner they chased down the vessel, the better.

The Master sighed through his mind like a fickle breeze,

sometimes a murmur, sometimes a roar, but always with a hand clasped about his soul, ready to drag him inexorably toward his prey. But the time was not right.

Sniv shrugged off the dark wind and summoned up a thin whistle as he sauntered forth to find someone who might welcome his long suppressed hunger.

Coming across a small group gathered about a little fire, he paused, hovering just outside their circle. Three men lounged on the ground, each with a woman draped about him. Several others gathered around them, listening intently.

Sniv sidled closer, and a girl caught his eye, giving him a shy smile. Sniv shivered in delicious anticipation, his lust rising as his mind conjured images of her writhing naked under him. Her smile deepened, as if she knew what he was thinking and by some miracle did not object. He took a step closer.

"Hey, I know you," exclaimed one of the men by the fire. "I've seen you up front with that bossy one, who thinks he owns us."

Sniv gave a cautious nod. "So?"

"So, what are you doing down here with us lowly peasants?"

Sniv shrugged. "Perhaps I don't like being ordered about."

"You looking to join us then?"

"Maybe. If I think you can do better for me."

"Come sit, then."

"What's your plan?" he said as he lowered himself down by the fire.

"That depends on you," the man replied. "I'm Hark, by the way."

"Sniv," said Sniv. "And I'm sick of waiting about, following that... the cloaked one."

"Revealer," said Hark with a sniff.

"What?"

"That's what they call themselves. They're some kind of cross between soldiers and spies and witches all rolled into one."

"Whatever," said Sniv. "Glad we don't have them in Stolen City."

"We might if we don't do something about it."

"What do you mean?"

"Haven't you heard the Master?"

Sniv shrugged again. "He wants us to get rid of someone."

"One of them," said Hark. "Some big shot getting too big for himself. He's got the souls that were in these bodies. If we get rid of him, these bodies will be ours forever."

"How do you know that? Genton never said anything about that!"

"Some of us listen better than others," said Hark. "Now that we're over that damned sea, we can catch our prey in a few days if we move fast."

"What are you going to do?"

"Can't you feel it? These bodies know when their souls are near. He's coming closer and we plan to act. No more wandering around. We destroy the vessel, the souls are lost and we truly own these bodies. We leave tonight. Are you in?"

"Absolutely," said Sniv. "On one condition."

"She's yours," said Hark, lifting a hand to signal lazily.

"How did you..."

"Like I said, some of us listen."

As he spoke, the young woman Sniv had noticed before stepped into the circle, her huge brown eyes regarding him under hooded lashes.

"Misa, I won't order you to bed him, but he's yours if you want him," said Hark with a smirk.

Misa smiled, sending Sniv into a flutter of excitement as his whole being responded with an urgency built on years of suppression and thwarted lust.

The girl slinked her way to his side, standing over him and lifting her skirt to show a slender calf. Sniv licked his lips, longing to touch her but terrified that she would pull away like they always did. She held out a hand and he cautiously reached out to take it.

She pulled at his hand, guiding it, letting his hesitant fingers touch the soft skin of her leg under her skirt and urging him to move upward.

Then she stepped over him and slid down onto his lap. Sniv let out a startled whimper as she untied his belt and loosened his trousers.

She covered his terrified sounds with her mouth on his, and the urgent need exploded over him as his hungry body responded. He barely heard the chuckles of his new companions as he experienced his first love right in their midst.

* * *

SIXTEEN

The Awakener took up a defensive pose at his wife's back, while the rest of the company closed in from all sides. This would be a tough bout, but he hoped to show how the strength of the marriage bond could increase their chance of success in an unfair fight.

Fighting as a pair was both difficult and rewarding. The new technique involved using the permanent mind link already established to become hyper aware and fight as one mind on two fronts. The first couple advanced.

The Adept Jumally, legendary in the College as the mysterious Iron, and her partner, Tikki, known as Path. Jum fought with pure strength, preferring hand-to-hand combat to swinging a sword. Evelar switched his grip on his own blade to send it pommel first at the tall woman's head.

But Tikki stepped in, swinging a small iron mallet on a long handle, using it to knock the sword away before it found its target. Evelar parried the blows as Miyam readied her sword to face Reep, closing in with his wife Berkana, known as Iris.

Behind the Awakener, Reeperly was reaching for his daggers, sheathed in his boots. Miyam threw her own knife but missed her target. In a flurry of movement, Evelar was in front of her, batting Reeperly's knives out of the air before they could hit home. Miyam spun to face Tikki, closing in with her deadly little mallet swinging over her head.

Miyam touched a switch on her harmless looking

wristband and a tiny knife, unseen in the thick of battle, flew toward the smaller woman. With a flick of the wrist, Miyam sent the mote knife dipping in to cut the cord that held Tikki's weapon secure, and it flung off into the bushes by the road.

Jum rushed to her partner's rescue, but Evelar intercepted her, taking on the woman's challenge to engage her in hand fighting. Miyam turned again, in time to catch the spinning fabric of Berkana's cloak, feeling the iron balls that weighted its hem clatter across her armband.

Recovering, she sent the mote knife toward the woman, ready to claim the point with a cut. But a new combatant sent his own weapon of choice into the fray. The Journeyer Jossep had drawn a crossbow and sent a dart straight at the tiny knife, knocking it off course.

His second dart came hard on the first, and was deflected on the sword of the Awakener. Then there came a blinding flash, a bolt of blue striking Evelar across the forehead, and he fell to the ground, body convulsing. Standing above him, Miyam held her hands aloft, two index fingers crossed to signal time out.

"I'm sorry!" the youngest member of their company cried. "I didn't mean to hurt him!"

"It's alright, Navear," Miyam smiled. "You performed exactly as you should."

"But he's been so troubled, and now I've made him worse," the girl blubbered.

"You caught him by surprise. What was that weapon?"

"Just this," said the girl, holding out her hand.

Miyam remembered seeing her use the weapon once before, to light a candle during training, but the girl had hidden it. Now she saw it was a small band of gold, with a circular piece resting on the palm.

"What is that? What was that light?"

"May I see?" said another voice.

Atwin approached from where he had observed the bout, Netta following with the children. The girl hesitated, but offered her hand with a shy smile and flushed cheeks.

Atwin took her hand gently between his own and slipped the simple band off to examine it. He frowned for a moment, then his eyes opened wide.

"Netta, look at this," he murmured. "I think it is an amulet."

"You mean like ours?" The Princess came closer, taking it from him to turn it over in her hands. "Where did you get this?"

Navear shrugged. "It belonged to my mother, but... I don't know how it works. I just... think about what I want and it does it."

A groan drew their attention as the Awakener tried to rise, and Netta handed the strange weapon back to the girl. Evelar was clutching at his temples and strange grunts issued from his mouth, followed by jumbled words and half phrases.

"It's coming, they're close, I can feel it, coming near, somewhere..."

"See?" Navear cried. "What have I done?"

"It's not you, Bell, this is something different," said Miyam. "This is the voices again."

Suddenly a loud cry and a great commotion crashed in on them. Navear screamed and Netta gasped, clutching the children to her as several people charged at them from all directions.

"Netta," Atwin cried. "Get the children in behind the gate."

Netta retreated into the palace courtyard while the revealers formed a circle around Evelar, creating a protective human shield. Strange voices continued to call out from

Evelar's mouth as a true battle raged around him.

The attackers charged in, driven by some wild compulsion to get to the Awakener. They almost did not engage the defenders, forcing their way through without concern for their own safety, hardly even noticing their injuries.

"No, don't hurt them, let them be," Evelar's voices clamoured. "We need them, they are ours, give them back to us."

The attackers countered with nonsensical cries of their own. "Get him, stop them from taking us, let us have our lives, these bodies are ours."

Somehow in all the noise, the Awakener had risen from his stupour. Evelar held out a hand, eyes blazing with power.

"I order thee to stop!" cried the voice of Kayus from Evelar's mouth. "Thy time is not now, this place is not right."

The attackers cried out in protest. "Master we come, this is our right, let us have him, we deserve to be free."

"I tell thee I will allow it not! Get thee hence!"

To the observers, it appeared the world stood still, the Awakener and the attackers in frozen tableau. But within the minds of the combatants something happened. The Master had come, and It would set them free.

The spirit took hold of their minds, severing the threads that held them bound, calling Its servants home. The possessed stood still, staring at nothing, silent and possessed no more, their bodies emptied of the souls that had animated them. Then Evelar clamped his hands over his ears, and his eyes flashed gold.

Taking control of the vessel, the Sandman ripped the amulet from around his neck, and holding it in one hand he touched it briefly with the other, sending a green glow floating to the ground.

Then he approached one of the comatose bodies, pulled open its tunic, and pressed the amulet to its chest. There was a brief blue glow from the amulet, and he pulled it away to press it to his own forehead.

The blue glowed out again, then he faced the same vacant body and pressed the amulet to that body's forehead. Now it glowed white. He held it there for a moment, until the body blinked its eyes, and comprehension illuminated the face as conscious thought flooded back.

The Sandman touched the amulet one last time and the green flared out to dissolve in the air. Then he proceeded to repeat the procedure with each of the vacant bodies, eyes flashing gold all the while, sending the lost souls back to themselves.

Then after one last touch that sent green drifting toward the ground to dissipate into the air, he sank to the ground, clutching at his head while the attackers looked about in bewilderment. They grasped at themselves, feeling their own bodies with trembling hands, with eyes wide and looks of amazement.

"I'm back," said one.

"We're free," said another.

"But... how?" said a third.

"You are returned to your own bodies," said the Awakener softly. "Your puppet master has set you free."

Miyam ran to him, sinking down beside him and staring into his warm brown eyes. "You're still you? I swear the Sandman had you."

"Perhaps briefly. I don't remember much."

"Are they all gone?" she whispered.

He shook his head. "No, only these few. And the rest are angry to be overlooked."

"How did he do it? And Why?"

"I wish I knew."

The man who had been Sniv licked his lips, staring at the young woman by his side. She was beautiful, and his body responded to her presence as if he should know her. Had known her.

He shook his head in confusion, blinked his eyes in an attempt to remember who she was. But he was sure he had never met her before, despite his body's erotic response.

"I'm sorry," he murmured. "Have we met? I feel like I should know you."

She smiled. "I feel the same, but... I'm certain we've never met. What happened?"

"I... don't know," he whispered.

"I feel like I missed something. Something... good."

"Me too," he smiled. "But... we've met now."

She let out a little breathless giggle. "Yes, we have. I'm Kira."

"Trask," he breathed. "And I'm very, very glad to meet you, Kira."

Ash fell about the town as flames licked at the treetops, crackling in their fury. The colonists redoubled their efforts shooting the water cannon as the science officer battled with the spent terraforming capsule, tapping commands into the fading connection.

Finally, bursting forth from the middle of the newly formed crater sea, a weak beam of light shot into the clouds. Almost instantly, the clouds broke and the rain fell, quenching the raging fire. With faces upturned to the sky, the colonists dropped their buckets and hoses.

"Now do you see why we need this technology?" the Commander jeered. "Those creatures need to be stopped."

"They don't know what they're doing," said the Sandman. "We're the ones who invaded their home."

"They're dangerous. They threaten everything we're

trying to build here. Tomorrow we fire up the shuttles and chase them down."

"And do what, exactly? Kill them? This is their planet. I won't be a party to genocide."

"Would you rather they pick us off one by one? Or worse, set their blazes against us?"

"Just let them be, Kay. They'll back down. They're only animals, they can't organise a defence."

"The capsule has no power left and the terraforming can only herd them so far before they fight back."

"Fight back? They're innocent creatures, they have no concept of fighting back."

"So what would you propose?"

The Sandman shook his head. "Herd them if you must, but don't kill them."

"I'll do what needs to be done," said Kay. "And you will stop questioning my authority. Our future is at stake, and our children's legacy must be preserved."

'Sand, wake up,' a voice cried.

The Sandman blinked as the disembodied voice floated into his mind. "Who is that? What do you want?"

'Sand, please come back.'

"I'm not going anywhere," he mumbled.

'Sandman, let him go!'

He felt a great mental push, and suddenly the memory was gone and he was left in darkness once more.

Sand took back his mind and opened his eyes. In the moonlight from the window he could see Miyam's face hovering over him, her lovely brow creased in worry.

"What's wrong, Mym?" he murmured.

"Evelar, you scared me half to death! You were talking all thees and thous in your sleep."

"I was?"

"Just like you do when Sandman tries to take over."

"Strange," he murmured. "It doesn't sound like that in my head."

"But you were talking like the ancients. I thought Sandman had you again."

"There weren't any old words, it seemed perfectly normal to me."

"How can that be?"

"It was a dream, my love. He was remembering. I suppose from his point of view it does sound normal. Like an accent that you can't hear yourself."

Miyam shook her head. "I don't like this. We need to call off this mission and get back to the College, where we can get you some help."

"I told you, I'm fine."

"I'm making this decision, Evelar. We're going to Drasmil with Netta and Atwin, then we'll head north from there."

"We can't cancel the new classes, Mym, you know that."

"Reep and Berkana are staying in Shirall to continue the outsider classes here."

"But we have the third school to set up in Nella. The people need to learn to protect themselves or we'll see more of these possessions."

"Don't worry about Nella. Jumally can handle it, with Tikki helping. They can head south from here, do some testing at Tellemot and send them back here to Reeperly and Berkana, then head on to Zelona and Nella."

"You've got it all worked out, haven't you."

"No point arguing, dear. That attack yesterday proves it's getting too dangerous, and we're putting Zaviar at risk. You need to get this problem sorted."

The imposing walls of Drasmil stretched before them. Across the crenellated walk, guards stood motionless. From the gate a small retinue sortied forth to meet the little group of travellers. Miyam glanced at the Awakener beside her with a frown. He sat his horse in a slump, his hands loose at the reins. He stared blankly, his mouth moving silently in time with the voices in his head.

As Miyam reached across to take the reins from his limp grasp Evelar sat upright, staring eyes flashing gold briefly. She kicked her mare forward and began to lead him on, toward the safety of the King's palace. But he resisted, hands clutching at the reins. He kicked in with his heels and the stallion bolted.

"What?" Miyam gasped.

Urging Cheena forward, Miyam held her son close and followed after the Awakener, spurring her mare to a canter. She heard the two journeyers following but ignored their calls. With Jumally and Tikki already far south on their way to Nella, and Reep and Berkana left behind in Shirall, she had to catch him before he did something that would put them all in danger.

Deep down she feared he was lost once more, but something forced her to continue following as he galloped toward the setting sun at breakneck speed. She had almost lost him in the blinding light of sunset when he appeared in distant silhouette, swaying on the big stallion's back. Heart in mouth, she watched helpless as he toppled from the saddle. Several figures scurried in, lifting him between them and disappearing into the sun.

"No!" she screamed, kicking Cheena to a gallop.

The stallion reared as she approached, and her mare whinnied in response. The big horse landed and stood leg-locked while his ears flicked back and forth. Eyes blurred, Miyam slid down, setting her little boy on his feet and approaching the black stallion.

"Hush, Lumen," she murmured as she scratched at his ears. "Where did they go, hmmm?"

The big horse nuzzled at her and she smiled in spite of herself.

"What happened?"

Miyam sucked in her breath. "Someone took him, Joss."

"Who?" said Navear.

Miyam held her breath for a moment, forcing down the panic. "I don't know, Bell," she whispered.

Two riders thundered up, skidding to a halt beside them.

"Mym, what is going on?" the Princess said anxiously.

"Evelar's gone, Netta," Miyam replied. "Someone took him."

"How? Who could subdue Evelar? He is too strong for that."

"I think..." Miyam shivered. "I think the voices were taking over again. He wasn't himself."

"Well then, I guess we need to call off our visit," said Atwin with a wry grin. "Let us get after them."

"No, Atwin. You can't just rush off now, you have to be king."

"That is unimportant, not when you need us."

"No, you've already been gone too long. We'll handle it."

"Well, if you are sure..."

Miyam was not sure, but she tried to look confident in the face of their concerned stares. Then she turned to the youngsters, trying to put on a brave face. Bell smiled. Joss cocked his head, waiting for orders.

Miyam took a deep breath, clearing her face of all expression, though her stomach was tied in knots and her throat seemed to close painfully. The revealer's mask had never come easily, never quite hiding her true feelings, but her natural confidence would take over if she could just think for a moment.

"We should look for tracks," she said quietly.

Joss gave a curt nod and set off, searching the surrounding bushes for signs of the captors. Navear touched a hand to Miyam's arm, making her jump.

"Can you *hear* him?" she said.

Miyam sent out a questing thought. Somewhere, the echo of the Awakener floated on the air, calling faintly, but she could not establish a link. Slipping into her own subconscious, she stepped across the miles, using the permanent connection through the centre of her being. The chaos of his mind hit her, a cacophony of voices all screaming in rage.

'They're here! Give us back! Get them out, they're ours!'

She closed her eyes, trying to break through, but although the link was live and active, it was cold and empty, no familiar mental voice welcoming her with its caress. The silence made the clamouring voices seem all the more intrusive. Holding her breath to stifle a sob, she shook her head, trying to ignore the girl's sympathetic expression.

"I've got something," Joss called. "They went south, a whole lot of them."

"Well, let's get going then," said Navear. "Right, Mym?"

Miyam blinked, hearing the shortened name through a fog. She opened her mouth to speak but no words came and she wiped at her eyes as she nodded. Turning to hide her face, she fumbled with Cheena's saddle, rigging a lead line and attaching it to the stallion's reins. She felt a touch on her arm.

"Give me Zaviar," said Netta with a smile. "The least I can do is keep him safe for you."

Miyam bit her lip, lifting her little son to hold him tight against her chest, blinking back tears.

"He will be fine, Mym, I promise," Netta said.

"But he needs me," Miyam wailed.

"You revealers ween early, do you not? I still have milk,

I can nurse him if he needs it. He cannot go with you, it is too dangerous, you know that."

Unable to speak, Miyam nodded, reluctantly loosening her grip and allowing her friend to take her son from her arms.

"Keep him safe for me," she whispered over the lump in her throat. "If anything happens..."

"Nothing will happen. He will be safe with me while you rescue his father, and then you will return to us. Everything will be alright."

Miyam nodded again, blinking back tears. She pulled herself up into the saddle, clicking her tongue and giving a flick of the reins. She tried to ignore Zavvy's cries as his mother rode away from him, and her faithful mare followed the two journeyers along the trail.

* * *

SEVENTEEN

Evelar blinked against the haze that threatened to cover his vision yet again. Something had hold of him under the arms, and his heels dragged along the ground. Two voices screamed within his mind, drowning out all other thought.

'This one's mine! Let me out!'

'I want to be free, let me get out!'

Evelar shook his head and gasped at the pain in his neck. His head hung painfully, bounced about by the motion of being dragged between two men. Straining to see their faces, Evelar shivered at the sheer agony he saw there.

"I can't take this, he makes my skin crawl," one man moaned.

"Let me kill him, please, Genton," the other whined.

"Nobody will do anything of the sort," someone barked. "Alright, time to swap."

The hard ground hit him in the back as the men let him drop, knocking the wind out of him. Evelar groaned, gasping for breath as two more men dragged the others away. The first two clutched at him with grasping fingers while their heads shook and their faces scrunched up in anguish.

"Let go, you fool," one of the new men grumbled, prying the man's fingers loose.

"Why can't we just kill him now?" the other newcomer whined.

"Not yet!" the unseen man snapped. "The Master says

it's not time."

"Everyone who touches him goes mad! These bodies want their souls back. Sooner or later someone's going to crack."

"The first person to draw a knife will feel my blade in his back."

Evelar felt his arms lifted, the ground falling away again, and his vision blurred as two new voices screamed their pleas to be free. Closing his eyes, he let himself float, sinking down into his subconscious mind, where the noise of hundreds of voices murmuring seemed like silence.

'Wilt thou stop, this vessel is mine.'

Evelar pushed at the more powerful presence of the Sandman, bracing himself against the door to his conscious mind to prevent the interloper gaining control. He held himself there, in a pocket of calm between the chaos of the outside world and the swirling cloud of foreign minds that threatened to push him into insanity. The minds within clamoured for attention, voices tumbling over each other.

'Our bodies are right there, so close! Let us out! Why won't you set us free? Give us back our lives!'

'I don't know how!' Evelar screamed into the crowd.

The cacophony subsided as the Sandman chuckled.

The settlement thrived under the alien sun, the colonists building a new life in a rapidly growing town, nestled in a lush green eden of their own making. The settlement had been birthed in fire, burned by the only indigenous life form as the creatures fought back against the terraforming.

The Sandman let his eye rove over the town with a flush of pride in what they had achieved. It was not exactly the town that had been planned, using the technology they brought with them, rather than living off the land as had been intended. Their despotic new leader had seen to that. It was a deviation that would eventually fail, when the power cells ran out and the machinery stopped working. But the great Commander Kay swept all opposition aside.

"He will see his error. The new generation will need to live off the land."

The Sandman smiled at the woman beside him, his beloved wife. He touched a hand to her rounded belly, thinking forward to the birth. His first true son would soon be born. The first non-clone child in uncounted generations. With the new colony finally on its feet, the Sandman's task was complete. He could retire, safe in the knowledge that he alone had brought his people safely to their new home, with memories intact and bodies mostly undamaged by the constant cloning.

"But will he change his ways before the people rebel?" he sighed. "I hear the whispers. They're not happy about this deviation. They expected to give up all technology for a simpler life."

"I worry about that too. Lately there is a lot of angry talk. I fear it will be soon."

"Sir! You must come!"

"What is it?" said the Sandman with a groan.

"Trouble, Sir. Some of the men are marching on the council building, calling for the Commander."

'Sooner than we even imagined,' the Sandman thought to his wife. "I'm coming," he said aloud.

Down in the town square, a crowd was forming, calling threats. Pushing his way through the angry throng, the Sandman held up a hand for quiet. Amid grumbles and continued heckling, the mob slowly calmed enough for him to be heard.

"Please, think about what you are doing," he called. "You don't want to destroy what we have built here."

"It's already destroyed," a man cried. "This place is

nothing like what we signed on for."

"Without our technology, the fire demons would have destroyed us all," someone protested.

"We'll never survive here if we don't get rid of this stuff," called another. "It doesn't belong."

"Small minded, provincial thinking," a voice scoffed.

The Sandman spun to face the Commander. "They do have a point, Kay."

"Commander Kay, thank you very much."

"An obsolete title that you stole in the first place."

"How dare you," the Commander cried over the roars of approval from the crowd.

"Calm down, everyone!" the Sandman yelled.

"You're the one who's obsolete, Sandman. Time for you to do the sleeping."

The Sandman heard the scream almost before he felt the blast rip through his chest. Dust floated in a cloud around him, clearing to show his wife's agonised face staring down at him. She was shouting something, eyes wide and tears leaving streaks in the dust on her cheeks.

There was a great thundering vibration in the earth beneath him, shadows flickering across his vision. Through the ringing in his ears, he could almost hear the roar of the mob as they passed over him in their charge.

He blinked against the dust of their passage, dust that seemed to grow denser with each impossible breath. Gasping for air, lungs seeming to constrict under a crushing weight, he tried to hear what his beloved was saying. He struggled to focus on her hands, red with blood.

"Get you to the lab, before it's too late!" he heard the tail end of her sentence.

He tried to shake his head. A darkness floated before his eyes and her voice faded away. The world shifted and he glided toward the council building. A confused array of chaotic images drifted by, people fighting, a man fleeing.

Then he was looking up at the bright lights of his lab, and his beloved hovered once more, a golden chain in her hands. He tried to protest but she hushed him, her voice coming from afar.

'It's time to sleep, love,' her whispering voice slipped into his mind. 'You're dying.'

'I don't want to go. I have no clone-son.'

'I will bring you back, love, I promise. But for now you need to sleep.'

That was his last memory before waking in this too-mature body, forced to fight for possession from within. If he could just gain control he might learn what had passed, and why. But all those other voices sapped his strength and took his reason. He must win through.

The sun was setting over the northern mountains when Genton and his raiding party finally rejoined the rest of the possessed. Concealed in the brush nearby, Nashta frowned. The men had disappeared one night without a word and left the rest of the travellers to fend for themselves.

"Where do you think they went?"

Nashta jumped at the voice and turned to face the woman. "Fransi, what have I told you about that? You can't keep following me."

"I'll do what I like. Staying close to you keeps me safe from them."

"What makes you think you're any safer with me?"

She snorted. "I know you only want me for my body. And you're too much of a prude to do anything about it."

Nashta shivered. Being a prude had nothing to do with it. Being close to her was an exquisite torture that left him trembling with desire and filled with anguish for the love he had lost. But he was not about to let her see that.

"You're safe now that Sniv has run off. You don't need me any more."

"I need you more than ever," she murmured as she sidled in close. "I need you every time I so much as glimpse you hiding in the bushes. I need you so much I can't walk straight. And if you don't get over yourself soon I just might have to satisfy my need with someone else."

He groaned as her soft curves pressed hard against him, stirring his lust. The thought of her lying with another man filled him with dread.

"You would never do that," he moaned.

"Wouldn't I? I could snap my fingers and have anyone I wanted. It's a pity I don't want anyone else, but I'm sure I could manage if it stopped this damned ache in my... what do girls call that part?"

"Fransi, stop it," he snapped.

"Forget about your lost girlfriend. She's gone and I'm here, ready and willing. So ready, and oh so willing."

"They've got someone with them."

"Forget about them, damn you."

She touched her mouth to his and something inside him snapped. He clutched at her, returning the kiss with all the urgency he had tried to suppress. He felt her fumbling with his clothing and did not try to stop her, his own hands working on their own to reach her soft skin.

Lost in the anticipation of the moment, he gave in to his pent up longing, eager for its release. Some time later, he came to his senses with a groan of chagrin, her soft chuckle bringing his mind sharply into focus.

"So that's what it feels like for a woman," the girl murmured. "I must say, that's a little secret they never tell their men."

"It won't happen again," he snapped, bursting to his feet as he straightened his clothing.

"Oh, why not?" she pouted, looking up at him.

He averted his gaze, her half-naked body and ruffled clothing enticing him to a repeat of recent events. He stumbled away, ignoring her protests.

Crashing blindly through the scrub, he burst into the camp and pulled up short. Before him, a crowd of possessed encircled a prone figure in the midnight blue cloak of a revealer. Seeing the black edge of the Awakener's cloak, Nashta hurried forward only to be blocked by Genton and his cronies.

"What have you done?" he cried.

"Only what the Master wanted. Captured the vessel."

"Vessel? What's that supposed to mean? He's hurt."

"He was like that when we found him, we haven't touched him."

"You expect me to believe that?"

"Nashta, calm down," said Fransi, coming up behind with a touch to his arm.

"You knew!" he growled, turning on her. "You distracted me."

She shook her head. "No, it wasn't like that."

"Who did that to him? Who?"

"Not us. He fell from his horse before we took him," said Genton. "He's barely been conscious the whole time."

"Let me see him, I can heal him."

Genton's men blocked him. "I'm afraid I can't allow that. We'd have a riot on our hands."

Nashta cursed. "You can't just leave him like that. He could be dying."

Genton threw back his head and laughed. "That's the idea."

Nashta glared at him, summoning up all his psychic power in a blast that sent the man reeling, clutching at his head. Then, while Genton's men were rushing to his aid,

Nashta hurried to the Awakener's still form.

Apart from some light bruising about his head consistent with a fall, there were no visible injuries. But behind his closed eyelids, his eyes flicked and rolled, and his limbs twitched almost in time with the movement of his eyes. Nashta touched his fingertips to the Awakener's temples and opened a mental channel.

'Sir? Can you hear me?'

Silence. Nashta delved deeper, finding his way down toward the subconscious mind. Finding the metaphorical doorway, he gave a mental tap and listened for a response. He could hear voices drifting through the barrier. He pushed against it, forcing the door to give way.

'Shut that door!'

The barrier slammed shut against him. Nashta hesitated, then tried again.

'Sir?' Nashta sent through the crack he made.

'Nashta? Is that you?' a familiar mental voice called.

'Tinny?'

'Quiet!' came the Awakener's voice. 'Out! I'm coming!'

Again the door was closed tightly against him, and this time no pressure would allow him access.

Reluctantly, Nashta pulled out and released his grip on the Awakener's temples. He sat back on his heels and watched, his mind racing. He had heard her voice. Tineya was there, inside the Awakener's head. But how? He was so shocked he almost missed the flicker of the man's eyelids and the troubled eyes gazing up at him.

"Tong, what are you doing here?" he whispered.

"I'm sorry, Sir. I've been... helping them. The possessed."

"Helping them do what?"

"I... don't know, Sir. I just have to do it. I... didn't expect them to kidnap you, Sir."

"I don't have time to worry about that, Tong. I need you

to get me away from here."

"I can't, Sir. I'm all alone here. They'd kill me without a thought."

"The voices are frantic, Tong. These are their bodies and they want them back. But I don't know how to help them. As long as I'm close to their stolen bodies, I can't function. All my strength is spent on keeping the voices under control."

"What do you want me to do, Sir?"

"Get Mist," he gasped. "And hurry."

"Yes, Sir!"

"And Nashta," he said. "Stop calling me Sir."

Then his eyes closed and he drifted away. Nashta lurched to his feet and stormed toward Genton, who sat with head in hands while his cronies fussed around him. As Nashta approached, the men formed up in front of their leader, faces hostile.

Nashta concentrated all his anger in a short mental blast that sent them stumbling back. He grabbed their leader by the scruff and dragged him to his feet, pushing him backward until he crashed into a tree. He held him there and glared into his face.

"If any harm comes to him," Nashta spat. "You won't live to regret it."

Then he released the man and stormed off down the narrow bush track. Someone followed, but he ignored the scurrying footsteps.

"Nashta, wait," Fransi called. "Please."

Nashta spun to face her, ready with an angry retort, but something held his tongue. If she knew he had spoken to Tinny, that she was alive and he planned to bring her back one day, what would she do?

He had to keep that body safe and untouched. Which meant keeping her close and not letting her run into the arms of some other man. He swallowed down his hurt pride and buried his anger. He allowed her to see a twitch of a smile, enough to encourage her to follow. Then he turned without a word and led her away from the camp.

* * *

EIGHTEEN

Riding Cheena with Lumen trotting along beside, Miyam could almost forget that Evelar was missing. But each time she glanced across and saw the empty saddle on Lumen's back, her breath caught in her throat and tears welled in her eyes.

Taking a deep breath, she forced the fear down and regained her composure, hiding her anguish behind a placid mask. It would not do for the two journeyers to see her in that state. They may be only a few scant years her junior, but they looked to her for guidance and leadership, and she was not about to disappoint them.

Jossep was proving to be a master tracker, and Miyam felt her beloved drawing nearer with each and every mile they travelled. He made no reply when she sent out her tendrils of thought, but the fact that she could still find his presence gave her reassurance. He might be unresponsive, but he was not lost; the Sandman had not won yet.

Ahead, Joss had paused and jumped down from his horse, examining the ground. As Miyam watched, Navear slid down beside him. Catching them up, Miyam frowned at their confused faces.

"What's wrong?" she said, cold dread lending an edge to her tone.

"The trail is gone," said Jossep. "Wiped clean."

"As if they knew we were following," Navear said quietly.

"Are you sure?"

Joss shrugged. "I'm sorry, Mym."

"But who would do that? Nobody can completely obliterate a trail."

"A revealer can."

Miyam's head snapped up at the new voice.

"Tong?" she gasped. "What are you doing here? Did you erase the trail?"

"Yes, I did," he said. "But only because I had to."

"Look at you lot," said a woman at his side. "All those colours. Green, blue, red, and the black one back at the camp. With those dark cloaks you're like some kind of gloomy rainbow…"

"Tineya?" Miyam gasped.

"No, my name is Fransi, though Nashta says this was her body."

"Why did you hide the trail?" Miyam snarled at Nashta.

He held up his hands in a calming gesture. "Calm down, Mist. You don't need the trail. I know where to find them."

"You do? How?"

"I've been helping them."

"Helping? You mean you're leading them? You took Evelar?"

"No, of course not," he said. "I've been following, helping when necessary, but only that. I had no idea they planned to take him. In fact I was furious when I found out."

"So what do the colours mean?"

"I think that can wait, Fransi," said Nashta.

"No, I mean it. What's the rainbow for?"

"Hush, Fransi. The colours denote rank. Now can we get on with business?"

"Rank?" she mused. "So… who's the boss then?"

"Fransi…"

"I don't understand, Sir," said Navear. "What's going on?"

"Sir?" said Fransi with a smirk. "So you're the boss?"

"I am the most senior here, but that's not important right now." He turned to Miyam. "We need to work out how to get the Awakener away from them."

"The Awakener? Is that the black one? Is he the boss?"

"Fransi, hush!" Nashta snapped.

"Where is Evelar?" said Miyam. "Why didn't you rescue him yourself?"

"There are too many guarding him, and he is unable to save himself."

"You mean he's possessed again? Or is it the voices?"

"I don't quite understand it. The outsider students' bodies are possessed with minds from another place. The minds in the Awakener's head are the true owners of those bodies."

Miyam's eyes opened wide. "So that's where they came from!"

"Right now, the bodies are unstable because he is so close and their minds are calling them. And the Awakener is engaged in a struggle for his sanity. It's a volatile situation, I'm afraid."

"I must find him!"

"So..." mused Fransi. "If I joined you, what colour would I be?"

"Fransi!" Nashta barked. "Mist, he asked for you. He must have a lot of faith in you. I think you should follow me."

He turned to walk down the track, but Miyam called him back.

"Tong, why don't you take Lumen, it will be faster."

Nashta thanked her and helped Fransi up onto the big stallion's back, then swung up behind her.

"So can I choose my colour or do I have to pass some sort of test?"

Nashta growled his frustration and kicked in with his heels. The horse surged forward as if knowing he was being taken to his master. Miyam and the two journeyers followed.

As night fell, the revealers came to a halt. A bright glow filtered its way through the trees, and Jossep pointed to the scuffed ground and broken branches.

'The camp must be just ahead,' his mental voice whispered in the minds of the group.

Creeping closer, they paused at the edge of the clearing. The bulk of the camp was silent, its residents already slipping into exhausted sleep. A fire blazed and a group of men sat together near a dark lump on the ground.

"Evelar!" Miyam hissed, then clamped a hand over her mouth.

"What was that?" one of the guards said.

"Nothing, just the vessel."

"I wish he'd shut up," the guard moaned.

"I'll shut him up," said the second guard, rising to his feet with knife in hand.

"Back to your post," a voice growled from the darkness.

"Sorry, Gent," the man mumbled as he scrunched down again.

'We have to do something,' Miyam sent silently to her companions.

'Can you contact him?' Navear asked.

'I'll try, Bell.'

Miyam closed her eyes and sank down into her subconscious centre, slipping through the link into the mind of her beloved. The voices slammed into her with all their chaotic ramblings.

'It's her! What is she doing? Is she going to help us? Get us out!'

'Hush!' she commanded. *'Where is he?'*

'Blocking us! Keeping us trapped. He won't let us out!'

'Stop it. I doubt he knows how to free you.'

'He said that. He can't help. Can you help?'

'Evelar, where are you?' her thought bounced about.

'Here, my love...' she heard the echo of his voice come floating back.

'Help us! Let us out! We want our bodies back.'

Shutting out the voices, Miyam floated through the subconscious pathways toward the door to the conscious mind. She felt his love encircling her mind, a caressing thought warming her soul. He hovered just inside the barrier, blocking access to his consciousness. No wonder he appeared unresponsive.

'I need to get away, my love,' he whispered. 'You need to help me.'

'I'm here.'

'I have to keep the door closed. I can only turn my back for a few moments.'

'What do you want me to do?'

'Distract the guards, help me get away.'

'How?'

'I trust you. I know you'll find a way.'

Miyam retraced her steps, ignoring the voices and returning to her own mind.

Opening her eyes she glanced from one worried face to another.

'He knows we're here,' she thought at them. 'He's ready, but he can only wake for a moment. We need to be quick.'

'We need to distract the guards,' Nashta replied. 'Mist and Bell, see what you can do. Make them sleep if you can.'

Miyam nodded, sharing a look with Navear.

'Joss,' Nashta continued. 'You come with me. Together we can drag him out.'

"Wait," Fransi whispered, almost silently. They had forgotten Genton, sitting just out of the light of the fire watching his guards to make sure they did no harm to the prisoner.

'I'll take him out first,' said Nashta, including her in his thought.

Fransi's thought floated about, unfocussed but readable. She would take care of Genton.

'No, Fransi, it's too dangerous.'

An image formed in the girl's mind. She planned to distract him by offering herself.

'No!' Nashta snapped, causing the others to flinch at the power behind his thought. *'I won't allow it.'*

Fransi shrugged. She knew Genton fancied her. It would be an easy thing to take his attention while they took their friend to safety. She would not take no for an answer. Before anyone could stop her, she stepped out into the clearing. The guards looked up and one sneered while the other leered.

"Well if it isn't the little traitor. The priest-man's pet."

"You don't need him, dearie. If the priest-man's dropped you, you can have me."

"Be patient, boys," she teased. "Play your cards right, you might get a chance. Where's Genton?"

"Forget Genton, come join us."

"Quit it, you two," Genton snarled from the darkness. "Where have you been, Fransi?"

The girl put on a broad smile and sauntered off toward the voice. Behind her, the revealers put their plan into action.

Miyam closed her eyes and reached out mentally to one of the guards, trusting Navear to attend to the other. She slipped into his mind and easily found the switch, sending him into a deep sleep. Opening her eyes, she saw both guards supine beside the fire. Fransi's giggle floated out of the darkness.

Just outside the glow of the fire, two dark figures slinked invisibly toward where the Awakener lay. Silently, Miyam reached out to her beloved and he opened his eyes. Glancing about, he carefully moved an arm, lifting himself onto hands and knees.

Crawling ever so slowly he moved out of the circle of firelight to meet the waiting shadows. As Miyam watched with breath held anxiously, Nashta and Jossep helped Evelar to his feet and led him toward the trees.Somewhere behind them, Fransi cried out and Genton bellowed.

"Where is the vessel? What have you done, bitch?"

The rescuers pushed onward, hurrying to the safety of the trees.

"It wasn't me, Genton. Please, don't be angry with me."

"Guards, wake up! Get after him!"

"Take him," Nashta hissed. "Let me deal with this. You have to get him away."

"But what about you, Sir?" Jossep said.

"Don't worry about me, I have Genton under control. Just go."

Miyam took Nashta's place at Evelar's side and together they half-dragged him away from the camp.

"You!" the voice of Genton screamed. "Where's the vessel?"

"I told you I wouldn't let you harm him," Nashta replied.

"What have you done, priest-man?"

"I've solved your problem. You know he was too dangerous to keep here. Sooner or later one of your men would have cracked and done him an injury, probably killed him. What would your master have done then?"

"You had no right! Guards, get after them."

Hearing crashing footsteps, the rescuers hurried on, toward where the horses waited. Jossep helped Evelar climb onto his stallion's back, and Miyam swung up behind him.

"Bell, will you lead Cheena," Miyam said and Navear nodded.

Grasping the reins around the slumping body of the Awakener, Miyam kicked in with her heels and Lumen bounded away. Trusting the others to follow, she led the way past the camp and down the track as the guards cried out behind her.

After riding at full gallop for several miles, the rescuers allowed the winded horses to slow to a walk. Sliding down to the ground, Miyam helped Evelar alight and led him to a log by the side of the track. As he slumped down, Miyam rubbed at her aching shoulders and flexed her arms to loosen her protesting muscles. Then she knelt before him and touched her fingers to his temples. He smiled and took her hands, kissing her palms before clasping them in his own.

"I'm alright, my love," he murmured. "But we must keep going. We must put as much distance as we can between us and the possessed."

"The voices?"

"Easing, but still agitated. I can almost relax a little. Where are we?"

"Somewhere northwest of Mytar, I think."

He nodded. "Good. Let's continue south through the mountains and meet up with the river Nort. We can join Jumally and Tikki in Nella Fillenga."

"You're not seriously suggesting we carry on as normal?" Miyam cried. "Evelar, we almost lost you twice over!"

"We can't exactly go north, can we? Not if we want to outrun the possessed."

She sighed. "No, I suppose not."

"Don't worry," he smiled. "I'm not lost yet."

"Here," Jossep handed them each a small packet. "Trail

cakes."

Evelar nodded his thanks and hauled himself to his feet. Watching him move wearily toward his horse, Miyam tried to hold back her concern. Of its own accord, one hand clutched at him as he passed and he paused to smile. She slipped into the circle of his arms and rested her head against his chest with a heavy sigh.

With his arm about her, leading her to the horses, giving the outward appearance of his old strength, she could almost believe everything would be alright. He helped her onto Cheena's back, then pulled himself up onto Lumen and kicked the big horse forward.

Somewhere high in the Dragon Mountains, a small group of revealers settled down in a sheltered hollow by the path. They lit no fire, aware that somewhere to the north the possessed watched for any sign. Jossep handed out dried meat and stale bread, and they ate in silence. Then he stretched out on a blanket beside his young wife. Hearing their exaggerated yawns, Miyam smiled in spite of herself. She rose to her feet and wandered away from the couple, finding Evelar staring out over the valley as he leaned against a tree.

"You should sleep," she murmured. "I can take first watch."

"I don't dare sleep," he replied with a frown. "But why don't you go join the others, there's no reason why you can't grab a few hours."

"I don't think they're sleeping," she said.

A soft giggle, quickly stifled, floated on the wind.

"Oh," Evelar smirked.

"Besides," said Miyam. "I'm not letting you out of my sight."

"Well, if you insist," he said, one eyebrow raised. "But

something else is bothering you."

She let out a long, slow sigh. "I'm just missing Zavvy. I wasn't ready to leave him behind."

"I know, but Netta was right to take him."

"Yes, but I'm sore from not feeding him."

"I can fix that," he smirked.

She let out a laugh. "I'm sure you could." She slipped in under his cloak to snuggle against him. "Do we really need to keep watch? I get the feeling your voices will let you know if the possessed get too near."

"How very astute of you, my love," he chuckled.

He pulled her closer, mouth hovering near hers. "I think those youngsters have the right idea. Who knows when we'll have another moment like this."

"I'm sure you'll find a way."

"I'd rather not take that chance," he murmured.

* * *

It was deep night when Jumally awoke in the guest quarters she shared with her wife Tikki in the palace at Tellemot. Something was tugging at her mind, something that had been growing stronger over the past few days, like an itch between her ears that she couldn't scratch.

Searching within, she followed the itch, determined to root it out. Digging deeper, she found a furrow, a slight fold that warped her mental pathways. Tracing the flaw, she found something tugging at the fabric of her mindscape, sending ripples outward from a central point.

Something was dragging at her mind, pulling gently. Examining closer, she felt around the centre of the disturbance. Some kind of barb seemed to be buried in her mindscape. She tugged at it, and it gave slightly. The hook resisted the pull, its attached thread fighting against her.

She pulled harder, dragging it out of the fabric of her mind, releasing the strain with a sense of relief. She released it, sensing it spring away, flung from her mind. She brushed at the slight flaw the hook left behind, shuddering. Then she floated back to her conscious mind to wake Tikki.

"What is it, Jum?" she whispered sleepily.

"I need to check something," Jumally replied. "May I look in your mind?"

"Of course, love, you don't need to ask.

Jumally touched her fingertips to Tikki's temples, probing within, hoping she would not find a similar hook. But as she sank deeper, the same furrows began to appear. With a feeling of dread, she found the hook and released it.

"Oh, that feels better!" Tikki exclaimed. "What did you do?"

"Something had hooked into your mind. I found the same thing in my own head."

"What? I don't understand. Who would do that?"

"I don't know, but I think we should warn the others."

* * *

As the revealers rode down through the pass toward the southern foothills, the Wild Plain stretched out before them, its three mighty rivers ribboning their way toward their union far to the south.

Miyam did not catch the exact moment when her fears became real. With Evelar beside her as he always should be, she had allowed herself to relax, to hope that the worst of his problems were over. But then, she caught a twitch, out of the corner of her eye. Glancing toward him, she saw another, an almost imperceptible shake of the head, a flicker behind his eyes.

"Evelar?"

He did not respond for a moment, then he blinked, shivered, and turned glazed eyes toward her.

"No," she whispered. "Not again. Evelar, you need to stop them."

He gave a shudder and his eyes cleared, making contact with hers. "I'm sorry, my love," he whispered.

"Don't do this," she moaned. "Don't let them in."

"There's more of them, Mym," he gasped. "New ones."

"New..." She jumped down and rushed to his side. "Joss! Help me!"

The young man appeared beside her to catch the Awakener as he fell. He lowered Evelar to the ground and Miyam knelt beside him.

"Bell, I need you," Miyam cried.

"I'm right here," the girl said. "What can I do?"

"Feed me strength. Whatever you can manage. Joss, I need you too. Hold him still."

Reaching out to catch his twitching head between her hands, Miyam sent her mind into the chaos inside his head.

Voices rattled around, each one trying to be heard.

'Where am I? What is this place? What happened?'

Miyam tried to hush them. But more voices cried out, new ones appearing in a wave of panic.

'Help me! I'm lost! Why can't I see?'

'Please, be calm,' Miyam thought into the noise. 'Evelar, what can I do?'

She felt his presence engulf her in the warmth of his love. 'You can't stop them,' his familiar voice whispered. 'There are too many.'

'Evelar, don't give in. We controlled them before, we can do it again.'

'Get thee hence,' a voice thundered through the mental pathways. 'This vessel is mine.'

'No, Sandman, let him be,' Miyam cried into the noise. 'Evelar, you have to fight him!'

'Mym, I can't,' Evelar whispered. 'There's too many. I don't have the strength.'

'Sand, you need to try! I won't let you go. Bell, I need

more strength.'

But something pushed at her thought, sending her crashing back into her own head.

Holding back the sobs, she tried again, but his mind was closed tight against her. His brown eyes fluttered, a gold spark flaring before his eyelids closed.

"Joss, I need more," she whimpered.

"We can't," the young man cried. "We're not strong enough, Mym."

"No," she screamed. "I won't lose him again!"

"I'm sorry, Mym," said Navear, one gentle hand resting on her shoulder.

Miyam rocked back on her heels, sobbing desperately. Through the haze of tears, she clutched at her husband's still form, sending out a searching thought. But he lay unresponsive, his beloved presence pushed down beneath the turmoil within.

"We'll have to let him fight on his own," Jossep said. "Let him be."

She shook her head. "I'm not leaving him. I want to be here when he wakes up."

A shiver threatened to send her into another paroxism of sobs. What if the Sandman won? She quickly buried that thought. Evelar would win. He was Sand, the most powerful revealer the College had ever known. He was the Awakener, whose coming had been foretold by the counsellor spirits themselves. He would win through. He had to.

* * *

NINETEEN

Huddled in the corner of the stark, white room, the boy watched as the holy-one twitched and giggled. The huge body lay supine on the bed, the whole upper torso buried in a glittering sea of gold. The eyes were closed, but from the mouth issued strange grunts and cackles, interspersed with long, shuddering seizures.

Taking a deep breath, the boy closed his eyes and sent out his thought with a timid yet determined touch. Within the mind of the holy-one, hundreds of strands radiated outward, reaching over the miles to somewhere unknown. The holy-one's consciousness flitted and danced among the strings, a triumphant laughter plucking at the gossamer threads to produce a discordant non-melody.

Settling down silently on the strings, the boy listened. Along the strings, a stream of conscious thought flitted and hummed. Each one a different soul, somehow tethered within the mind of the holy-one. And somewhere above, the holy-one gathered all those thoughts, sending back an insistent message, an order of unwavering power. Now. Catch. Kill.

* * *

Miyam sat cross-legged beside the unconscious body of her beloved husband, her head hanging low in the half-sleep of a revealer on watch. Her mind floated in a waking fog, fully aware but standing back, watching and listening without resting on any one thought.

Small sounds from the world around flitted over her,

touching without staying. The call of a bird, the hum of an insect, the sounds of love from her young companions. Nothing intruded as it passed, except for the light breathing of the man she watched. A soft groan, almost imperceptible, and she opened her eyes. The head twitched, an arm flicked. The eyelids fluttered.

"Evelar?" she breathed.

Another groan, long and low. His mouth opened for tongue to lick at parched lips. Miyam offered water and he swallowed by reflex. Then he sighed and settled back into his stupor.

Leaning forward, Miyam touched fingertips gently to his temples, sending a soft mental touch into his mind. Something pushed at her, forcing her back. Then his eyes snapped open, a gold fire flashing in their piercing gaze.

Releasing his head with a gasp, Miyam scurried backward, out of reach of the man's grasping hand. He rose up on one elbow, those golden eyes taking in everything. Miyam stood, shaking her head in denial.

"No, it can't be," she whispered.

"Thou must know," he said. "This has to be."

"No. I will never believe it. Give him back!"

The Sandman threw back his head and laughed. "As I did tell thee already. Never shall I do so."

"What do you want?" she said.

"Answer me this," he replied. "Who art thou? And wherefore ist my wife?"

"I... I am your wife. His wife."

"Thou hast the look of her. But thou art not my wife."

Miyam gave an involuntary grunt, feeling the rejection like a blow to the stomach. Even knowing the words came from a stranger imposing his mind on her beloved's body, the sight of his face twisting and his mouth forming the words hit her right in the heart. It was not her Sand, it was not Evelar. He was buried somewhere inside and she would find a way to bring him back.

"Leave her alone," said Jossep, appearing by her side.

"Mym, come away," said Navear, taking her by the arm. "Let Joss deal with him."

Miyam blinked back the tears, and allowed the girl to lead her away. But her ears strained to hear as Jossep quizzed the Sandman.

"Now, perhaps you can help us understand."

The man snorted his derision. "Thou thinkest to placate me, boy? Give me answer. Wherefore ist my wife?"

"Sir, I don't understand."

"Art thou a simpleton, boy? She did promise to wake me. I am awakened."

"Perhaps you could explain, Sir. Why are you taking possession of the Awakener?"

"Why dost thou call him this, if not for me? I am the Awakener of Souls, I did bring the people home and did wake them from their slumber. They did call me Sandman, the one who bringeth sleep and waketh with the dawn."

"But why are you here now?"

"Thou truly knowest me not? How many turns of the sun did I sleep?"

"You've been unconscious for two days."

"No, simpleton. My soul did sleep. What count were the years?"

"I'm sorry, I don't know what you mean. How can a soul sleep?"

"With this!" He clasped the amulet at his neck. "Mine old vessel was destroyed. Then did my soul-sleep begin, to await the growth of the clone-seed which did become this vessel. But too late was I awakened, and the vessel did fight me."

"What does that mean?"

The man rubbed at his eyes, heaving a sigh before continuing. "Always it was our goal to let the soul-tech die. That I can attest. Thy lack of comprehension doth suggest a passage of time. But what length of years? A hundred? More? And by what circumstance was I awakened?"

Jossep shook his head. "I don't know, Sir."

Somewhere in the darkness a woman wailed. Nearby, voices whispered and scattered thoughts intruded. He reached out with the power of his mind, searching. The way out was blocked by an impenetrable barrier.

No help would be coming from the outside world. If he was to escape this prison within, he had to find help. Perhaps the weeping woman could help. Perhaps she would know what had happened. But he already knew.

Floating closer to the woman's lament, he sent a thought. The wailing stopped, replaced by a soft whimpering. He delved deeper, wrapping her pain in a soothing thought. He recognised the feel of her mind, but he could not fathom why she was there.

'I know you,' she whispered. 'You're the Awakener.'

'And you are Tineya,' he replied.

'Sir,' she whispered, voice rising in a wail. 'I heard Nashta. But I can't find him.'

'He's not here. You heard him calling from outside. But how can you be here?'

'I've been here since the beginning, amongst the other voices. But you never noticed before.'

'But why are you here?'

'Because you touched my mind, just like the others. All of them were tested by you.'

'What are you talking about?'

'Don't you see? We are your students, we all attended your classes. And now we are here. How could you not know

that?'

'I guess I never made the connection. But how did you get here?'

'It was the Master. The holy-one. You touched our minds and It sank Its hooks to pull us here.'

'So it's all my fault. This mess is because of me. And now the Sandman has control.'

'No, Sir. The Sandman is an opportunist, but the Master has control.'

'Then who is the Sandman? Where did he come from?'

'He was already here.'

'Already... Then he is the one who started it.'

'Sir,' she sighed. 'Will you help us?'

'I will try, Tineya. But you must also help me. When the time comes.'

'Of course we will. But what will you do?'

'The Sandman's memories will tell me what I need to know.'

Sand wandered through the Sandman's memories, dipping into each scene and flitting past, searching for something to help him understand. So many were simple life memories, with nothing more than everyday hopes and dreams, albeit in a strange world from another time. He searched for something that explained the Sandman's presence in his mind, and the motivation behind the strange spirit's possession of his body.

After sifting through uncountable memories of an alien life, Sand encountered a bright white world, clear and pure, crisp and colourless. He paused. Something about that place seemed familiar.

As he delved into the memory, a feeling of utter peace settled over him, a quiet contemplation of everything and nothing in complete silence. As he sank into that world, he remembered a time when his mind floated in just such a place, relieved of all the pressures of physical life. And he remembered his return to life, called back to earth by his beloved wife to continue his mission.

As Sand remembered his return, the white world seemed to twist and spin, stretching out as something pulled. He reminded himself that this was not his memory, but that of the Sandman, and somehow he was pulled from that place.

The white dissolved around him, and he found himself alone in the darkness, trapped in a tiny corner of thought while disembodied voices echoed around him. He could feel the Sandman's confusion, emanating from his spirit, full of ache and torment.

Tapping into that remembered thought stream, Sand followed the Sandman's reasoning. He had been in soul-sleep. His beloved wife had sent him there after the revolt that saw his vessel murdered. But now, through activation of the amulet, he had been released from storage.

He should be hearing the soothing words of awakening, delivered by his love to help him transition from soul-sleep into his new vessel, ready for a new life. But something was wrong. The vessel had not accepted him and now he was trapped within, his soul buried beneath the new mind created by the vessel, a new soul fully established in a strong adult body. His awakening had come too late.

Sand took hold of the memory, exploring the thought of the amulet. It could only be the amulet he wore about his neck, the one his sister had worn for so long before she was killed. Somehow, it had activated when he, Sand, had taken it. But what did that mean? A simple trinket with the power to wake a dead soul?

He forced himself to remember the first amulet he had encountered, the Queen's Amulet Leena, worn for generations by the queens of Shirall, carrying the soul of ancient King

Rexa's queen. And the second amulet, the subject of Princess Nettayna's quest, the King's amulet Naali, carrying the soul of King Rexa himself, now worn by King Atwin. Sand had never thought to question his own amulet, had never considered that it too might carry some long dead soul.

But why would the soul of the Sandman be released into his body? The King and queen were never invaded by their amulet souls. They acted as guides and mentors, but never were they bent on possession. He had to find out what had made his amulet behave differently.

If the amulet could impose the Sandman's soul on his body, there must be a connection. And if the link could be followed one way, it must be possible to travel the other. Sand would have to find the path to the amulet. Only then could he uncover the secrets it held.

Miyam stared out into the darkness, her whole being attuned to the coming danger. She tried to ignore the Sandman as he paced, his hands clenching and that horrid archaic voice mumbling out of the Awakener's mouth.

Too much time had passed waiting for Evelar to awake, and now the possessed were close. Perhaps Evelar could break through, use the distraction of the voices in the same way the Sandman had.

"Should we wait?" Navear whispered at Miyam's side.

Miyam licked her lips. "We can't," she groaned.

"Why not? Let the voices take over again, and give Evelar a chance to come back."

"I know," Miyam sighed. "But we can't risk it. The possessed will kill him if they catch him. We have to run."

"Oh thou infernal shades, wilt thou not be silent?" the Sandman muttered. "How does one think with this monstrous noise?"

Navear giggled and Miyam smiled in spite of herself.

They heard Jossep calming the man.

"The possessed are close, and the souls want their bodies back."

"What dost thou propose I do?"

"We have to get moving before they catch up. The closer they get, the worse those voices will be."

"Then why, pray tell, do we stand here witless?"

"Mym?" said Jossep.

Miyam turned reluctantly and hesitated, then she gave a sharp nod. She whistled for Cheena and the mare approached. She swung up into the saddle and watched the others. While Navear and Jossep mounted up, the Sandman regarded the big stallion with a look of bewilderment.

"Thou wouldst have me ride that?"

"That's usually the idea, Sir," said Jossep.

"How wouldst thou suggest I achieve such a thing?"

"Don't you know how?"

"When I did fall into soul-sleep, our first horses were not yet full grown." He reached a hesitant hand to touch the horse.

"Well, you'll have to learn fast if you want to escape the possessed. Just put your foot in the stirrup and... pull yourself up."

Miyam kicked in her heels and moved off, passing the flustered Sandman with barely a sideways glance. As she passed Jossep she sent a silent thought.

'Help him, Joss. Remember whose body that is.'

Then she led the way back to the path and turned to the south, following the river as it cut its way across the plain. Somewhere behind, a grunt and a gasp, followed by a skittering of hooves. Then a sharp cry and the stallion thundered past, the Sandman clutching its neck in both arms.

"Joss, how is that helping?" she exclaimed. "What if he

falls?"

"Lumen won't let him fall. He's a smart horse, he knows what's going on. He'll stop eventually."

"Well," said Navear with a giggle. "At least he's going in the right direction."

* * *

TWENTY

The holy-one's eyes snapped open. "Boy! Bring me my souls."

The boy scurried to the wall. He ran his hand over the smooth surface, searching for the door without success.

"Make haste, boy."

"But Sir..."

"Thy hand doth know the method."

The boy closed his eyes and touched the wall, feeling his fingertips tingle. He found the place and gave a little push. The door sprang open.

"Which one, Sir?"

"It is of no consequence."

The boy grabbed at the golden chains, hearing the whispering of the trapped souls. Pulling one out at random, he felt its whispers grow stronger, felt a strange pulling sensation as the soul eagerly sought admission into his mind.

Blocking instinctively, the boy hurried over to the holy-one, draping the amulet about the priest's neck to lie amongst the hundreds already festooned about the holy-one's supine form.

"Another," said the old priest. "Keep on, boy, stop thou not."

The boy rushed back to the closet, pulling out another and taking it to the holy-one, following it with another. For hours, the boy carried amulets, their whispering souls growing louder with each moment, then falling silent as the holy-one drew them in. Each voice attempted to capture the boy, and each voice was repelled by his strong young mind.

But the holy-one welcomed them, sending them out along the strings. When the holy-one at last called a halt the closet was almost empty, the last few amulets sending out lonely whispers, begging for release.

The glow of the amulets smothering the priest's body lit the room with a blue haze, blinding to look upon. Under their weight, the holy-one struggled for breath after ragged breath. The boy brought soup and spooned it into the Master's slack mouth, then hovered uncertainly, twisting his hands as he waited for his next order. His young mind followed the holy-one to the faraway souls in their new vessels, listening to the Master's relentless call.

* * *

"Sir, they're waking up!"

Reeperly followed the servant out to the main courtyard, dreading what he might find. If this event followed the same pattern as Eeasto, the students would be waking up changed, possessed by some other soul. And without the timely warning from Jumally, he felt sure he and Iris would have been thus possessed too.

Berkana touched his arm, her own concern clear in her eyes. Without the help of the Maestro or the Awakener, Reeperly knew he would never control the violent tendencies of the possessed. He smiled at his wife, but his outward confidence did not make it below the surface. She smiled in return, offering reassurance.

"You will make the right decision, dear," she said.

Bursting out into the sunshine, the couple paused. The new students mingled together, half dazed, their recent unresponsive state vanquished by something new. Reeperly approached a young man, formerly a promising student who had faced a bright future in service to the College as an outside contact.

"Fondess?" he said. "Are you alright?"

The youngster gave him a bewildered look. "I'm sorry? My name's Antoni, but... where am I?"

Reeperly took a step backward, then tilted his head. "Where are you from, Antoni?"

"Stolen City. But I was old and sick, dying I think. Then the holy-one came and I was trapped somewhere white. That's all I remember before waking up here." He looked down at his hands, then felt his own face. "And I seem to have been made young again."

"What's happening?" said a squat, middle aged woman, bursting in on them. "I'm an old woman! I was a man, in my prime, now this. Where am I?"

"It's the holy-one's promise!" a man cried. "We have our new bodies."

"New?" said the woman. "I hardly call this new!"

"Now wait," said Reeperly, holding up a hand. "This is only temporary. These bodies are not yours."

"They are now," said Antoni with a sneer. "You won't be taking them from us."

"The holy-one calls!" cried a young woman. "Can you hear?"

"Let's go!" yelled another.

The crowd surged for the outer gate, coming up hard against the bars and calling out in their urgency.

"Let us out! You can't keep us here."

Reeperly licked his lips. "Please, don't be hasty. We need to find out what happened so we can fix it."

Antoni turned on him, rushing at him with a look of pure disdain. "You won't stop us. We have to heed the call."

"I'm sorry," Reeperly muttered. "I can't let you go."

Antoni made a sign with his hand and two men grabbed

the revealer by the arms.

"No, don't hurt him," Berkana cried. "We'll let you go."

"No, Iris, you can't," Reeperly gasped.

"The Maestro let the others go. You have to do the same. They'll kill you, Reep!"

As if to illustrate the point, Antoni slammed a fist into the revealer's face. Then he gestured for the captors to drag him toward the gate.

"Either you give the order to open the gate, or we kill the guard and open it anyway, then we kill you."

Blinking blood out of his eyes, Reeperly shuddered at the empty hatred on the young man's face. "Open it," he called to the gatekeeper.

As the gate opened, the possessed pushed forward, heedless of the man in their path. The gatekeeper ducked back into his guardhouse, but Reeperly had no such retreat. He battled to stay upright as the possessed surged past, buffeting against him.

One heavyset man collided into him, knocking him to the ground and trampling over him. Fighting panic, Reeperly curled into a ball, clasping his head in his arms as the crowd clambered over him, heedless of his presence.

When the last of the crowd had passed, he lay huddled on the ground, groaning. He flinched at a light touch on his back, fearing another booted foot. Then he uncurled, raising his head to meet his wife's worried gaze.

"Are you alright?" she whispered.

He gave a nod, then groaned, clutching at his head.

"Let me see," she said.

He raised his face once more and she examined his cut, clicking her tongue. Her loving hands roved over him, prodding and poking.

"I don't think there's anything broken," she murmured. "Do you?"

He smiled. "I'm fine. Just bruises and a sore head."

"Let's get that seen to. You need a stitch or two."

"What do we do now?" he said as she helped him.

She smiled. "Let's find the Awakener."

* * *

The holy-one sent out a thought, searching for the Awakener, ready for more minds to hook. The enemy mind hovered just out of reach. Following the familiar pathways, the priest sent those tendrils of nothingness into the enemy. But something was in the way.

Something caught those mental fingers, sucked them in and then spat them out. The spirit of nothing tried again, slipping through the spongy resistance toward the enemy's mind. Then the barrier constricted, pushed back, and the thoughts bounced away.

The holy-one considered. There had to be a reason the door was closed. The enemy had never known of the holy-one's presence, but the interloper did. That strangely familiar mental touch, like a visitor from the distant past.

The intruder must have gained control of the enemy's mind, and his natural protective block now stood between the spirit and Its prey. The spirit of nothingness abandoned Its enemy. Dancing along the tethers to where the loyal followers waited, the holy-one hatched a new plan. There was no longer any reason to keep the enemy alive.

No more souls would be hooked, no more bodies to be emptied. The last of the amulets would have to remain in the closet, their captured souls forever sleeping. It was time to release the minions, allow them their greatest desire and get rid of the Awakener once and for all.

Then the souls would forever claim their new vessels, forever in debt to the holy-one, loyal to the end. The Awakener would be gone, never to threaten the spirit again, leaving It free to take the next step.

The interloper, too, would be gone, that ancient foe taken at the same moment, two enemies at one strike. And the holy-one would be free to make the final move, in a plan that had spanned a thousand years.

The holy-one lay under the burden of hundreds of glowing amulets, mind wandering among the loyal souls. Sent out to take possession of their new bodies, the souls eagerly listened to the holy-one's message. Find your fellows. Join together and hunt down the enemy. The holy-one laughed as the souls went forth, knowing they would follow without question.

* * *

As the possessed travelled down out of the foothills to gasp at the great plain before them, the wind brought smells of grain and promise. Somewhere down there, the enemy moved.

"We have new instructions," said Genton to the troops. "We camp here and wait."

"What?" said the new lackey. "But we're so close."

"Can't you feel the change? The Master has a new plan. We wait here."

"What for?"

Genton shrugged. "I don't know. But are you willing to go against the Master?"

"I know why Sniv ran off with those others. Sick of all this waiting. We could have claimed our bodies weeks ago, but you let the enemy vessel get away. Now you expect us to lose him again?"

"I don't argue with the Master. I prefer to keep my sanity intact."

"Well I'm not waiting."

"Fine, off you go. You won't last more than a day."

The lackey grumbled but melted back into the camp to wait out this latest delay.

*

Nashta watched from the sidelines as Genton paced in front of his men, building up their enthusiasm with words of encouragement and the occasional dressing down. The scouts had come back with news of a large rabble approaching, and Nashta suspected there would be fighting before nightfall.

No amount of cajoling on his part had swayed the possessed from their path, the call of the Master too strong. But this new force was a mystery. Beneath the expectant energy the self-appointed commander seemed calm, almost serene. He lined up his men along the plain and waited, his constant stream of words keeping the excited men under control.

"You don't need to worry," said Fransi. "Genton won't let anything bad happen."

"Won't let... You speak as if he's some holy man, untouchable and all powerful."

"Don't be silly," she snorted. "He knows the Master's plan. He knows these newcomers are more likely to be friends than enemies."

"They don't seem very friendly from what I've seen."

As if to illustrate his point, a loud cry echoed across the plain, followed by a rumbling and a roar of voices.

"Just wait and see."

"Come out of danger, at least. You don't need to risk your safety in this fight."

"My safety?" she snorted. "You mean the safety of this vessel, which you intend to take from me at the first opportunity."

The earth shook under the pounding of feet, the air rang with cries of triumph and derision. The possessed shuffled and cowered back as Genton roared at them to stand their ground. Nashta pulled at Fransi's arm.

"Just come away," he said.

Pulling back into a thicket by the roadside, Nashta found a good stout tree and began to climb.

"What are you doing, silly man?" Fransi giggled.

Nashta reached down to grasp her wrist.

"Come on," he said as he pulled her up.

Moving higher and settling into a sturdy fork of a branch, Nashta stared out over the plain. Fransi grumbled beside him but fell silent when he growled at her. Out on the plain, a cloud of dust rolled rapidly closer, a gaggle of animated voices tumbling over each other above the rumbling of countless footsteps.

The waiting possessed milled about, held in place against the urge to run only by the curses of their leader. The new force came closer. Nashta held his breath. Fransi mumbled, and Genton roared. The possessed shivered as the dust cloud hit them. The ranks of the opposing force came on behind the dust.

As the two groups met, Nashta steeled himself for the sounds of battle. The two forces merged, the front ranks giving way on both sides and melding, the newcomers sliding through the possessed like the dust that preceded them. Cries of triumph filled the air, with happy laughter and eager words of welcome. Nashta let out his breath as the two forces became one.

"See?" said Fransi. "I told you there was nothing to worry about."

Genton lounged back, watching the newcomer through lowered eyelids. He studied the youngster, who had by some quirk of fate assumed leadership of the newly awakened. Somehow he had formed the rabble into a cohesive group, with all the purpose and direction that Genton himself had never quite achieved.

His men still questioned his every decision, even after he had proved himself at the land bridge and kept them alive for months in a world that did not want them.

"Quite the camp you have here," said the lad. "Comfortable in a minimalist kind of way."

"We don't intend to stay here, if that's what you mean."

"From what I hear, you had the enemy cornered before you gave up."

"We didn't give up," Genton snarled. "The Master called us back to wait for you."

"You do everything the Master says, do you? Like a little lackey?"

Genton forced himself to laugh at the boy. "You're lucky. You haven't had to go against the call yet. We had to spend weeks travelling in the wrong direction before we got here. It wasn't a walk in the park."

Antoni snorted. "What happened? The Master give you a talking to? The Master isn't here, you can do what you like."

"You don't know half what the Master can do. Don't scoff until you've felt it yourself."

"Sure, a disembodied spirit takes over and makes you kill yourself, I'll believe that when I see it."

Genton smiled. "Oh, you will." He raised his voice. "Porkis!"

The old man shuffled over and slumped before the two leaders, giving a grunt of acknowledgement for Genton.

"Why don't you take Antoni north for a few days, let him see the sea."

"Sir?" Porkis grunted.

"He doesn't believe how far we've come."

"But... the Master... can't..."

"Oh don't worry, Porkis, I'm sure you won't get that far. He'll soon want to turn around once the call kicks in."

"No," said Antoni, hands raised. "I believe you. I don't need to see the sea."

Genton waved a hand and Porkis grunted, moving away as fast as his old legs would shuffle.

"I'm glad to hear you say that, Antoni," said Genton with a smile. "I'd hate to have to leave without you."

He waved a hand again and two men appeared. Genton murmured a few words and they rushed off.

"What are you doing?" said Antoni with narrowed eyes.

"I just gave the order to strike camp."

"What... now? We only just got here."

"No point getting comfortable. You said it yourself. The enemy is getting away."

"But... the sun's gone down. My men are tired, we need food and rest."

"We've rested long enough. And you can forage on the way."

* * *

TWENTY ONE

Echoes of thought touched the white place only briefly, the outside world a distant flicker seen through fog. The impressions disappeared on waking, seemingly lost forever, like the fleeting glimpse of a dream.

But the amulet captured it all and stored it, ready for the day it might be needed. The Sandman might not have had access to the information, but it was there for the finding. Something touched the edges of the fog, an event that sent a spark of action into the awareness within.

An almost familiar spirit brushed against the white world, opening a thin channel, a curling tendril of clarity within the fog. At last, a compatible vessel, a mother for the implant. The trapped soul reached out through that opened channel, feeling its way slowly and sending out a questing thought.

'Come to me...'

The passing soul paused, feeling the connection on a visceral level, sensing something, yet unaware. Flitting past, the soul receded, moving on. The soul in the white reached out again, more insistent this time.

'Find me...'

And the perfect vessel returned, listening to the call from the fog. Closer, she came, the mother to be, eager yet unknowing, drawn to the call from the white.

'I'm here... I'm yours... Take me...'

And there she was, her perfect hand taking hold of the charm, bringing it close, slipping it over her soft neck. The white world exploded with colour, channelled through her beautiful young mind.

'Ah, my beloved, thou art perfect.'

'Who are you?'

'I am thine forever, and thou shalt be mine.'

'But who are you?'

'I am thy love, thy mate, thy son, thy reason. And thou shalt be my mother.'

'But... I am an acolyte, I will be the new Sand Mother, I cannot...'

'Thy path is now with me. Thou shalt find me a father.'

And the girl went out into the world, gave up her service to the holy woman, and searched for a mate. Her hunger took her into the world of men, driven by the trapped soul, his whispered words forever driving her on, rejecting and rejecting until one day she found him.

Mind poisoned by the whisperings of her secret companion, she discovered love. She let herself believe her love was true, and in the blink of an eye he took her to wife. And in the act of love, when the body filled with lust, and conditions were ripe for the implant, the amulet touched her bare skin, pressed between the lovers, pricking at her breast, and the clone-seed found its vessel.

Slipping down into her, the seed worked its way slowly to the inner nest, burrowing in and making its home, next to the truly conceived child, where they grew in tandem until the day of birth. A cuckoo twin to be raised in love, and the perfect vessel for the soul to take, when the time was right.

The river Nort snaked its way south toward the high cliffs and fjords of Nella Fillenga. Following the great river, the revealers held the horses at an ambling gait for hours, slowing to a walk only rarely. The Sandman seemed to relax into the rhythm and his tormented look receded as they lengthened the miles between themselves and the possessed. While Jossep took the lead, scouting the path, Miyam sat back, watching.

From behind, Miyam could imagine that the beloved form of the Awakener was unchanged, the intruder no more than a bad dream. He had removed the Awakener's cloak, claiming it was an annoyance that got in the way and made him hot in the sun.

The sight of him without it only served to heighten her misery, as she recalled the more intimate moments of their life together, his vocational attachment to the cloak something he only relaxed in private.

Navear rode beside the Sandman, answering his questions and countering with her own. Miyam tried to quell an irrational sense of jealousy, but the sight of the younger girl in her place, however innocent, cut deep into her soul. She tried not to listen, but her carefully hidden curiosity kept her hanging on their every word.

"Tell me about your world," the girl said.

"I fear my world is but a distant memory. There is nothing of it here."

"Was it so very different?"

"Ah, child, it was. A spark of new life just beginning to bloom. Thou wouldst not believe."

"New life? What does that mean?"

"When we did find this world, it was baked and barren, poisoned by creatures of fire."

"You mean the kalkar?"

"Thou didst name them?" he said. "To mine eyes they were nothing but danger, a race of fire to be extinguished."

"But how could you do that?"

"They were nought but animals, subjecting their own world to destruction. We did heal a small part, thus driving them back."

"Animals? They're thinking, feeling, intelligent people."

"Dost thou jest? They did hunt us in mindless savagery."

"They defended themselves!"

"They did threaten our very survival. We did drive them away."

"Then what happened?"

"There was one of our number," he explained. "Who did want to retain our knowledge, never let our outdated ways die. It was he that sent me into soul-sleep."

"So, you really don't know what happened?"

"I can assume, by thy current lapse in memory, that thy people did defeat mine enemy and destroy the machines we carried here from our old world. But I cannot say how that may have occurred."

"And you say you don't know how you got here?"

"The how, I do know. The circumstance, I know not."

"I don't understand. How is the circumstance different?"

"Poor child, thy comprehension is far beneath the concept."

"Well, excuse me for being an uneducated savage!"

The Sandman let out an exasperated sigh. "Thou dost misunderstand. Thou art uneducated, yes, but thou art a product of thy time."

"And how does that make my comprehension so slow that you cannot explain it to me? Perhaps you doubt your own ability to convey the concept accurately!"

The Sandman groaned. "I must apologise, I did speak out of frustration."

"So, take a deep breath and try again. How did you come to be here?"

"It was accomplished by this," he pulled at the chain about his neck, holding the amulet aloft.

Navear stared at the golden charm, then glanced down at her hand and the device she carried there. "How?" she whispered.

"The soul-space doth reside within, a place wherein the soul doth sleep. Contained alongside was the clone-seed, the instructions for building this vessel, taken from mine own body at the time of my death."

"A copy, then? With your mind intact and ready."

"Thou art perceptive. I see I did misjudge thee."

Miyam frowned. A copy? It did not make sense. How could that body be a copy of another, the Sandman's old body? He was her love, her life, her everything. Evelar was not a copy!

"Somehow," continued the Sandman. "The clone-seed did find a host, a mother body in which to grow. But the soul did remain entrapped. It is intended, when the time is right, for amulet to be paired with vessel, that the soul might take possession before the seed grows too mature, but after the danger of childhood. The transfer did not occur. Until now."

Miyam could not listen any more. Retreating into herself, she burrowed down into the centre of her being, shutting out the world. Slipping deep into her secret place, she found someone waiting. Someone who encased her in his love and smoothed away the pain.

'How can you be here?' she whispered into the dark.

'Did you forget the link, my love?'

'No, but...'

'I am still here, still inside my own head, as he was before.'

'Why don't you come back?'

'I don't have the strength. He holds me back, as I held him back when he was the one who was trapped. Until he weakens I can't return. Even this link is difficult.'

'Did you hear through me? Did you hear what he said?'

'Yes.'

'Is it true?'

'According to his memories, yes.'

'But how? You're Evelar, you're not some copy of him.'

'I don't understand it completely, but I'm learning more.'

'I want you back,' she wailed.

'I know, my love. But I can't stay here. I don't want to be locked out completely.'

'Alright, but... how long?'

'I don't know.'

As his voice faded, Miyam allowed herself to rise out of herself, opening tear-filled eyes to watch again, heedless of the moisture on her cheeks.

As the moon rose high they made camp by the river. Miyam set about making the fire and preparing a meal, trying to ignore the incessant talking, shutting out that archaic phrasing from the mouth of her beloved.

"I must know but one thing," the Sandman said. "How did the vessel come by the amulet?"

"I don't know," said Navear. "Mym?"

Miyam glanced at her young friend. "Yes, Bell?"

"How did Evelar get the amulet?"

"Oh. It was his sister's."

"Wherefore did the sister obtain it?" said the Sandman.

"It was their mother's."

"Where might I find this mother?"

"She's long dead," Miyam snapped, turning back to her task.

"He was raised in the desert, with the nomads," Navear said.

"Ah. Then must we find these desert people. They will give the answers I seek."

"It's out of our way," Miyam growled. "We're going to Nella."

"Thou shalt do as I say!"

"I'll do no such thing. I'm in charge here."

"Let me talk to her, Sir," Navear murmured.

Miyam turned her back, ignoring the girl's approach. When Navear touched her arm, she pulled it away.

"Mym, I know this is hard," the girl whispered. "But it's a good idea."

"We're going to Nella, where Iron and Path can help us bring him back."

"Perhaps they can, but what if they can't?"

"We'll deal with that if it happens."

"And waste time doing so," Navear said.

Miyam bristled, mouth opening with a retort.

"Just hear me, Mym."

Miyam paused, closed her mouth on her angry impulse, and gave a curt nod.

"What if the desert is what he needs?"

Miyam cocked her head.

"The place he knows best of all, and the Sandman will be out of comfort. The desert is not for the uninitiated. I suspect he will weaken and Sand will return."

"Bell, I know you're trying, but it's as much a gamble as Nella."

"Just think about it. We don't have to turn yet."

"I won't change my mind, Bell."

"Alright. But don't you want to know about the amulet too?"

The revealers continued south, following the river across the immense Wild Plain. Ignoring the whispers of her companions, Miyam set the path with stubborn determination. She was going to get her beloved back.

They would reach Nella Fillenga in a few days and Jumally, the infamous revealer known as Iron, would know what to do. She knew the Sandman had other plans, but he would not get his way.

Miyam set about making camp, letting Jossep collect firewood while Navear prepared the roots and greens they had foraged along the riverbank. She didn't care what the Sandman was doing.

It was so much easier to forget his presence than to face the confusion of his all too familiar form worn by a stranger. Thus she was unprepared when a hand clamped over her mouth from behind, another clasping her about the waist, pinning her arms. Eyes wild, she cursed the emotion that had dulled her edge.

"Make thou not a sound," the Sandman hissed. "Thou shalt take me where I would require, with nought of thy stubborn refusal."

She tried to shake her head, struggling to get her arms free.

"Cease thy struggles," he snapped. "Thy friends are subdued and thou art alone."

She flinched away from his iron grip, but he twisted and held her more tightly. A crashing through the scrub brought Jossep at a run, Navear close on his heels.

"How ist that thou art free?" the Sandman gasped. "I did bind thee."

"We're revealers," Jossep snorted. "You can't hold us that easily."

Jossep aimed his crossbow and Navear held a hand out, a blue glow ready to be released.

'No!' Miyam called mentally. 'Don't hurt him!'

Miyam forced herself to relax, and his grip loosened in response, just enough to allow movement in her right arm. With a tiny flick of the wrist, she activated her mote knife and set the tiny blade to hover in mid-air while she considered where to strike.

She did not want to damage him, just give him something

to think about. Before he could realise her movements had meaning, she sent the knife flying, to dip and strike at his hand where it still covered her mouth. Just a little scratch, but enough to make him cry out and release her.

"What hast thou done?"

Then he grabbed her wrist, turning it painfully to examine the metal band covering her right forearm.

"I knowest this weapon!"

Miyam twisted out of his grasp and flicked her wrist to bring the knife back to hover, but it lay lifeless on the ground at his feet. She tried again, with no response. He bent to pick up the elegant leaf shaped knife, a double-edged, double-pointed blade barely two inches long. Miyam backed away, meeting the two younger revealers and allowing them to step in front with their weapons at the ready.

"Take thy blade," he said, holding out the little knife. "I will not take it from thee. But I would know how thou comest to hold it."

Reaching forward with a trembling hand, Miyam took the mote knife and slipped it into its hidden sheath in her blue headscarf. She licked her lips, considering.

'Tell him,' a beloved voice whispered in her mind.

'But...'

'He is lost and confused and he genuinely needs to know.'

'I can't.'

'Look at him. What do you see?'

'I see you, but... he's not you,' she wailed into the silence.

'He is not the evil man we believed, my love. Help him.'

Then the voice was gone, and she felt more alone than ever. Blinking back sudden tears, she gulped air while her mind raced. How could Evelar want her to help him, the man who had destroyed her life?

"Wilt thou tell me?" the Sandman said, his face pleading.

"It... belonged to my mother," Miyam stuttered. "And her mother, and hers before, and as far back as anyone can remember."

"So, a treasure beyond price, passed down through the ages. This weapon did belong to my wife."

"What?" Miyam gasped.

"I did say thou dost resemble her. Might I suggest thou art her progeny."

"Are you saying I am descended from... you?" she let out a little moan. "That can't be! It's not possible!"

He placed a finger to his lips. Taking his amulet in one hand, he reached for her. Trembling violently, Miyam touched her hand to his and he closed his fingers about hers.

The amulet glowed through his other hand as he concentrated. Miyam watched his face, the heavy thumping of her heart sending painful spasms throughout her torso.

Finally, he shook his head.

"No," he whispered. "Thou art not from me. This amulet doth hold the pattern for my clone-seed, and there is no match in you."

"But you said I was descended from your wife."

"This I do suspect. Thy weapon doth need a pattern match. If the pattern were lacking, the weapon would fail."

"But it just did fail..."

"No, it did lose charge. It doth need sunlight. Dost thou not know how the weapon doth work?"

She shook her head. "I was told it powers itself from my own psychic energy."

"Thy teaching was flawed. Much time must have passed."

"But how could I be descended only from her? Are you sure?"

"Be thou assured, thy love is pure. And mine was false."

Miyam's breath caught in her throat. "You can't know that."

"Thou art proof. My love did live on without me, bear children to another after my demise. Thus was I left in soul-sleep, never to be awakened. I was forgot."

"I... I'm sorry."

"Now dost thou see? Dost thou understand why I must solve the riddle? How came it to pass that I was awakened? I must seek the keepers of the amulet. Only there will I find the answer."

* * *

TWENTY TWO

"What was life like, before you found yourself here?"

Fransi frowned in the darkness. "I wish you wouldn't ask, Nashta."

"Was it really so bad?" He murmured as he leaned back against a tree.

She cocked her head. "You really don't understand, do you?"

"I accept that you were living somewhere far away, and that you made some deal with this master person to get a new life. But why?"

She sighed, staring at the glimmer of firelight from the camp. "Every one of us was dying, Nashta. Whether from disease or starvation or just our own deformed bodies. Anything would be better than that. So we gave up our souls, willingly, before the moment of death."

"Why would you do that? And how was it done?"

"It wasn't the Master then. We only learnt that name once we came here. It was the holy-one, the age-old progenitor. We all came from the holy-one, and we all owed our lives to the holy-one. So we gave nothing that didn't already belong to the holy-one. The holy-one became the Master."

"Who is he that he holds such power over you? You could have refused."

"The holy-one is not he. The holy-one has no sex, yet yearns to be whole. So the holy-one made us in an attempt to grow a new body. The holy-one gave us life, cared for us, promised to make it all better."

"Why all the sickness, the deformity?"

"The holy-one was copied too many times, the soul transferred too often and too young. Many of the good copies died in a great uprising, until the holy-one was forced into the last survivor, the sexless one. And from that one the holy-one made us, forever trying to create a perfect one, to raise for the next transfer."

"How do you know all this?"

"Bedtime stories. My mother was a slave in his fortress, helping the women who were implanted with the copies."

"It sounds... I can't imagine what it was like."

"Now do you see? We must have our reward. Our new lives, just as the holy-one promised."

"I wish I could help you, but I can't allow you to keep those bodies. Not now that I know they're still alive."

"You don't have that choice," she cried. "Once the enemy is gone, these bodies will be ours forever. You can't stop them following the call."

"I can't let them kill the Awakener."

She burst to her feet, ready to storm back to the camp, but at the edge of the trees she hesitated, the shivering fear holding her back. Sniv might be gone, but Genton still watched her with covetous eyes, waiting for the right moment to prove his power.

She turned to face Nashta, peering into the darkness, but he had dissolved into the shadows. She licked her lips, knowing he could see her.

"Why is your friend so important?" she whispered into the blackness.

"He is the most powerful revealer the world has ever known. His coming was foretold by the ancients. He will teach the truth and change the world forever."

"So he's a holy man? Like our master."

"No! Not like that at all. Why does the Master want him dead?"

"I told you..."

"No," he said. "You told me why you want him dead. Why does the Master?"

"I... because of the promise..."

"No," he snorted. "This is personal, between your master and him. And it's an unfair fight."

"What will you do? Lurk out here in the dark and stop us with your stares? You can't do a thing."

"I can warn him. I already helped him escape once."

"So leave. We don't need you here."

"I can't leave you here."

"Oh my hero," she scoffed. "Too scared to touch me, too jealous to let me find someone else. Make up your mind."

"Keep your voice down, we don't want them to hear."

"They know you're here, you fool. You can't lead us all this way then melt away as if you were never here."

"It's not my crusade. I'm only here to protect you."

"I don't need your protection," she lied.

He shrugged. "I didn't ask you to come out here and sit with me."

"Fine!" she snapped. "I won't."

She stumbled away, back to the camp and the dubious safety of the fire.

Genton trudged along at the head of his ragtag army, eyes focused on the distant horizon. Somewhere ahead, the enemy lurked, but the link to the old souls had faded now. With almost four hundred followers and no faster means of travel than their own feet, the chance of catching a small group of mounted prey was almost nil. Yet they must catch them.

"Genton, the people are grumbling again."

"We don't stop, Antoni."

"But..."

"No buts. Keep them walking. Any way you can."

"The sun is going down. Can't we rest early tonight? At least give me that to encourage them."

"We stop at midnight, as usual."

"Surely you realise, without the compulsion of these bodies for their souls, the people are losing faith. Even with the Master whispering, they have lost the urge to travel."

"Remind them how it felt to move against the Master's call. They'll soon perk up."

"Either that, or they'll realise what a slave driver you are. A change of leadership might be just what they need."

"You think you could do better? I'd like to see you try."

"Just watch your back, that's all."

Dismissing the man with a wave, Genton looked about. Fransi moved past him, pretending not to listen. He pursed his lips, fists clenched. Always listening, trying to spy for that revealer. He would have to show her some humility one day.

"Where's loverboy, Fransi?" he called.

"Don't know, don't care," she snapped, trudging forward as if she had not been eavesdropping.

Genton chuckled. "Had a little tiff, have we?"

Fransi did not answer, staring ahead. Genton lengthened his stride to catch her. She ignored him, eyes fixed on the horizon, lower lip caught in her teeth.

"Where is he? I could use some help right now. They trust him."

"Haven't seen him."

"Come to think of it... I haven't either. Not for days. Has he finally left us, do you think?"

She gave a little shrug. Genton peered at her face, noticing the eyelids fluttering as she tried to hold back tears.

"Actually, you haven't been slipping away at night lately either. Just hovering at the edge of the fire. Has he left you here?"

She said nothing, but the tears spilled down her cheeks.

"Poor sweetheart," he simpered. "Never mind. You still have me."

Fransi hung back from the bustle of camp, watching as the fire was built, the blankets rolled out and the long-awaited stew bubbled in the pot. With no sign of Nashta, and Genton now eyeing her possessively, Fransi dreaded the first watch.

She contemplated slipping away, but the thought that one of the scouts might find her alone kept her close to the leader. At least he cared enough to protect her from the less scrupulous among the troupe. Genton approached with a bowl of piping hot stew.

"Come and sit, sweetheart," he murmured.

She bristled at the false endearment, wishing he would stop using it. But she had begun to realise that it was more than bravado on his part. She suspected he might actually mean it.

When she refused to follow him to the fire he shrugged, handed her the bowl, and took his place with his men. Fransi turned her back and sat on the ground to eat, staring into the darkness as if her wishful gaze might make the revealer materialise. Behind her, the camp grew silent, but she remained awake, willing him to come back to her. A hand on her shoulder brought her out of her daze.

"Come to the fire, sweetheart," Genton said gently. "I hate to see you shivering like this."

Fransi shook her head stubbornly.

"He's not there," he said. "You know that, don't you."

She nodded glumly, remembering her last words to him. She had told him to go, that she didn't need him. And he had believed her.

"Come on," said Genton, taking her hand and pulling her to her feet.

She followed him to the fire. Before allowing her to sit, he turned to face her, taking both hands in his. His eyes stared into hers, filled with earnest longing.

"I'm not going to force you," he whispered. "But I'd like you to give me a chance."

Then he leant forward and touched his mouth to hers. She stiffened, but his arms closed about her and she let herself relax. Her mind tripped over the thought that Nashta might be watching. Part of her hoped he was, just so he could feel the pain of rejection she had been feeling.

Another part hoped he did not see, because it would hurt him too much. No part considered how she herself might be feeling. She felt no spark, no desire to return the same ardent caresses Genton now offered her. But something inside threatened to snap.

If she just imagined, let herself believe this was Nashta, then maybe Genton would do. Maybe her aching need would ease. She forced herself to feel his hands, to welcome the searching fingers as they made their way under her tunic.

She suppressed the crawling sensation of his touch and thought only of the one time she had felt her lover's caress, when he had given in to their mutual desire and she had learnt that she loved him.

She tried to believe it was him again. But the calloused hands scraped her skin, and the grizzled chin pricked at her face. Then his rough hands found the skin between her thighs, and the bulge of his need pressed against her, and her mind rebelled.

"No!" she cried.

She could never let him defile her. Pushing against him with both hands she struggled free and backed away, staring at the man. He came after her, face twisted in rage and lust, hands clutching at her.

She scurried backward, shaking her head, but he came on relentlessly. Her foot caught on something and she stumbled. She clambered to her feet, but he was upon her, hands gripping her wrists as he pushed her backward. She felt her back hit something hard as his mouth came close. She shook her head, twisting her face away.

"I thought..." she gasped. "You said you wouldn't force me!"

"That was before you led me on, sweetheart," he growled.

She tried to push him away, but he caught her hand, pushing her arm up to slam against the tree at her back. His arm held her in place while his other hand fumbled with her clothing.

Someone was screaming, high with panic. Was that her voice? She had never imagined it would be so easy to scream. But then another voice joined her, a male voice screaming in pain.

It was Genton. Eyes wide, she stared at the knife that pinned his hand to the tree. She watched him reach up to grab the hilt, but another hand beat him to it.

"I told you not to touch her," someone snarled.

Fransi's breath caught at the familiar voice, her heart beating hard in her breast. A flurry of movement and the knife was gone. Someone took her by the hand and pulled her away from a screaming Genton. He dragged her away from the firelight, into the protective blanket of night.

He led her through the trees, down into a moonlit meadow, where a dark shape moved to meet them. She heard a faint snort, a jingling of harness. Nashta's gentle hands guided her foot to the stirrup, pushed her body up into the saddle. Then he swung up behind her and his arms snaked around her to take the reins.

"Shall we go?" he said.

"I thought you were gone," she sobbed. "I thought you had left me."

"Never," he whispered. "I just went to buy a horse."

She giggled in spite of herself. "I'm glad you came back."

"Really? You seemed to be getting along fine without me."

She shivered. "I'm sorry I told you to go away. I couldn't admit I needed help. This female thing is so confusing sometimes."

"You're doing just fine."

"No, I'm not," she sighed. "Look, I know I can never replace the woman you love, but I'm here in her body, and I love you. I could never accept anyone else."

"I know. And I'm sorry I can't love you in the same way. But I'm here for you, and always will be. And I could never accept anyone else either."

Genton nursed his injured hand with a sulky pout and a mightily wounded pride. Just watching him tend his battered ego was enough to set Antoni's teeth on edge. It was time to teach the fool a lesson.

He had driven his followers to the brink of exhaustion with no reward and no sign of an end. With most of the followers ready for a change, Antoni had no doubt his plan would go without a hitch. His captains were in place, and all it would need was a nudge to send the people over the edge.

Antoni stood over the man as he tossed in his sleep. With little more than a faint sense of curiosity, he lifted his foot and planted his heavily booted toe in Genton's ribs. Then, before the man could catch his breath, Antoni motioned to his men. Genton was pulled roughly to his feet, both arms pinned behind his back. He grunted as his newly cracked ribs made their presence known. Antoni smiled.

"What's the meaning of this?" Genton snarled.

Antoni raised an eyebrow. "Surely you saw this coming."

Genton twisted, then screamed as a fist slammed into his stomach.

"It's over, Gent. Your ineffectual reign is nothing more than a bad memory."

"What are you talking about? The people follow me without question. You have no right..."

Another fist stopped his voice and his breath caught in a wheeze around a dislodged diaphragm.

"They don't follow you, fool. They tolerate you because there's no-one else. They followed the revealer you chased away."

"I... kept us... on track..."

"On track? I've heard what people say. How you let that man take them weeks off the path, nearly drowning them all. How you spent all your time chasing that little mistress of his as if she would choose you over him?"

"She never was his mistress. She was stringing him along just like she did me, and Sniv before me."

"That shows how little you know, fool. They were lovers. What do you think she did sneaking off to be with him every night? You let your feelings for her cloud your judgement and lead you astray."

"I was never clouded! I am taking us exactly where the Master wants us to go."

Antoni spat in his face. "Letting the enemy get away then twiddling your thumbs while he escaped? Driving them to the point of collapse, refusing rest stops, starving them. What made you think you could ever inspire their loyalty?"

Antoni gave a signal and the men dragged Genton

backward until he slammed into a tree. They tugged his arms back around the trunk and tied the wrists behind. Genton scrabbled with his feet, trying to get free, heels scraping in the dirt.

"No point wriggling like that, you'll only hurt yourself."

"What are you going to do with me?"

Antoni considered. "You know, I really can't say. I certainly can't take you with us, to spread your apathetic blubbering."

"Let me go, Antoni. I'll let you take over, I won't fight you. Please."

"Oh, shut him up," Antoni growled.

One of the men approached Genton with a dirty rag in one hand. As Genton shook his head, the man forced the rag into his mouth, then pulled the ends tight, wrapping them around the tree and tying them together, pinning Genton's head to the trunk.

"Now perhaps we can get some sleep," said Antoni. "We leave at first light."

And after a quiet night, the travellers struck out for the southern range. As the people passed the man tied to the tree, they kicked, spat, trampled and generally damaged him in passing. Antoni stood to one side, smiling his unassuming smile, showing not a flinch at the blows that rained down on the defenceless man.

He watched everything, and when it was over and the last of the troupe had moved off down the path, he sauntered over to bend down and stare in fascination. Wide staring eyes, seeing nothing. Cuts and bruises from head to foot, and a wide gash spurting a red fountain from his neck.

Antoni could not remember the killing blow, but he smiled in satisfaction. That was one problem solved. He untied the rag that held the head upright, then held it under the spurting artery to catch the blood. Face impassive,

Antoni washed the rag in the life of a fool, turning it over and over to catch the lush red stream.

When the rag was saturated and his hands were red with blood, the fountain had slowed to a trickle. Antoni straightened, spreading the rag out between his hands and gazing at the beautiful dark red cloth.

He raised it between his hands, touching it to his forehead. Holding the ends reverently, he wrapped the gruesome sash about his head, tying it at the back in a parody of the tame revealer's headscarf. As the sticky ooze trickled down his face and through his hair, he bent and wiped his hands in the grass.

* * *

TWENTY THREE

Miyam sat her horse in the middle of the crossroads, watching as Jossep and Navear continued south toward Nella Fillenga. She shivered in irrational fear, reminding herself that they were capable young revealers. Their minds had been cleared of the mysterious hooks Jumally had discovered, and they were not the target of her enemy; there was nothing more to fear.

When the pair had shrunk almost out of sight, she turned and led the man in Evelar's body along the eastern road toward the foothills of the Dragon Mountains. If the young couple moved quickly, they could fetch Jumally and Tikki and bring them back across the pass to catch up before she led the Sandman out into the desert. She intended to give them every chance to do so.

Moving at a walk, Miyam pointed Cheena at the mountains. In the early afternoon light, the distant hills appeared to shimmer in welcome, and as the day wore on toward dusk the shadows stretched out before them, seeming to point the way. By nightfall they were camping in the shadow of the first range.

"I see not why thou art holding us back," the man said as she handed him a bowl.

"I'm keeping the horses rested," she said. "We have a long and difficult crossing ahead, it would not do to have them winded before we even begin."

"Dost thou tell true? Or ist a falsehood designed to

deceive?"

"This is not the place I would have chosen to cross. But you insisted."

"That I did. With sound reason and urgent need."

"I promised to help you and I will. But we do it my way."

By which, she meant as slowly as possible, but he need not know that. For the better part of a week they climbed slowly into the mountains. As they rode higher, Miyam no longer needed to keep the pace slow; the twisting path did that for her.

By the time they reached the highest ridge, they were walking, leading the horses over rocky ground that threatened injury with every step. It was at this highest point that Miyam stopped, straining to hear something unexpected.

'Miyam, can you hear me?'

She cocked her head, sending out a reply and listening intently.

"What ist?" the Sandman said.

"Hush, I'm listening."

"For what dost thou list?"

"Quiet!" she snapped.

'Where is the Awakener?' came the faint voice. *'I can't reach him.'*

'He is unable to communicate,' she sent out into the silence. *'Who are you? You're so faint I can't tell.'*

'Nashta. I'm following. Can you wait?'

'I'm going as slowly as I can. What's going on?'

'I'm trying to catch you. I'll explain then.'

Miyam let out a long, slow breath. What could the man be up to this time? Ignoring the Sandman's curious stare, she flicked the reins and pointed Cheena across the ridge.

Four days later, she stood on a peak, looking out over the sands of the Barren Wastes. Just a few more ridges and they would be there. If she could stretch that out into a few more days, all the better.

"Ist the desert?" said the Sandman. "Where shall we find the people?"

"Don't be too hasty," she replied. "We have several days yet before we actually set foot on the sands."

"But there it is, right before us."

"Travelling downhill can be more dangerous than climbing, you know. The last thing we need is a lame horse."

Miyam stood staring out across the cold desert night, folding her arms against the cool wind while the bonfire behind her sent the heat of a furnace to warm her back. Between two extremes, she held on to a small glimmer of hope, walking the line between despair and determination.

As one threatened to topple her, the other held her upright, and eventually one would have to win. The nomads would see the beacon fire, and come to investigate. Then she would get her beloved back.

"What are you doing?" a voice behind snapped her fragile calm.

She spun about. "Nashta! What are you doing here?"

"I've been trying to call you for days. I had no idea how close you were, but then I saw that fire. You need to put it out, now."

She shook her head. "It's a signal for the nomads."

"The possessed will see it."

"I have to take that risk. Besides, he's stable so they can't be too close."

"They're right on our tail!"

"What? You led them here?"

"No, I mean... we left them weeks ago, but something has changed. They're moving so much faster now."

"We?"

He gestured to a young woman who hovered outside the light of the fire.

"Tineya?"

"She calls herself Fransi, remember. That's why I stayed with them. To guard her."

"He's here, isn't he?" the girl stammered. "This body wants its soul back. It makes it hard to think."

"I hoped maybe the Awakener could help her."

"So you thought to lead the rest of them here?" Miyam snapped.

"We could hardly keep ahead of them, even mounted."

"Nashta, how could you do that?"

"I had no choice. I had to warn you."

"What do you mean?"

"They're determined to catch you. They intend to kill the Awakener."

"They already tried that, if you remember."

"No, they didn't. They held him but they never tried to kill him. Now something is different. They really mean it this time. And they know exactly where he is, all the time."

"Nashta, I can't move from here. I can't walk out into the desert without the nomads. Evelar knew how to do that, but I don't."

"He's right here, what are you talking about."

"It's only his body. The Sandman has taken over, and he's determined to find the nomads."

"Who is the Sandman?"

Amid a chorus of murmured pleading, the girl searched for one voice, one friend who might help her. Trapped in this invisible world of sensory starvation, closed off from the living world, time seemed to stand still.

The only times the outside encroached were those moments touched with pain and utter desperation, when the longed for body was close. So close yet so untouchable.

Somewhere in the gaggle of voices, someone knew the secret of their liberation. But finding that one voice could wait. She could feel her own lost body, driving her mad with the desire to be free.

A thought flicked past. The host no more, trapped now like everyone else. He claimed he did not know the secret of their entrapment, but the girl knew better. Was it not his mind, his body?

But he was moving away, slipping down into the deepest part of the dark world, a presence so powerful yet so helpless, just as trapped as all the rest. The girl followed the echo of the thought, tracking the mind of the Awakener as he sank into the very centre of the mind, a place the girl had never before penetrated.

He was there, just out of thought, masked by a barrier of such subtle architecture as to be almost invisible, camouflaged against the wider landscape of the mind. The girl fluttered against it, pushing without success, until she found the opening, a sliver of a gap where her questing thought slipped through with ease.

Something was there, not quite the Awakener's mind, yet him and more. The Awakener and someone else, mixed yet separate, two souls residing in the same place. Floating closer, the girl sensed another presence, heard whispered voices in conversation.

She strained to hear, drifting closer to the oblivious thought forms of the Awakener and his wife. In her eagerness to discover the secret of this bizarre twinning of souls, she floated too close. When her questing mind touched the mind of the wife, she found herself in another place, another mind. A mind silent and aware, with none of the distracting voices to destroy the peace.

The girl drifted upward, rising to the surface in a rush

as if she were floating in water, to break through into the air with a gasp. She could see, out into the real world through the woman's eyes.

There was a great fire against a black sky, filling the night with its roaring crackle of flame, and beneath it the sound of horses moving about somewhere nearby. There by the fire, she saw people. A man who should be the Awakener, yet somehow was not. And a couple, a young but mature woman cradled in the arms of an older man. Her man, holding... her body?

The girl felt herself pulled back, a powerful force taking hold of her before she could make sense of the scene. Sucked back through the mind of the woman, through that invisible connection to the other mind, she fought the pull in vain.

She burst through that hidden door, back into the flamboyantly noisy world of the Awakener's prison. He said nothing directly, but she felt a great wave of disapproving anger wash over her, followed by an overwhelming feeling of danger. Above it all, an intense mental image, silent but clear, of a locked door never to be opened again.

Somewhere to the west, a large band of travellers moved at double time, feet marching a quickstep in time to a chanting rhythm. At their head a young man trotted, hair matted with dried blood from the sash about his head. Grim-faced he called the beat, echoed by his followers. The mountains loomed ahead but the leader kept on, driving the possessed with wild words of victory and fortune.

Coming back to herself, Miyam opened her eyes to meet the wondering stares of Fransi and the Sandman.

"Thank you, Nashta," she said. "I have been unable to search since Evelar lost his mind."

"I don't understand," said Fransi. "What did you do?"

"We projected our minds," Nashta explained. "We took

a journey of the spirit, to seek our enemy and learn their position."

"And?"

"They are mere days away, a week or ten days maybe. The pass might slow them but the way they are moving it won't be much."

"How can they have caught us so fast? We nearly killed that poor horse."

"Something has changed. Someone new leads them. I did not see Genton anywhere."

"How dost thou know this?"

"It's something all revealers are trained to do," said Miyam.

"I must know how this is done. When I did sleep, the power in our minds was newly found. This is much more."

"How can that be?" said Miyam with a frown. "If Evelar is truly a copy of you, then you should have known this power. He is the most powerful revealer the world has ever known."

"Mayhap the clone-seed was altered. It was our practise to enhance each successive cycle, to keep the copies strong. My wife did believe we should cultivate the power."

"Or perhaps you had simply not yet discovered your power."

"That would be a pity indeed, for then I might have defeated mine enemy and survived to see mine offspring."

"Nevertheless," Nashta interrupted. "We have a few days' grace. Hopefully, the nomads will come for the signal before the possessed get too close."

Miyam wandered away from the fire to stare out into the desert. She longed for more time, to give Evelar a chance to fight back. If the possessed came too close, maybe the voices would take over and give him that chance. The Sandman's lack of training would see him lose the fight much more quickly than Evelar had.

Closing her eyes, Miyam settled down into her own mind, slipping through the link to find her beloved waiting in the silence.

'Did you see?' she whispered.

'Yes, my love. Let them come.'

'Do you think you can defeat him?'

'Once the voices start, you must keep him there, no matter how close the possessed get. It's the only way I can break through.'

'Please try, Sand. I miss you so much.'

The voices clamoured to be heard. Sand moved amongst them, whispering, cajoling. He had to make them see that they needed to work together. The bodies were close now, and the souls battered themselves against the confines of their prison.

'Let us out. They come. Give us our lives. Set us free.'

'I can't do that from in here,' Sand sent the thought out amongst them.

'Help us. Don't keep us here. Why won't you help us?'

'I'll help. But you must help me.'

'Yes, yes, help us. We will do as you ask. Help.'

'If we work together, we are strong. Those bodies are yours, but I can't find the secret from here. I need to get control. Will you help me defeat the Sandman and send him back into the amulet?'

'Yes, yes. Help you to help us. We will, we will.'

Sand let his consciousness drift, continuing his search for the origin of the spirits. He knew they had come from his students, but how? He felt Tineya following again. Perhaps she knew more than she realised. He wrapped her thought pattern in his power, probing for any clue.

'Stop that!' she cried.

'Who is the Master?'

'I don't know.'

'How did the Master bring you here? You said it was when I touched your mind.'

'Yes, the hook. I didn't know it was there until it began pulling, and then I snapped, out of my body and into this place.'

'That happened during travel, when I was far away from you. How?'

'There was a stretching, a pulling in my head, then falling, swirling, spinning away. Then I was here.'

'So the Master tethered you to me, letting the connection stretch out until it snapped. The same thing happens to a revealer who astral searches too far from his body. You lose your connection. So, your mind was linked to mine somehow and when I travelled away from your body you were pulled with me, losing your connection.'

'If you say so.'

'I need to follow the hook, back to your master.'

'The Master is not here. The Master wants our bodies, not our minds. The Master watches from afar, but does not come here any more.'

'So I need your body.'

'My body is near. I saw her. I feel her, always calling, so near yet so far. She is with you now.'

'Then I must go. Please don't follow me again, Tineya. It's too dangerous.'

Sand released her and floated away, sensing her curiosity, feeling her receding. He slipped deep into his subconscious centre to find Mist. He slipped through the gateway and into his wife's mind. She welcomed him as she always did, with love and longing.

'Mym, I need you to do something.'

'Of course I will, whatever you need, you know that.'

'It's my fault, Mym. I missed the obvious again. The voices came from the bodies of my students.'

'Yes, dear, I know that.'

'But it was me. It was the act of touching their minds that hooked them. I had a visitor, someone other than the Sandman, who is known by the souls as the Master.'

'Yes, I've heard Fransi talk about him. She's the one in Tineya's body. They sometimes call him the holy-one.'

'They say it is not a him, no gender, just the Master.'

'I remember someone else like that.'

'That's what worries me. Remember you said you heard Kayus? What if this master is Kayus?'

'If that's true, we are all in trouble.'

'I need you to find out for me.'

'Me? How can I do that?'

'Tineya says the Master is no longer here in my head. That It watches the bodies now. I think the tether might still be there in the physical minds of the possessed. That must be how the Master controls them. You can find it and follow it back to its source.'

The Sandman paced, hands over ears. The possessed were getting closer, and Miyam worried what he might do to escape the voices. Miyam squatted in front of Fransi, wondering how to convince her to let her into her mind. The girl twitched and grunted, often incoherant, her body rebelling against her mind with the proximity of Tineya's soul.

She knew Fransi fought against the urge to do violence, to stop the pull of the body. Evelar's idea could help her find the answers, maybe even a solution. She had already explained to Nashta and he was ready to help, but the girl had no reason to agree.

"If you let me do this," Miyam smiled. "It might help

me find a way to stop the conflict, perhaps even block that body's pull toward its soul. If you want to stay with us, you need to find a way to be calm."

"What should I do, Nashta?" the girl sobbed.

"I think it's a good idea," he smiled. "I promise it won't hurt, and we won't try to send you away. We just want information, so we can help you."

"I don't know what to believe. You could be lying for all I know."

"Perhaps. And all I can say is this. Do you trust me?"

"Of course I do!"

"Then let us do this."

She chewed at her bottom lip, eyes moist with unshed tears. Then she gave a little nod. Miyam reached out and touched her hands to the girl's temples. She felt Nashta's hand on her shoulder, and his mind link with her. Accepting the extra power, she delved into the girl's mind, searching for the hook.

There, in the fabric of the girl's mind, a ripple in the surface of thought. A collection of waves, radiating out from a fixed point, growing stronger as she moved closer to the point of convergence. And there it was, a connection, a tether, hooked into the very essence of the mind. A thread, so fine and yet so strong, like a spider's gossamer web. She rested against that line, feeling it vibrate with power.

She traced the string, following. It seemed to go on forever, so very far away. She clutched at Nashta's willing meld, fighting back the fear. She would not get lost, she would keep hold of the thread and not lose her way. She fought the urge to spring back to herself. The thread hummed and drew her onward until something welcomed her. A presence pulled her in, a cackling laughter filling her mind.

'Thou art welcome, little one!'

Her thought fluttered with fear and she backed away.

One taste was all she needed. She knew that voice, had felt that touch. Had hoped to never feel it again.

'Tell mine enemy his nemesis doth await. Tell thy beloved I wait for thee. Come to me that I might vanquish thee!'

Miyam flew back along the string, terror lending speed to her escape. She held down the trembling fear that threatened to snap her control, thinking only of the return that seemed to take so very long.

When she finally returned to herself, she pulled away from the girl, scrambling backward, blubbering in her fear.

"What?" said Fransi, eyes darting from one terrified face to the other.

"It... it's nothing," Nashta mumbled. "Don't worry."

"What did you see?"

Miyam shook her head, scrambling to her feet and stumbling away. Kayus. Evelar was right. She had found Kayus and It was waiting, ready with a new threat to destroy the Awakener. She glanced to the place the Sandman was sitting by the fire. But he was not there. She searched around, panic hitting in the pit of her stomach. He was nowhere to be seen.

TWENTY FOUR

The Sandman watched as the woman delved inside the other girl's head. He knew instinctively that she was looking for a way to calm the noise inside his head, and he knew intellectually that there was some link to the mysterious master within the girl's mind. But that did not stop the voices that threatened to drive him insane.

They were so close now, the possessed bodies, and the voices knew it. He remembered what it had been like the last time, when he had been trapped in there with them. But this was different. They clamoured and whispered, filling his head and drowning out all thought. He felt the pressure against that mental barrier, threatening to burst out of the subconscious to take over his waking mind.

He wondered how the other soul had resisted for so long. When he had been using the distraction to break free and take over, he had felt the man's power fading and the final possession had been so easy. But how could he stop it happening all over again? He risked losing the fragile control he had, that mental door constantly battered by the other minds within.

This was why the woman delayed. She knew the struggle her Awakener had endured, knew how easily the mind could be overthrown. As the possessed bodies came ever closer, the noise grew louder, the insistent pushing more unbearable with every moment.

He had to get away. If he stayed even one more day, the

voices would weaken him, and the other soul would regain control over the vessel.

While the woman and her companions were preoccupied, while they concentrated on their esoteric journey into the mind, he could slip away. Somewhere out there were the answers. Someone who could tell him why the amulet had revived him in this strange new world.

He missed his beloved wife, even as his heart stung at her evident betrayal. He missed his old life, with its safe, comfortable technology. Now he understood a little, of the objections his old friend turned enemy had tried to convey. These people were primitive, not exactly savage but lacking in all the basic knowledge that had brought them to this world in the first place. He had to find out what had happened.

Even as his mind simmered and wandered, his feet took him, running in the only direction his body understood; away from the possessed. He stumbled out over the sands, feet finding their way of their own accord. Completely unaware of anything but his driving need to get away, he forced his legs to keep moving, fighting the soft sand beneath his feet.

He noticed nothing, not the baking sun on his head, nor the blinding sand, not the raging thirst, nor the ache in his limbs. Even when he fell, he dragged his body forward on hands and trembling knees.

Building the fire into a great blaze, they left it burning at the edge of the desert, its bright flame licking the sky, shining out against the dark bulk of the mountains. They walked out onto the sands, leading the three horses laden with water in oiled leather sacks.

With face set in determination, Miyam led the others, their worry evident on their faces. Even Nashta, who prided himself on his knowledge of the world, never lax in reminding everyone how much he had travelled, seemed lost.

They followed the faint tracks left by the Sandman, moving northwest in a meandering path that became more erratic as the hours wore on. In the desert heat, without water, he would not survive a day. Miyam searched the horizon for any sign, her worry dragging her ever forward.

As the sun climbed toward its zenith, she raised her blue-lined hood, retying the revealer's sash to hold it in place. She glanced toward Nashta and he copied her, tying his red sash about his own hood. Miyam handed a blanket to Fransi and the girl gave her a look of confusion.

"Out here, you must cover up or die," Miyam said. "Even a blanket is better than the sun."

The girl shrugged, but draped the blanket over herself without a word. Miyam passed her a water bag and she drank thirstily. The small group continued on until, some time after midday, they saw a dark lump on the top of a rise.

Miyam hurried forward, struggling up the side of the dune, following the long, dragging tracks. Gasping for breath, she reached the summit and dropped to her knees beside the still form of the Sandman. She turned him over and lifted his head, forcing a dribble of water between his parched lips.

"Is he alright?" Fransi gasped as she came up the hill.

Miyam nodded, too shocked to speak. She should have been prepared for this, but seeing her beloved husband's body so near death shook her to the core. She may not care for the Sandman, but she loved this body, and nothing would stop her trying to protect it from harm.

"What do you need me to do?" said Nashta.

Miyam forced herself to answer. "Use the poles we cut earlier. Make a shelter with the blankets. We camp here. I just hope the nomads find us soon."

Eyes dry with grit flickered and opened on a blinding bright world. Parched lips parted and a sandpaper tongue searched for moisture. A trickle of heavenly liquid soothed sand blasted throat. A croak that scratched its way up from seared lungs sufficed for gratitude.

"Don't talk," a woman whispered.

He moved his head, realising it rested in someone's lap. Looking up into the woman's beautiful face he offered a smile and she returned it with a broad grin. She offered more water, and allowed more this time, letting him drink his fill.

He caught hold of her hand, taking the water from her to place it by his side. Then he brought the hand to his mouth to kiss the soft palm. She gasped and tried to pull away.

"Don't," he said.

He felt her reaction deep in his skull as her surprise hit him unshielded. He suppressed a groan at the ache brought on by her emotional response to that one word.

"Sorry," she whispered. "Is it really you?"

He rose up on one elbow, fighting dizziness to get closer to her worried face. He stared into her eyes, sending his love to wash over her troubled mind.

"Your eyes are brown..." she sighed. "Oh, Evelar!"

He rose up higher, planting his mouth firmly on hers. But the urgency of her response threw him off balance and they ended in a tumbled heap in the sand, her delighted giggle sending sparks into his heart. He settled back into her lap and cuddled her hands to his chest.

"Welcome back," she murmured.

"I don't know for how long," he replied, voice hoarse.

"No, don't say that."

"The possessed are very close."

"Don't try to talk…"

"I have to, my love. I only managed to break through because he was so close to death. What happened?"

"He tried to get away from the voices by running out into the desert."

"They can be hard to resist. I thought I had the souls on my side, but as soon as their bodies came near they went crazy and turned on me, mad with their drive to escape."

"It's not over, then?"

"I'm afraid not. The possessed are so near, they'll start up again soon."

"And he'll take over again?" she moaned.

"He'll certainly try. And until I can work out how to get him back into the amulet, I have no real defence. It's very hard to block the door from the outside."

"What are we going to do?" she wailed.

"We'll think of something. We always do," he smiled. "I just hope the scouts find us soon. How long have you been out here?"

"We set the fire at the edge of the sands about two weeks ago. The Sandman ran away two days ago."

"Then it shouldn't be too long. Just sit tight and hold off the possessed as long as you can."

"Don't speak as if you're going away," she sobbed.

"I might have to, my love. I have a fight ahead that I may not win. Yet."

"I don't want to lose you again. I can't bear seeing your face every day and knowing it's not really you."

He smiled, reaching up to brush a tear from her cheek. "Just knowing you're here, protecting me even when I'm not myself, is enough to keep me going. Seeing you is a blessing I will carry with me into the chaos of my mind, to sustain me when hope fails."

Miyam emerged from the shelter, rubbing at eyes red with fatigue and sorrow. She did not notice the little group sitting about the camp fire until her name was called. She glanced in their direction, seeing Nashta and his possessed woman, then realising that her companions had been joined by several newcomers. Jossep and Navear had brought Jumally and Tikki.

"How is he?" said Navear quietly.

Miyam smiled at the girl's concern. "He's sleeping. He says the possessed are very close."

"Is he..." She let the words trail off.

"Yes, Bell," said Miyam with a sigh. "He is himself. For now."

Jumally unfolded from her place beside Tikki, moving in smooth strides to join Miyam. She held out a hand.

"May I?"

Miyam nodded, and the older woman touched her hand to the side of her face, rubbing gently at her temple before sending a subtle finger of thought into her mind. Miyam felt her worries dissolve under the woman's treatment, her fears relaxing into calm. Tears of relief formed in her eyes and Jumally pulled her into a close embrace.

"Thank you, Iron," Miyam whispered, bemused by the aloof woman's tender ministrations.

"We must all rely on each other now," Jumally smiled as she released her. "You are not alone."

Jumally led her toward the fire. As Miyam sat amongst her friends, Navear handed her a stick of dried meat and hard cheese with a slice of crusty bread.

"We are all here for you," Jossep said. "And look..."

As he signalled, someone stepped out of the shadows by the horses, many more horses than she remembered, and a second figure followed close behind.

"Reep?" Miyam whispered. "Iris? How did you..."

"We started after you as soon as the students rebelled at Shirall," said Reeperly with a grin. "It's a good thing we caught you before those possessed did."

"I don't know how much good it will do, even with ten of us," Miyam sighed. "There are hundreds of them, and Evelar is in no condition to fight."

"You're revealers," Fransi murmured. "With your minds and your rainbow, you can do anything."

Nashta wrapped an arm about the possessed girl's shoulders in a silent gesture of gratitude.

"We won't have to hold them off for long," he said. "I saw smoke to the east at sunset. The nomads are coming."

The Awakener curled in a ball on the sand, hands pressed to ears, strange mumblings bursting from his mouth. Fransi watched him with puzzlement, her body fighting her urge to do him harm. She had prided herself in her calm acceptance of the situation, refusing to give in to the violence shown by the other possessed when in the presence of the vessel.

But now, with him so close and her body's soul crying to be freed, her sense of self-preservation kicked in, warring with her resolve. She backed into a corner of the shelter and sat against the blanket wall, pulling her knees up to her chest, eyes fixed on the man who held her rival soul in his addled mind.

Outside the shelter, the revealers formed a circle, taking hands and closing eyes, shutting out the cries of the approaching army of possessed. Somewhere nearby, the nomads approached. They had to believe that, or give up then and there. Nashta and Jumally took the lead, their strong minds linking together to bring in the others.

Gathering in the power, they built a concentrated ball of white light, filling it with a protective energy that hummed in their minds. Letting the ball expand, they held it in formation, forming a shield of light at the outer limit of the circle. Then they pushed it out further, the power growing to encompass the entire camp.

The noise of the approaching possessed dulled to a whisper, but the vibration of their running feet grew stronger with every moment. In the centre of the white, another ball grew, shaped by the minds of the revealers in full gestalt. A faint blue glow deepened and coalesced, expanding toward the edges of the white shield. The blue ball blinked through the barrier of white and continued to expand, reaching out to where the possessed still ran.

In a powerful wave of thought, it hit them unseen, sinking into their minds and filling them with calm. The enraged cries settled, petering out in a bewildered murmur. The possessed faltered, feet falling still. They milled about in confusion, their bloodthirsty rage neutralised in an instant.

But one among them shook off the enchantment almost before it took hold. Raising his voice in a cry of rage, he moved amongst the possessed slapping their faces, yelling into their ears, breaking the spell. Slowly the possessed shook off the blue fog, faces twisting in anger at their leader's ungentle coaxing.

The revealers began creating a new ball, at first a soft yellow within the white shield. As it grew, it took on an orange hue, fuelled by the destructive power of thought. Larger and darker it grew, passing out of the protective sphere and washing over the reanimated army of possessed.

Screams erupted where it hit, people clutching at their heads, some toppling into the sand, writhing in pain.

Again, the leader moved among them, dragging them to their feet, snatching hands away from ears to yell his encouragement. The possessed rallied again, and the revealers began the unthinkable task of creating a new ball, full of black fire. The possessed charged forward, almost upon them.

The first rank hit the protective shield and bounced back, landing winded in the sand. The black ball grew, almost to the edge of the white shield. The possessed charged again. The black fire burst forth. The leading edge washed over the front line. People fell.

Somewhere in the gestalt mind of the revealers, a woman cried out in agony as the enemy died. The collective fell apart, the revealers each grieving the loss of so many innocent souls. The possessed rallied, a force hardly diminished.

Strengthened by the death before them, they stepped over the bodies of their fallen comrades. The revealers let the shield fall and stood watching them come. The possessed were upon them, ready to take lives in order to reach their quarry. The revealers drew weapons, holding the possessed at bay through physical means.

But their numbers were too few to withstand the onslaught. In the shelter behind, someone screamed. Miyam heard the scream like a stab wound to the gut. She backed away and ran. Inside the shelter, she found Fransi standing over the body of Evelar, a knife raised.

The unconscious revealer writhed in the sand, screams ripping out of his senseless mouth as the souls within felt the death of their bodies. Fransi's face twisted, her hands shook, but she did not make the killing thrust. Miyam whispered soothing words and stepped up to take the knife from her unresisting hands.

From outside, a new noise broke in on them. Whoops and shrieks, war cries and thudding feet. Miyam rushed out to a scene of utter bedlam. A new force rushed in on the enemy, pushing them back from the camp, leaving fallen possessed in their wake. As the enemy turned and fled, the nomads pulled up to watch them go, surrounded by the dead and dying.

By sheer force of numbers, the nomads had sent the possessed into a rout. But in the midst of the dead, one man remained, walking among them. He stopped at each body, bent, and something flashed in the light. He hacked at the heads of the dead, and when he stood up, something in his hand dripped blood into the sand.

"What is he doing?" Miyam whispered.

Reeperly came up beside her. "I think he's... collecting trophies."

TWENTY FIVE

The leader of the nomad force approached Miyam with a smile and a ready hand. When he spoke, his heavy accent brought a tear to her eye. She rarely noticed Evelar's accent; he had lived away from the desert so long his tones had mellowed.

"Ontaro," she smiled. "I'm so glad you found us, though you cut it a bit fine."

He returned her smile. "I apologise for our tardy arrival, my lady. What brings you to the sands with such an enemy on your heels?"

She signalled for him to follow. Leading him into the makeshift shelter, she ignored Nashta, comforting the sobbing girl in the corner, and gestured to the prone form of Evelar. Ontaro knelt beside him with a frown.

"What is wrong with him?"

"He is... not himself. He battles within his mind for power over his body."

"I do not understand."

"I'm sorry, I can't explain it myself. We only hope that his father and Old One might be able to help."

"Old One is ill and failing fast. His age is too great. But perhaps my brother can help."

"Anything Chief Entranos can do will be welcomed."

Evelar's unconscious body was strapped across the back of a camel, in front of its hump, while Miyam took her place behind. Reeperly and his wife chose to stay with the slower horses, leading them at a walk with the help of two nomad guides. The younger couple, Jossep and Navear, eagerly accepted the offer to each ride a camel in front of one of the nomad warriors. Jumally and Tikki shared an animal, mounting with a confidence that suggested long experience.

Ontaro rode beside Miyam, his concern reaching into her troubled psyche. On his other side rode Jossep and Navear, both avidly taking everything in from in front of the nomad riders. Navear stared about, eyes wide in excitement, her gaze often resting on the nomad leader almost without pause. Finally, Ontaro addressed her.

"You have the look of the sands, child," he smiled. "Have you a connection with the people?"

"My mother," she replied. "My name is Navear, which I'm told was also her name, though she died when I was very young. She was taken as bondslave to the chief of the Wetsnow tribe in the Dragon Mountains."

"Navear!" he gasped. "Can it be?"

"What's wrong?" the girl whispered.

Ontaro let out a great whoop of delight. His men glanced at him with surprise as he grinned at the girl. He called something in his own tongue and the men let out a cheer. The nomad riding behind Navear gave her a hearty pat on the back.

"What's going on?" Navear said, looking about nervously.

"I think..." Miyam replied. "He said something about a homecoming. Something lost is found."

"You are right," Ontaro replied with a grin. "But not something. Someone. Navear was my sister."

"Your sis..." Navear gasped. "You are my uncle?"

He laughed delightedly. "It appears so, my child."

Navear stared, her mouth open in surprise. "But...

how?"

"How did she end up with Wetsnow? It was a treaty agreement."

"She was a nobody, a slave..."

"No, my dear. Bondslave is what the mountain people called it, but it was a treaty between two chiefs, a daughter for a son. Your mother secured peace after years of border dispute."

"She did? I never..."

"Welcome home," Ontaro smiled.

Waking to warmth beneath his head, the Sandman blinked open his eyes, staring upward at the shelter above, some kind of animal skin stretched over a tall central pole. The woman offered water, a hesitant smile playing on her lips.

"I thank thee."

Her expression changed, disappointment flashing behind her eyes before she stifled it, settling on a blank, almost serene stare.

"Thou did think perhaps I might be forever gone."

"You put us all in danger, running out into the desert like that. Would death have been better than returning life to my husband?"

"I wish thou wouldst allow me to woo thy regard."

She frowned. "How do you propose to do that? You stole my husband's body."

"Nay, he did steal mine."

With a snort of disgust, she pulled her legs out from under him, letting his head crash into the sand as she stood and stormed out of the tent. The Sandman lifted himself up on one elbow, gazing after the woman with a smile playing on his lips.

Dragging his legs under himself, he staggered to his

feet, fighting a moment of intense vertigo. Planting his feet firmly beneath him, he followed the woman out of the tent. The midday sun hit him in the face and he gasped, blinking for a moment as his eyes adjusted to the blinding light.

All about, the bustle of camp met him, a large group of men lounging about under little tents, light brown animal skin cloaks held up in front by a short staff. They murmured together in groups while the sun blazed down. To one side, a herd of large animals hung their heads in rest. Were they camels?

The Sandman could not remember camels in the colony, but perhaps they were bred from stored material after he went into soul-sleep. The animal reanimation program had begun with only a few of the most useful breeds, but encompassed a long-term program of a much wider range of species.

The woman stood staring out over the dunes. He shuffled his way toward her, feeling suddenly timid and unsure, an unfamiliar feeling that set him on edge. She ignored his approach, arms crossed over her heavy cloak, with its blue edged hood framing her lovely face. Her cheeks were wet, her eyes shining with tears that spilled over unheeded.

Cautiously, he slipped an arm about her shoulders and she stiffened, but he pulled her close against her protests. She let out a sob, but allowed his arm to remain. He gazed out over the sands, remembering the first time he had seen this desert. The last stand of the fire demons against the terraforming, their fire holding the new forests at bay.

The usurper had led the colonists in an orgy of genocidal hunting, forcing the creatures back, using water as a weapon, rounding them up until they had no fight left. The last of the natives had turned and fled, leaving this last remnant of their habitat permanently scarred by their passing.

Yet somehow people lived here, managed to eke out some kind of existence. He had no idea what to expect from the nomads who had stolen away his wife, but he had to believe they could help. Somehow, they would have the answers.

"What doth trouble that one?"

The Sandman indicated Nashta standing alone as he watched Fransi moving among the horses. His expression was at once wistful and agonised, full of pain and regret.

"Why don't you go ask him?" Miyam replied. "You might find people treat you better if you make an effort to fit in."

He flashed her a pained look, but her suggestion had merit. He approached the man in the ridiculous red-bordered cloak, not looking to see if she followed, but absurdly hoping she did. Nashta barely noticed him, but the Sandman stood beside him anyway, trying to work out what was so fascinating about the woman he watched.

"Thou art troubled," he tried.

Nashta huffed, flashing him a bewildered look. "I just can't get used to that," he said. "You aren't right, you know. You should not be here."

The Sandman shrugged, unsure what to make of that. How could his rebirth not be right? It was meant to be. The vessel's new persona was an aberration, a simple mistake of fortune.

"I heard you removed some of the possessed, and returned the rightful souls to their bodies. Could you do it again?"

"The transfer ist but a trick of the soul-tech amulet. But I cannot expel the intruder. That was not of my doing."

"Could you bring Tineya back?"

"It would be unwise. Her vessel doth contain another. There would be conflict within the mind."

"She would be like you?"

"That is so. Thou would not wish it on thy love."

"She can handle it. Ask her, she's in there somewhere. She will say the same. She can best Fransi."

"That one would allow it not."

"Don't worry, I can deal with her."

The Sandman sighed, wondering why he should help this fool. "I cannot use the mind-speak. I have not the skill."

"If you had ever loved, you would do it for me. For us."

The Sandman considered. This man thought him a heartless intruder, taking possession with no thought for the soul he had ousted. Perhaps he was right. But he had loved, and hoped to love again if the vessel's wife would have him. It would not hurt to grant one lover's wish.

"Bring thou her to me."

Nashta sprang into action. The Sandman glanced about, feeling Miyam's eyes on him. He caught her searching look, felt her probing thought. She truly believed he was incapable of compassion. Perhaps he needed to show her that he did indeed have a heart.

Nashta approached the possessed girl, reached a hand out to touch her face. She leant into his hand, welcoming his caress. Then she closed her eyes and fell limp into his arms. Nashta scooped her up and carried her toward the Sandman.

Removing his amulet, the Sandman pressed the cleansing mechanism, just to be sure it had not picked up his own code through general wear. A short puff of green cleaned the code chamber. He pulled at the neck of the young woman's tunic, bearing the skin, and touched the amulet to her chest.

He felt the faint click as the microscopic needle penetrated her skin, and the blue glow indicated a sample had been collected successfully. Touching the amulet to his own forehead, he listened, waiting for the soul to respond.

'It's mine! Oh yes, please, take me home!'

The amulet glowed blue again, showing that the soul had recognised its code and been drawn out of the body, into storage. The Sandman touched the amulet to the young woman's forehead, waiting for the transfer.

Finally, the white glow indicated a successful implant, the soul returned to its body. It was now up to her to battle for dominance. The Sandman cleaned the code from the amulet once more, the green mist floating down and dissipating into the air.

"Is it done?" said Nashta breathlessly.

The Sandman nodded as he slipped the gold chain back over his own head. He caught Miyam looking at him, her eyes wide and her mouth parted slightly. She looked beautiful, with those flashing green eyes glassed over with unshed tears. He did not know whether to be pleased or shamed by her reaction. She gave a small shake of the head, and his heart sank.

"Why?" she moaned. "Why will you do it for him, yet refuse me? Why won't you give me back my husband?"

For many days they travelled, across a scorching landscape, resting only at midday and midnight. The nomads found hidden water each time they camped, obviously following a well-known path, though the revealers could see no markers or permanent oases. Finally, they reached the top of a rise and stared down over the tent city of the nomads, stretched out beneath the sheltering branches of an almighty oak tree, hundreds of feet tall.

"You moved the camp!" Miyam gasped.

"When your princess broke the spell, bringing the mother tree out of hiding, we decided to move into her protection," said Ontaro. "It's taken a while to get here, with the kalkar war, but now she has given us the blessing of her shelter and the security of a permanent home."

Miyam clicked at her mount and the camel knelt in the sand for her to slide down. She walked away, leaving the Sandman to sit uncertainly, before he slipped down and followed her. Ontaro was already halfway down the slope, with the rest of the group now leading their camels in his wake. Navear appeared beside Miyam with a grin plastered across her face. Jossep hovered, seeming unsure how to handle his wife's newfound exuberance.

"I never dreamed I would find relatives," she whispered.

"Or that you already had found one," Miyam replied.

"What do you mean?"

"Haven't you realised yet?" Miyam laughed. "Evelar's father is nephew to Old One. Ontaro's cousin."

Navear frowned. "My mother's too?"

"That's right."

"My mother and Evelar's father were cousins? So... we are too? Some kind of cousin?"

"Second cousins, I think."

Jossep slipped an arm about her. "My wife is related to the Awakener?" he said with a bemused grin.

Ontaro hurried back to take hold of Navear's arm. "Come along, child," he said. "Come and meet your grandfather."

"My..." she glanced at Jossep and his grin widened.

"And granddaughter of a great chief!" he crowed. "How lucky am I?"

As the two young revealers hurried off with Ontaro, Miyam continued into the tent city, feeling the drop in temperature as she entered the shade of the great tree. There under the branches, the tent city thrived. Women gossipped as they stitched elaborate designs on cloth for clothing. Children ran amongst the tents, laughing as they played, while older children sat watching the leather makers at work, or helping the smith make colourful glass beads. She saw a man approaching and recognised Evelar's father, Shevron. Miyam smiled and accepted his embrace.

"Welcome home, daughter," Shevron smiled.

"Thank you, Sir," she replied.

"My son," he beamed at the man in Evelar's body.

"Whofore art thou?" the Sandman said.

Shevron's face clouded over and Miyam pulled him to one side. "I'm sorry, sir, but... he's not himself."

"I can see that. What happened?"

"He has been invaded by another soul, who claims to be the rightful owner of his body. Evelar has been locked in mental battle with the intruder. Right now, the other soul is in control."

Shevron frowned. "Bring him to my tent."

Miyam signalled for the Sandman to follow, but as they moved deeper into the camp she saw an enormous woman staring from where she stood beside the great tree's massive trunk. She gave a small nod, and Miyam returned the gesture.

"I'm sorry, Sir, but Sand Mother wants me."

"Of course she does," said Shevron with a smile. "Don't worry, you can leave him with me. I'll talk some sense into him."

"Sir, I don't think you understand..."

"Oh, I do, my dear. Don't you worry. Off you go."

Miyam backed away with hesitant steps, feeling the mental pull of Sand Mother but unwilling to leave the Sandman unattended.

"Come along, boy," Shevron was saying. "Sit here by me and we'll have a chat."

As Miyam watched, the Sandman gave in to the old man's ministrations, sitting where he indicated without protest. Miyam let out a sigh and turned to meet the huge woman's stare. Her feet moved on their own and she headed toward Sand Mother's tent.

Nestled beneath a large overhanging branch, the tent of Sand Mother seemed to blend into the foliage, becoming one with the great tree. At the apex, where smoke drifted out of the aeration holes near the top of the central pole, the tree reached down with its fibrous tendrils, a fine lattice of growth encasing the uppermost portion of the tent.

"The mother tree gives of herself to protect us," Sand Mother murmured. "In time, we will have no need of tents, her own limbs forming nests to embrace us."

As Miyam gazed up into the branches, a little creature peeked out at her, big grin plastered over a goblin-like gnome face.

"Leshma..." she breathed.

"Who, my dear?"

"The guardian of the tree."

"She has a guardian?"

"There..."

But as she pointed, the creature disappeared. Scanning the branches, she saw the little face peek out in a new place. High in the branches, Leshma touched a bent finger to his lips and closed one round eye.

"Never mind," Miyam murmured.

Sand Mother motioned to a bowl resting on the sand near the closed door, and Miyam bent to scoop a handful of water. As she did so, a drip struck her hand and she glanced upward to see a pendulous branch hovering just above the bowl, another droplet forming on its downward pointing tip.

"The Mother Tree sustains herself by drawing water up from far below the sands, and she has chosen to share it with us."

Miyam stared up into the spreading branches. "I thank

you, Mother, for your gift of water," she whispered, fancying she heard a rustling whisper in return.

"Come, my dear," said Sand Mother, leading her into the tent.

Sand Mother gestured to a pile of cushions and Miyam sat while the old woman sprinkled a fine powder over the coals in the hearth. A thick smoke rose, filling the room with its fragrant fog. Miyam felt her body begin to relax, and her mind cleared.

"Now," said Sand Mother as she let her huge body sink into the cushions. "Tell me what is bothering you."

Miyam considered where to start. "Evelar," she sighed.

Sand Mother nodded. "I felt the change in him."

"His essence is unchanged, but his body is in turmoil. The Sandman has taken him."

"And who is the Sandman?"

"We don't know. He has invaded his mind, and stolen his body. We don't know how."

"Does this Sandman know?"

"He... I think he is confused, and does not know the whole of it. He says he needs answers and he thinks that this is the place to find them."

"Why does he think this?"

"Because of the amulet. The one his mother wore, that he now carries."

"Ah," Sand Mother mused. "Perhaps he is right."

"But what can you do?"

Sand Mother chuckled. Rolling over onto hands and knees, she grasped the central pole and hauled herself upright, the whole structure shuddering under her weight. Miyam scrambled to her feet but the old woman waved her back down.

"I need to speak with this Sandman."

"You? But you never..."

"There is no never, child. If I said never, I would never see the surprise on their faces. These men need to be surprised every so often, don't you think?"

Seated outside Shevron's tent, the Sandman listened to the old man's ramblings with only half a mind. Something pricked at the back of his head. He shook the feeling away and redoubled his efforts to appear interested. But the man had ceased talking and now stared at something beyond the Sandman.

Turning to follow the old man's gaze, he saw an enormous woman staring directly at him. Her eyes tugged at his mind, sending tingles into his limbs, forcing him to move them.

"You must go to her, boy," Shevron said in a strangled whisper.

Sandman nodded, rising to his feet almost against his will. The camp had fallen silent, all noise had ceased, all voices quelled. Glancing around, he saw that every face was turned toward the woman, eyes wide and mouths agape.

Even the children stood silent and still, staring at the man who was called by Sand Mother. His feet moved and he found himself walking toward the woman, all thought of resistance washed away. He felt every stare as he traversed the short distance to the waiting woman.

She gave a huge smile, her wise old gaze roving over the watching people, and one by one they hung their heads and turned away in embarrassment. She lifted the flap and gestured, and he entered the tent ahead of her.

TWENTY SIX

Sand Mother settled into the cushions once more, motioning for the Sandman to sit. As he took his place, Miyam shrank away from him, unwilling to share the intimacy of Sand Mother's presence. She felt Sand Mother's eyes on her and hung her head.

"Why do you dislike this man?"

"He stole his body. He took my husband from me."

"He is still the same man."

"No. It's the same body, as I well know, and it tears me apart. But the mind is not his. He is a stranger and I cannot bear it."

Sand Mother turned her gaze on the Sandman. "I feel you do not dislike this woman."

"This vessel doth love her with its every fibre. With its very essence it hungers for her."

"You seem to feel there is a distinction between the your mind and your body."

"This vessel did build a life in my place. I know this woman not. But I cannot deny her effect on this vessel."

"Why have you done this?"

"This vessel was ever mine by right."

"And who gave you that right?"

"It is mine."

"How did you get here?"

"The clone-seed did grow to become this vessel. The vessel took the amulet, wherein my soul did sleep. I was awakened."

"But how? What is this amulet?"

"This," he replied, bringing the amulet out of his shirt and holding it up on its fine gold chain."

"Ah," said Sand Mother. "And how did you come by this charm?"

"I can answer that," Miyam said. "Evelar took it from his sister when she died. It came from their mother."

"The mother did receive the seed, to grow and birth the vessel. But my soul did sleep too long."

Sand Mother nodded. "This explains something that has troubled me for a very long time. Evelar's mother was my acolyte. But one day she changed. Her vocation dissipated and she could think only of love. Am I right in assuming this seed you speak of was stored inside the amulet?"

"Thou dost assume correctly."

"This amulet was in my care. She must have found it and taken it, though how and why is a mystery, since it was hidden away. I did not discover its loss for many years. But why would she steal something like that? It was not in her character."

"The amulet did call to her. It did recognise a compatible host for the seed. How came thee by the amulet?"

"It has been in the care of Sand Mother for countless generations. Along with certain other artifacts of our distant past."

"Thou sayest generations? How ist that I did sleep for so long?"

Sand Mother considered for a moment. Then she grasped the central pole and dragged her vast bulk to her feet. She shuffled toward the back of the tent and began pulling cushions and blankets away from her sleeping platform.

Tearing the skin from the frame, she lifted several

wooden slats to reveal a large chest. Digging into her ample bosom, she pulled out a small gold key on a chain and unlocked the box.

When she came back to the hearth, she held a large sack, shimmering with colourful glass beads sewn in elaborate patterns, covering its surface. Finally seated amongst the cushions once more, Sand Mother looked up into their curious faces. She opened the bag and carefully brought out a dusty old scroll.

Holding it reverently for a moment, she laid it on the mat in front of her. As she slowly unrolled it, the leather parchment crackled, and the musty smell of ages wafted into the air to mix with the smoke of the fire. She perused the ancient manuscript, running her fingertips lightly across its cracked surface. Then, without ceremony or preamble, she began to read, a long and fantastical history beyond comprehension.

In the privacy of the tent that was set aside for their use, the revealers came together to link minds in discussion of their situation. Nashta set Tineya at the door to keep guard while the rest gathered in a circle about the hearth.

"First," said Nashta. "We need to decide what to do about the Sandman. He needs to be controlled and the Awakener needs our help to do so. He has not succeeded on his own."

"Now that we are all together, we should have enough strength to send him away," said Reeperly.

"But we tried that before and he came back, dear," said Berkana. "We need to lock him out for good."

"But surely such decisions should be made with Miyam in attendance?" said Tikki.

"Miyam needs us to make plans for her, Tikki." said Jumally firmly. "We all know she's not coping."

"Jossep is still with Navear and her new family," said Berkana. "How can we make any decisions without them?"

"The Journeyers will go along with whatever we decide here," Nashta said. "So what should we do?"

"As my wife so eloquently reminded us, any attempt to push the Sandman down will be just as temporary as the last," said Reeperly. "Unless we can find a way to shut him out."

"In order to do that, we need to know where he came from," Jumally sighed.

"It was the amulet," said Nashta with a grimace.

"The... How do you know that?" said Reeperly.

He shrugged. "Miyam explained it all, while we were waiting for you lot to join us."

"Can you explain it to us?" said Jumally wryly.

"I don't know much. It's the same as Leena and Naali, the amulets of Shirall. It holds a living soul, just as they hold the ancient King Rexa and his queen. Somehow, this soul was able to escape and infect Evelar."

Reeperly whistled. "That's some powerful magic right there."

Nashta made a dismissive noise. "No magic. Just ancient technology, long lost to us."

"But how does it work?" said Tikki.

Nashta shrugged. "No idea."

"We need to get the Sandman back into this amulet," Reeperly mused. "But how?"

"Without knowing how the technology works, how can we control it?" Berkana sighed.

"There is someone who could control it," said Jumally. "Two people actually."

Tikki's eyes lit up. "You're right, Jum! You always were the clever one."

"No more clever than you, my dearest."

"Who?" said Nashta in exasperation.

"She's right!" cried Berkana. "Can't you guess?"

"No, I don't play guessing games," Nashta grouched.

"Netta and Atwin, of course," said Berkana with a grin.

"Why didn't I think of that?" Reeperly smiled.

"Well then," Nashta said. "It might be time for some long-range communication. Reeperly, will you take the lead, they know you."

As one, the revealers joined hands and closed their eyes. With Reeperly as the focus, the five minds merged, augmenting the power.

Reeperly reached out a thought, pulling the other minds with him. Breaking free of the physical constraints of his body, he travelled over the sands, heading north toward the mountains. Reaching the Heights, he floated over and continued, finding the ancient city of Shirall. For a moment his thought flickered as he realised the minds he sought might not be there. They might be still at Drasmil. But he searched on and found a familiar thought pattern.

'Your Majesty?'

The mind showed no surprise, just a welcome and a query. 'Who is this?'

'It's Reeperly, with the others. We need your advice concerning the Awakener.'

'What has happened? You did find him, did you not?'

'Oh yes, Your Majesty. But his mind is suffering behind the intruder's grasp. We believe you are our best hope for a solution.'

'I will help in any way I can, but I had thought this was a matter for the revealers.'

'Ordinarily, it would be, but you and your wife have a special skill that we do not. You control the amulets.'

'What have the amulets to do with your quest?'

'Evelar's condition is caused by amulet power.'

'It is? I was not aware of that.'

'Nor were we, until recently.'

'Well then, that settles it. Where are you? And what of the possessed?'

'The possessed have given up the chase, for now. We're in the Barren Wastes with the nomads. They're camped under a tree the like of which I have never seen before.'

'Yes, I know the place. We shall join you there.'

"I beg thee halt," the Sandman said. "If thou please, wouldst thou repeat that last?"

"Certainly," said Sand Mother. "From 'letting go'?"

"A might further if thou wouldst."

Sand Mother scanned the scroll to find her place and began to read again.

"His task complete, the Sandman sought his rest,

Taking into dreams the people's quest.

Knowledge stored of lifetimes on the way,

To keep them safe until another day."

"Halt," the Sandman said. "Mine enemy did strike me down. My rest was forced upon me. How can this slander be borne?"

"I cannot attest for the truth of this document, it is hundreds of years old."

"Hundreds? How many hundreds do you count?"

"Certainly more than eight," Sand Mother shrugged. "Perhaps a thousand years."

"Asleep a thousand years? Then my wife did truly forsake me. And what of my son?"

"We'll get to that. Shall I finish reading?"

The Sandman frowned, but gave a curt nod, and Sand Mother continued.

"When hope is fading and the darkness falls,

The Sandman will awake to hear the call.

To lead his people to a new beginning,
When it seems there is no hope of winning.
"The memory of ages long ago,
A life the Sandman must choose or forgo.
Telling past and bringing back to life,
That people know and so avert the strife.
"It is said the Sandman waits alone,
Dreaming of the new life soon to come.
The truth will be revealed to those held dear,
And when the past is vanquished, all is clear."

The last lines fell into a heavy silence while the Sandman chewed on the final image.

"What does it mean?" Miyam whispered into the hush.

"It doth mean nothing."

"On the contrary, it says quite a lot," Sand Mother smiled. "It suggests that the writer of this hoped you would return, that a plan was set in place to bring you back when the time was right."

"My time it was. My task complete."

"If you truly are the Sandman returned to life," said Sand Mother. "Then I have something more for you."

"Thou dost?"

"Perhaps it will shed some light on the events after your demise."

Sand Mother lifted the scroll, turned it over, and laid it before the Sandman. On the reverse of the ancient scroll, someone had scrawled a long, rambling note.

"It is in the oldest dialect I have ever seen, and to read it would take more effort than I can muster. Would you read it to us?"

The Sandman touched the scroll with reverent fingers, mouthing the words before he began to speak.

"To my father," he began. *"I write in the belief that thou might one day hold this parchment in thy hands. No doubt*

thou hast come to the realisation that my mother did betray thy memory and make a new home without thee.

For myself, I too did believe this, for I did not know the truth. But thy betrayal did not come at the hands of thy wife.

Thy sleep did give thee more than time, it gave thee life. For thou art the sole remaining member of the star bound crew. The rest did lose their lives, their souls in storage forever. Our last tech did send them above to return no more.

But thou mayst appeal to them for counsel. Our homes, our dignity, our fledgeling city, all taken by treachery. Kay did plot to take the very trappings of our lives, the instruments, the memories, the soul-tech itself, to use for his own nefarious ends.

This parchment was crafted to remind us of thee, and with it went thy soul-store, the only remaining soul-tech, both hidden against the enemy, in the hope that one day thou mayst return to exact our revenge.

Thou art the keeper of our lives, the holder of our history, and thou art our hope for the future. Take thee this knowledge, teach thee this story, and mayst thou right these wrongs. Know thou art not forgot.

Thy loving son, in hope for thy future, in eternity."

"Collect thy comrades," the Sandman exclaimed. "Mine enemy hast wreaked havoc long enough."

Miyam exchanged a look with Sand Mother as he stormed out of the tent.

"We must keep him here," Miyam sobbed. "We need to give Evelar time to break free."

"Don't worry, my dear. I feel your friends have a plan stirring."

With a smile for Sand Mother, Miyam hurried after the Sandman. He rushed straight for the horses where they dozed near the edge of the tree's shadow. But before she could catch him, a man stepped out from one of the tents as she passed. She vaguely registered the red border of a revealer's cloak and paused, half watching the Sandman as she greeted Reeperly.

"What's he up to?"

"He has it in his head to go chasing after his old enemy. But Reep, I think I just worked out something. Sand Mother had some old scrolls, and a letter from a thousand years ago addressed to the Sandman. He really has been somehow stored and reanimated."

"I think we all pretty much believe him now," Reeperly smiled. "But what have you worked out?"

"The letter mentioned his enemy by name. Kay. Nothing more. But what if that's a shortened name? What if it's short for Kayus?"

Reeperly let out a low whistle. "What makes you say that?"

"Well, we know Kayus is behind the souls and the possessed. Nashta helped me follow the threads in Fransi's mind, to find the puppet master. Who do you think it was?"

"Kayus," Reeperly nodded. "So you think Kayus has something to do with the Sandman too?"

"Actually, no, I think that's a coincidence. But perhaps the amulet knew Kayus was up to something. Did you know it's more than just the soul?"

"More?"

"The amulet stored both the soul, and the material necessary to impregnate a woman with a seed, to grow a new body, to house the old soul."

"It what? But that means..."

"He really does have a right to take Evelar's body. But because Evelar's mother passed the amulet to her daughter, and not directly to him, the soul never took possession and Evelar grew up in his own way, with his own soul."

"But you said the amulet knew something."

"From what I could understand of what he said, when a compatible woman came near, the amulet called to her, seduced her to leave her vocation with Sand Mother and become mother to the seed. I don't think it was entirely coincidental."

"So what do we do now?"

"The Sandman wants to go after Kayus. But we're not ready, are we? We need Evelar."

"It's a good thing we've called for help, then, isn't it?"

"You called... Netta and Atwin?"

He gave a nod. Miyam let out a squeal and threw her arms about him. "Oh thank you, Reep!"

Reeperly chuckled. "I assume that means you have a plan?"

"Not me. Evelar."

"Evelar? How?"

She grinned and tapped a finger to her forehead.

"You're in contact?" he gasped. "Why didn't you say anything?"

"Come on, let's get planning."

"But what about him?" He indicated the Sandman fussing about with the horses.

"I don't think he'll run off again. Almost dying can really make people respect the desert."

The Sandman fidgeted and frowned, attempting to pace in the confines of the shared tent while the revealers sat discussing plans. They were just sitting there, wasting time when they should be getting started. They did not have the most basic understanding of the technology involved, nor how the enemy had gained such control over so many minds.

"Well why don't you enlighten us, if you have so much

more understanding than us," the vessel's wife snapped.

The Sandman cursed his loud thoughts. He could not get used to people routinely using their minds to delve into each other's heads. He wished he had the skill to block them, but the upstart soul had somehow walled off those parts of his memory. Intellectually, he knew this body had great power, engineered into his physical code, but that power remained frustratingly inaccessible.

"How is Kayus doing this?" said the older male in the red trimmed hood.

The Sandman sighed, settling down on the cushions for yet another lecture in soul-tech. "Kay doth use amulet power. First he doth collect souls from dying clone-sons, then he doth send them out to inhabit the mindless drones."

"But how did he create the drones?" The other red one frowned.

"He got into Evelar's head," said Miyam quietly. "Every time he touched one of the students with his mind, Kayus sank his hooks, and because they were linked to Evelar they were pulled away from their own bodies when he travelled too far."

"The hooks Jumally found!" Reeperly said.

She shrugged. "He took a while to work it out."

"I don't get it," the little green girl said. "He's supposed to be the strongest revealer in all of history. How could this Kayus get inside his head without him knowing?"

"It's the Master of nothingness, completely invisible," Miyam replied.

The Sandman let out a laugh. "Dost thou not know the truth of mine enemy's power? It is created by altering code within the clone-seed. Thy precious love is but one step away from thee, one generation of altered code. Kay hath spent a thousand years enhancing the power. Thy most powerful example has but a tenth of Kay's strength and subtlety."

"Then we have no chance," the little girl sighed.

"Thou must take the fight to Kay. Thy minds are no match this far removed. Deny Kay the soul-tech and the possessions will fail."

"By soul-tech you mean amulets, I presume," Nashta said. "Am I right in assuming he... I mean It has an amulet for each of the possessed?"

"I posit that theory," the Sandman sniffed.

"But how does Kayus control so many?"

"Kay controls because all are the same code, created for the purpose. A personal army, ready and loyal and all linked to one mind. A formidable enemy."

"Then it's a good thing we've called in the experts."

TWENTY SEVEN

The Sandman stood staring out over the desert sands. This waiting dragged at his sanity, pushing him to desperation. But it seemed things were about to change, with the newcomers who had appeared in the night to send the revealers into excited chatter. The vessel's wife in particular seemed happier, more willing to be kind.

He wanted her to be happy. Her loyalty to her lost love warmed his heart and gave him hope for a future in this strange new life. She would grow used to him, her physical attraction guiding the way to a deeper attachment. If only she would give him a chance to prove himself.

Hearing his name, he turned to see her approaching with a small child on her hip. His heart flipped over in his chest at sight of the boy as the vessel reacted on a visceral level. She smiled and the Sandman felt his mouth turn up in a grin of its own accord. She tilted her head, eyes searching his, but the light quickly faded and her expression closed over on her disappointment. When would she stop searching for him?

"Papa!" the little boy cried.

The Sandman blinked in surprise. "Whom is this child?" he whispered.

"This is your son, Zaviar," Miyam smiled.

"Nay, not so. My son was lost a millenium past."

"Physically, he is your son," the woman said.

'Papa sick?' a little voice sighed inside his head.

"He doth talk in my mind!"

"Yes, he does that. It's easier than speech at his age."

'Mama sad. Help Papa.'

"What doth he want from me?"

"Nothing. He wants to help you get better."

"I need not to be healed. Wherefore hast he come?"

"He came with Netta and Atwin, to meet his grandfather." She set the boy down and pointed him back toward the camp. "Run and find Auntie Netta, sweetie. She will take you to Poppy Shevron."

'Yes, Mama,' the boy mind-spoke and toddled off, calling silently to Auntie Netta as he went.

"Why dost thou show me this child?"

"He is a baby, and he needs his father. I had allowed myself to forget that to him you haven't changed. I have been selfish."

He narrowed his eyes at her. "What dost thou say?"

"I'm saying, I want to try to make this work. I know you will never give up his body. I need to accept that."

He tried to control his breathing, hiding his excitement from her calculating gaze. "Thou art giving thyself to me?"

"Yes. If you will have me."

His heart chattered as she touched her hand to his chest. He felt the prick of the amulet, but disregarded it. This woman would not know she had just sampled his code. It was not important. Not nearly so important as this woman could be.

This woman was his one chance to reclaim his lost life. This woman, descended from his beloved wife. The child to replace his lost son. This beautiful woman who now offered herself to him. He reached out a hesitant hand and she took it in her own. She lifted herself up on her toes and touched her lips to his.

His arms went about her completely on their own, his

body reacting in the only way it could, her somehow familiar form fitting itself perfectly against him. He returned the kiss with an ardent fervour, releasing all the desire he had suppressed.

A great noise filled his head, the sound of hundreds of voices yelling all at once. A great wave washed over him, his mind overwhelmed by other souls, pushing from all directions. The force of the voices coalesced and took on a single direction, forcing him down, into darkness. He felt his hold on consciousness ripped away, the door to the world slammed shut on his desperate struggle. And the pushing, pulling, driving force continued unabated, forcing him down deeper.

The flood carried him along, the raging force growing yet more fierce as the way seemed to narrow. Funnelled through a tiny gap in the fabric of the mind, the world exploded in a bright white light. No more dark, comfortable mindscape, he looked out over a white world, devoid of all colour, stark and quiet. No voices clamoured to be heard, no thoughts wrapped him in their presence. He recognised this place. He dreaded this place. He tried to turn, to flee back to the safety of the vessel's mind, but his way was blocked.

'No!' he cried into the silence. 'Not this place!'

Out on the desert sands, at the edge of the tent city of the nomads, Miyam looked down at the unconscious body of her beloved husband. She fell to her knees beside him, unaware of the tears staining her cheeks. Reaching out with trembling hands, she searched for the gold chain about his neck, pulling it up over his head.

Looking at it for a moment, she let all her fear and heartache wash over her, before raising a hand to hurl it as far as she could. But before she could release the golden charm, a hand stopped hers and took the amulet from her grasp.

"Better keep hold of this, just in case," Reeperly murmured as he released her hand.

Miyam let out a shuddering breath. "Let's get him inside," she whispered.

She watched through a blur as her friends lifted his body and carried it away. She sat still, staring at the imprint in the sand, as the tears fell. She jumped at a hand on her shoulder.

"Are you alright, Mym?"

She nodded, and smiled up at Navear. The girl took her arm and helped her to rise.

"I'm sure he'll be fine," Navear smiled.

Miyam gave a sigh, and allowed the girl to lead her toward the tent. Inside, Evelar's body had been laid out by the hearth, appearing to be merely asleep. Miyam sank down beside him, afraid to hope that the plan had worked. She stared at his face, listening for his shallow breath and willing him to wake. Around them, the other revealers settled in a circle, ready to support her. And so the vigil began.

At first, he was aware only of warmth, and softness beneath his head. He could hear someone breathing nearby, a peaceful, sleepy sound. Beneath that he felt, more than heard, more breathing; other presences gathered all around. Allowing his eyes to open, he looked up, seeing only shadows above the glow of the fire.

He rolled his head to the side to see a woman seated beside him, head down and eyes closed. Her breathing was low and soft, but regular, not the shallow breath of true sleep. He lifted a hand and her eyes snapped open, staring in abject fear.

He touched his hand to her face, wiping away the single

tear that trickled over her perfect cheek. Moving slowly, he lifted himself up to sit before her, staring into her troubled eyes. He longed to kiss her, but he knew he had to move slowly, to assure her that he was himself.

"Don't cry, my love," he whispered.

She caught her breath on a sob, eyes widening. Those beautiful green eyes, filled with something he had missed more than anything else. Her love shone through the tears. She let out a small sigh, ending in a suppressed squeak.

"Evelar?"

He grinned at her, enjoying her reaction. Then she was in his arms, clutching at him, wrapping herself about him. He chuckled into her hair and she wriggled against him, twisting into a more comfortable position. Only then did he allow his mouth to find hers. He barely heard the other occupants of the tent as they stirred from their slumber. But Miyam pulled back to look at them as they gathered around.

"Is it him?" Navear said.

Miyam snuggled in against him and he smiled.

"It's me," he said.

The gathered revealers broke into smiles and relieved laughter, talking all at once in their eagerness.

"My friends," Evelar smiled. "I thank you all for your help. I know you have a lot of questions, and we have plans to make. But right now, I'd like to spend some time with my wife."

"Of course you would," Reeperly said. "We'll leave you to it."

"But it's still dark outside!" Jossep exclaimed.

"The sun is rising," said Jumally stiffly. "And none of us have trained in days. Now would be a good time."

Jossep grumbled but took Navear's hand and headed for the door, followed by the others. At the door, Reeperly turned to smile at them.

"Have fun, you two," he winked.

Miyam giggled. Evelar sent him out with a wave of his hand, then turned to his wife, pulling her close.

"Now," he said. "What's this I hear of you kissing another man?"

"It was your idea!" she cried.

He covered her indignant pout with a kiss and she melted against him.

Miyam smiled as her little son toddled about after Princess Shedissa, who led him on a squealing chase about the trunk of the great tree. Stopping in front of Sand Mother where she sat in the sand outside her tent, the children clambered into the huge woman's lap. Sand Mother laughed and sent them on their way. Miyam turned her gaze back to the little group gathered by the chief's tent.

"I must say, you had me worried, son," Shevron was saying. "And now you say you want to head off on another dangerous quest against this... who did you say?"

"Not just any quest, father," said Evelar. "Kayus was the cause of the last kalkar war, which almost destroyed us all."

"But you defeated him."

"Not entirely. But we did think we would have more time."

"I do not like it."

"Dissa!" Netta cried suddenly. "Get down from there!"

Miyam looked up to see the children scampering along a branch above Sand Mother's tent. She burst to her feet and rushed after Netta.

"Zavvy, stop where you are! Don't move, I'll get you down."

'Mama silly,' the boy thought at her.

"Zaviar, don't you speak to your mother that way," Evelar growled.

As Miyam watched with breath held on a racing heart, Zaviar stumbled and slipped sideways off the branch. She gasped and rushed toward him, but as she watched he seemed to float in mid-air. An invisible force lifted him up and plonked him down on the branch where he sat giggling down at his mother.

'See, Mama?' the baby gurgled. *'Leshie catch.'*

"What?"

Miyam stared up into the branches to see a little wizened face peeping out at her. Netta let out a sharp giggle and Leshma winked at them.

"Well, that is different," said Netta with a smile. "You children play nice."

Together they returned to the meeting, countering the surprised stares with broad smiles.

"You're going to let them play up there?" said Tikki. "They're babies!"

"They're perfectly safe," said Miyam.

"Safe?" said Jumally. "They are eight foot in the air. They could be killed."

"Not with Leshma in charge."

"Who?"

Atwin let out a laugh. "That explains it."

"Shall we get back to business then?" Evelar said, taking his wife's hand and pulling her down beside him.

"If you're sure..." Berkana frowned.

"So," Nashta said. "We take the fight to Kayus."

"Kayus controls the possessed," said Evelar. "It does so using amulet power, somehow augmented to reach from wherever It hides."

"We find and neutralise the amulets," said Atwin. "And sever the link that keeps the possessed in control. Then we can get their souls out of Evelar's head and back into their own bodies."

"What about Kayus?" Reeperly said. "It's not going to let us just walk on over and spoil Its plans."

"And with all those hooks in Evelar's head, Kayus will know we are coming," Atwin frowned.

"Kayus wants him to come," said Miyam. "Already the possessed have given up the fight and are right now racing to their master. Kayus wants him dead, to reward Its loyal followers with new life."

"But why? What does It care for them?" Nashta said.

"They're a captive army, ready to fight for their master," Reeperly grimaced. "We are a handful of revealers with no plan."

"You may have as many of my warriors as you need," said Chief Entranos.

"That's very kind of you, Sir," Evelar smiled. "But I'm hoping to conclude this without entering into battle."

"I learnt the importance of world affairs during the kalkar invasion. I won't fail you this time."

"I'd hardly call my mental breakdown 'world affairs', Sir."

"You should value yourself more highly, my son," said Shevron quietly. "I know the rest of the world does."

"Quite right," said Reeperly with a grin.

A murmur of assent rippled through the group, their smiles and nods of agreement bathing the troubled Awakener in the warmth of their regard. Miyam beamed at him, snuggling in under his arm to slip her arms about his waist.

'I should think you would know how highly I value you,' she whispered mentally.

"We all feel the same way, my friend," Atwin smiled. "You will just have to accept our help and get on with it."

"All we need now is a plan," said Reeperly. "Or perhaps a compass that points to the possessed."

"We have better than that," said Nashta, glancing at Tineya huddling silently behind him. "We have Fransi. Her pull to the Master is all we need."

"Who me?" the girl gasped.

Stepping out of Sand Mother's tent after a final counselling session, Miyam bent to catch the little body that hurled itself into her arms. Laughing, she swung the boy about before settling him on her hip for a cuddle.

'Mama happy!' he mind-spoke at her.

"Yes, sweetie, I'm happy now."

'Papa sad,' he sent with a pout.

"He is?" she sighed. "Let's go find him, shall we?"

'Yes, Mama.'

She sent out a probing thought and received an immediate response. But the mental voice seemed heavy and dull, not his usual vibrant presence. Following the thought, she carried Zaviar out past the sheltering branches of the great tree. Out on the sands, high on the crest of a dune, a black shape squatted. Returning to the tent the revealers shared, she dug in Evelar's pack to pull out a heavy bundle of midnight blue fabric.

"Come along, Zavvy," she smiled. "Let's cheer up your Papa."

Zaviar grinned and held up his arms to be lifted once more. Miyam pulled her own blue edged hood over her head and tied it with the sash, then tucked the cloth bundle under one arm and picked up the boy, making her way back out into the bright desert sun.

She trudged her way up the high dune toward the lonely figure, coming up behind him as he stared out over the sands. Zaviar wriggled out of her arms and threw himself into his father's unresponsive lap. Evelar held him absently, no smile registering the boy's presence.

'Papa?'

Evelar sighed. "Hello, little man," he murmured.

Miyam squatted down before him, searching his eyes for a response. He avoided her gaze, staring out into the bright desert haze.

"Evelar, what's wrong?"

His eyes flicked toward her for a moment then darted away.

"What's troubling you? Is it the search for Kayus that has you worried?"

He moved his head slightly, a small shake.

"Then what? You know you don't need to keep it from me. Do I have to pull it from your mind?"

"No," he sighed, letting his troubled eyes meet hers. "I just..."

"You don't have to say it. Let me see."

She touched a tender hand to his temple, searching his churning thoughts. Confusion. Shattered confidence, and self doubt. This was not like him. What had caused such a reversal?

"I learned a lot, while I was trapped inside," he whispered. "I explored the Sandman's memories, his whole life, his purpose, and what it means to me. I am merely a copy of him. I'm not a real person, Mym. I was never meant to be."

"How can you say that?" she gasped. "Look at what you've achieved. We would all be slaves of the kalkar, if it weren't for you. We would be suffering under the thumb of Kayus himself, if not for you."

"I'm a shadow, existing only because the Sandman lived and died and created a copy for his own rebirth. I am nothing."

She stared at him for a moment, then hauled back and slapped him across the face. He blinked, clasping his cheek, eyes filled with sorrow.

"Don't ever call yourself nothing!" she cried. "You are everything to me, and to your son. You are our whole world. You are the saviour of that world and everyone in that world knows your name."

"It was the Sandman who created that power in the first place. Not me."

"Do you really believe that? When the Sandman was in control, he had no idea how to use that power. He was lost and afraid and alone. You took the power and made it your own. Nobody else could have done what you have done. And everybody loves you for it."

"How can anybody love a copy?"

"You are not a copy! You are Evelar of the Sands. You are son of Shevron, who is nephew to old one. You are my husband and Zaviar's father. You are Sand of the College, the Awakener, greatest revealer in the whole of history. You did all of that. Not the Sandman. We love you, Evelar, as you are right now, not what you might have been if the Sandman had his way."

He let out a heavy sigh, raising his tortured eyes to finally, really meet hers, with all his doubt and all his love warring with a tenuous hope. "Do you mean that?"

"Of course I do, why would I not? I love you, Evelar. Just you, always and forever. Now stand up."

He blinked, staring for a moment. Then he rose to his feet, and Miyam shook out the cloth she had brought, laying his precious revealer's cloak over his shoulders. She lifted the hood over his head, and tied the black sash of his rank about the hood to hold it in place.

"There," she smiled. "That's my husband, right there. My Sand."

A reluctant smile tugged at his mouth, and she returned the smile.

"Feel better?" she said. "More like yourself?"

His smile broke into a grin, and he chuckled. "Yes, my love. My beautiful, clever Mist. How can you know my heart so well?"

"How could I not? Don't I hold it in my hand?"

His laugh echoed out over the dunes and he pulled her into his arms, his mouth finding hers in a perfect kiss. At their knees, the little boy wrapped his arms about both their legs.

'Papa better!' he gurgled into their minds.

* * *

TWENTY EIGHT

Dancing across the gossamer strings, the holy-one felt for the change in direction. The enemy was too well protected, and the loyalty of the reborn had been sorely tested. Too many had been lost, and the plan was in danger of failing.

'Come to me,' the Master called. 'The enemy will follow and we shall vanquish him together.'

And so the minions came, forgetting their vendetta, ending their hunt; they came closer with every day. The Master tugged at the strings, dragging the souls by their tethered hooks, drawing them toward their homeland.

'Come to me,' the Master cajoled. 'And I will give thee thy lives.'

The loyal souls drifted onward, crying in their sorrow for the lost, wailing in pain for their defeat. And exalting in joy at the Master's call.

'Come to me,' the Master ordered. 'Bring thy bodies home.'

Antoni jogged at the head of the demoralised army of the reborn. The injured were carried without protest, the healthy eager in their urge to follow the call. At least he no longer needed to whip them into action. They moved of their own accord, the Master's call pulling them ever onward, stopping only when their exhausted bodies collapsed beneath them, and staggering onward before those same bodies were fully ready to continue.

Each morning, the rising sun blasted into their faces, blinding them with its glory. Every afternoon, that same sun beat down on their backs, blistering skin and sucking moisture from their veins. They pushed on, the impassable mountains to their right, the dreaded desert to their left.

Trapped between the two, on a little-used highway with sand drifting across the cobbles, they let the landscape take them the only way they could travel, mercifully leading them in precisely the direction they so wanted to go. Within a day they had completely forgotten the former target, leaving the revealers to go their own way.

The pull of the Master took them eastward and south, through an unfamiliar land with no guide but their instinct and the road. So it was that they at last came out of the desert, into a land of cultivated fields and grazing cattle. Antoni sent two of his nameless army ahead, to scout for civilisation.

They returned with stories of a great city nestled at the edge of the desert, with ocean behind and the mountains casting their shadow over a bustling port full of fishermen bringing in their catch.

"And what about the call? Where does it go from here?"

"It keeps going, sir. Out across the water."

Antoni mused for a moment. "Did you talk to any locals? What's out there?"

"Just south of here, there's a chain of islands heading east, spanning right across the sea."

"Where does it lead?"

"A great land, destroyed by the burning ones."

"Sounds familiar," Antoni grimaced. "And you say the Master calls from there? Could it be the way home?"

"It does sound like the land around Stolen City. But how do we get there? We tried to get boats last time, and nobody would carry us."

"We could use the islands," said Antoni. "Hop across, camping on dry land along the way."

"Please, sir, don't make us use rafts again."

"Of course not, I'm not stupid," Antoni scoffed. "You said there were fishing boats. How big? Big enough to carry all that lot?"

"Maybe. There were one or two big ones. If we get them after they've emptied their load."

"Then that's what we'll do. Tonight, you'll take a small group and grab one. We'll head down the coast a ways and meet you. We'll use the islands and ferry if we have to."

A small group of men slinked through the moonlit night, dashing from shadow to shadow, inching closer to the largest boats in the fishing fleet, a small collection of trawlers moored in deep water near the end of a long break wall. Scuttling along the wall, the men approached a mighty boat, perfect to carry all the reborn in one trip.

"I don't see anyone on deck," one of the men hissed, ready to rush out.

"Wait, Chock," another snapped. "Look."

Three dark shapes had appeared on the prow, their voices carrying over the water. Chock ducked back down.

"It's only three," he whispered. We can take 'em."

"No, Chock. Ship like that'll 'ave more, these're jus' the ones on watch. There'll be more below."

"But none of the others is big enough."

"One or two might be, at a pinch. These things're made to carry a heavy cargo."

Chock sniffed. "Alright, Scud, what about that one?"

Scud peered at the next boat, its lantern swaying in the light swell. "Small, but might do."

"No guards."

Scud nodded. "Alright, you lot, let's try that'n."

The men scurried across to the next boat, hiding behind bollards and boulders.

"There," another man pointed. "At the stern."

A lone shape sat motionless against the rail.

"Leave 'im to me," Chock hissed.

The others watched as Chock slinked along the wharf, then jumped lightly across onto the deck. The guard did not stir, and a light snore floated across to the watchers. Chock slipped up behind the guard, the lantern light flashing off a blade. A quick cut, a push, and the guard flopped over the side and splashed into the water.

"Who's that?" someone cried from the ship's cabin.

Chock froze in place, gave a cough, called out. "Jus' me, Cap'n."

"Well keep it down out there, some of us are trying to sleep."

"Yessir!"

Chock signalled for the others to jump aboard, while he headed for the cabin. A thud, a grunt, and he backed out of the cabin, dragging something heavy. He pulled it to the rail and tumbled it over the side.

"No more on board," a man called.

"Keep it down," Scud hissed.

"Let's get going," Chock said. "Anybody know how to sail?"

Antoni watched the boat heave to, listing dangerously on the surf. The hull hit the sand with a sickening crunch and men cried out in the night.

"Careful, you fools!" Antoni snapped.

He waved men forward to rush at the boat, hauling on ropes to drag it higher onto the beach.

"Not too far!" Antoni shouted. "We don't want to get stuck."

"Sir, there's still cargo on board," Scud called from the deck. "Should we bring it out?"

"What sort of cargo?"

"Umm... Fish? Sir."

"Well then leave it, what else do you expect to feed these people, seaweed?"

"Nothing wrong with seaweed, sir."

"Just... leave it and start loading up."

The reborn army hurried to fill the boat with all manner of supplies, collected along the road, then the people piled on. One woman stood back, whimpering in fear.

"It's too full," she cried. "We'll all drown."

"Just get on, woman."

"But..."

"Don't you feel it?"

She mumbled something incoherent, her lip trembling. Then she scrambled forward and reached for the hands ready to pull her up. Even when the boat groaned with passengers, they continued climbing the ropes, squeezing in, pushing against the crowd until they filled the hold and all available space.

As the moon passed overhead, sinking toward the horizon, the swell took hold of the hull, pulling sand out from under the groaning vessel, catching at the stubborn wood in the undertow. Men worked about the bow, digging at the sand with bare hands, creating a channel for the water to fill. Slowly, the boat began to move.

"Keep digging," Antoni cried.

The waves crashed against the hull, dragging at the wallowing boat until suddenly it shifted, and the sand let go. One man screamed, caught in the path of the stern as it slewed into the waves. The men rushed forward, clutching at the hapless victim as he was dumped under the swell.

When they finally pulled him free, his vacant eyes stared

back at them while his life blood drained from a gash to his head. Antoni pulled at the man by his hair, dragging him up onto the beach. A hank of hair came away in his hand, a bloody scrap of skin clinging to it. Antoni licked his lips, feeling the blood lust taking hold.

He stared at it for a long moment, eyes blurring with the red fever. He wound the gruesome threads about his hand, skin and all, and slipped it into his pocket. Antoni and his helpers scrambled aboard and clutched to the rail as the next few waves pulled the boat further into the swell. Finally, the boat floated free, and someone trimmed the sail to catch the light dawn breeze.

"We're on our way, Sir," Scud yelled from the wheel. "Don't worry folks, yer in good 'ands."

The waves lapped at the rail, the dangerously overloaded boat wallowing low in the water. The ranks let out a cheer as the wind caught the sail and took them out toward the rising sun. Pushing his way to the stern, Antoni settled himself down against the rail. He bared his left arm, his hand running reverently over the rough scars in parallel lines all the way up his arm from wrist to bicep, finely stitched hairs forming a fuzz over the cuts.

He drew his knife and placed it above the uppermost cut. He set his mouth in a thin line and pulled the knife across the skin, watching the blood flow in a dark stream down his arm, bathing the cuts that had come before it. Letting the blood flow, he pulled out the hank of hair off the drowned man.

From another pocket, he found a tiny leather pouch. Opening it, he selected a fine, silver needle. He chose a good long strand of hair, pulled it from the scrap of scalp, and threaded the needle with it. Then he stuck his knife between his teeth and proceeded to sew up the cut he had made.

*

As the setting sun sent sparkles across the rippling water, the heavily burdened fishing boat pulled in to a tiny beach on a tiny island in the middle of a vast ocean. A wet and sorry band of reborn tumbled out of the boat to throw themselves onto the sand. Antoni moved among them, kicking them into action, and slowly a bedraggled camp grew up on the shore.

A group pealed off to explore while another band started building a fire. Piles of fish brought up from the hold lay close by, and Antoni delegated another group to gut them, ready to be skewered and cooked whole.After a surprisingly hearty meal, the troupe fell silent as exhaustion set in, and soon the only sound among the reborn was the occasional snore.

Before dawn the next day, they piled onto the boat once more, putting their lives in the flimsy care of a boat made to carry a fraction of their number. Rough seas washed over them, soaking them to the skin and threatening to throw them overboard. Every island they passed called to them, offering safety and dry land, but they followed a greater drive, a mutual, overriding compulsion to continue sailing east, into the unknown.

They stopped only when tides allowed, and only when fighting brought the threat of death to them all as they were driven mad by the confines of the boat. Countless days passed. Countless tiny islands, some with little more than sand and a few scrubby trees, some green and teaming with life.

And all the while, Antoni kicked and cajoled and cursed, driving them onward with a stubborn refusal to hear their complaints. Any criticism was readily met with blood, but somehow no fatal injuries occured. Antoni enjoyed drawing blood just to see it pumping out, that red fountain bringing a look of pure joy. But he liked to keep his victims alive, to prolong the thrill of the bloodletting.

At last, a new land greeted the rising sun, a great shore stretching in either direction as far as the eye could see. A treeless plain, wide and brown, covering a whole continent with tall grassland waving in the breeze. After their dreadful voyage, nothing was more welcome, and as the boat pulled up on the sand they spilled out to kiss the ground and crawl through the sand to sprawl out in the grass.

Dawn broke on a silent camp, the fire reduced to embers, the people sleeping in the trampled grass, oblivious to the passing of the night. In their exhaustion they slept like the dead, and for once even Antoni showed no inclination to move on. The Master called but still they slept, until the sun climbed toward its zenith.

Arising from his stupor, Antoni stared toward the edge of camp, and the dread creatures who had appeared while he slept. In every direction the fire demons had gathered, surrounding them in a smoldering wall of alien flesh, standing dormant in the morning sunlight.

Antoni approached one of the fell things, wrinkling his nose at the sulfurous smell. He had heard stories of the demons, of their burning touch. But he had never seen one up close. The creature stood totally still, a strange fleshy cloak draped about it, its head completely covered. It seemed unaware, somehow shut down, yet it almost glowed with the heat it gave off, and a miasma of smoke rose about it.

Antoni grimaced, hands itching to touch it but held back by an instinct of self preservation. He backed away, and set about kicking the people to their feet. He sent the first two to make a way through the surrounding demons, while the rest of the reborn huddled in groups within the sizzling circle. But then the screaming started.

Rushing toward the noise, Antoni and several others pulled up short at the edge of the circle in time to see the men fall to the ground. The two men lay blackened and smoking at the feet of the sleeping demon. Antoni bent to examine the bodies, reduced to a stinking pile of sticky ash. He licked his lips, mind racing. He reached a hand down to sift through the black stuff. No hair.

He rubbed it between his fingers. Maybe the ash would do. He drew his knife, pushed up his sleeve and made a new cut, then took a handful of ash from one of the bodies and rubbed it into the wound. After repeating the process with the second dead man, he sheathed his knife and rose to his feet. Staring down at them for a moment, he took a deep breath, then turned his emotionless gaze on the watching reborn.

The men may have lost their lives, but they had managed to push the demon far enough to open a gap, through which the reborn could escape. With sneers and curses, Antoni rallied the troops, driving them out of the dread circle of demons, and striking out across the plain, following the call of the Master.

* * *

Huddled in a corner of the brightly lit room, the boy pressed his hands to his ears. On the creaking bed, the holy-one lay supine beneath hundreds of glowing golden amulets, mouth moving in silent exaltation. The boy tried to shut out the sound of the holy-one's incessant cajoling call. He tried to block the insistent tug of the reborn souls, all eager to join with their master.

Every day the noise grew louder, as the reborn army drew closer. And each day the holy-one cackled and danced in the silent world of an overflowing mindscape. The boy blocked the overflow, as the holy-one leaked soul energy, the amulets catching only a portion of the feedback from the projected souls.

The boy hoped the new bodies would get there soon. He shivered at another wordless cry from the holy-one, the gurgling triumph sending a shiver up the boy's spine. Once more he thought of leaving, just running away while the holy-one was unable to stop him. But something held him there. The holy-one had a hook in him too, and he desperately dreaded the thought of severing it.

So the boy hovered about the Master, offering a watery broth and wiping the spittle from the holy-one's chin, listening with a morbid fascination to the ramblings of a mad priest. Priest of what?

The boy was finally beginning to question the meaning of his life. A life the holy-one constantly claimed for some future possession the boy had no intention of granting. If the holy-one were not so incapacitated by the grand plan, the boy would never dare think such things. But then, perhaps it was not some wordless sin. Perhaps he was entitled to hope.

* * *

TWENTY NINE

"I am still unsure," Netta moaned. "Should we not take Dissa back to Shirall first?"

"Don't worry about the children," Shevron smiled. "They'll be little nomads by the time you get back."

Miyam sighed. She knew they would be safe, especially with Leshma on guard, and there were plenty of other children to play with. But she dreaded leaving Zaviar again. She shared a look with Netta, knowing she felt the same way.

"We can't take the time," Evelar said. "I'm sorry, Netta, but Zelona is the better option."

"I am sure they will be fine," Atwin said, arm about his worried wife. "Certainly they will be safer here than walking into danger with us."

"I do understand, Netta," Miyam said. "Zavvy has changed so much in the few weeks since we left him with you, and I don't want to miss any more."

'Safe, Mama,' the little boy whispered in her mind.

Miyam hugged him closer. "I know."

'Poppy Shevvy nice.'

Miyam giggled in spite of herself.

"What did he say?" asked Shevron.

"He says you're nice. He calls you Poppy Shevvy," she grinned.

Shevron let out a great roar of laughter, making Zaviar giggle in response. "I think I like that," Shevron smiled.

'Papa need go,' Zaviar sent. *'Fix head.'*

It was Evelar's turn to laugh. "Yes, little man, I need to fix my broken head."

"Sir," said Jossep as he ran up to the little group. "The supplies are all packed and the horses loaded up."

"Well done, Joss," said Evelar. "Tell the others we leave directly after the midday snooze."

"Will do, Sir."

As Jossep hurried off, Evelar turned to Netta. "We need to communicate with your aunt in Zelona. Do you think you can lead the spell?"

"Of course. But I will be glad when we take your teachings to Zelona; it would be nice to use mindspeak instead of the communication spell. It is so loud."

"All in good time. We just need to get over this little hump first."

"Let's do it during rest time," said Miyam. "We can gather in our tent without disturbing anyone."

Miyam took one last look at her little boy, sleeping peacefully in the hot tent. Beside him, the little princess snoozed fitfully, and on the other side of the hearth, Sand Mother lounged in her cushions, watching silently. Beside Miyam, Netta bent to kiss her daughter's forehead, and Shedissa sleepily wrapped her arms about her mother's neck. Netta whispered reassurance and she settled again.

Kneeling by Zaviar, Miyam fought the urge to scoop him into her arms. Instead she stroked his hair, kissed his forehead, and heaved herself up. She shared a look with her friend, seeing the tears that mirrored her own. She gave Sand Mother a nod and stumbled from the tent, Netta close on her heels. Outside, Evelar waited, with Atwin by his side.

"Are you alright, my love?" he murmured.

Miyam nodded, not trusting herself to speak. Seeing the

sorrow in his own eyes, she slipped into his arms, letting her tears fall. She tried not to hear Netta sobbing into her husband's chest, her own anguish made more intense at the sound of her friend's sorrow. But she drew a deep breath, straightened her back, and met Evelar's gaze with a smile.

"It's time to go," she said.

"Onward to Zelona," Evelar replied.

Two weeks later, a band of travellers emerged from the desert, followed by a large force of nomad warriors. As they continued further into the cultivated fields, past farmsteads and small villages, they drew stares from the occupants. Nine revealers, accompanied by three others, two of them obviously noble, and a host of warriors rarely seen in a provincial setting, were enough to set tongues wagging and eyes popping.

Outside the great city of Zelona, the nomads pitched their tents and set up camp while the revealers and their friends continued into the town. Leaving the heavily laden horses at the camp, they walked through the outskirts of the city, collecting locals as they went.

The dark blue cloaks of the revealers, their rainbow colours flashing as they flapped in the breeze, brought children running to see them, their excited chatter lending a carnival feel to the whole event. Soon streets were lined with people, staring and pointing, while children ran along behind, waving to their families and friends, turning the usually invisible revealers into the subject of a great parade.

Tineya giggled at the looks of consternation on their faces, enjoying their attempts to cover their surprise with stony masks of calm. Finally, they reached the palace in the middle of the city, arriving at the gate with a crowd of spectators. Atwin stepped up to speak to the guard.

"Would you be so kind as to tell King Lenent that King

Atwin of Drasmil and his wife, Princess Nettayna of Shirall, are here to see him and his lovely queen."

The guard blinked, then bowed and ran off. Turning to face the crowd, Atwin lent back against the bars of the gate with a smirk. The revealers hovered uncertainly, seemingly lost without the chance to melt into the background.

All this attention would be good for them. After all, they wanted to be more visible to the common people, to recruit more members and expand their outsider classes. What better way than a parade through the streets of an isolated city like Zelona.

The revealers and the crowd settled into an uncomfortable silence, returning each other's stares with equal amounts of bewilderment and awe. But before too long the guard returned and opened the gate. The crowd closed in, only to be growled at by the guard as the travellers slipped through into the relative peace of the palace courtyard, where a page hurried to meet them.

"If you would follow me, Your Majesty," the boy squeaked.

The travellers allowed the page to lead them into the palace, passing the great hall and into the private corridors behind. At a large oaken door, the boy raised a trembling hand to knock. At a sound from within, he swung the door wide and signalled for the group to enter. As they filed in, the page pulled the door closed and left them alone with the King of Zelona.

"Welcome, my friends," said King Lenent. "Come, sit, enjoy some refreshment. My wife will be along soon."

The travellers arranged themselves on couches and chairs that had been placed about the large sitting room, while servants offered glasses of wine and plates of savoury treats.

"Thank you, Your Majesty," Atwin smiled.

"Think nothing of it, Your Majesty," said Lenent with a

lopsided grin. "I welcome you to my humble city."

"How is my aunt, Your Majesty?" said Netta.

"Oh, you shall see, Your Majesty. Or..." he hesitated. "Do you prefer Your Highness? I never quite know how to deal with double titles like yours."

"I prefer to use the title of my birthright," Netta smiled. "I am not quite ready to be a majesty yet."

"Then highness it is," Lenent grinned. "And here is my beautiful bride."

He jumped up to take his wife's hand as she entered, smiling broadly. The Queen moved slowly toward the group, one hand pressed to her back as her enormous belly preceded her. Netta gasped, rising quickly to rush to her aunt's side.

"Oh, Aunt Averil, how wonderful!" she gushed.

The King led her to a hard chair beside his couch and helped her to sit.

"Forgive me if I do not join you in comfort," the Queen said. "I find I cannot rise once I land in one of those soft couches."

"When are you due?" said Netta.

"My time is almost upon me, my dear," the Queen smiled. "An heir for my dearest Len at last."

"I would be happy to live out my days with you, heir or not, my heart," Lenent smiled.

"Still, we had worried that we may have left it too late," Averil said. "I am glad to be finally giving Len the family I denied him for so long."

"You had other responsibilities, my heart. We always knew we were in for a long wait."

"I am so happy for you," Netta smiled. "Kandi will be so pleased. I am surprised she did not tell me."

"My daughter has had her own troubles. She is lucky to have such a loving husband in Calib. But she will be here to meet her new brother within the month," said Averil. "And how long will you stay?"

"Not long, your majesty," Atwin said. "I am afraid we must be away on the morning tide. If the ship is ready?"

"All provisioned and awaiting your embarkation," Lenent replied. "But please, stay for the evening meal at least."

"We would be honoured, Your Majesty," said Netta with a smile.

It seemed a lifetime since Ontaro stood on the dock, staring out over the great water for only the second time in his life. His ancestors had called it the Water of Wonder. The last time he had gazed upon it, the bounty of such a wide expanse had filled him with awe. But this time he knew the truth, that this water was as desolate as the sands of his homeland, undrinkable and virtually impassible.

His men had gathered behind him, some staring with that same awe while others, veterans of the kalkar war, gazed on it with hardened eyes. It had been a struggle to convince the younger men that the insignificant craft would carry them in safety.

After sailing for two weeks in the direction of the rising sun, it was a relief to see land stretching along the horizon at daybreak. Two weeks of sickness and indignity in the stifling hot hold, with no access to fresh water beyond what had been stowed aboard.

For nomads used to rationing water, it should have been an easy voyage, but the fear of never finding land, the awareness that their intimate knowledge of fresh water and where to find it was no use there, had worn heavily on the men.

The ship pulled into a secluded bay as sunrise slanted across the bow. And there to greet them as the blazing sun broke over the water, a line of steaming figures stood like statues in silhouette across the top of the headland, their covered faces turned toward the inbound ship. Ontaro shivered, his memory of the creatures still fresh and raw. Too many had lost their lives to those demons.

"Kalkar!" someone whispered.

"What now?" groaned another. "We can't fight them. Can we?"

"It's daylight. We can get past them while they are dormant," Ontaro said.

"No need," said Evelar. "They are our allies now."

"Then why are they lined up waiting for us?" the first speaker snarled.

"Why if not to kill us, repel our invasion?" another man replied.

"To welcome us," said Evelar.

Ontaro frowned. Evelar might be kin, but he was still a stranger to most of the men. His life had taken him far from the people. Yet, he was a warrior of great renown in his chosen home, and no matter how far he had strayed, he was still the son of Shevron.

"I choose to trust you, son of my cousin," Ontaro intoned. "Do not make me regret my trust."

As the ship cast anchor in the bay, longboats were put over the side and the long process of ferrying passengers to shore began. The first to disembark were the nomad scouts, hand picked for their skill in tracking. Each group to make landfall took on tasks to set up camp, gathering firewood, foraging for food, clearing scrub for a campsite. Only when all the nomads were safely ashore did the revealers make the trip.

"Do they always do that?" Tineya shivered. "Gaze down on you like sentinels at the gates of hell?"

"They are merely announcing their presence," said Miyam. "They could blend into the landscape and you would never see them, but they choose to show themselves."

"Seems more threatening than reassuring to me."

"I know it seems that way," Nashta said, slipping an arm about her waist. "But Miyam is right. They are at their most vulnerable when they sleep."

"I know more than most how threatening their theatrics can be," said Netta with a smile. "But in this case, there is no threat intended."

"How can you know that?"

"Because they are telling us," said Nashta. "Open your mind, Tinny."

"The kalkar have a psychic link that joins them all together," said Miyam. "Their individual minds are subsumed in a group consciousness with one overriding thought. Right now, that thought is a song of welcome."

Tineya closed her eyes to concentrate. "It's beautiful," she whispered.

"So what do we do now?" said Reeperly, joining the group with his wife Berkana in tow.

"We wait, and we rest," said Evelar. "When they wake, we talk."

The flames licked the treetops, roaring their anger to the night sky. The people ran, leaving everything behind. The man grabbed his woman's arm, dragging her along despite her protests, her gasping breath tearing at his heart as she clutched her rounded belly with her free hand.

Behind them the town burned, the demon fire eating at everything. Above, huge dark shapes swooped over the fleeing colonists on membranous wings. Who could have known that the demons could fly?

The fire creatures had been vanquished, banished to the last bastion of their habitat, collecting in such numbers that the land beneath them turned to sand. But now they fought back, destroying everything the colonists had built. They had been so blind, thinking they could renounce their technology and live off the land.

With such a native threat, there should have been a system in place for their own protection. But nobody had dreamed they would fight back in such an organised assault. And now they ran for their lives, praying only to stay alive until sunrise.

His eyes snapped open as his breath gasped out. He sat up, glancing at the woman by his side before staring out at the red fire of sunset over the ocean. He felt her hand on his arm, her breath on his neck.

"What's wrong?" she whispered.

"Just a dream, my love. An ancient memory."

"But Evelar, I thought he was gone."

"His memories are still there, ready to surface at any time. I never know when something might trigger them. He really suffered at the hands of the kalkar."

"Will we ever be free of him?"

"I don't know." Evelar smiled at his wife, smoothing her frown with a gentle finger, seeing the glow of the sunset reflected in her eyes.

"We should make our way up the hill," he said. "It's time to talk to the kalkar."

On top of the bluff, surrounded by sizzling statues that gave off enough heat to warm the air around them, the revealers waited for the last gasp of the sun. One last shaft of light flickered through the clouds and was gone, leaving only the half-light of dusk, and the cliffs echoed with a loud crackle of sound.

The steaming figures began to move, bony hands spreading enfolding wings, and lifting hoods of membranous skin, to reveal scaly, alien faces. The thin fabric of wings and hood settled in a fall of flesh, looking for all the world like a heavy cloak.

Two of the creatures stepped forward, and the larger male spoke in fluent human, though with a throaty rasp.

"We welcome you to our homeland, Awakener."

"We thank you for your welcome," said Evelar. "And vow to leave your land in peace when our present task is done."

"We thank you for your vow. I am Seven Supprack Asfar." He signalled to the female by his side. "I believe you already know my mate."

"I greet you, Four Zjobock Dhort," Evelar smiled.

"Thank you," the female rasped. "And I welcome you."

"Your voice!" Miyam cried. "You allowed your throat to be cut."

"Yes, Miyam," the female said. "It is our way. And with Seven Supprack Asfar I had nothing to fear in the mating ritual. He is the mate of my choosing and he would not fatally wound me."

"Then I am glad for you."

"I thank you. And now we must discuss the reason for your visit."

"Some days ago," said Seven. "We discovered a large band of humans. They landed near here, and travelled across the plain toward the sun of sleep."

"Still moving east," Evelar nodded. "Tineya, is that where the pull takes you?"

The girl frowned. "I believe so. I cannot be sure without waking Fransi. I'd rather not, if you don't mind."

Evelar chuckled. "I can quite understand that."

"Why would they go east?" asked Miyam. "There are only the mountains, and the hatching caves."

"You only travelled as far as the caves the last time you were here," Four said. "But there is land beyond our home, more plains where the sun heralds our sleep."

"And," said Seven. "There are humans."

"There are?" said Nashta with a frown. "Since when?"

"Almost as long as there have been humans on our world. But they fester and fail, not prospering like your people at all. Just one small city full of decay."

"Fransi's memories are full of this place," said Tineya.

"I knew they came a long way," said Nashta. "But what power could send them so very far?"

"We believe it is also the home of the one we once called the Leader," said Four.

Miyam nodded. "That makes sense. The Leader is behind the migration you saw, though It is known as the Master now."

"Ah," said Seven. "Then we offer ourselves, to help in any way we can."

"Are you sure you want to expose yourselves to the Leader once more?"

"We can do no better service to our race than to eliminate the dreaded Leader once and for all."

* * *

THIRTY

The reborn army forged ahead, climbing high into the mountain spine of their homeland with eager anticipation. Soon they would be home, the Master would restore them to full possession of their new bodies, and they would reunite with their lost families to build a new, pain free life.

But Antoni shepherded his human flock against increasing resistance and a frustration that sapped his strength and took his sanity. He worried that the mountain pass might spell the end of his control over the mob.

"Sir, we need to rest. Please."

"Move it!" he snapped.

"But sir, we can't. The Master calls, but our vessels won't cooperate."

Antoni turned on the man. "If you want to fight the enemy here in the mountains, go ahead, but you'll never make it to Stolen City. He'll pick us off one by one."

The whispering rippled back through the ranks, each individual passing it on. Occasionally it stopped.

"I can't go on," a nameless reborn would cry. "My feet won't move."

"But the Master pulls, just never lets up."

"The Master promised. Just keep moving."

And by some miracle they did. But the tearing feeling deep within grew stronger with every day. Finally, the high pass was behind them and the travel became easier. The Master's iron fist closed about the hearts of the reborn, and their bodily desire to confront the keeper of their rival souls eased. They could almost smell the city now, and the downhill path was surprisingly smooth and well kept.

"I've heard about the mountain road," one man murmured. "Never thought it was real though."

"Still want to wait for the enemy?" Antoni snarled.

"Oh no, sir, he can wait. I want to see my family."

* * *

Evelar sat his horse with a vacant stare, eyes focused on nothing while the voices in his head urged him onward. The grey mountains loomed ahead, their snow covered peaks lost in the cloud. It seemed they were always in shadow now. But the lost souls knew the source of the hooks was close.

'It's getting closer now. Please, hurry, let me find it. Give me my life!'

Evelar pressed his hands to his ears in an attempt to silence the crowd. He felt Miyam's hand on his arm and an instant calm washed over him. He pushed the voices down and smiled at his wife.

"Thank you, my love," he sighed. "Every step brings us closer to the possessed."

"I just hope we're not walking into trouble," she replied. "Every time we get close I lose you."

"There's no Sandman to take over now, so long as I stay away from that amulet."

"I don't know," she sighed. "I have a feeling he has one more card to play."

"What could he do? We don't need him now."

"Don't we? We still don't know how to control the amulet, nor how to get those souls back into their bodies."

"We neutralise Kayus, the possessions are severed, and then we free the souls. What is there to know?"

Miyam frowned. "I think you're too confident. Or perhaps

that's a front. You don't need to hide your worry from me."

"I know, my love. But perhaps I need to hide it from myself."

* * *

The boy paced the floor, stopping after each lap to stare out the tiny window at the city below. Somewhere down there, the reborn were massing, looking for a way into the city. Then they would come to their master, searching for their salvation. The boy shivered, wishing he could shake the feeling of unease.

Those poor souls, trapped in a prison of the Master's making, no way to escape and no hope of getting their lives back. Their bodies stolen and their minds driven mad by the urge to find a way home.

If the holy-one's plan came to pass, the boy would be possessed in just the same way, but he would be trapped still within his own body, a slave to the Master. He did not want to die.

A pulse of energy hit him, a commanding thought. *'Comest thou here, boy.'*

His mind rebelled, but his body followed the Master's call and his feet moved of their own accord. He shuffled forward, blinking at the light from all the amulets, toward the great bulk lying on the bed.

'Take it,' the holy-one thought at him. *'Takest thou the amulet and give thyself to my future.'*

The boy whimpered, desperate to escape but compelled to act. He knew which amulet it was, had dreaded this moment his whole life. The holy-one wanted access to his body, now that the amulets weighed the old body down, keeping it immobile. The boy shook his head, fighting the force that drove him onward. He watched his hands reach out and select one particular chain and lift it off the holy-one's neck.

'Thou art a good boy,' the holy-one thought. *'It will soon be time for thee to give they life.'*

The boy shivered at the power of the thought. He had no hope of resisting, his life-long training too strong to break. But he would not give in without a fight.

If the holy-one wanted his life he would have to take it by force. Nevertheless, his fingers spread the chain, and his hands draped it over his own neck. The great mind of the Master cackled its way into his brain, taking up residence in the very centre of his being. And the memories flooded in.

* * *

The slums of Stolen City squatted along the valley floor, surrounded by rolling hills and terraced pastures. The reborn gathered on the crest of a rise, staring down at their long lost home. The holy-one had been right. Here they were, in perfect new bodies, alive and well and home at last. A great cry rang out, hundreds of voices shouting their joy.

They surged down the hill, oblivious to the startled stares of the field workers, plunging into the streets like an invading horde against an unprotected foe. Antoni let them go. He had no right to hold them now.

Heading slowly into the city, Antoni drank in the sights of home. The dirty streets, the tumbledown houses, the beggars in their rags. Everyone was a beggar there, yet somehow he noticed the squalor now. His feet took him down into the darkest corner of the city, where people existed cheek by jowl in lean-to shacks built one on top of another.

Children scurried past on shortened legs, or crab-walked on stumps. Young women stared out of bent faces with barrel bodies, their hands pointing with missing fingers. Men moved to guard their women, and Antoni suddenly realised how strange he must seem to them, with his perfect new body. Why had he never noticed the pain in their faces?

He had been so caught up in his own despairing life, he had ignored the people around him. Finally, he turned a corner and approached a nondescript shack built onto the end wall of a tenement block. He paused as a young girl clambered out of the shelter on hands and knees, and settled outside the shack to begin tearing at a bundle of reeds, making strips for her half-finished basket.

Her stubby fingers fumbled with the grasses, and she took hold of a reed with her teeth to split the end, pulling at it to tear it lengthwise. The girl ignored the cuts to her fingers and the corner of her mouth, laying the reeds in a neat pile beside her work.

"I thought I told you to use the mouthguard and gloves I made for you," Antoni sighed.

The girl looked up, her mismatched eyes showing her confusion as she jutted out her already pointy chin.

"Who are you?" she accused. "Don't come any closer or I'll call my husband."

"Husband? You're ten!"

"Well, not husband yet. But he will be when I'm old enough. He protects me and everyone knows I'm his, so back off."

"But it's me, it's Papa."

Her eyes narrowed, and her thin mouth almost disappeared behind her chin.

"My papa is dead."

"But I've come back, just as the holy-one promised."

She snorted her derision. "Nobody believes that. It's just a hope for the dying, to ease their suffering."

Antoni sidled closer. "You used to believe it. Look at me. It's true, Sami. Ask me anything."

She cocked her head. "What did my papa tell me just before the holy-one came for him?"

"I said… 'Look to the hills, every morning, and one day I will come'."

"Anyone could have told you that. Anyone could have heard it and told you what to say."

"Then why ask me? Is there nothing that will convince you?"

"My papa is dead," she snapped. "And so are you!"

Antoni felt hands on his arms, lifting him off his feet. He cried out in pain as the scars down his left arm pulled, the hair-thread stitches ripping into the festering skin. He flailed his legs, but his captor held him in a grip of iron.

"What do you think you're doing?" a man growled in a thick, heavy voice. "That girl is mine."

"I…I'm her father, I swear."

The man tossed him like a sack, and he landed with a painful crunch. He clutched at his trophy cuts and his hand came away bloody. The man came after him, thickly muscled arms ready to throw him again, but Antoni scurried out of his reach and ran.

* * *

The battered town sprawled along the river like a miasma. It reached its fingers of corruption out into the denuded landscape, encroaching on the sickly crops. People worked in the fields, tilling the soil with a slow shuffle, even the oxen behind the plough seeming to drag their feet. The closer they came, the more wrong the people seemed.

"Those poor people," Navear moaned.

"Why are they like that?" Jossep replied.

"It looks like inbreeding," said Reeperly. "But on a massive scale."

"It's the only town we've seen anywhere on this continent," said Jumally. "Perhaps these are the only humans here."

"We'll have to wait for the kalkar," said Miyam. "Ask

them if they know of any others."

"Tinny," said Nashta. "Can you speak to Fransi?"

Tineya shivered. "Must I? She won't cooperate. She wants me gone."

"We need to know what we are walking into, and Evelar is busy with his own demons."

"Please," said Miyam. "Only you can help us."

Tineya sighed. "Alright, I'll try."

She closed her eyes and the others watched as she concentrated. Then her eyes snapped open.

"What do you want to know?" she snarled.

"Don't be like that, Fransi," said Nashta.

"Why shouldn't I? You pushed me aside, got rid of me so you could be with your little piece of fluff."

"Fransi, are you going to help me or not?"

Fransi frowned. "Alright, but only because I can't refuse you, Nashta."

"Thank you," he smiled. "Who are these people and why are they how they are?"

"I don't understand."

"You know, all wrong, deformed and sick."

"They are?" Fransi said, genuinely surprised. "Well, I suppose they are. I never noticed it before."

"How could you not notice?"

"They're normal! Well, normal for us. Everyone is like that, it's how we lived. Why do you think we wanted new bodies?"

"But why?" Reeperly said. "What caused it?"

"It was the holy-one. The Master. Constantly growing new copies but getting it wrong. Almost every man in Stolen City is a copy of the holy-one gone wrong. They are born in the citadel, but the ones that turn out damaged are expelled into the city, where they live out their lives, having damaged families and passing on their deformities. Every generation gets worse."

"So... the inbreeding is compounded by the high number of copies," said Reeperly. "Being damaged, they add their problems to the already depleted stock."

"It's terrible," said Tikki. "How can anyone live like that?"

"When it's all you know," said Fransi. "What else can you do? The holy-one offered hope, and new bodies."

"I think I understand now," said Nashta. "Thank you Fransi. You may go now."

"But... No, I don't want to go!"

"Please, Fransi, you know my world is not yours. We will find your salvation, I promise."

"But then I can't be with you," she moaned.

"Fransi, you know this has to be."

"I can't say no to you," she sobbed. "You're cruel."

Then she closed her eyes and when they opened again Tineya was back, looking about in bewilderment.

"Let's camp here," said Miyam. "Wait for the kalkar to catch up. I don't think I'm ready to face that city."

Outside the rotting city, the nomads formed ranks in front of the kalkar. With no firelight to guide them, they thanked the full moon for lighting their way in the darkness. In their midst, the revealers prepared to head into the town, Fransi ready to lead them, Netta and Atwin ready to offer their amulet power.

To one side, Evelar stood silent, eyes glazed over as he stared into the darkness, just an occasional twitch showing that he still breathed. And in the outskirts of the city, a force stared back, all the possessed lined up to accept their nemesis.

"Now remember," said Nashta. "You warriors are a distraction, to draw the defenders out here while we infiltrate the fortress."

"Use the kalkar as a last defense," said Miyam. "They will be dormant, unable to actively fight, but they are formidable even in that state."

"Fear alone will keep the townsfolk at bay," Reeperly added.

"And please," said Miyam. "Try not to kill any of the possessed. Every death is one more soul without a body to return to."

In the half-light of approaching dawn, they watched as the city came to life. People stumbled out of their hovels to go about their business, some heading out to the fields, where they passed the newcomers with barely a glance.

But a few noticed, and one or two turned to shuffle-hurry back into the town. Those people brought more to gawk at the gathered warriors. Leading the big stallion, Lumen, Miyam approached the Awakener, and he mounted mechanically. Pulling herself up behind him, she whispered into his chaotic mind.

'Are you ready?'

'Yes, my love.'

"Let's move," she said aloud to her companions.

As the sun rose behind the city, twelve invaders rode into the dawn. Using the shadows, they passed the people of the city, moving slowly through the streets toward the central tower and its surrounding citadel.

Behind them, the possessed turned their heads, sensing their departure from the coming battle. Their feet began to move, their minds battling with their bodies. Torn between the mission to dispose of the vessel and their beloved families who rushed out to meet the invading warriors, they vacillated.

With a heavy heart, Ontaro gave the order to attack. The people stumbled back before the charge and the possessed turned away from the enemy to join their loved ones in protecting the city.

Unaware that their own humanity had turned them from their master's call, the possessed joined the battle, ready to defend the only home they knew, for the future of their families and their new lives.

THIRTY ONE

The possessed and the deformed, an uneasy alliance of fear, stood trembling as the invading warriors charged. One man yelled his defiance, and the ragtag army replied with a whimper of terror.

The man yelled again, calling on their desire for freedom and a better life. The possessed took control of the townspeople, dragging them into the fray. And then the warriors were on them, stabbing with their spears and slashing with their knives. The defenders fell back under the onslaught, screaming in their terror. The nomads pushed forward, right into the city streets.

"Stand your ground!" someone yelled.

But the townsmen paid him no heed. Stumbling over each other in their desire to get away, they pushed through the ranks of the possessed, ignoring the grasping hands of people who claimed to be their lost kin.

"Think about your children back there in your hovels," the leader of the possessed cried. "Think about your old people, unable to fight. Protect them now."

"What do you think we're doing, you fool?" a voice came from the fleeing crowd.

The inhabitants of the city disappeared into the maze of streets, ignoring the cries of the crazy man who would get them all killed. Antoni rounded on the ranks of the possessed, milling about in confusion at the cowardice of the townspeople. He snarled his anger into their faces.

"If you want to see your families live another day, turn about and chase those nomad dogs out of our city!"

The possessed let out a cheer. And the nomads paused in their advance.

"They falter!" cried Antoni. "Now push them back. Take back our home."

The possessed surged at the invader, closing in to engage them one on one. But wherever they turned, the warriors refused to meet their challenge.

"Remember your orders," their leader cried.

And in response, Antoni yelled victory to his possessed army. "They don't want to fight! Get after them!"

The warriors no longer had the advantage of courage, and the defenders had the superior numbers. Lifting his great horn, the nomad leader sounded a loud blast. As one, his men fell back, peeling off to the sides to reform ranks behind the smoking line of kalkar.

The creatures stood immobile, smoke rising in the morning sunlight, lending a tang to the air. The possessed pulled up short against the sizzling wall, the creatures forming an impenetrable barrier behind which the nomads huddled.

"Sir, we should be out there fighting," a warrior snarled.

"You know our orders," Ontaro snapped. "Nobody dies. Let the kalkar do their part."

"But what can they do? They're asleep."

Hearing the exchange from his place in front of the kalkar wall, Antoni let out a laugh of triumph.

"They refuse to fight! And these things are no match for us. Take them down!"

Two men willingly stepped forward and placed hands on one of the sizzling creatures. But even as they pushed, the smoke engulfed them and screams rang out over the field.

"No!" cried Ontaro. "You'll be killed."

Antoni watched in fascination as the men's hands turned black. The skin bubbled off their fingers and the smell of burnt flesh filled the air. Watching avidly, actually seeing the event as it happened this time, Antoni held his breath, taking it all in. Blackened beyond recognition, the bodies fell at the feet of the creature they had tried to attack.

With a hand raised in the air, Antoni called off his possessed, and they settled back to stare at the horror before them. Stepping in close, Antoni breathed deeply, sucking in the acrid smoke. He bent to rub his hands in the blackened flesh of the men, collecting the ash for his next cuts.

* * *

Somewhere in the bowels of the city, a small group approached the citadel of the holy-one. As the narrow suburban streets, with their foetid gutters and rotting hovels, gave way to wider avenues of stunted trees and cobbled pavements, they began to think they might win through. But ahead, an unholy force gathered, ready to repel them.

Men with bent faces and stumps for limbs. Men with blind eyes or screaming minds. Men with such pain in their expression. And yet, somewhere behind the deformities, every face was the same.

'Time to fight,' Miyam whispered into her husband's mind.

Evelar lifted his head, clasped the hilt of his sword and pulled. Raising it above his head he kicked in with his heels and led the charge. Riding behind him, Miyam drew with her left hand and held him about the waist with the other, and together they ploughed into the waiting copies.

The rest of the company joined the fray, hacking at the defenders from horseback. The defenders fought back with bare hands and carving knives, their faces twisted in righteous fervour. But they were no match for a well-trained company of revealers.

Leaving the decimated defenders behind, the company moved on toward the citadel wall, faces grim as they hid their sorrow behind the placid mask of the revealer at work. Approaching the nondescript plate-iron gate, they expected a challenge, but there was no guard. Miyam searched for a lock or a handle, but there seemed no way to open it.

"Why don't we just break it down?" said Nashta.

Suiting action to word, he rushed at the gate, shoulder at the ready.

"Wait!" Miyam cried.

But her warning came too late. Nashta hit the metal with a sickening crunch, and was thrown back by an invisible force. He landed some ten feet back from the wall and lay groaning as Tineya rushed to his aid.

"There's a psychic lock, you fool!" Reeperly cried. "Didn't you feel it?"

Nashta let out another groan. Shaking her head, Miyam stepped up to the gate. She ran her fingers gently over the smooth metal panel, searching for a clue to the opening mechanism. She frowned, playing with a small section near the centre.

"Netta," she said. "What do you think of this?"

The Princess stepped up and felt where she indicated.

"A depression," she nodded. "Round, about the size of an amulet?"

"That's what I thought. Do you think you could open it?"

"I can try."

Netta drew out her amulet and stepped in close to the metal gate, pressing the charm into the barely visible depression. She closed her eyes and concentrated, but nothing happened. She stepped back, shaking her head.

"The amulet fits, but something is not right. Something is missing."

Evelar let out a long sigh, his habitual mask hiding his true feelings. Miyam moved to stand before him, searching his face.

"What is it?" she murmured. "Evelar?"

"It's an ancient lock," he sighed, his voice seeming to come from very far away. "This citadel is stolen technology. It is the landing craft that brought them down from the sky ship. Only a few souls are able to open it."

"I don't like the sound of that," Miyam said. "How does it work?"

"An amulet," he replied. "Carried by the matching physical body, and the mature mind. All three are needed to open it. But not just any mind. Only members of the original crew of the colony ship that brought them here."

"We can arrange that," said Reeperly, digging into his pack. "We have this."

He held out the Sandman's amulet. Evelar took an involuntary step backward as the gold flashed in the sunlight.

"Reep, put that thing away," Miyam snapped.

"I'm sorry, Mym," said Reeperly. "But this is what is needed. Without the Sandman we can't get in, and our whole mission is lost."

"We allow the Sandman to return and we lose Evelar. And he'll never let go."

"We subdued him before. We can again."

"No!" Miyam cried. "I won't allow it."

"Mym," said Evelar softly. "Reep is right."

Miyam rounded on him. "No! You can't let him back in, Evelar."

"I don't want to. But I don't think I have a choice."

Miyam shook her head, tears threatening to spill over.

"I can't lose you again," she sobbed.

"I need to get these voices out of my head. The answer is inside this citadel. We have to get in, and we need the Sandman to do it."

Miyam jumped at a hand on her shoulder. "I know it's difficult," said Jumally at her ear. "But he's trying to do the right thing. We're all here for you, and we won't let the Sandman win."

Miyam drew a shuddering breath. She stared into her husband's brown eyes, filled with love for her. He reached out to touch her face, to brush the tears away. Then she fell into his arms, clutching at him as she sobbed her despair into his chest.

'Everything will be alright, my love,' he thought into her mind. *'I promise.'*

Then he pulled back, reaching out to take the amulet from his friend's grasp. The change was instant. As the presence in the amulet whispered at him, he lifted the chain to drop it about his neck, letting the golden charm rest against his chest. The amulet flared blue for a moment, then his eyes flashed gold and the laugh of the Sandman burst from his mouth.

"So," he cackled. "Thou hast chosen to give me my freedom."

"Only for a moment," Miyam snapped. "We need you to open this door."

"And why wouldst thou think I might do so? Thou hast cast me out, refused me my right."

"Behind that door is your greatest enemy," Miyam said.

"True?" he exclaimed, raising one eyebrow. "Well now, forsooth, that doth change everything."

The Sandman stepped up to the door, lifted the amulet and pressed it to the depression. A blue light engulfed him, shimmering in the sunlight. A soft note sounded in the air, and then the metal gate slid sideways to disappear into the wall.

Ahead lay a long white tunnel, lit along its roof at intervals by bright white lights. The Sandman stepped inside without hesitation, and strode into the strange citadel. Leaving the horses tethered outside, the rest of the companions followed in trepidation.

The strange white building was bathed in silence. Not a sound disturbed the echoes as the companions followed the Sandman through twisting corridors that seemed to double back on themselves and take them further backward than forward with each step.

No guards rushed to detain them, no shouts of alert put an end to their passage. The winding tunnels seemed to lead them deeper into the building, yet she sensed that they travelled a very short distance in reality.

Miyam glanced about nervously, but forced herself to trust that the Sandman knew what he was doing. The building seemed familiar, like she had been here before, but that was impossible. Although she had been somewhere like this, when she was taken up to the home of the forgotten spirits at the end of the kalkar war, when Evelar had been killed and she had called him back to life. She had almost forgotten, and now she realised that place had been a colony ship such as this.

Finally they reached the inner most chamber. The Sandman burst in without ceremony, setting off no alarms and finding no resistance. In a corner of the room, an enormous body lay still, completely buried under the weight of hundreds of amulets, shimmering in the harsh white light. In front of the body stood a small boy.

"So, Kay, thou hast fashioned thyself a new vessel and thou hast possessed it too soon. Just as thou art wont to do."

"And thou, Sandman, hast taken thy body too late. Thy vessel hath been a worthy adversary. Art thou as worthy?"

"Whyfore hast thou done this? Thou hast taken the soul-tech that was rightfully thy fellows', denied them of rebirth and taken their hope for future generations."

"Thy precious colony was doomed, Sandman. They were blind and I did choose my own path with those enlightened souls that did follow me."

"Thy path hast led thee down the road to corruption and extinction. Thy Stolen City teeters on the brink of ruin and thou dost sit here capturing souls."

"I did attempt to reward them, to give them the lives they did deserve."

"Thou did so under false pretense. Thy flawed reason hast deluded thee."

"And thy trust hast led thee into despair."

With that, the face of the boy twisted, and the revealers felt the surge of energy as Kayus struck out with his mind. The Sandman crumpled, hands clutched to his head. The boy Kayus struck again, and again, the sheer power of the mental blast sending the Sandman sliding along the floor to strike against the far wall.

Then the maniacal laugh of Kayus erupted from the boy's young mouth. Miyam knelt by the Sandman, reaching into his mind to bring him back to consciousness. The voices were silent, but somewhere inside, Evelar waited.

"Sandman, you need to let him out."

The Sandman shook his head stubbornly.

"You don't have the training," Miyam pleaded. "You can't fight Kayus, but Evelar can."

The Sandman let out a sharp breath, then gave a curt nod. Then Evelar looked out at his wife with his warm brown eyes. Miyam smiled and helped him to his feet. Behind them, the laughter of Kayus grew more and more insane.

"I welcome thee, Awakener," the boy said.

Taking his wife's hand, Evelar turned to face his enemy. Behind him, his companions took positions, joining hands to enhance their connection. They willingly offered their minds to their hero and as he harnessed their power, the enemy struck again.

This time, the power crackled in the air but the Awakener did not falter. He struck back, and it was the boy's turn to reel away from the blast. Kayus rallied, and sent out a new barrage of mental agony, but Evelar blocked the attack and parried with a blast of his own. For what seemed an age, they traded blows, but soon the boy's body began to falter.

"Stop," Miyam cried. "The poor child is suffering."

"That child is Kayus!"

"No, he's a child possessed by Kayus."

"You're right, my love. Let me try something else."

He gathered his allies together, and as Kayus rallied for another blow, he sent a tendril of thought deep into the boy's mind, searching for the subdued consciousness of the child.

'Help me!' a tiny voice whispered.

'We'll help you,' Evelar called. *'Come to us.'*

The boy came, full of joy at his rescuers. There in the silence of the child's mind, Evelar told him what to do. And he happily skipped off to do it. Withdrawing from the mind of the child, the revealers gathered their power to strike at the enemy, blow after blow, sending the little body reeling back to land against the wall, unconscious.

Then something amazing happened. The boy opened his eyes and smiled, pulling off his amulet. He slipped it over the head of the holy-one on the bed, and the huge body awoke, the voice of kayus growling its rage. The room crackled with power as Kayus gathered all his strength for a massive strike.

"Cut away the amulets!" cried the boy. "Quickly."

Atwin stepped forward, sword drawn. He slipped its point under the gold chains and severed them, ten at a time. Netta stepped in and swept them onto the floor as he cut them.

With each cut, the voice of Kayus screamed, nonsensical words spurting out in a stream of vitriol. By the time the last of the amulets were removed, the only sound from the mouth of the holy-one was a mindless babbling, punctuated with cries of trapped souls.

"She's gone!" cried Tineya. "I'm me, all alone, no Fransi whispering at me!"

She threw herself at Nashta and he grabbed her up, swinging her about in celebration.

"What happened?" Miyam gasped.

"The threads are cut," the boy said. "The souls the Master collected have come back, and now they are all inside the Master's head with no way to get out."

"How did you know it would do that?"

"I have watched the Master my whole life. I know everything."

THIRTY TWO

The boy scurried away from his old master, hiding behind his saviours. The holy-one screamed his rage and, relieved of the burden of amulets, tried to rise. But the corpulent body resisted and the trapped souls clamoured, and the holy-one fell back in exhaustion. The boy whimpered in fear.

"Come on," Reeperly sighed. "Let's leave It to Its misery."

"Take the amulets," cried the boy. "Don't leave them where the Master can get them."

As the rescuers gathered up the golden charms like so much treasure, filling their packs with them, the boy hurried to the back wall and opened a concealed cupboard, taking out more amulets and stuffing them in a sack he had produced as if by magic.

"Let's go," he gasped. "Please, hurry!"

Strange cries and grunts came from the lump on the bed, voices talking over each other in an attempt to be heard. Beneath them, the voice of Kayus screamed for silence and was ignored. The companions hurried from the room, carrying their treasure with them.

The boy led them through the corridors, around corners on a twisting course through the maze until they finally reached the outer door. Rushing out into the sunlight, they mounted the horses and headed away from the citadel, its open gate yawning balefully at them as they left.

Outside the citadel, a host of vacant people hovered,

staring without seeing, standing without moving, appearing to wait for something, yet completely unconscious. And then the Awakener began to scream, the voices of the lost souls crying out of his mouth at the proximity of their now empty bodies.

"Help us! Set us free! Our bodies are waiting!"

"They look like they were heading toward the citadel," Reeperly mused. "Do you think they realised the Master was under attack?"

"It looks like they were on their way," Jumally said. "Perhaps their master was calling for help."

"But they didn't get there," said Tikki.

"They are no longer possessed," said Jossep. "When the souls were pulled back to the Master these bodies reverted to their waking coma."

"But what do we do now?" said Miyam. "Evelar?"

But the Awakener was unresponsive, hands over ears. Miyam slipped down and helped him to the ground, where he sank in a heap, rolling about in agony as the trapped souls yelled for freedom.

"Wait a minute," said Nashta. "We have all these amulets. Remember how the Sandman freed Tineya?"

"Let's get back to the camp and see what we can do," said Miyam. "We'll send the nomads up here to herd these people."

"And what about Kayus?" said Reeperly.

"I think I know what to do," said Miyam with a wink.

Miyam watched as her friends carefully carried Evelar into the tent, then hurried to meet Ontaro and his captains. She explained the situation and he immediately delegated a team to bring the empty bodies out of the city. Then she stared out toward the mountains and the setting sun beyond, waiting for the kalkar to wake.

She walked along the sizzling line, searching for a familiar form, a difficult task with their hood flaps covering their faces. Standing before the one she thought was the individual she sought, she stood vigil. As the shadows lengthened, she stood as immobile as the kalkar.

Finally, the last shaft of light blinked from the sky, leaving the half-light of dusk. In a wave of crackling sound, the kalkar came to life. Clawed hands reached for hood flaps to push them back from scaled faces, phosphorescent markings glowing out in the fading light, every one individual. Flaccid skin membranes pumped full of acidic ichor to spread out wide as delicately thin wings, then slowly deflated again to fall about skeletal bodies like a cloak of skin.

"Miyam," said the individual before her.

"Four Zjobock Dhort," Miyam smiled. "I have a favour to ask."

"We are here to help," Four said in a raspy yet somehow feminine voice.

"In the city there is a citadel, a place of metal and lights, cold and unwelcoming. Within is a collection of corridors and rooms hiding all kinds of unfathomable things. Things that pose a threat to our very way of life, if they were to fall once more into the wrong hands. For our own safety, we need those things destroyed."

"We will smote them with our fire."

"Burn the white citadel and all it contains. But let the city be."

"We shall do as you say."

Miyam smiled. "Also within you will find an individual, a human of sorts. It was once your dreaded Leader."

"We shall smote It also," Four snarled.

"No. It is mad, and dangerous, but without its technology it will be a threat no more. Frighten It, but let It survive.

Chase It out into Its corrupted city, but let none of Its possessions go with It."

"It shall be done."

"Do this, and you shall be freed of your debt to us. Your people will be redeemed in our eyes and our alliance will be equal from this day forth."

"We accept your terms, Miyam of the humans. And we thank you for this chance to call you friend."

In the cacophony of his mind, Evelar flitted about, trying to calm the trapped souls. But the noise only grew louder and more insistent. Somewhere another voice laughed in triumph. He felt himself carried along on the tide of emotion, a great wave of hope and eager anticipation as the souls realised their bodies were close and free.

But their enthusiasm proved even more distracting than their despair, and no matter how he fought he could not gain control over their thoughts. The souls of the victims could sense their bodies nearby, and they began to fight for release from Evelar's mind.

Keeping guard at the door to his conscious mind, Evelar blocked the attempts of that other presence to gain access. The souls pulled at him from all sides, dragging and clawing in their attempts to get free, searching for a way out.

He felt himself swept away, down into the darkest corners of his mind while the crowd surged upward. Chasing after them, he fought his way through the crowd back up to his conscious door, only to find it closed tight. The crowd pushed him back again and he screamed at them to allow him through. But he could not be heard over the din.

In the waking mind, the Sandman settled into place with a warm glow of contentment as the vessel's living senses returned. He took a deep breath, a smile tugging at his mouth as he explored the sensation. The smell of woodsmoke and animal hide, underlaid with the stench of the city beyond the camp. The smell of meat cooking. And something else, an acrid tang in the air.

He listened, enjoying the human babble. The sound of warriors sparring, voices chattering and people laughing. The soft murmur of women nearby. One voice comfortingly familiar, a voice he had come to like, perhaps even love.

"Evelar?" she whispered.

A triumphant laugh bubbled up from within his chest, bursting out of him in a deep throated chuckle. He opened his eyes to see the beautiful face staring down at him. Her loving eyes changed, her expression growing hard, and he felt a pang of regret. This woman would never accept him.

"You," she spat. "How dare you."

He laughed even harder, relishing her anger. He would enjoy breaking her.

From the centre of the squalid city, a column of smoke rose into the night sky. The revealers gathered in their tent to discuss the final dilemma; how to reanimate the lost souls. The Sandman smirked at them, hiding his glee behind hooded eyes. The fools would never work it out, and he stubbornly sat on the knowledge.

His eyes widened as they tipped out bags in a golden stream, forming a glittering pile of amulets the like of which even he had never seen. Not in one place at one time, at any rate. His enemy must have collected every amulet ever produced. The rest of the stolen technology was now destroyed by fire, but here was wealth beyond imagining, power to control the minds of hundreds of clone-seeds.

"How do we use these to restore the souls of our people?" said Reeperly.

The Sandman shrugged. He had no intention of telling them.

"Do you intend to keep them all inside your head?" said Nashta. "I should think you would want to get rid of them."

The Sandman shrugged again. He was getting used to them now. It would be a shame to send them away. Although... they did pose a threat. They could turn on him with the slightest provocation, and he might find himself expelled in their stead. He frowned. Perhaps he should help them.

"Thou hast persuaded me," he sighed. "Cleanse them of their existing codes. Then thou mayst use them."

"And how do we do that?"

The Sandman let out a dismissive noise, giving a final shrug before curling up in the cushions and closing his eyes. Let them work it out. He listened to their confused murmurings for a while, enjoying his power to play them like puppets. No wonder Kay had grown drunk on power.

"He touched it," said Nashta. "Something floated away."

"Yes, I remember the same thing when he did it the first time," said Reeperly. "When he restored the souls to that group who attacked us back in Shirall."

"But what exactly did he do?" said Jumally, turning an amulet over in her hands.

"Let me see, Jum," said Tikki.

She ran a finger over the back of the charm, then pulled it away sharply. She slid the same finger around the rim. Something clicked and a green vapour escaped.

"How did you do that?" Jossep gasped.

"You clever girl," said Jumally proudly.

"There's a catch on the side, too small to see but you can feel it. Just watch the back, there's something there too, sharp like a needle."

"That must be how it collects the code," said Miyam. "Remember we used that to pull him out of Evelar's body that last time."

"So, we clean them first, yes?" said Nashta. "That lever must be the release mechanism to flush the code."

"Let's get on with it, then," said Miyam. "We have quite a few to get through."

They worked through the night, cleaning amulets until their their fingers were raw and their eyes burned. Until at last the only ones that remained were the extras the boy had brought, still safely in his sack, clutched in his arms as he slept.

"I don't think we need those," Reeperly said. "They weren't on the holy-one's body, they were separate."

"Don't wake him," Miyam sighed. "But do wake the Sandman. Let's get this over with."

Dragging the Sandman out into the cold pre-dawn camp, Nashta and Reeperly led the rest of the companions, who carried armfuls of amulets. As they made their way silently through the sleeping camp, only the smouldering kalkar, milling about in silence, showed any life.

Glancing across to where the creatures gathered, Miyam gave a small nod to Four, who returned the gesture and turned back to her pack mates and their unheard communion. On the edge of camp, the formerly possessed stood in unresponsive stupor, like the dead walking.

"What now?" said Nashta.

"If thou wouldst collect samples," said the Sandman. "And bring them thou to me."

The companions did as they were bid, pressing the amulets one at a time to the flesh of the comatose bodies, then taking them to the Sandman. He took each amulet and pressed it to his forehead. A brief white glow and he passed it back, sending it back to the body that had been sampled. And slowly, the soulless bodies came back to life, their souls restored. By midday, most of the bodies were sitting about, enjoying warm broth as the nomads took charge, giving them comfort in their confusion. At last, it seemed all the bodies had been reborn, but a substantial pile of amulets remained.

"Are they all gone from your head?" Miyam whispered.

The Sandman shook his head. "There are but a small number remaining. These amulets to them do belong."

"They must be people who died along the way," said Reeperly. "Quite a few were killed in the desert, remember."

"How do we remove them?"

"Thou must find the code, or the soul cannot be called."

"How does it work?" Jumally said.

"The code doth contain a marker, that doth match the soul. Only the right code will call the soul."

"Then we must take the amulets home with us," said Reeperly. "To find those missing bodies."

"Perhaps not," said Ontaro as he approached the group. "I think you need to see this."

He signalled to a young man who hovered hesitantly behind. As he stepped forward, the Sandman sprang to his feet and rushed at the lad, who stumbled backward. The Sandman snatched a filthy scarf from around the young man's head. He scooped up an amulet from the pile and pressed it into the cloth, stiff with dried blood. Then he pressed the amulet to his forehead to remove the soul.

"The voices do clamour and cry out," the Sandman said. "This boy doth carry more code."

Whimpering, the young man held out his left arm, and pushed up his sleeve with the other hand. Along the length of the arm were parallel cuts, one after the other, each red and puckered with infection, held together with fine thread. The uppermost cuts gaped wide, blackened and oozing. The Sandman raised an eyebrow.

"Oh you poor child," Jumally whispered.

"Is that hair?" said Navear with a shudder.

The Sandman grabbed at the arm, and the boy screamed.

"Wait," Miyam cried. "The poor lad's in agony. Let me treat him first."

"Thou wouldst disturb the codes," the Sandman protested.

"At least let me ease his pain."

She touched her fingertips to the young man's temples, and his face relaxed. She lowered him unconscious to the ground, settling beside him and pulling his head into her lap. Then she gave a nod and the Sandman began the long process of extracting the code from the boy's wounds. When he had done, the pile of empty amulets had been filled with souls. All but one. Clutching that last amulet, the Sandman sniffed, tasting the air.

"Are they all gone now?" Miyam sighed.

"Just the one doth remain," said the Sandman. "And that one doth sense the code."

The Sandman raced off, searching amongst the reborn. Miyam had no doubt he would find the code, probably some forgotten keepsake in someone's pocket, a lock of hair maybe. Miyam allowed her companions to take the young man and tend his wounds, but she remained there in the dirt, her head low in her despair.

"Mym?" said Navear.

She looked up, seeing the other women gathered in concern. Navear, young but with such a good heart. Tikki and Jumally, chalk and cheese but so much a pair that one never seemed whole without the other. Berkana, quiet and usually silent, never far from her husband. Tineya, troubled but with an unswerving sense of loyalty. And Netta, dear friend and confidante, never pushing but always ready to help. Miyam could not hold back the tears.

"Mym, what is it?" said Netta, kneeling in front of her.

Miyam shook her head. "Don't you see? Without the voices to provide a distraction, without their massed power within his mind... We will never force the Sandman out. We can never get Evelar back!"

THIRTY THREE

Taking the focus of the meld, Miyam led the revealers down into her subconscious mind, through the door to her inner self, and skipped across into Evelar's innermost centre of being. Calling in the silence of his mind, she felt him embrace her thought. He took hold of her presence, dragging her with him.

Together, the conglomerate rose up, toward the door to conscious thought. There, the Sandman hovered. In a direct attack, with no subtlety and no subterfuge, the revealers slammed into the Sandman's thought form, latching on and dragging him down. But their combined mind slipped through the Sandman's presence, finding no purchase. It was merely an echo, a guard placed to keep them at bay while the real soul remained ensconced in the conscious mind of the vessel.

The revealers rushed at the barrier, forcing their collective will against the mental door. The ghost soul seemed to only grow stronger. The Sandman had finally learned a few things from Evelar's well trained mind, and now he was using everything against them. He pushed back.

The revealers braced against the force, but somehow the Sandman pushed them down, deep into the subconscious mind. They fought back, and the echo of the Sandman dissipated. But another stood in its place. And another. A whole line of echoes, each imbued with the full power of the trained revealer.

Each time the joined minds of the companions took one

down, another took its place. And slowly they sank even further. When the conglomerate could no longer fight back, their mental exhaustion dangerously high, they settled into the innermost centre, slipping out of Evelar's mind and back to Miyam's.

As they departed, they heard the voice of Evelar, sighing its regret. He could not follow, for fear of being locked out permanently. He would hide away inside his mind, waiting for the chance to win through.

'Don't give up, my love,' he whispered. 'We will find a way.'

Blocking her mind against the messy communication spell, Miyam curled into a ball in the cushions. She did not want to hear the others making plans, sending for extra ships to carry the formerly possessed victims home. She did not want to listen to their happy report of the successful mission. It had not been a success for her.

She had lost her beloved husband to a stranger, with no hope of ever getting him back. She had no reason to celebrate. When the noise of communication was gone, she uncurled to stare unseeing at the camel hide tent above her, its central pole pointing through the smoke hole and taking her thoughts upward with the smoke. He was out there, strolling through the city of the clones, making plans for a future none would ever have suspected.

He wanted to stay there and create his own empire, rebuilding the technology. His ambition was terrifying, and he intended to keep her by his side. She could not continue without Evelar. Her life would be worthless, never again a joining of minds. If not for her son, waiting in the desert, she would choose a final drastic solution to end the heartache.

She would not stay there, even knowing Evelar was still trapped inside somewhere. She could not watch a stranger grow old in her beloved husband's body. As the tears spilled over, she ignored the sound of someone entering the tent.

"Miyam," said Nashta. "We plan to leave before dawn tomorrow, as soon as the people are rested and ready."

Miyam said nothing, letting the words wash over her.

"Tineya and I are going with them. We started with them, and we need to finish it. Get them safely home."

Miyam made no response. It was unimportant.

"We've collected all the amulets. I don't know what you want to do with them, but perhaps the others will think of something."

Miyam's gaze flickered toward him then bounced away.

"They're too dangerous to leave lying around."

What did she care about a pile of amulets that had been the instrument of her undoing. They could not hurt her more than they already had.

"I think the others are staying with you for a while. They seem to think they will find a way for you to be happy. I hope you can rescue Evelar, I really do. But I need to go."

Miyam sighed.

"Ontaro is staying too, with his nomads. He feels loyal to Evelar and will help if he can."

Miyam stared in silence, not caring what he said, wishing he would just go.

"I'm sorry," he sighed, and left her alone.

As the sun set on a subdued camp, the kalkar awoke from their daily sleep. Four Zjobock Dhort moved through the camp, ignoring the people that instinctively moved out of her way. She was searching for one human, the woman whom she had come to regard as a friend. Finally, the woman appeared from one of the tents, her sad face haunting in the twilight. Four approached her with an approximation of a human smile.

"Miyam, we take our leave," said Four.

The woman smiled. "I thank you for your help, Four Zjobock Dhort. Please convey my gratitude to your pack. And my thanks to your mate."

"I will. But you are unhappy, Miyam. May I offer my help, on a personal level?"

"I thank you," Miyam said. "But my troubles are human. They cannot be solved by your pack."

"Perhaps not. But I sense your problem is not physical. I think you know the power of our group mind. Perhaps we could help after all?"

Miyam opened her mouth to protest, but then her eyes narrowed as she considered. Four listened to the woman's thought process, hearing her mind at work. Miyam's eyes opened wide and she let out a laugh.

"Four, you are amazing! I think you might have a point."

The Sandman approached the woman, searching her face for a clue to her state of mind. He knew she felt trapped and betrayed, and that she did not believe he could make her happy. But he wanted to prove himself, if she would just let him. She sat by the camp fire, her friends around, and he feared another attempt on his soul. But she held up a hand in a reassuring gesture.

"You're safe," she said. "I just want to talk."

He grunted his distrust, but sat nearby, ready to listen.

"I know you want me to accept you," she began. "You want me to take over from your lost wife. You want my son to replace your own lost son. I understand your need to find a way to build a new life."

"Dost thou accept me then?"

"I wasn't finished. You must realise, we can't allow you to take over from Kayus. The technology must remain lost. Our world cannot be endangered by it any more."

"I would use it not for evil."

"It would corrupt you. You want to live forever, building copies and taking them over, just as Kayus did. But you have already lived long enough."

"Who art thou to tell me how I should live?"

"I am your wife. And you are blinded by your old ways. Your ways are ancient and exalted, but they are not compatible with life in our world."

"What would thou propose I do?"

"Live forever, but not by copies and possessions. Become a beacon for our people, an advisor for the College of the Art, just as King Rexa advises the kings of Shirall."

"Thou would have me return to the soul-store? Trapped for eternity in that white place?"

"You wouldn't be trapped. You would experience life through the bearers of the amulet, a new Awakener every generation."

"I shall not yield. I choose life, not thy eternal prison."

"If you won't do it for me, do it for your son. And for the new child."

"New child? Thou art with child?"

"Do it for her," she whispered. "Give her back her father."

His mind raced. If she spoke truth, he would be a father again. Why should he give that up? He shook his head. He could not choose to leave now. If she had thought this news would change his mind, she was sorely mistaken. He was determined more than ever to make it work.

As he ruminated, a boy clambered into his lap, Kay's final clone-son. He stared at the boy, trying to work out why he insinuated himself on his person. Before he could react, the boy touched his face, fingertips finding his temples. The Sandman raised his hands to remove the boy, but then his mind exploded in fire.

Retreating in agony, the Sandman pushed against the

invasion. The boy brought destruction into his soul. The boy let the fire demons into his head! The Sandman battled against the terror, but everywhere he touched his mind burned. The fire demons filled his head, taking away his reason.

All his defensive barriers crumbled to ash, the darkness of his mind choking in smoke. His mental echoes that filled the spaces of his mind were snuffed out one by one as demons ravaged his very thoughts. He fled before them, looking only for escape from the burning.

Sinking down and down, deep into the corners of the vessel's mindscape, the Sandman found a door. He could not remember seeing it before, but it must have been there. Perhaps he could slip through, hide himself from the onslaught and return when they gave up their invasion.

He approached it down a long thought-funnel, feeling its familiar comfort, knowing he had indeed been there before. It felt right somehow. He touched the metaphorical door, feeling its smoothness, its luscious texture, almost sensuous. He pushed and it opened easily, as if it were meant just for him.

Behind him, the fire demons raged, screaming at him as they came, but the new space called him, offering peace and contentment beyond his wildest dreams. He slipped inside and closed the door. Only then did he notice the white. No, not that place!

He turned to escape, but the demons bashed against the door, its smooth surface warming to their attack. He whimpered, knowing he was trapped.

In the Awakener's lap, the boy pulled at the golden chain, ripping it from the man's neck. Evelar opened his eyes, gasping in the shock of awakening. The boy grinned at him as he touched the amulet, releasing a green vapour into the air. Then he slipped the gold charm into Evelar's belt pouch, giving it a final pat as he smiled up at him.

"How did you do that?" Evelar whispered.

The boy grinned again. "I told you, I know everything."

"What's your name?"

The boy shrugged. "The Master only called me boy."

"What about your mother?"

"She died a long time ago. But... I think she called me Skitter."

"Skitter," Evelar mused. "Then that is what we will call you."

The boy grinned, then his face fell into contemplation. "Sir, I... I spent my whole life serving the holy-one. What do I do now?"

"How old are you, Skitter?"

"I... I think... about ten, sir."

"Well then, Skitter. How would you like to come with us? You are very powerful, and we can train you to use your power, and use it to help people."

The boy's eyes lit up. "I'd like that!"

"Good," said Evelar. "Then it's settled. But right now, Skitter, I'd like to cuddle my wife."

Skitter grinned as he clambered up and scampered off. Evelar raised his eyes to gaze at Miyam. Her eyes glowed with happiness, and she flew into his arms.

In the half-light of dawn, the revealers stood in a circle, a pile of golden charms glittering before them as the first ray of sun hit them. The once-possessed followed the departing night westward on the first leg of the long journey home. Nashta and Tineya remained only to see this last act concluded, and then they would follow, to guide them. The nomads busied themselves dismantling the camp and preparing the horses, and the kalkar had departed sometime in the night.

"Are we sure this is the right thing to do?" said Jumally

quietly.

"I did wonder if it would not be kinder to present the remaining souls to their families," said Navear timidly.

"I suspected you might feel that way," said Miyam with a smile. "But the amulets are too dangerous. And isn't it more kind to free the souls, rather than leave them imprisoned forever?"

"There are other amulets with trapped souls," Navear pouted. "Are we going to free them too?"

"That is a decision for their bearers, in consultation with their advisors. It is not our choice to make."

"I assure you," said Evelar. "This is the only way to free the souls and ensure they can't be enslaved. And we must destroy the amulets."

"This is the right thing to do, sweets," said Joss.

She sighed. "I know. Let's do it then."

The revealers joined hands, giving their power to the Awakener, who took the focus with practised ease. Letting the power build, he raised his hands, pulling the others with him so that they all reached out together, into the centre of the circle.

He concentrated the power, and sent it in a long, hot beam, to burn down on the pile of amulets. Slowly, the pile of gold grew hot and began to melt. Still the revealers sent heat into the metal. The gold formed a puddle, bubbling and glowing red. Still Evelar focused the beam.

The molten gold glowed white hot, and somewhere in the bright pool a white vapour began to rise, lifting the souls free to float above. The mist spread over the circle, floating higher, to dissipate into the air. But still the beam continued.

Evelar pulled in even more power from his followers, and the steaming pool bubbled more frantically, the molten gold reaching such a heat that it too began to float away into the ether as smoke. Slowly, the pool shrank, the bubbling receded, and when the revealers dissolved their meld nothing remained of the gold but a burnt patch of ground.

Evelar let out a sigh. "It is done."

"Time to go home," said Reeperly.

Miyam turned to gaze at the rotting city, just waking from its slumber. "I wonder what will happen to them?"

"They will live on," said Jumally. "But I think they will need help if they are to survive much longer."

"A task for another day," said Berkana. "The Maestro will know what to do."

* * *

Sand finished the last sentence and dropped the pen into the inkwell. He sat back, perusing the words as the ink dried. Two years of work, finally finished. The untold story of the beginning of history, the first people to inhabit the world. And the story of the people who risked everything to build a new life.

It was a story of ambition, life and love, and triumph over adversity. It was the story of the Awakener and his beloved wife, of how they battled against the odds to bring history to light. Not less, it was the story of the Sandman and his nemesis Kay, who became known as Kayus, the most feared spirit to ever threaten the world.

It was the story of history. And it was done. He gazed at the last page, sealing away the memories and closing the book on the past. The golden amulet flashed at him in the sunlight from the open window, where sounds of childish laughter wafted up from the garden.

He grasped the amulet and pressed it to the front of the book. It flared for a moment and then remained fused there. And there it would remain until the next Awakener was ready to claim it. Sand rose to his feet and strode to the door, opening it and calling down the corridor for an apprentice.

Returning to the window, he gazed out, watching the children play in the grass. The woman looked up, sensing his eyes on her, and smiled. He returned the smile, his mind searching for hers.

'Are you finished, dear?' she thought into his mind.

'Yes, my love,' he sighed in reply.

A knock at the door heralded the Apprentice and he called him over to take the book.

"Take this to the Maestro," Sand said. "He'll know what to do."

The Apprentice gave a nod and hurried away. The Maestro would see that the book was shared, copies made and distributed to the royal libraries all over Sharné. One day, a new Awakener would wear the amulet again, teaching the history held within the book, so that the world would never forget their origins, nor the people who fought to keep them free and safe.

But that was not his task. He had rediscovered the truth, told the story and preserved it for the future. Now it was time to live his own life. He was the Awakener, and he would continue his task to teach the world about the mind and the powers within.

But more importantly, he was Sand of the College, and Evelar of the desert. Son of Shevron, who was nephew to Old One. He was the husband of Miyam of Martose, known in the College as Mist. And he was the father of Zaviar, who would be the next king of Shirall after King Atwin. And Tivoli, his little Tilly, the beautiful little girl who looked just like her mother. His family needed him now, and he would give them his undivided love and attention, for the rest of his days.

Climbing up onto his desk, he stepped out of the window

and climbed down the drainpipe, straight into the garden, avoiding the questioning stares of other revealers relaxing in the common rooms. The children ran toward him and he turned to watch them come.

Zaviar, growing into a fine young lad, and Tivoli, gambolling after her brother on wobbly toddler feet. He spread his arms wide and they ran into his embrace. Lifting them up together, he swung them around, feeling their giggles deep in his chest. Setting them down, he met his wife in a loving embrace, his mouth finding hers in a passionate kiss, letting her feel all his love and commitment in that one act.

"Are you really, finally finished?" she whispered.

"Yes, my love," he smiled. "I am all yours, forever."

The children clasped at his legs, gazing up at him with their adorable little faces.

"Can you play now, Papa?" Zavvy cried.

"Yes, little man," he replied. "I'm ready to be Papa now."

Tilly clapped her pudgy baby hands, giggling out her excitement.

"Your children have missed you," Mist said.

"I have missed them," he said. "And I can't wait to make some more…"

Mist let out a delighted laugh, that bubbling giggle that went right to his heart and filled his soul with joy.

"We're glad to have you back," she said.

"I'm glad to be back," he smiled.

And with that, Sand let go of the past and stepped into the future, bathed in the love of his family.

THE END

Ella Mortimer

The Curse of Mycenae
A new historical novel from the author
of the Race of Fire trilogy.

Klytemestra has good reason to hate her husband. The great Agamemnon, who killed her first husband and new-born son, and dragged her off to
Mycenae to be his queen.

When Klytie's sister, Helene, runs away with Paris to far off Troy, Agamemnon begins a decade-long campaign against the country that harbours the lovers.

Klytie is left abandoned and alone, her hatred settling as a black cloud over her heart. Finally, she accepts the advances of Aegisthus, her husband's cousin and true heir to the usurped crown Agamemnon wears, who seeks his own revenge upon the King.

When they learn that the King is on his way home, their perilous position becomes clear.
But is it enough to justify murder?

APPENDIX

CHARACTER SKETCHES

MIYAM

EVELAR

NETTA

ATWIN

NASHTA

TINEYA/FRANSI

THE BOY

ANTONI